Final Resting Place?

The house must have been a fairytale cottage once—a beautiful Victorian with a tower and arched windows—but the years had not been kind. The porch, which looked like it had been a pleasant, shady place to loaf on warm summer evenings, sagged ominously. The front door had a window in the top half, and while I stood there trying to decide whether I should knock or employ the ancient twisting doorbell, I went up on my tippy-toes and peeked through the window. And saw a pair of feet in black dress shoes and matching socks sticking out of a door halfway down the hall.

I'll be the first to admit that I have a vivid imagination, honed by years of watching bad TV shows, and for a second or two, the world stood still while I tried to process the fact that there appeared to be a dead body in Aunt Inga's house. Immediately, I was certain that someone had murdered my poor aunt. Why my elderly aunt should be wearing men's dress shoes and charcoal gray trousers I didn't really know, but I wasn't thinking too clearly at the moment. I could feel the blood draining out of my head, and when I put a hand on the door to steady myself, it opened with a long, drawn-out squeal of hinges; the kind of sound you hear in horror movies.

I wasn't sure whether to be relieved or even more surprised when the corpse moved.

—Acknowledgments—

This book would not have come into being without the help, support, and encouragement of a lot of people. Great big thanks to the following: My brilliant agent, Stephany Evans. She is one of a kind, as an agent, a writer, and a human being, and I'm so lucky to have found her. My wonderful editor, Jessica Wade. She could have entrusted Avery's story to someone else, but she chose me. I hope I've made her proud! My publicists, Leslie Henkel with the Penguin Group (USA) and Tom Robinson with Author and Book Media. This book would be nowhere without them! Fellow writers Tasha Alexander, Diana Killian, and Hank Phillippi Ryan. They've been incredibly generous with their time and advice, in addition to being the kind of writers, and the kind of women, I want to be when I grow up. Jamie Dierks, my critique partner. Without her, this book wouldn't be what it is. My buddies at the ITW Debut Authors. They've all, individually and together, helped me make it through the year in one piece. Robert Czapliewicz, handyman *extraordinaire*. He has helped me renovate every house I've ever owned and taught me everything I know about Doing-It-Myself. My first grade teacher, Mrs. Fullman. She told my parents I'd grow up to be an author. It took a while, but look at me now! My friends and family, near and far. Especially, my husband and my two boys. They're perfect and beautiful and the best family anyone could wish for, and they deserve far more than thanks, both for being who they are and for letting me be who I am.

FATAL
Fixer-Upper

JENNIE BENTLEY

BERKLEY PRIME CRIME, NEW YORK

THE BERKLEY PUBLISHING GROUP
Published by the Penguin Group
Penguin Group (USA) Inc.
375 Hudson Street, New York, New York 10014, USA
Penguin Group (Canada), 90 Eglinton Avenue East, Suite 700, Toronto, Ontario M4P 2Y3, Canada
(a division of Pearson Penguin Canada Inc.)
Penguin Books Ltd., 80 Strand, London WC2R 0RL, England
Penguin Group Ireland, 25 St. Stephen's Green, Dublin 2, Ireland (a division of Penguin Books Ltd.)
Penguin Group (Australia), 250 Camberwell Road, Camberwell, Victoria 3124, Australia
(a division of Pearson Australia Group Pty. Ltd.)
Penguin Books India Pvt. Ltd., 11 Community Centre, Panchsheel Park, New Delhi—110 017, India
Penguin Group (NZ), 67 Apollo Drive, Rosedale, North Shore 0632, New Zealand
(a division of Pearson New Zealand Ltd.)
Penguin Books (South Africa) (Pty.) Ltd., 24 Sturdee Avenue, Rosebank, Johannesburg 2196,
South Africa

Penguin Books Ltd., Registered Offices: 80 Strand, London WC2R 0RL, England

This is a work of fiction. Names, characters, places, and incidents either are the product of the author's imagination or are used fictitiously, and any resemblance to actual persons, living or dead, business establishments, events, or locales is entirely coincidental. The publisher does not have any control over and does not assume any responsibility for author or third-party websites or their content.

PUBLISHER'S NOTE: Neither the publisher nor the author is engaged in rendering professional advice or services to the individual reader. The ideas, projects, and suggestions contained in this book are not intended as a substitute for consulting with a professional. Neither the author nor the publisher shall be liable or responsible for any loss or damage allegedly arising from any information or suggestion in this book.

FATAL FIXER-UPPER

A Berkley Prime Crime Book / published by arrangement with the author

PRINTING HISTORY
Berkley Prime Crime mass-market edition / November 2008

Copyright © 2008 by Penguin Group (USA) Inc.
Cover illustration by Paperdog Studio.
Cover logo by axb group.
Cover design by Rita Frangie.
Interior text design by Laura K. Corless.

ISBN: 978-0-425-22457-1

BERKLEY® PRIME CRIME
Berkley Prime Crime Books are published by The Berkley Publishing Group,
a division of Penguin Group (USA) Inc.,
375 Hudson Street, New York, New York 10014.
BERKLEY PRIME CRIME and the BERKLEY PRIME CRIME design are trademarks of Penguin
Group (USA) Inc.

PRINTED IN THE UNITED STATES OF AMERICA

10 9 8 7 6 5 4 3 2 1

The letter from Aunt Inga arrived, as the saying goes, a day late and a dollar short. Or not a whole dollar, exactly, but Aunt Inga must have missed a few of the recent postal increases, because the stamp was short by several cents, and that was probably why it had taken the letter almost two weeks to get from Maine to New York City.

The mailman arrived just as I was putting the finishing touches on the hand-printed and hand-sewn upholstery I had created for a reproduction Gustavian love seat I was getting ready to put in the display window of Aubert Designs on Madison Avenue in New York City. (Gustavian furniture is a sort of simplified, Scandinavian rococo, FYI.) I'm the resident textile designer for Aubert Designs. Philippe Aubert designs furniture—high-end, handcrafted, reproduction furniture. My job is to enhance Philippe's creations with my own custom-designed fabrics. He's been on something of a Gustavian kick lately, and the piece I was working on had the distinctive arched and scrolled backrest and carved gilt-wood frame. My fabric, by contrast, was hip and modern, with a pattern of overlapping lipstick kisses in three shades of pink. Gustav was probably rotating in his grave, and Philippe hadn't been too positive about the idea either, when I'd first pitched it to him. But I was happy to see that the lipstick kisses looked just as good with the curved gilt wood as I had hoped.

Just as I was putting in the last few stitches, the door opened, and the mailman walked in. He looked from me to the stack of mail in his hand. "You Avery Marie Baker?"

I jabbed the needle into the underside of the love seat, where the mark it made wouldn't be noticed, and got to my feet. "I am. What have you got?"

He extended the other grubby hand. "Postage due. There's only a thirty-seven-cent stamp on this letter."

"Oh. Sure." I dug in a pocket of my jeans and came up with a dime. "Keep the change."

"Too kind." He pocketed the dime and shuffled out after handing over the stack of mail. I dumped the rest on Tara's empty chair—she's the receptionist—and sat down on the lipstick-upholstered love seat to open my letter.

The envelope was ecru and thick; it looked like it came from the kind of old-fashioned correspondence set people used back in the days before telephones and e-mail took over the world. The letter seemed to have originated some-where in the state of Maine, and my name and address were written in a shaky, elegant hand with what looked like real ink. The kind that comes out of a fountain pen. I slit the envelope open with a pair of upholstery shears. Philippe would have objected had he seen my cavalier use of his tools, but he'd gone to lunch (without me), so I did it anyway. It beat getting up to look for a letter opener; especially on Tara's desk, which looked like a whirlwind had blown past it. Whatever else Tara had going for her—as if I didn't know— she wasn't much of an office manager.

There was only a single sheet of writing paper inside the envelope, also thick and ecru in color. The message was short, dated two weeks ago, and written in the same shaky hand as the outside of the envelope:

My dear niece,

I trust this finds you well and that you are happy in your life in New York.

You may be surprised to hear from me after all this time. That is, if you even remember visiting me when you were a child.

I am writing in the hope that you might be able to find the time to come to Waterfield to see me sometime soon? As I attempt to put my affairs in order before my life draws to a close, there are things I feel compelled to share with you. It is time for secrets to be told, for the truth to come out, and wrongs to be put right.

Your affectionate aunt,
Inga Marie Morton
43 Bayberry Lane
Waterfield, ME

I was still sitting on the love seat ten minutes later, lost in thought, when the door from the street opened, letting in the aroma and miasma typical of New York City, no matter the time or season. Along with it came Philippe Aubert, resident genius, my boss—and boyfriend.

Philippe, as you've probably gathered, is French. Aggressively so. He keeps his wavy brown hair long enough to pull back into an artistic ponytail when he's working, and when he's not, he keeps it confined by that most French of French headgear, a beret. Today, he was dressed in skintight leather pants and a black leather blazer, with a flowing white poet shirt, open halfway down his muscular chest. On anyone else, the getup would have looked ridiculous. But Philippe looked good enough to eat, like he had stepped off the cover of a romance novel, and I resisted the temptation to pinch myself to make sure I wasn't dreaming.

"Hello, *chérie*." He sauntered over and bent down to greet me. His lips tasted of wine, and he smelled of musky aftershave. I was just a touch breathless by the time he straightened up and looked around. "Where is everybody?"

It took me a second to get my voice to cooperate. "Tara went to lunch. Just after you. And Kevin is delivering the checkered fainting couch."

"Ah." Philippe grimaced. The checkered fainting couch was a sore subject.

A fainting couch is perhaps more commonly known as a *chaise longue*, a long chair in French, or a lounging chair in good old-fashioned English. They've been around for millennia; Ramses the Great and Julius Caesar used to lie around on chaise longues, nibbling on grapes and being fanned by slaves. In more recent years they have been used primarily by women, since until just a hundred years ago or so, women's stays were often too tight to allow them to bend comfortably. Instead, they'd recline, fanning themselves and trying to keep from fainting. Philippe's couch was a reproduction of a rococo chaise longue, but as with the love seat, I had prevailed upon him to let me cover it with a less historically accurate fabric. Once he'd come back to his senses, he tried to back off of the promise, but it was too late. The couch was upholstered in eye-popping shades of bubblegum pink, lemon yellow, and orange, with black trim and tassels, and to Philippe's shock and my decorously hidden delight, someone had purchased it the very same day we put it in the display window. Some woman walking by on the street decided she just had to have it, and now Kevin was off delivering it to its new home. Even with the money in the bank, however, Philippe wasn't entirely convinced that letting me cover it with harlequin-patterned candy colors had been the right thing to do.

The bell above the door jingled again, this time admitting Tara. She's a leggy blonde in her early twenties, with straight, baby-fine hair and round blue eyes, and she resents the fact that I'm romantically involved with Philippe. She also resents the fact that I'm a designer, while she's a receptionist. I'm not sure which she resents more, but I know for a fact that she can't stand me. Her look when she came in and saw me suggested someone sinking her teeth into an apple and finding a worm. When she looked at Philippe, however, her expression changed to one of adoring hero worship. "Hi, Philippe," she breathed.

I rolled my eyes and turned my attention back to the love seat, but not before I had seen Philippe wink and ask her if she'd enjoyed her lunch. Tara giggled, "Oh, ye-e-es!"

• • •

Work got under way after that, and it wasn't until that evening that I had a chance to tell Philippe about my summons from Aunt Inga. To my surprise, he was a lot more excited about it than I was. "Who knows, *chérie*?" he said, with one of his Gallic shrugs, "maybe she is planning to make you her heir."

We were sitting across from each other at a romantic table for two at Le Coq au Vin, a tiny hole in the wall on the Upper West Side. I snorted into my glass. "And maybe not. I don't really remember meeting her, so why would she leave anything to me?"

"Why would she ask you to visit?" Philippe asked reasonably.

I shrugged. "I have no idea, but when I get home tonight, I intend to call my mother and ask her. Mom was a Morton before she married, and she grew up in Maine. That's where the letter came from. Aunt Inga must be one of Mother's relatives."

"Does your mother's family have money, *mon amie*?"

I shook my head. "None that I know of. We aren't poor, but we're not rich, either. My grandfather was an accountant, I think. I have no idea what Aunt Inga is or was. We don't stay in great touch with that side, but if there were millionaires in the family, I'm sure I would have heard." I wouldn't still be renting an apartment, for one thing. I'd own a beautiful little condo in the West Village instead.

"Still," Philippe said, tapping his fingernail gently against the side of his glass, "it would not hurt to go see your aunt, *non*?"

"I suppose not," I said unwillingly, "but I'm not going to go up there to try to insinuate myself into her will, if that's what you're thinking."

"Of course not," Philippe agreed, looking at me with soulful blue eyes, "but aren't you the least bit curious, *chérie*? What big secret could your aunt have that she wants to share with you? In person, not in a letter. What confession could she want to make that she doesn't want to take to the grave?"

They seemed like rhetorical questions, so I didn't bother answering. "I thought you'd tell me you needed me here," I said instead. I was a little hurt, frankly, that he hadn't. "With the big commission for the Hamiltons coming up at the end of the week, and everything."

"The Hamiltons' dining room set is finished," Philippe assured me, with a wave of his hand as if to shoo it away. "Any last-minute repairs or adjustments, Tara can do."

"Tara."

My tone must have been weighted, because Philippe smiled. "Do not be jealous, *ma petite*. It does not become you." He leaned across the table to put his hand over mine.

"Of course not." I smiled back, linking my fingers through his. I knew I had no reason to be jealous. I just didn't like the way Tara was always making eyes at him. That wasn't my gripe at the moment, though. "It's just that she's not a designer, Philippe. And I'd hate for her to do something to ruin all our hard work. The Hamiltons' dining room set is going to be beautiful, but not if Tara attaches any loose trim with black thread and those enormous stitches of hers."

Philippe took his hand away and leaned back in his chair again. "I will take care of Tara while you're away," he promised. "Are you ready to go, *chérie*?"

"Go?" I repeated, surprised. Philippe is never the one who wants to go. He's always happy to socialize into the wee hours. Leaving a restaurant before dessert and coffee is unheard of.

"Calling your mother is more important than cake, *chérie*." He hustled me out of the restaurant and down the sidewalk. "Your *pauvre tante*, she is up there in Maine, perhaps old and sick, and you are stuffing your face instead of arranging to go see her."

"I wasn't stuffing my face," I protested. I never stuff my face. I'm short; I have to watch my weight, or I'll end up looking like one of those Weebles, as broad as I'm tall.

Nevertheless, he did have a point, so when he walked me to the door of my building and declined my invitation to come up for a cup of coffee, I masked my pout as best I could and headed upstairs by myself. After kicking off my shoes and curling up on the couch (oyster silk blend with black piping, printed with cross sections of enormous black and green kiwifruit), I grabbed the phone and dialed California.

"Oh, yes," Mother said when I had told her about the letter I'd gotten from Aunt Inga. "It's just a few weeks since she wrote me to ask for your address. I gave her your work address in case she wanted to send a package. The perils of living in a building without a doorman. Why I remember—"

I interrupted her. "So you know her?" I admit it, I'd been halfway expecting my mother to tell me that we had no Inga Morton in the family, and that someone was playing a joke on me.

"Of course I know her, dear. She's my aunt."

"I thought she was my aunt."

"She's both of our aunts," Mother said. "Her father and my grandfather were brothers, I believe. That would make her my aunt, and your great-aunt once or twice removed. Something like that."

"How old is she?" If she was a contemporary of my mother's grandfather, then she had to be a hundred, at least. No wonder she was worried about her life drawing to a close.

Mother thought for a second. "Ninety-eight last September, I believe."

"And you stay in touch with her?"

"I try," Mother said, "although she hasn't made it easy, poor dear. She's a bit of a recluse, you understand. Doesn't like people, not even family. Not that one can blame her, considering what some of the family is like."

"I beg your pardon?" I said.

Mother ignored me. "I guess she must have had some sort of life when she was young, but for as long as I've known her, she's been standoffish, to say the least. Other than a card every Christmas, she never reached out to us. The last time I contacted her was last summer, when I invited her to The Wedding."

The Wedding—capitalized—had been hers, not mine, as perhaps it should have been, given our respective ages. I'm thirty-one and have never been married, due to a series of unfortunate love affairs in my early and mid-twenties. I had to kiss a lot of frogs—or at least men who looked like them—before I found Philippe.

But I digress. My mother is fifty-six, and this was her second marriage. After my father passed away, Mother stayed single for years, putting me through high school and college. It's only in the last few years that she's started dating again. Three years ago, she met a wonderful man named Noel, and last year they got married in a sunset ceremony on the beach in California. I'd been there for the wedding, of course, as maid of honor, but I couldn't remember seeing Aunt Inga. Or more accurately, I couldn't remember seeing any little old ladies I didn't know shuffling through the sand. I said as much.

"Oh, she couldn't make it," Mother explained. "At her age, I guess I can't blame her for not wanting to drive to

Portland to get on a plane, then flying across the country. But she sent a card and a set of the prettiest antique lobster utensils I've ever seen. Fit for a queen!"

"That was nice of her," I said. "I guess people eat a lot of lobster in Maine."

"Maine lobster is famous," Mother agreed. Even after all these years, she pronounced it with the native Mainer's dropped r: *lobstah.*

"So how come I never heard of Aunt Inga before?"

"Of course you've heard of Aunt Inga, Avery," Mother said. "You even met her once. We drove up to Maine and spent a few days with her the summer you turned five. Don't you remember?"

"We did?" I thought back. The summer I turned five was twenty-six years ago, so it had been a while. "I don't think so, no."

I could hear Mother's oversized earring clink against the receiver, and I could picture her, sitting on her patio, looking out over the Pacific, the ocean breeze ruffling her short hair. "There were cats," she said, obviously trying to coax some kind of memory out of me. "Lots of cats. Five, at least. You played with them. Big cats with bushy tails."

"Oh, Lord," I said. As the song goes, it was all coming back to me now. Or maybe not all, but enough. We had rented a car and driven to Maine in the sweltering heat of summer, my mother and I—Daddy had been working—and it had been a long and agonizing drive, back in the days before in-car DVD players and Game Boys. Add to that the fact that I'd gotten violently nauseous whenever I tried to draw or look at a book, and it had made for a grueling experience for both of us.

Of Waterfield itself, I remembered very little. There had

been cats, yes, and they had let me stroke and pet them until they got tired of me, and then they'd disappeared around the house toward the woods or across the road toward downtown and the harbor, their tails waving in the air like medieval plumes. There were also some vague memories of dirt and rocks and some mean little boys, although that could have been my imagination. But Aunt Inga herself was pretty much a blur in my mind, and my recollection of the house wasn't much better. It had seemed like a big, rambling place, full of dusty old things, but it was hard to say whether that was because I was smaller then, and used to life in a compact New York apartment, or whether it had actually been a large house.

"I remember the cats," I said, "and a little about the trip, but I don't really remember Aunt Inga or the house."

"Oh, it's wonderful, dear!" Mother sounded delighted that I'd asked. "A marvelous Victorian cottage with a tower and arched windows. And Waterfield is this lovely, picturesque little town on the coast. The third-oldest town in Maine, if you can believe it. And of course Aunt Inga's a real character. She never married, you know; it was just her and her cats for as long as I can remember. She's always been very reluctant to have anyone else in her home, and it was a fight getting her to agree to put us up when we came. Although I think by the time we left, she might have been a little sad to see us go. At least it seemed that way to me at the time."

"So what do you think she wants with me now?" I asked.

Mother was quiet for a moment. "She was very vague in her letter. There's only one way to find out, isn't there?" she said.

I made a face. "I could call."

"You could, except Aunt Inga doesn't have a phone. That's why she wrote instead of calling you."

That figured. "Do you know of any reason why she might want to talk to me? I mean, if she's only seen me once in thirty-one years...?

"I have no idea," Mother said, "but if she'd told me, it wouldn't be a secret, now would it?"

Obviously. "But I can't just leave..." I said plaintively.

"You're dating your boss," Mother pointed out with just a hint of asperity. She doesn't like Philippe. She thinks he's too flamboyant, too flirtatious, and too good-looking to be trustworthy. "Surely Philippe will give you a few days off to take care of a family emergency." *As any halfway-decent person would,* her tone said.

"Of course he would," I said loyally. "In fact, he's already told me that he thinks I should go. I'm not sure I'd call it an emergency, though. Whatever she has to say to me isn't likely to be anything life-changing. Plus I don't have any money to spend on travel. Airplane tickets aren't cheap, you know, especially last minute, like this."

Being a designer sounds a lot more impressive—and lucrative—than it is. I don't actually make a whole lot of money. In fact, I could probably make more waitressing at Le Coq au Vin.

"So rent a car and drive up," Mother said. "Rental cars aren't that expensive. You've kept your driver's license current, haven't you?"

"I have." And a big pain it had been, too. Most New Yorkers aren't stupid enough to keep cars—the monthly garage rentals are insane; it costs as much to park the car as it does to park oneself—so my ability to practice had been severely limited. I wasn't about to rent a car just so I could practice my driving, and Philippe hadn't been eager to allow me behind the wheel of his beloved Porsche. "But I can't drive to Maine," I added. "It's almost in Canada. Practically the end of the world. Don't you remember how awful the trip was back when I was five? It'll take days."

"Six hours," mother said. "Waterfield is three hundred and fifty miles from New York. If you leave now, you can be there before dawn."

"You're kidding!" I said and then caught myself. "Well, even if I did decide to go, I'm not ready to leave now. I'd have to rent a car first. And pack. And figure out where I'm going. Are you sure it's only six hours?" It had felt like an eternity back when I was a child.

"Positive," Mother said. "Although it felt a lot longer when I had to stop every twenty minutes so you could throw up. It took us most of the day, I think."

I twisted my face. "Thanks for reminding me."

Still, I should probably do the right thing and go. My great-aunt had taken the trouble to write and ask for me. She had mentioned family secrets and confessions, and like most people, things like that make me curious. Plus, now that Mother had described it, I wanted to see the marvelous little cottage I had visited as a child and the picturesque little town it sat in. I'm a New Yorker born and bred, and I love the city, but sometimes it's nice to breathe fresh air, too.

"Why don't you get busy renting a car?" Mother suggested. "If you leave at seven tomorrow morning, you can be in Waterfield by lunchtime. Let me know how it goes." She didn't bother with a good-bye, just hung up in my ear. I made another face as I crawled off the couch and over to the computer to Google car rental agencies.

The third-oldest town in Maine turned out to be a pretty place, if one's tastes should happen to run to provincial towns on the outer edge of the back beyond. Mine don't particularly, but it was undeniably attractive, with its steep, cobblestoned streets and mixture of Victorian cottages and stately Colonial and Federal-style homes, interspersed with the inevitable weathered New England saltboxes. The air was fresh, too, with a hint of salt from the ocean. It looked like a nice place to visit, maybe even hang around for a day or two, but I wouldn't want to live there. There were no chic clothing stores, no theaters, no trendy restaurants, no Starbucks...just a bunch of houses, and the occasional antique shop or tearoom, with names like the Ancient Mariner and Thea's Teas. All in all, too quaint for words.

The tinny, automated voice that had guided me onto the

Cross Bronx Expressway and all the way to Aunt Inga's house finished the job by almost killing me just as I was getting to my destination. I was turning the corner of Outlook Avenue and Bayberry Lane, where Aunt Inga's house was, when suddenly a huge black pickup truck erupted out of the cul-de-sac and almost clipped the front of my zippy little convertible VW Beetle.

The driver of the pickup didn't even glance my way, and the windows were tinted almost as black as the paint itself, so I couldn't get a good look at him or her. There was a white magnet sign on the door advertising some kind of business, but I wasn't able to read it. While I was still trying to catch my breath, the truck accelerated and disappeared down the hill toward the center of town. I watched the taillights glow red as it braked for a token tenth of a second at the four-way stop halfway down the hill. And then the sight of Aunt Inga's house blew everything else out of my head.

Mother's description of Aunt Inga had prepared me for the fact that the house would probably be in some need of repair. Aunt Inga was old, childless, reclusive, and not well off, so there had to be things—probably a lot of things—she wasn't able to keep up with. Things she couldn't do herself and things she couldn't afford to pay anyone else to do, with no family around to help out. I expected an overgrown yard, a few loose roof shingles, overflowing gutters, and maybe some rotted boards. The reality was so much worse than anything I could have imagined that for a second, I just stared, appalled.

The house must have been beautiful once. Like Mother had said, it was a fairy-tale Victorian cottage with a tower and arched windows. Unless my mandatory architecture classes betrayed me, I was looking at a Second Empire Victorian. Basically an Italianate style, identified by a square tower, mansard roof, and tall, narrow windows, arched or rounded on top. Named for the reign of Napoleon III (1852–1870), Second Empire was the first true architectural style of the Victorian era in the U.S.

Unfortunately, the wonderful house that Mother remembered had deteriorated more than a little in the past twenty-six years. The windows were tall and narrow, four over four, but several of the panes were broken. The mansard roof was laid in an intricate flower pattern, but many of the old shingles were missing. The front porch looked like it was meant to be a pleasant, shady place to loaf on warm summer evenings, but at the moment the floor sagged ominously and looked none too safe. The paint had peeled and faded so far that it was impossible to guess the original color. And don't even get me started on the yard. Cultured heritage rosebushes were choked with weeds, and lilac trees were rubbing elbows with thistles. The small birdbath on the front lawn was almost invisible. The grass was easily a foot tall, obscuring the walkway from the sidewalk up to the front of the house. I couldn't tell whether I'd have to walk on brick, flagstone, gravel, or just plain packed dirt to get to the front door.

A ten-year-old Cadillac in immaculate condition sat at the curb, and because I was so busy looking at the house, I almost plowed right into it. Only the good Lord and quick reflexes saved me, but even so, the front bumper of the Beetle kissed the back bumper of the Caddy before I backed up again to a decorous two-foot distance.

Swinging my legs out from the Beetle's interior, a little stiff after six hours behind the wheel, I shuffled carefully through the tall weeds along the invisible front walk.

The entrance to the house was inside the tower in a dusky corner of the porch. The Victorian front door had a window in the top half, and while I stood there trying to decide whether I should knock or employ the ancient twisting doorbell, I went up on my tippy-toes and peeked through the window. And saw a pair of feet in black dress shoes and matching socks sticking out of a door halfway down the hall.

I'll be the first to admit that I have a vivid imagination, honed by years of watching bad TV shows, and for a second or two, the world stood still while I tried to process the fact that there appeared to be a dead body in Aunt Inga's house. Immediately, I was certain that the person in the black pickup had murdered my poor aunt—probably bashed her over the head with the proverbial blunt instrument—and left her to die on the floor. Why my elderly aunt should be wearing size ten men's dress shoes and charcoal gray trousers I didn't really know, but I wasn't thinking too clearly at the moment. I could feel the blood draining out of my head, leaving me light-headed and dizzy. When I put a hand on the door to steady myself, it opened with a long, drawn-out squeal of hinges; the kind of sound you hear in horror movies.

I wasn't sure whether to be relieved or even more surprised when the corpse moved. The feet disappeared, and a few moments later, a shocked face peered out into the hallway. I stared back, wide-eyed.

Whoever it was, it wasn't my Aunt Inga. This was a man; old, but not as ancient as my aunt. He might have been around seventy or seventy-five, a spare man with gray hair combed over the top of his head, nattily dressed in a dark suit with a white shirt and a striped tie. There was dust on his knees. I tore my eyes away from it and up to his face. "Excuse me. My name is Avery Baker. I'm looking for my aunt."

For a second he just looked at me. I couldn't tell whether he was dazed—from that blow on the head I'd hypothesized—or just surprised. In hindsight, I realize he probably just couldn't see me too well in the semidarkness of the hallway, and my appearance had shocked him. "Miss Baker?" he repeated finally.

I nodded. "I'm looking for my aunt. Inga Morton. She wrote and asked me to come see her."

The gentleman brushed off his sleeves before he came toward me. "I'm sorry, Miss Baker. I guess you haven't heard."

"Heard what?"

"I'm afraid Miss Morton has passed away."

For a second the house, the porch, everything, spun crazily. "Passed away?" I repeated stupidly. "You mean she's dead?"

The man nodded. "My condolences, Miss Baker. Were you and your aunt close?"

"Not really." I shook my head, partly to dispel the dizziness. "I'd only met her once. But she can't be dead. She's expecting me. She wrote me a letter just last week."

"I'm afraid Miss Morton died two days ago," the gentleman said. He looked me up and down for a moment before he added, "Would you like to come in for a moment and sit down? You look upset."

"Please." I brushed past him into the house and, spying an old love seat in the room on the left, went over to it and collapsed onto the worn velvet. The old guy watched me from his vantage point in the middle of the hallway. After a minute or so, he stepped over to the doorway. "You did say that your name is Avery Baker?"

I nodded. "My mother was Rosemary Morton, until she

married my father. Inga Morton was her aunt a few times removed. Or something."

"And she contacted you recently? Did you exchange letters on a regular basis?"

I shook my head. "Aunt Inga and my mother stayed in touch," I said, even if the staying in touch had been confined to once a year, for Christmas, "but I haven't seen her for years. Or heard from her, either."

"What did she want when she asked you to visit?"

"No idea," I said, leaning my head against the gray velvet back of the old sofa. I felt very shaken. Honestly, I wasn't entirely sure why the idea of Aunt Inga's death had affected me so strongly. I hadn't known her, and she'd had a long life; it was probably just time for her to go. It had sounded like she was preparing for it, anyway, with her letter to me and her mention of coming clean before dying. "She just said she had something to talk to me about."

"I see," the old gentleman said. He was staring into the distance. I contemplated him for a moment.

"I'm sorry, sir, but who are you?"

"My apologies, Miss Baker." He came closer and extended a hand. "My name is Graham Rodgers. I'm her attorney."

"Nice to meet you," I said, standing up to shake hands. "I don't suppose you have any idea what my aunt wanted to tell me?"

Mr. Rodgers hesitated. "I'm afraid not, Miss Baker."

"Were you looking for something?"

He glanced over at me, startled, and I added, apologetically, "I saw you. On the floor, earlier."

He gathered himself. "Oh, yes. Indeed, Miss Baker, I was. I was looking for any will your aunt may have written."

"If you're the family attorney, don't you have one on file?"

"Indeed I do, Miss Baker. The office does have a will on file, which I drew up for your aunt some years ago. But it is customary for the executor of the estate to go through any paperwork to ensure that the decedent has not had a change of heart."

"I see," I said. "I guess you probably looked through the desk, then?" The desk stood in the middle of the room we were in, a yellow oak monstrosity from the 1970s, hideously out of place in the high-ceilinged Victorian room.

But Mr. Rodgers admitted that he had, in fact, not. "The room across the hall," he explained, "was where your aunt spent most of her time. I thought it best to start there."

"May I?" I walked down the hall to the door I'd seen him sticking out of earlier, and peered in.

Once upon a time, this must have been the formal dining room. It had lovely crown molding and an elaborate chair rail, not to mention a heavily carved fireplace on one wall. With proper dining room furniture—something like what Philippe had designed for the Hamiltons, with a jazzier, more upbeat fabric on the chairs—it would look fabulous. However, at this time, the room was dominated by Aunt Inga's bed, a hideous postmodern construction of sleek yellow oak, similar to the desk in the parlor. It must have been left untouched after Aunt Inga died, because it still sported the rose-printed sheets she must have favored. The pillow even bore the imprint of a head. "Did she die in that bed?" I asked, my voice hushed.

Mr. Rodgers shook his head. "She was found over there, on the floor." He gestured toward the front hall, where I'd come in. "The police ruled it an accident. Apparently she was on her way down the stairs and lost her balance."

"And fell?" How horrible.

"I'm afraid so," Mr. Rodgers said with a practiced, sympathetic look.

I forced a smile and looked around. The rest of the room was filled with what must have been Aunt Inga's treasures or her favorite and most necessary things. A microwave, unplugged, stood on a rolling cart in one corner, along with an instant coffeemaker. A stack of colorful magazines sat on the bedside table next to a cup of dark sludge and a small plate with only some fossilized crumbs left. On top of the pile was a biography of Marie Antoinette, written by the same woman who wrote that best-selling novel about Elizabeth I a year or two back. A pair of fuzzy old-lady slippers was left halfway under the bed, toes pointing in, and an old-fashioned nightgown, yellow with white lace, was folded neatly across the footboard. A medical supply walker stood at the foot of the bed, and a manual wheelchair sat in the corner.

"Unless she had an appointment with her doctor," Mr. Rodgers said, "or an appointment with the veterinarian, she saw no one and rarely left the house."

"My mother told me she was reclusive." I nodded. "Did you know her well?"

Mr. Rodgers gave the dignified lawyerly equivalent of a shrug. "As well as anyone. We had lunch together every Friday."

"I see." I had a last look around the dining room before I went back out into the hallway. "Would you mind if I hung around a little longer? I don't want to get in your way, but I spent some time here as a child, and I'd like to say good-bye." Not to mention that I was curious. What could my aunt have wanted to tell me?

Mr. Rodgers hesitated, but in the end, there wasn't a

whole lot he could say. He may have been tempted to warn me against sticking anything in my pocket, but if so, he managed to refrain from saying it. Not that there was a whole lot of items sitting around I'd like to have, frankly.

The rooms in the rest of the house had been closed off, with covers over the furniture and a velvety layer of dust over anything that wasn't covered. The upstairs consisted of three bedrooms and a bathroom, with a footed tub and cracked vinyl on the floor. The downstairs had the front parlor, where the desk was, the dining room, where Aunt Inga's bed was, another living room, and the kitchen. The wood floors throughout the house were scuffed and dull, with gouges and scratches. The wallpaper was faded and peeling, the paint was chipping, and everything that could sag or crack was sagging and cracking. It was depressing beyond belief.

By the time I came back downstairs again, Mr. Rodgers had apparently finished his search of Aunt Inga's room and had moved on to the desk in the parlor. I came in just as he pulled out the top drawer, the shallow, middle one running along the underside of the top of the desk. I saw him freeze, and then I saw him reach in and pull out an envelope, the same kind of thick ecru envelope I had received in the mail.

"What's that?" I asked.

Maybe Mr. Rodgers was hard of hearing and hadn't realized I was there, because he jumped, clutching the envelope convulsively.

"Is it a will?"

"It's a letter," Mr. Rodgers said somewhat reluctantly. I moved closer, and he added, "It has your name on it."

"It does?" I grabbed for it.

He held on a second too long, and I ended up snatching it out of his fingers.

"Sorry."

My name was written across the envelope in the same elegant hand as the letter I'd received in New York, and my hands were shaking as I ripped it open. Maybe Aunt Inga had written down everything she had wanted to tell me, and I'd figure out what her secret was after all.

The envelope contained another sheet of that same ecru writing paper, covered with my aunt's loopy, elegant script.

I, Inga Marie Morton, hereby leave all my property, my house, and everything in it, to my great-niece, Avery Marie Baker. Everything I own is to convey directly to my niece upon my death, without benefit of probate. I feel confident that my niece will be able to handle everything and will know exactly what to do about all my possessions, and furthermore, that she is the only person who will properly take care of matters as relate to Jemmy and Inky. Signed, the 18th day of May, Inga Marie Morton.

"Wow," I said, torn between being shocked, upset, and just a little amused. I was an heiress after all, just as Philippe had predicted. Wouldn't he be surprised when I told him? Of course, what I'd inherited was a run-down pseudo-shack in the middle of nowhere, full of bad furniture and framed pictures of cats, but still, I was an heiress.

Mr. Rodgers looked poleaxed, like someone had sucker-punched him in the stomach.

I added, "Are you all right, Mr. Rodgers?"

He glanced over at me, then seemed to pull himself together. "Indeed, Miss Baker, I am. A little surprised, I must say."

"You're not the only one." I looked at the letter in my hand again. "It's not witnessed. Is it legal?"

"The state of Maine does recognize a holographic will," Mr. Rodgers said with the air of someone quoting, "whether witnessed or not, as long as the signature and material provisions are in the handwriting of the testator. Section 2-503."

"Well, this is Aunt Inga's handwriting. Same as in the letter I got. So it's legal?"

The lawyer nodded. "It is indeed, Miss Baker. My congratulations."

"Thanks," I said, looking around, "I think."

"Of course," Mr. Rodgers added, "there will have to be a waiting period before you can take possession. To give anyone with claims against the estate the opportunity to come forward."

"What sort of claims? You mean, like other relatives?"

He nodded. "Indeed, Miss Baker. Relatives. Lienholders. Or anyone who ever lent your aunt something that they want to ensure does not become part of the estate."

"I see," I said. "If, for instance, that book in the other room, the one about Marie Antoinette, is a library book, the Waterfield Library will want to make sure I don't inherit it along with everything else."

"Exactly," Mr. Rodgers said, sounding pleased that I was catching on so quickly. "But assuming everything goes smoothly, and no one makes any claims, after the waiting period is over, the house and personal property will be yours to do with as you please."

"Gosh," I said, wondering what I'd do with a house in Maine and how I could most easily get rid of it.

Mr. Rodgers must have read my mind. "Perhaps you would prefer me to handle the matter? I can arrange to have Miss Morton's possessions removed to a storage facility and the house offered for sale for you. That way, you may return to New York immediately, and you won't have to worry about the details of the estate."

That sounded good. In fact, it sounded marvelous, but before I had the chance to say so, there was a knock at the door. "Are you expecting someone?" I asked instead.

Mr. Rodgers said he wasn't. "May I?" He indicated the door.

"Please." I stepped out of the way, and as such, my first impression of Melissa James was of her voice. It was a soft and feminine purr, with an undertone as crisp as a brand-new, crinkly dollar bill.

"Good afternoon, Graham."

"Good afternoon, Miss James," Mr. Rodgers answered politely.

"Such horrible news about Miss Morton. I could hardly believe it."

While she spoke, she slid smoothly past Mr. Rodgers into the front hall, and I got my first look at her. And I admit it: it was dislike at first glance. She was everything I wasn't, and everything I'd always wanted to be. It didn't help, either, that she looked quite a lot like Tara, Philippe's receptionist. Or Tara's older sister, anyway, since Tara was all of twenty-two, and Melissa was my age, at least.

Like me (and Tara), she was a blue-eyed blonde, and like Tara—but unlike me—she was tall and shapely. Where my hair is a long tangle of bright yellow crimps, hers was a shining cap of pale moonlight, cut in a precise wedge along her elegant jaw. And where my eyes are the soft blue of chlorinated water, hers were a deep, vivid cerulean, immaculately made up. My nose is pert, with a dusting of freckles, hers was straight and elegant. And in addition to her God-given attributes, she clearly had excellent taste and enough money to indulge it. She had on a lovely, cream-colored designer suit that must have set her back quite a few hundred dollars, and she made me feel like a dirty-faced urchin in the cropped jeans and hand-painted cotton top I'd put on for the drive.

"This is Miss Avery Baker," Mr. Rodgers said. "Inga Morton's niece . . . and heir."

Melissa's lovely eyes widened and registered shock for a moment, although she didn't say anything.

Mr. Rodgers continued, "Miss Baker, this is Miss Melissa James with Waterfield Realty."

I nodded politely and insincerely. Melissa did the same, looking down at me from her lofty height of five foot eight or thereabouts. I stared as hard as I could at the roots of her hair, but either she had an excellent stylist, or the shiny pale color was her own.

"Miss Baker has just driven up from New York," Mr. Rodgers added, skipping lightly over the fact that when I left New York, I had no idea my aunt was even dead, let alone that I was her heir.

"My condolences, Miss Baker," Melissa James said politely. "Were you and your aunt close?"

I shook my head. "Not particularly, no. She and my mother stayed in touch, though."

"And you live in New York City?"

I nodded.

She whipped a business card out of her pocket and held it out to me. "If you decide to sell the house, Avery—you don't mind if I call you Avery, do you?—I would love to help you. In fact, I have a client who is prepared to make you an offer of one hundred thousand dollars right now." She smiled.

"A hundred thousand?" I repeated, dismayed. "That's all it would bring?"

Not that a hundred thousand is pocket change, of course. But a hundred thousand dollars for a whole house, when one-bedroom apartments in New York go for six times that?

"I'm afraid so," Melissa said sympathetically. "This house hasn't been updated since it was built a hundred and fifty years ago. Renovating it would be a massive job, even for someone who knows what to do, and it would cost a fortune. An investor would have to get it cheap to make it worth his while. Accepting one hundred thousand dollars would allow you to sell the house quickly and be able to move on. That *is* what you want to do, isn't it?"

Those blue eyes drilled into me. I felt the way I did when I was a teenager, and my math teacher caught me sketching designs in class instead of working on trigonometry: *"Graduating with good grades,* is *what you want to do, isn't it, Avery Marie?"*

"Of course it is," I said. "I live in New York. I have friends there, and an apartment, and a career. I don't need a house in Maine." Even if my aunt had left it to me and hinted at deep, dark family secrets and things needing to be set right.

"Wonderful." Melissa showed me all her lovely, white teeth again. "Let me get a contract from the car, and we'll get it filled out."

I nodded, but before Melissa could turn on her heel and slither out, Mr. Rodgers cleared his throat. "Just a moment, Miss James. Miss Morton's will specified no probate, but there has to be a one-week waiting period to allow any claimants time to come forward. Miss Baker will be in no position to sign anything for a week, at least."

Melissa pouted, but there was, after all, not much she could do. She turned to me. "Where are you staying, Avery?"

"I thought I would be staying here..." I began, but before I could explain that that was before I realized Aunt Inga had died, she interrupted.

"Oh, you can't possibly stay here! This place isn't fit for man or beast."

"My aunt lived here," I said, stung. I felt the same way myself, but it wasn't Melissa's place to say so.

She continued as if she hadn't heard me. "You've just got to stay with Kate."

"Kate?" I glanced over at Mr. Rodgers for an explanation.

"Caitlin McGillicutty," Mr. Rodgers said. "She operates a bed-and-breakfast in town."

Melissa nodded. "It's just the most darling place, Avery. I sold it to her. It was my first big sale, five or six years ago, and she's just done wonders with it. It's a little pricey, but if you tell her I sent you, I'm sure she'll give you a discount. If she has any rooms available, of course. The Waterfield Inn is the most popular B and B in town."

I hesitated. If Melissa thought it was a little pricey, it was probably way beyond what I ought to be spending for a night's lodging. Maybe I had better look for a Motel 6 or a Days Inn; something downtrodden and cheap. If something as plebeian as a cut-rate motel existed in this quaint, old-fashioned town.

"I feel certain Miss Gillicutty will be able to accommodate you," Mr. Rodgers said, misunderstanding the reason for my hesitation. "The height of the tourist season hasn't started yet, and it is the middle of the week. I doubt every room in her very nice inn is filled."

"If you want," Melissa chirped, "I can take you down there and talk to her for you. I'm sure she'll do her best for another client of mine." She smiled.

"Thanks," I said, "but I'm sure I can figure it out on my own."

"In that case, just let me know when you're ready to sell. Nice to have met you, Avery. Graham, always a pleasure." She gave Mr. Rodgers a dazzling smile and sashayed to the door, hips and hair swinging. Her car was waiting at the curb. It was a late-model Mercedes-Benz, the same creamy color as her suit, and I waited until she had tucked her long legs under the steering wheel and had pulled away before I turned to Mr. Rodgers.

"She didn't waste any time, did she?"

Aunt Inga was probably not even in the ground yet, and Melissa James was already trying to muscle in on her house.

"Miss James is one of the most successful real estate professionals in Waterfield," Mr. Rodgers said.

With tactics like these, I wasn't surprised. The obituary had probably run in today's paper, and the lovely and successful Miss James had descended like a vulture on the remains.

"Is my aunt even buried yet?" I demanded. "Or couldn't she even wait that long?"

"Miss Morton is at the medical examiner's office in Portland," Mr. Rodgers said, neatly sidestepping the question. "It is a necessary complication with any unexpected death, I'm afraid."

"They're cutting her open?"

Mr. Rodgers hesitated. "I feel certain they will be respectful, Miss Baker."

And how, exactly, would they manage to do that? I wondered. "When will the body be released? Will I have to arrange the funeral?"

Mr. Rodgers shook his head. "Miss Morton already made her own arrangements with the funeral home and the chapel. There is to be no memorial service, no flowers, and no graveside ceremony. Miss Morton wanted to be buried quietly, like she lived."

"So I can't even be there?" That didn't seem fair. After driving all the way up here, only to be cheated out of seeing my aunt because of her untimely death, I wouldn't even get to say a final good-bye.

"I'm afraid not, Miss Baker," Mr. Rodgers said. "Miss Morton was adamant about not wanting a fuss."

"Fine." My voice, I'm sorry to say, was snippy. "It's too late for me to drive back to New York tonight, so I guess I may as well spend the night. Where may I find this B and B that Melissa James talked about?"

"I'll drive down there now," Mr. Rodgers said helpfully, "and you can follow me. That way, you won't get lost. These steep, winding roads can be challenging for someone who is not familiar with them."

"That'd be great," I said, feeling ashamed of my own bad attitude when he was so nice. "Thanks."

Mr. Rodgers smiled, his cool, gray eyes crinkling at the corners. "It is my pleasure, Miss Baker. My very great pleasure. Now, shall we?" He gestured toward our two cars waiting patiently at the curb. I nodded and preceded him down the path to the sidewalk.

• • •

The first thing I did when I got in the car was call California. Mother picked up on the first ring, excited to find out what was going on. "Hi, Avery. Are you in Waterfield? Did the drive go OK? How's Aunt Inga?"

I took a deep breath, hating what I had to do. "I'm in Waterfield. The drive was fine. But Aunt Inga is dead. I'm sorry, Mom."

"Dead?" my mother repeated, her voice shaky.

I nodded into the phone. "I'm afraid so."

"But... how?"

"Apparently she had an accident. When I got here, her lawyer was at the house, and he told me she had fallen down the stairs."

"Old Horace Cooper?" Mother said, diverted. "Wasn't he even older than Aunt Inga? How can he still be practicing?"

"Not Horace Cooper. This was someone named Graham Rodgers."

"And he told you Aunt Inga is dead?"

"He did. And he didn't say anything about suspicious circumstances, so I guess it was just an accident."

"Well, what else could it be?" Mother asked reasonably, rallying a little. "I guess you have no idea what she wanted to talk to you about then, do you?"

"Unfortunately not. But get this, Mom. We found a will, and she left everything to me. Her house and everything in it. I don't even have to wait for probate. Just a one-week waiting period for anyone who needs to, to file claims against the estate, and then it's all mine."

"Goodness gracious," Mother said.

"I know. Isn't it crazy? Why would she leave it all to me? But everything's a lot more run-down than the last time you were here—the house probably needs a ton of money's worth of repairs—but there was a Realtor there, who said she had a client who'd pay me a hundred thousand for it, just the way it is."

Mother hesitated for a moment. "So what are you going to do, Avery?"

"I'm not sure," I admitted. "A hundred thousand's a lot of money, even after taxes. Although it seems like it ought to be worth more, doesn't it? I'll have to think about it."

"You do that, dear," Mother said. She sounded relieved. "Keep me updated, OK?"

I promised I would, just as Mr. Rodgers's Cadillac pulled to the curb outside a white picket fence.

—3—

The Waterfield Inn turned out to be every bit as lovely—and expensive—as Melissa James had said. A true Queen Anne Victorian, the inn was a mix of architectural styles and angles. Two and a half stories tall with a square tower, like Aunt Inga's house, it also had a round tower with an onion dome, like the Kremlin in Moscow. The square tower had a mansard roof topped by a widow's walk. There was a bay window on the first floor; a wraparound porch; gingerbread trim; narrow, arched windows; and gables sticking out in every direction. In other words, the house had every Victorian excess imaginable—the very hallmark of the Queen Anne style—and everything was painted a sunny butter yellow with gleaming white accents.

Its proprietor was another pleasant surprise. I had imagined someone older—a retired schoolteacher or librarian, perhaps—with white hair and a prim cardigan, sitting behind an old-fashioned desk in the main entry of the inn, just waiting for me to arrive. The kind of person I could imagine moving to a place like Waterfield to start a B and B. Kate McGillicutty was something quite different.

My first impression was of her posterior, bent over a flower bed in the front yard of the inn. She was wearing tight jeans and a T-shirt, and when she straightened up, I saw that she was in her late thirties, with flaming copper curls, a freckled nose, and a broad smile, not to mention a figure that could have put Jane Russell to shame. "Hi there. What can I do for you?"

I told her who I was and explained that I had come to Waterfield to visit my aunt Inga but found things to be a little different from how I'd expected. "I thought I'd be staying with her, but under the circumstances..."

Kate had already heard about my aunt's death. She nodded. "Too uncomfortable. I understand."

Also too premature, but I didn't see the sense in mentioning that. "Melissa James suggested that you might have a room I could rent for the night."

Kate put a hand on her generous hips. "Did she, now? And did she suggest that I might give her a referral fee, too, for sending you here?"

"Not to me," I said, taken aback.

"Hrrumph! It's coming, I'm sure." She pulled her gardening gloves off and extended a hand. Her grasp was firm and strong, the grip of a woman not afraid of hard work. "Sorry about the attitude, but Melissa seems to think that because she was my Realtor when I moved here, she's entitled to referral fees for the rest of her natural life. I don't expect to receive part of her commission when I refer someone to her, so I don't know why she should expect to get part of my profit when she sends someone to me, but I shouldn't have taken it out on you."

"That's OK," I said. "From the way she talked, I assumed you two were close friends."

Kate snorted. "She wishes. No, our only connection is that she was my Realtor five years ago, and that we serve on a few of the same committees. We usually end up on different ends of the spectrum whenever there's a vote, too. Melissa wants to make Waterfield into a big town, with more business, more development, more people...I left Boston to get away from all that."

I nodded. I'd never willingly leave the hustle and bustle of Manhattan for this backwater, but I could understand why someone who valued the peace and quiet here might not want it to change.

"But you're not interested in all that," Kate added. "Come on in, and I'll show you the rooms." She tucked the gardening gloves into her back pocket and indicated that I should follow her. "We have five. Captain Cabot's Room, Mrs. Mary's Room, Anna Virginia's Room, John Andrew's Room, and the Widow's Walk. John Cabot was a sea captain in Waterfield a couple hundred years ago, and all the rooms are named for his family." As she was talking, she led me toward the front door, along a graveled path bordered by perennials in all the colors of the rainbow. "You can pick any room you'd like. Midweek like this I'm usually not busy at all. And you get the midweek discount, too." She smiled. "The weekends are a different story, of course. Come Friday, I'll be full up, and you'll be lucky to find a broom closet to sleep in. If you're still around by then, you're going to have to move into Shannon's room, because everything else is reserved."

"I'm sure that would be fine," I said. "Was Shannon another of the Cabots?"

Kate laughed, her bright hazel eyes dancing when she turned to look at me. "Shannon's my daughter. She's nineteen and studies history at Barnham College."

"Oh," I said, feeling stupid. "Pardon me."

She shrugged. "How could you know? Barnham is just a few miles down the road, so you probably passed it on your way into town. And don't worry about putting Shannon out; she's used to it. Half the time she's not here, anyway." She gestured me up the front steps to the porch.

"I see," I said. "I appreciate it, but I doubt it'll be necessary to impose upon her. I don't plan to be here long." If I couldn't do anything about Aunt Inga's house for the next week, I might as well be back in New York, enjoying my job and my boyfriend.

Kate nodded. "If you're Inga Morton's niece, I've got something that belongs to you."

"You do? What's that?"

"I'll show you after you're settled. Come on in." She opened the front door and ushered me into a high-ceilinged entry. I stopped and gasped.

The outside of the inn had been only the beginning. Inside, it was like stepping into a magazine spread. Persian rugs covered the polished oak floors, gorgeous tiled fireplaces held valuable knickknacks on their ornately carved mantels, and antique furniture abounded. Twelve-foot ceilings soared above my head, and soothing classical music played softly from hidden speakers. The air was permeated by the smell of fresh flowers, blooming in vases on every flat surface.

"Wow," I said, too impressed to come up with anything more articulate.

Kate beamed. "It's taken me five years to get it to this point, and I'm not finished by a long shot. There are still rooms on the third floor that I haven't touched, not to mention the servants' quarters above the carriage house out back. Once Shannon has flown the coop and it's just me, I plan to move out there and rent out every room in the main house. Let me show you the bedrooms."

She started up the curving staircase to the second floor with me tagging along behind, gawking right and left.

The guest rooms were just as lovely as the inn's common rooms, each with its own fireplace and private bath. I don't usually go in for feminine frills, but after careful consideration, I settled for Anna Virginia's Room, a gorgeous, peaceful retreat with frothy curtains, flowered wallpaper, and a four-poster bed with white canopies and lots of plump pillows that were just begging me to sink in. Looking at it, I suddenly felt a wave of fatigue wash over me, and all I wanted to do was crawl into that inviting bed and pull the down comforter up over my head.

"You look beat," Kate McGillicutty said in her direct way. "Maybe you should lie down and take a breather. You've probably had a lot going on in the past few days."

"You don't know the half of it," I answered. Between the late night last night and being up earlier than usual this morning, and then the long drive and the shock of finding out that my aunt had passed away, I felt bushed.

"Most B and Bs are only licensed to serve breakfast and boxed lunches. But there are several restaurants in walking distance. When you come back downstairs, I'll give you some recommendations."

I nodded. "That'd be great. Thanks."

Kate smiled. "Rest up. I'll see you later."

She closed the door behind her on the way out. I fell into

the soft comfort of the bed, closed my eyes, thinking for a moment that I should call Philippe but then deciding to surprise him with my news in person—and just like that, I was asleep.

• • •

When I woke up again, it was the next day. Bright sunshine was slanting through the white curtains, and I was still fully dressed, lying across the bed with my head buried in the lace-trimmed throw pillows. One of them had made a perfect impression of eyelet across my right cheek.

After a quick shower and blow-dry I felt a little more human again. Human enough to pay special attention to my attire. I was afraid I'd see Melissa James again at some point, and I was damned if I would let her make me feel like an unwashed urchin two days in a row. So I put on high-heeled, strappy sandals and a yellow polka-dotted sundress with black piping and a thick border of stylized Scottie dogs with red bows around their necks along the hem. A designer original, it was hand-cut and sewn by yours truly. There's not much I can do with my hair, but after slathering on some mascara and colored lip gloss, and hooking a pair of hoops through my earlobes, I descended the magnificent staircase and followed my nose to the dining room, my stomach growling in accompaniment to the clicking of my heels. I had slept right through dinner, and lunch yesterday hadn't been much of an affair, either—a Big Mac and French fries while I steered the car with the other hand—so I was ready for some real nourishment. And whatever it was smelled really good.

"There you are," Kate said with a welcoming smile when I stepped into the dining room. She was sitting at one of the small tables scattered throughout the room, across from a man in uniform. "I was starting to worry about you."

"Guess I must have been more tired than I thought," I answered apologetically. "I went to sleep right on top of the covers, fully dressed." I shifted my eyes to the man on the other side of the table. He was middle-aged—mid- to late forties, maybe—with dark hair shot through with gray and a weather-beaten face with crinkly crow's feet at the corners of the eyes. The uniform was navy blue and belonged to the police.

"This is Police Chief Wayne Rasmussen," Kate said. "Wayne, this is Avery Baker. She's Inga Morton's niece, up from New York."

Chief Rasmussen stood up to shake my hand and showed himself to be a lanky six foot four or five. "Nice to meet you, Miss Baker." His voice was deep and mellow and his handshake gentle.

"Likewise," I said, glancing at Kate. "Um…is everything all right?"

Chief Rasmussen folded himself back down onto the chair, his eyebrows tilting up at a comical angle. Kate giggled.

"Sure. Wayne's here for you, not me."

"Me?" I looked from one to the other of them. "Why?"

"Just to give you my condolences on the loss of your aunt," the chief said easily. "I guess Mr. Rodgers called to tell you she'd passed on?"

"Actually," I said, "when I came, I thought I was coming to see Aunt Inga. She sent me a letter a couple of weeks ago, inviting me up for a visit, but because she didn't put enough postage on it, I only got it the day before yesterday."

Chief Rasmussen's eyes sharpened. "Did it say anything of any consequence?"

"That depends on what you consider consequential, I guess. I have it here, if you want to see it." He nodded, and I dug it out of my bag and handed it over to him. He scanned it quickly, then read it over again more slowly before handing it back.

"Must have known she was close to the end, it seems. It's funny how people sense it sometimes. But I guess at almost one hundred, she had lived with the possibility for a while."

"I guess so," I agreed, folding the letter and stuffing it back into my bag. "Mr. Rodgers said she fell down the stairs?"

The chief of police nodded. "Death must have occurred pretty quickly. And she didn't feel any pain. Her neck was broken."

"Gosh," I said, and fell silent. It was good that she hadn't suffered but bad that it had happened at all, and while she was alone, too. If someone had been with her, maybe she could have been saved.

"Wayne was just stopping by to tell me he's heading out of town for the day," Kate said. "He's driving down to Boston to interview a witness in a missing person case."

"Oh?" I said, with a glance at Chief Rasmussen.

"Shannon and her friends are just devastated," Kate added. "They really liked Professor Wentworth."

"Professor Wentworth is the missing person?"

Chief Rasmussen nodded. "Ay-yup," he said, with the typical straightforwardness of a native Mainer.

Kate wasn't. "Martin Wentworth. He's a history professor at Barnham College. Nice man, very interested in the history of Waterfield. He drove Shannon home once, after a special project, and stayed for dinner. I told him about the Cabots and showed him some of the things we found when we were renovating the house. Did you know that when people built houses back in the day, they would leave something of their own in the construction for luck? We found a penny from 1889—the year the house was built—and a picture of Margaret Campbell among the insulation in the attic. Margaret was Anna Virginia's daughter, and it was her husband who built the house."

"That's interesting," I said.

"Isn't it? Old houses are great. It's so much fun bringing them back to what they should be. You know, undoing all the terrible things people perpetrate over the years. Paneling, shag carpets, acoustic ceilings, popcorn..." She shuddered. "This place was cut up into three apartments when I bought it, with three separate gas and electric meters and three rinky-dink kitchens. I spent a year converting it back to a single-family home before I could even think about starting to take in guests. Some of the things we found were incredible. Beautiful oak floors under four layers of vinyl in the kitchen, gorgeous silk wallpaper under the paneling in the front parlor, a claw-foot tub covered with drywall upstairs... That lovely ribbon tile in your bathroom was hidden under a couple of layers of vinyl, and the mantel over there," she nodded toward the gleaming mahogany fireplace on the far wall, "was painted with purple granite paint on top of at least five other layers. It took two weeks just to get it all off."

"It's beautiful now," I said.

"No thanks to me; that was all Derek's doing. Derek Ellis: he runs a local renovation and restoration company. But I'm keeping you from eating. There are English muffins and toast next to the toaster, coffee in the urn, orange juice in the pitcher, egg strata in the hot dish, and scones and Danish in the basket. Enjoy."

"Thank you," I said. "I will." I started to turn away, but

Kate just couldn't seem to keep herself from chattering, not that I minded.

"You look better today. More rested, and very nice, too."

"Yes, well…" I shrugged sheepishly. "Melissa James made me feel ratty yesterday, so I decided to try to do better today. I guess it should have been black, under the circumstances, but I didn't realize I'd have to wear mourning attire, and I didn't bring anything appropriate."

"Well, you look very nice," Kate said. "Doesn't she, Wayne?"

She turned to Wayne for his approval. He nodded, mouth full of English muffin with orange marmalade. After he had swallowed, he added, "Better get yourself some food, Miss Baker. Before I eat it all." He winked.

"Thank you," I said. "Um…good luck today. I hope you find the professor."

His face sobered. "So do I. Nice young fellow shouldn't just be able to walk out his front door and disappear. Not in my town."

I nodded. "It was nice to meet you, Chief Rasmussen. Excuse me. I'm going to get some breakfast."

Both of them nodded, and they went back to their low-voiced conversation while I filled my plate with a pile of the good things Kate had prepared.

By the time I had eaten my way through all of it, Chief Rasmussen was ready to leave. He gave Kate a chaste peck on the cheek and a not quite so chaste slap on the bottom before he sauntered toward the door and out. Kate came over and sat down on the opposite side of the table from me, her eyes still dancing merrily.

"Sorry," I apologized, "I didn't mean to interrupt your time together."

Kate grinned. She was wearing another pair of stretchy

jeans today, and a scoop-necked, sapphire blue T-shirt that pulled tight across her enviably ample chest. "You didn't. He'll be back this evening."

"He seems like a nice man," I said. Laid-back, comfortable, easy to talk to.

"As long as you're on the right side of the law. But yes, Wayne's the best."

"I don't expect he has a whole lot to do in a place like this?" Pretty, peaceful Waterfield didn't seem like a place with a flourishing criminal class.

Kate shook her head. "We're on the coast, and not too far from the Canadian border, so we see some attempted smuggling from time to time. It's a tradition hereabouts, dating back to Federal times. But mostly we have small-time crime. Shoplifting, drunk drivers, an occasional domestic disturbance. A couple of kids from the college getting into a fight over a girl...The last time we had a murder was, I think, four years ago, and everyone knew that crazy old Mr. Withers had just had enough of his golf buddy's gloating and hit him over the head with his nine iron." She took a sip of the coffee she had brought over to my table.

"This disappearance must be a big deal, then."

Kate nodded. "Everyone at the college is beside themselves. It's difficult to imagine that he would just walk out. But the alternative is even more unlikely. Who would have wanted to hurt such a nice young man?"

"Maybe he just had an accident," I suggested. "Went for a walk and fell off the edge of the cliffs, or something. There are cliffs here, right? I think I remember my mother telling me not to go near the cliffs when I was little."

"Oh, have you been here before?" Kate's eyes were bright.

I nodded. "When I was five. My mother and I came up to

visit Aunt Inga one summer. I don't remember much of it. Just the cats and the cliffs."

"The cats. Right." She took another sip of coffee.

"Uh-oh," I said. Mr. Rodgers hadn't mentioned cats, and I hadn't seen any evidence of them on my tour of the house, so I hadn't realized that they might still be here.

Kate nodded. "Remember yesterday, when I said I had something that belonged to you? After your aunt died, we brought her cats over here. Mr. Rodgers was her lawyer, so he's supposed to be handling things, but he doesn't seem to like them. Wayne lives in an apartment, and I couldn't bear the idea of taking them to the pound. They've been here for a couple of days. But they're digging in the yard and sharpening their claws on my furniture, and I can't keep them much longer. Would it be possible for you to take them with you when you leave?"

I could feel myself turning pale. "I live in an apartment, too. And I have a no-pet policy in my building. One cat might be possible—I could smuggle it in, and if it was fairly quiet and slept most of the time, maybe no one would notice that it was there—but if I remember correctly, Aunt Inga had a lot of cats. Five, I think my mother said."

"That was then," Kate said. "Now there are only two. But they're big cats, and not quiet at all. Especially if you plan to keep them inside. They're used to being able to roam. If you try to keep them locked up in a small apartment, I can pretty much guarantee that someone will figure out that they're there within twenty-four hours."

"So what am I supposed to do?"

She shrugged lightly. "I guess that depends on what your plans are."

"My plans," I said, "are to wait a week to make sure no

one else tries to claim they have rights to the house, and then sign Mr. Rodgers's papers and get it off my hands as quickly as possible. He didn't mention the cats were still around, so I guess I didn't realize I'd have to deal with them."

"Surprise," Kate said, with a catlike smile of her own. "Have you hired Melissa to list the house for sale for you? Is that how you met her?"

"She knocked on the door and said she had a client who was interested in buying it. I have no need for a house in Maine. I live in Manhattan."

Kate nodded. "Just out of curiosity, how much did she tell you the house was worth?"

I repeated the amount Melissa had mentioned and added, "Why? Didn't she tell me the truth?"

"I'm sure she did. She works with a lot of renovators and developers—including her boyfriend—and she knows exactly what they'll pay for something like that. They'll be fighting each other to get at that house. It's one of the few in the village that hasn't been renovated. Once it's back on the market—for two hundred fifty thousand dollars or three hundred thousand dollars, say—she'll sell it again, and double-dip the commission, too, if she can represent the new buyer as well. She stands to make plenty."

"Two hundred fifty thousand?" I repeated, my eyes big. Kate nodded.

"I paid just under two for this house five years ago. Of course, it's much bigger. But Waterfield is becoming a desirable—and expensive—place to live."

"Three hundred thousand?!"

I knew I sounded like a broken record, but I couldn't help myself. Kate grinned.

"If you don't mind some unsolicited advice, why don't

you reconsider your plan? Wayne took me over to your aunt's house the other day, to help him round up the cats, so I know what it looks like. If you clean out all the debris, and you just do basic repairs, you can probably get fifty or sixty thousand more than Melissa said. And if you have some time and a few grand to spare, you could turn it into quite a nice little place and probably make a good bit more." She leaned back in her chair.

"It sounds like a good idea," I admitted. "But I live in New York. And I don't know the first thing about renovating a house." I had no problem imagining what it might look like, what colors to paint the walls, the proper kinds of furniture and draperies to use, but I hadn't the faintest idea how to go about actually doing the work.

"It's not difficult," Kate said. "Just a lot of hard, manual labor. And you can always hire people to do the things you can't. You could even hire someone to do everything while you stay in New York, and just drive up once or twice over the summer to check progress."

She paused a moment, watching me think, before adding, "I can give you the number of the guy who helped me. His name is Derek Ellis. Local guy. Totally trustworthy, and very good with his hands." She didn't seem to be aware of the connotations of the remark, so I decided not to comment. In any case, she kept right on talking. "He's the one who restored the fireplace over there," she indicated the gleaming mantel I had admired earlier, "and the stained glass window on the landing. It had been painted over, and Derek cleaned all the paint off and brought it back."

"Expensive?" I asked.

"He is. But if he's not too busy, he might cut you a break. Especially under the circumstances." She grinned.

"What circumstances?" I asked, but before she could answer, the butler door between the dining room and the kitchen creaked open. I glanced over, expecting to see someone. The opening was just big enough for a slight body to squeeze through. I heard soft, padding footsteps, then the door swung shut again. Kate took one look at the expression on my face and burst out laughing.

"It's one of the cats. Nothing to worry about."

"Cat?"

I leaned down and peered through the table legs, and sure enough, it was a cat. The biggest cat I'd ever seen.

My friend Laura Lee in New York, a high-powered attorney, has one of those small, yippy dogs with a bow in its topknot. A Yorkshire terrier. It spends its days on a monogrammed pillow in Laura's office and its nights on Laura's bed. When Laura goes out, the dog goes with her, in a specially made, monogrammed purse that she carries everywhere. The dog's name is Muffin. This cat could have eaten three Muffins for breakfast and still had room for pancakes.

A brown tabby cat, it must have weighed a good twenty pounds. Long, thick fur made it look even bigger than it was. It had a ruff around its neck, tufted ears, more tufts of fur between its toes, and a long, bushy tail. Its eyes were big, round, and golden green, and they were fastened on Kate. The cat padded right up to the side of our table, sat down, tucked its luxurious tail around its haunches, and opened its mouth. What came out was less a meow than a chirping sort of trill, and in the back of my mind, a memory stirred. I'd met this cat, or one like it, before.

Kate nodded politely. "Good morning, Jemmy."

The cat turned his head to look at me. I smiled tentatively. "Hi, Jemmy. Nice to meet you."

Jemmy regarded me with disdain for a moment before turning his attention back to Kate, who told him, "If you'll come out to the kitchen, I'll give you your breakfast."

Jemmy meowed, a surprisingly soft, kittenish sound, given his size. He headed for the door, his tail waving like a knight's plume. "Excuse me," Kate said, following him. The door swung shut behind them both, and I heard the sound of water running and an electric can opener.

"Wow," I said when Kate came back a few minutes later, drying her hands on a dish towel she slung over her shoulder when she was finished. "That's the biggest cat I've ever seen."

She nodded. "Maine coon cat. Biggest breed there is."

"Coon cat?"

"There's a story that they came from cats and raccoons interbreeding, but that isn't biologically possible. Some people think they may be descended from Norwegian forest cats that the Vikings brought over from Scandinavia a thousand years ago. The two breeds have a lot in common. Tufted ears, big feet, long hair . . . There's also a story about an English sea captain named Coon, who sailed up and down the coast a couple hundred years ago with several long-haired cats. When the captain went ashore, so did the cats, and made kittens with the local cat ladies. Hence, Coon's cats. There are even people who think the Maine coon breed is descended from Marie Antoinette's cats at the French court. Apparently, she had a fascination with long-haired cats."

"These days it would probably be small, yappy dogs," I muttered, thinking of Laura Lee and Muffin.

Kate giggled. "I think she liked those, too. Anyway, Jemmy is one of your aunt Inga's cats. The other one is Inky. She's around here somewhere, too." She glanced around.

"Is she as big as Jemmy?" After seeing him, the thought of bringing them both back to New York seemed even more preposterous. The people in the apartment below me would be complaining about thudding footsteps above their heads all day.

"Not quite," Kate said. "The females are a little smaller than the males. Jemmy must be eighteen or nineteen pounds. Inky is probably only thirteen or fourteen."

"Only."

Kate shrugged, trying unsuccessfully to hold back another amused giggle. "Sorry, Avery. If you decide to stick around and renovate the house, they can move back in with you. Maybe you'll get attached to them and decide to stay."

Fat chance, I thought, but I didn't say it. "Or I could take them to the pound," I said, in spite of the fact that I didn't think I had it in me, any more than Kate did. She nodded, her eyes flat.

"You could. They're your cats. Or will be, once your week's waiting period is over. I'll keep them until then, if you need me to, but after that, you'll have to make other arrangements. Like I said, they're digging in my garden and scratching my furniture. Not to mention that a lot of people are allergic to them. I had a cancellation yesterday because of the cats."

"Gosh," I said, stricken, "I'm sorry. Would you like me to reimburse you for the loss?"

"Thanks, but that's not necessary. If you're going to renovate your aunt's house, you'll need all the money you can lay your hands on." She smiled, and with that oh, so encouraging parting remark, she grabbed my empty plate and wandered out into the kitchen to clean up the breakfast dishes. I grimaced.

– 4 –

There didn't seem to be any reason to stay in Waterfield any longer, so I turned the nose of the Beetle back toward New York. As I drove, I pondered what Kate had said.

The more I thought about it, the more sense her idea made. Why sell the house for a measly hundred grand if I could throw a little bit of money at it and maybe make three hundred thousand? Once the house was mine, I could borrow against the equity to finance the repairs, and if Kate's Mr. Ellis was willing to do the work without my even being there, I could just arrange to drop in once or twice over the summer to see how he was getting on. Simultaneously, I'd keep my job in New York and get to enjoy all the benefits of living in the city: restaurants, shops, theater, Philippe...

My first stop, once I'd dropped my bags at my apartment and the Beetle at the rental office, was my boyfriend's place.

I couldn't wait to tell him that he'd been right and that I was an heiress after all. I also couldn't wait to see him again. After just over four months together, I was still pinching myself regularly and asking myself how I could have been so lucky that this gorgeous, talented, successful man was into me.

Philippe lives in SoHo in a converted loft with enormously high ceilings, wide-open living areas, and sumptuous furniture and accessories. It's on the top floor, so it's a bit of a climb, but it's worth it. I was pausing for a second outside the door, catching my breath before knocking, when I heard a voice from inside. A female voice, raised in an excited squeal.

I froze, still as a statue, my raised fist hovering two inches from the door and my narrowed eyes fixed on nothing. A few seconds later, when the buzzing in my ears had abated, I recognized the squeal as belonging to Tara.

I could have taken the high road, I suppose, and walked away without making a fuss. I could have, but I didn't. Instead, I knocked on the door, and when Philippe opened it, bleary-eyed and gorgeous in a sumptuous silk dressing gown, I pushed past him into the apartment and swung on my heel.

"You son of a bitch! You didn't waste any time, did you? I haven't even been gone for two whole days, and you're already sleeping with someone else." I directed a glare over my shoulder to where Tara was perched on the arm of the sofa, wearing one of Philippe's shirts and nothing else, looking like a Victoria's Secret model. She smiled complacently, flipping her corn-silk hair over her shoulder and recrossing her long legs. I turned back to Philippe. "You're old enough to be her father, for God's sake!"

Tara pouted. Philippe rubbed his stubbly chin. From

what I could tell, he hadn't left the apartment all day. They'd probably started their love marathon right after work yesterday, just about the time I was learning that my aunt had died, and they'd been at it all night and all day, like rabbits.

"Avery, *ma petite chou*..." Philippe reached a conciliatory hand toward me. I stepped back.

"Don't call me your little cabbage, you bastard! And don't you touch me, either." I felt tears threaten and added, on a renewed burst of anger, "Dammit, Philippe, how could you do this to me?"

Philippe opened his mouth to answer, but I waved a hand to shut him up. If he gave me some glib, charming line about being a man, and French, and—Lord have mercy—having needs, I'd be tempted to give it right back to him, and I didn't feel like getting into it. I just wanted to get out before he could see me cry.

"You know, it's not important. I came to tell you that you were right. My aunt did put me in her will. She left me everything she owned, including a house in Maine. So what I really came to do was tell you I quit. I'll go over to the shop tonight and clear out my things; that way we won't have to deal with each other during business hours tomorrow."

I turned on my heel and walked to the door with all the dignity I could muster. "Avery!" Philippe said behind me, a note of alarm in his voice for the first time. I guess losing me as a designer was a lot more important to him than losing me as his girlfriend. Or maybe the fact that I was an heiress suddenly lent me some extra appeal I hadn't had twenty minutes ago, when he was bonking Tara.

"I have an idea," I said, turning. "Why don't you promote Tara into my job? She's got everything else, after all. And you'll need another designer, won't you? Someone without any experience or vision who'll turn out all the boring fabrics you want without any questions, unlike me. Yes, I think Tara will be perfect, don't you?"

I smiled brightly at them both, and then I ran down the stairs and out the door before either one of them could say another word.

. . .

I had thought that maybe, just maybe, Philippe would follow me to the gallery and try to make amends, but in that I was disappointed. Either Tara had seduced him back to bed, or I really didn't matter to him at all, heiress or not. I gathered my tools and a few personal items in a box, then carried it home on the subway, blinking back tears. Someone even asked, in flagrant disregard for New York's dog-eat-dog reputation, whether I was all right. Once I got back to my rent-controlled, little two-bedroom walk-up on Sixty-ninth Street, I curled up on the kiwi-patterned couch and called my mother.

"Oh, dear," she said when I told her about Philippe. "I'm so sorry, Avery."

"Me, too," I sniffed. "But I always knew, deep down, that it was too good to be true, you know. I mean, why would somebody like him like me?"

"What nonsense," Mother said. "The question you should ask is, why would someone like you like someone like him? You're a wonderful, loving person, and he's too slick and good-looking to be trustworthy; you know I've always said that."

"I know," I agreed with a sigh. "I guess I should have believed you. I just thought it would be different this time, you know?"

"I know, sweetie," Mother said sympathetically. "So what are you going to do now? Take the one hundred thousand dollars from Aunt Inga's house and use it to live on while you look for another design job?"

"That's a possibility, I guess. Although…" I slowed down as new and interesting possibilities opened up in front of me. "Although maybe I should go up to Maine and spend a month or two working on the house before I sell it. I was planning to pay someone to do the work for me while I stayed here, but it would be a lot cheaper if I could do some of the repairs myself, and since I'm out of a job anyway…"

"That sounds like a wonderful idea," Mother said warmly. "You've been putting in a lot of hours in your career the past couple of years, and apart from The Wedding last year, I can't remember the last time you took a vacation. It'll be good for you."

"Uh-huh." I wasn't exactly sure how she could equate renovating a house with taking a vacation, but she was probably right: it would be good for me. If nothing else, it would take me out of New York for a while. I wouldn't have to worry about running into Philippe at Le Coq au Vin or Tara at Bloomingdale's, and I also wouldn't have to worry about coming up with another design job in the middle of summer.

"You shouldn't have a problem finding someone to sub-let your apartment while you're gone," Mother continued. "Not where you live. The location's wonderful, and the rent hasn't gone up more than a few hundred dollars since I first moved into the place back when you were a baby."

I nodded. I still lived in the apartment where I'd grown up, although back then it had been Mother's and Dad's, and now it was mine. Relatively speaking, since it actually belonged to someone else, and I, like most New Yorkers, just rented.

"It sounds like you have a lot to do in the next few

days," Mother said, smoothly excusing herself from the conversation now that her mission was accomplished and I had something to think about other than Philippe and his betrayal. "Let me know how it goes and when you're leaving."

I promised I would, and we both hung up. I got to work.

Finding someone to sublet turned out to be even simpler than Mother thought. The day after the debacle with Philippe, Laura Lee called to talk. We arranged to get together for lunch the next day, with Muffin the dog in her bag under the table, surreptitiously accepting morsels of chicken.

"So spill," Laura said, after we had ordered our salads and the waiter had given us both our bottled spring water. "What happened?" One side of her stick-straight black hair fell forward as she twisted the cap off the water bottle, and she tucked it behind her ear with a pink-polished nail. I eyed both nails and hair enviously. I've long since given up on growing my fingernails long, let alone on keeping any polish I put on them from chipping off, but if there's one thing I'd sell my soul for, it's straight hair.

Twisting a tendril of my own kinky mop around my finger, I told her what had happened when I came back from Maine, and why I had made the on-the-spot decision to leave Aubert Designs. Laura didn't blame me at all. "The bastard," she said. "And with that little tramp, too. What could he possibly see in her?"

"She's young, pretty, and adores him?" I suggested.

"While you're ugly and old?" She rolled her eyes eloquently. "She's a bimbo, Avery, and he'll tire of her in a matter of weeks, if not sooner."

"It doesn't matter," I said with a shrug, although between you and me, it did.

Laura looked at me. "What are you going to do now?"

"I've decided to spend some time in Maine. I'm going to renovate my aunt's house and get it ready to sell." And it was going to be fun. I was going to go completely crazy and do everything I wanted to do, on a much larger scale than my small apartment had allowed.

Looking back on the past few months, I had realized that during the time I'd worked for Philippe, I'd had to put rather a lot of myself aside to make things run smoothly. I hadn't been given much room to grow and develop my own art; it had been more a matter of turning out the frankly boring fabrics and patterns Philippe wanted. If I was good, occasionally he'd let me come up with something more to my own taste, like the lipstick-kissed love seat. But when it came to a big, important commission, like the Hamiltons' dining room set, my input and expertise were unwanted and unappreciated. But now I had a chance to really put my mark on something without anyone telling me what I could and couldn't do, and by golly, I was going to do it! And the next guy who tried to tell me that his vision was better, more right, more appropriate than mine, would get it with both barrels.

"What are you going to do with your place while you're gone?" Laura wanted to know.

"I was hoping to sublet it for the summer," I answered.

She smiled. "I was hoping you'd say that. I have this friend . . ."

It turned out that Laura's old college roommate wanted to spend a few months in New York—she was changing careers and needed to do an internship—and I agreed to sublet my apartment to her for the duration. If I finished the repairs on Aunt Inga's house before Laura's friend was ready to go back home, I figured I'd just fly out to California and spend some time with Mother and Noel.

The ever-efficient Laura called her friend, got an excited squeal of approval, and drafted a lease agreement right then and there on a yellow legal pad she pulled from her briefcase. I signed it, and we were all set. We stopped at a hardware store and made a set of keys to pass on to her friend. She gave me a hug before she lifted the bag full of Muffin and minced off up Eighth Avenue on her three-inch heels.

It was that afternoon, after I had essentially signed away, at least temporarily, the one thing still keeping me in New York (apart from my friends and Central Park), that I got my first inkling that spending the summer in Waterfield might not be as simple and uncomplicated as I had envisioned. When I picked up my mail in the lobby on my way upstairs, among the circulars, bills, and trade magazines was a plain, white envelope with my name and address printed on the outside.

I turned it over in my hands as I stood in the lobby. At first glance it was eerily similar to the letter I'd gotten from Aunt Inga less than a week ago, only white instead of ecru, and on less impressive paper. The inscription was done in one of those computer-generated fonts made to look like handwriting, and the envelope lacked a sender's name or address. For a second I thought about ripping it in half and tossing it directly in the trash. I'd gotten similar mailings before, and they had invariably turned out to be solicitations. However, upon closer examination, I noticed that this had a real stamp—one with enough postage—as well as a bona fide postmark. The letter had originated in Waterfield. If someone had thought enough of it to pay for first-class postage to get it here, I should at least take a look at what was inside.

The envelope contained a single piece of copy paper, folded in thirds. When I unfolded it, expecting a letter of some kind, I stared in shock at the single sentence typed across the paper, in the same computer-generated font as the name and address on the outside:

> Stay away from Waterfield unless
> you want to end up like your aunt.

It was followed by a small icon of skull and crossbones. Just in case I had somehow missed the point, I guess.

• • •

For the next several days, I seriously considered changing my plans and not going to Waterfield after all.

I called Wayne Rasmussen and told him about the letter. He sounded concerned, and he asked me to fax him a copy, which I promptly did, promising to deliver the original in person when I came back up to Waterfield. Probably just a prank, he said, but he wanted to see it.

I showed the threatening letter to each of my friends, when I got together with them for the good-bye lunches and dinners I'd scheduled, and solicited their opinions on what I should do. But in the end, I didn't see that I had much choice. I had agreed, in writing, to let Laura's friend sublet my apartment, so even if I wanted to stay in New York, I couldn't stay there. Several of my friends offered to let me bunk with them, but given the small size of most New York apartments, we'd be on top of each other. Not to mention that they all had irritating habits. One smoked, one liked to bring her boyfriend home and have noisy sex, and one owned three rabbits, which stunk up her tiny place. And then there was the untidy one, the pack rat, whose sofa was always buried under piles of books, clothes, newspapers, and old Chinese take-out containers. And although Mother and Noel would undoubtedly be happy to have me, I didn't want to impose on them for the rest of the summer, either. So spooky letter with skull and crossbones not withstanding, I pretty much had to go to Waterfield. And hope against hope that when my unknown correspondent threatened me with a fate like my aunt's, he or she meant I would live to the ripe old age of ninety-eight and die accidentally in my own home.

A little over a week after the first time I'd cruised into town in my rented Bug, I was back in Waterfield. This time I'd taken a plane to Portland and a cab the rest of the way. The cab had three suitcases containing all my summer attire in the trunk. Only summer clothes, since I didn't plan to stick around long enough to need winter ones. The only other thing of note that I brought—other than my makeup bag and sewing machine—was a home equity line worth twenty thousand dollars that I'd taken out on Aunt Inga's house. I had called Mr. Rodgers to let him know I was coming back and to leave the key under the mat for me. He had in turn informed me that although someone had come forward and tried to claim that Aunt Inga had been non compos mentis when she wrote her holographic will, the claim had been easily routed, and the house and everything in it was mine.

I had been in touch with Kate and asked her to have her friend Mr. Ellis stop by the day after I arrived, so I could ascertain whether he wanted to help me with the repairs and whether I could afford him if he did. I had even contacted the post office and had my mail forwarded to Aunt Inga's address. I was all set, or so I thought.

My sunny disposition got its first check when the plane was delayed and I arrived in Portland four hours late. By the

time the cab pulled up to the front of the house, it was getting dark, and I had yet to change the sheets on Aunt Inga's
bed. The sight of the house squatting there like something
out of a horror movie didn't improve my mood. In fact, for
fifty cents I would have turned around and walked away.
But that was a luxury I couldn't afford. Laura's friend would
be moving into my apartment the next day, and since it was
Friday, Kate wouldn't have had any rooms available, even if
I had been willing to spend my limited funds on lodging.
Still, it took all the courage I had to dig the key out from
under the mat and insert it in the lock.

Mr. Rodgers had made sure that the electricity was on, so
things could have been worse. I turned on the light in the
hall and outside on the porch before I closed and locked the
door behind me.

The place didn't look that different from the last time I
was there. There was furniture on top of furniture, boxes
along the walls, knickknacks everywhere...I didn't remember it being quite so chaotic—at least half the boxes
were open, with their contents trailing out and across the
floor—but I'd been pretty overwhelmed last week, and it
wouldn't be surprising if my mind had glossed over some of
the more upsetting aspects of the visit. Plus, that had been in
broad daylight; everything seemed a lot creepier now in the
dark. Still, at the back of my mind, I had a feeling that something wasn't quite right. I managed to keep it together pretty
well, though, until I walked into the kitchen.

The last time I'd seen the kitchen it had cracked vinyl on
the floor, a rusted wall sink, chipping paint, and cabinets
that looked like they had been put together out of wood sal-
vaged from a shipwreck. Frankly, it had been too depressing to contemplate. But bad as it was last week, that's
all that had been wrong. This week, I stopped in the door-

way, gaping, my heart beating so hard in my chest I could hear it.

Shards of broken pottery, a sea of porcelain pieces, were strewn across the floor, as if an earthquake had hit Water-field while I'd been away, knocking all the flatware, glasses, and utensils out of the drawers and off the shelves onto the cracked vinyl, breaking whatever could break on im-pact. There were even some broken jars from the refrigera-tor among the mix, and the sour smell of pickles permeated the air.

I stood frozen for a second, in shock, before I backed slowly out the door. In the hallway, I turned tail and walked briskly to the front door, ears straining. I knew there hadn't been an earthquake in this part of the country in the past few days. Someone had lifted the plates, cups, and glasses off the shelves and flung them against the floor and walls to break them. Someone who had been in Aunt Inga's house while I was away. Someone who might still be here.

It took an eternity for my shaking hands to undo the lock on the front door, and every moment I stood there fumbling, I expected to hear footsteps behind me. But whoever had been here—kids, maybe?—was long gone. Still, I didn't draw a deep breath until I was outside on the sidewalk, well away from the house. Once I could breathe normally again, I pulled out my cell phone.

After I had introduced myself to the 911 operator and explained the situation, I settled down on the curb to wait for someone to arrive. Given the fact that it wasn't actually an emergency, I figured it would be a while, but less than ten minutes later a squad car came quietly rolling up the street. It parked a few feet away, and Police Chief Wayne Rasmus-sen unfolded his lanky length from behind the wheel. "Eve-ning, Miss Baker."

"Avery," I said, "please. Nice to see you again, Chief Rasmussen. Quite an honor, having the chief of police answering my call."

Wayne Rasmussen's lips quirked. "Recognized the address. Figured it was you." He looked around at the dark and overgrown yard and the light spilling out of the open front door, before turning his attention back to me. "Wanna tell me what happened?"

I nodded, still a little shaky. "Well, you know I've spent the past week in New York. Settling my affairs, as Mr. Rodgers put it." A little sinister, that expression. That's what people do before they die, isn't it? What Aunt Inga had been trying to do, when she asked me to visit. "The flight was delayed, or I would have been here hours ago. When I walked in, I discovered that someone had been in the house. There's broken china all over the kitchen floor. And after that letter…"

"Maybe Mr. Rodgers dropped a stack of plates?" Wayne suggested.

I shook my head. "Every plate, glass, and bowl in the house is broken. It looks like someone opened the cabinet doors and dumped everything."

Wayne Rasmussen glanced at the house. "I'll just take a look. You can wait right here."

"Don't mind if I do," I said, turning to watch as his long legs ate up the distance between the sidewalk and the porch. Just before he disappeared inside, he unholstered his gun, and I went back to chewing on my bottom lip.

He came back a few minutes later and stopped in front of me, rocking back on his heels, thumbs hooked under his belt. I squinted up at him. He nodded. "Sure doesn't look like any accident I ever saw. I'll get somebody out tomorrow to look things over. Maybe we can pick up some fingerprints or something. Or at least figure out how they got in. You take the key to New York with you?"

I shook my head. "Mr. Rodgers kept it. Just in case he needed to get in while I was gone, I guess." Not that I was accusing Mr. Rodgers of running amok in Aunt Inga's kitchen. "And because the house wasn't actually mine until now. The waiting period, remember?"

"How'd you get in, then, if Mr. Rodgers had the key?"

"I called him a few days ago," I explained, "to find out how things were going. When I told him I was coming back, we arranged that he would leave it under the mat."

"Could you tell if anything's missing?"

I smiled in disbelief. "You're kidding, right? I've only been here once, for a few minutes; I have no idea what Aunt Inga owned or didn't own. And you've seen the inside of the house; there's no way to know what's there and what isn't, or if something is gone that ought to be there."

Wayne nodded. "I'll see if Graham Rodgers made an inventory. Chances are it's just a case of vandalism, though. Kids or something. Never heard that Miss Morton owned anything anyone would have wanted."

"That's what Mr. Rodgers said," I confirmed.

We stood and sat quietly for a few seconds. "Don't suppose you wanna stay here?" Wayne broke the silence. I shook my head. "Why don't you get in the car. I'll take you down to Kate's. She'll put you up for the night."

"But it's Friday," I protested weakly. "The inn must be full."

"Shannon's probably spending the night down at the college again, so her room's empty. And Kate would give anyone who needed it the shirt off her back. Don't worry, she'll take care of you." He held out a hand. I allowed myself to be hauled to my feet and put into the police car.

. . .

When we got to the inn, Kate ushered us into her own personal quarters, away from the parlor and front porch, where those of her guests who weren't at dinner were whiling the time away chatting and watching TV. "You poor thing!" she exclaimed when Wayne had explained what I was doing there and what had happened. "No wonder you look like something one of the cats dragged in. Here, have a seat. Let me get you a drink. Of course you must stay here tonight. Shannon's never around anyway; she hasn't slept in her bed for three or four days. And you can't stay in that place until you've made sure that nobody can get in again. Wayne . . ."

Chief Rasmussen nodded. "I'll send Brandon out in the morning to look around. Probably won't find much, but we'll check it out." He turned to me. "Miss Baker—Avery—any idea who might have wanted to break into your aunt's house?"

I shook my head, wrapping my hands around the cup of sugary hot tea Kate had poured. "Teenagers? They knew the house was empty and wanted somewhere to hang out? Or someone who thought there might be something of value there, and who got angry when they didn't find anything to steal? She didn't own a computer, or a stereo, or even a TV, and the fridge can't be worth more than twenty-five dollars."

"Silver?" Kate suggested. "Jewelry?"

"If so, Mr. Rodgers didn't mention it. Or my mother, either."

"Unless Miss Morton was a lot better off than anyone knew," Wayne said, "I can't imagine anyone in town thinking there was anything in her house worth breaking in for.

Can you think of anyone who might have wanted to upset you?"

Wayne's gaze was firm. I shook my head. "No, of course not. I don't know anybody here. Except you two and Mr. Rodgers."

"And Melissa," Kate reminded me.

I hid a smile. The temptation to blame the perfect Miss James was almost irresistible, but I couldn't in good conscience sic the chief of police on her just because she reminded me of the girl who had stolen my boyfriend. "Why would Melissa James break into Aunt Inga's house and smash all her china?"

Kate shrugged. "I didn't say she would. But since you asked: maybe because you told her you'd let her sell your house and then you changed your mind?"

"Don't be silly," I scoffed. "She's a professional; she wouldn't do something like that. Would she?"

Kate and Wayne exchanged glances. "No way of knowing," Wayne said. "Don't know her well. She's from away. Hasn't been here but a few years."

Kate added, "I've heard some stories about her temper, though. From someone with firsthand experience. It wouldn't be the first time she's broken crockery."

"Still," I said, "I doubt she would have vandalized my house just because she didn't get to sell it. Surely other people must have turned down her offer of representation before." And I hadn't even really turned it down. Not yet. I just hadn't called her, was all.

Kate shrugged.

"Anyone else?" Wayne asked. "Do you think this could be connected to that letter?"

"Mr. Rodgers told me that someone had tried to contest

the will, although he wouldn't tell me who. I brought the letter for you." I dug my hand into the bright corduroy tote bag that doubles as my purse. Meanwhile, Kate cleared her throat diffidently.

Wayne turned to her.

"Yes, Kate?"

"I was just thinking . . . what about the twins?"

"The twins?" I repeated, glancing up.

Wayne sent Kate a quelling look but answered my question anyway, if a little reluctantly. "Kate is talking about Randall and Raymond Stenham. Local boys, owners of a construction company."

I looked from one to the other of them. "Why would they break into Aunt Inga's house?"

"They're upset," Kate explained.

"They'd have to be, to smash that much china. But why would two people I've never heard of break into my aunt's house and destroy her kitchen?"

"She was their aunt, too," Kate said. Wayne leaned back on the sofa, rolling his eyes. I stared.

"Excuse me?"

"She was their aunt. Or great-aunt, like she was to you. They're your cousins, a few times removed. Actually, the three of you and your mother were probably Inga's only living relatives. Wayne grew up here; he can explain it to you."

She looked at him. Wayne sighed but rose to the occasion. "Your mother was Rosemary Morton, right? Her father was John Morton. He had a sister named Catherine. Catherine married Hamish Kendall and had a daughter named Mary Elizabeth, who married Roger Stenham and became the mother of Randall and Raymond. They're a couple of years older than you, I think."

"I see," I said. "So my mother and their mother are second cousins?" Wayne nodded. "Why would they break into Aunt Inga's house and destroy her stuff?"

"They're angry," Kate said again. "They assumed they'd inherit."

"Why didn't they? Aunt Inga must have known them a lot better than me. Why didn't she leave the house to them instead?"

Kate and Wayne exchanged another look, this one of amusement. "Bad blood," Wayne said. "Isn't long ago that they tried to have her declared incompetent so they could get their hands on her property."

"Yikes!" That's a pretty brutal way to treat family. No wonder she'd decided to leave the house to me—a relative unknown—rather than to them. I guess maybe she'd figured I'd be the lesser of two evils, and even if I decided to sell the place, at least the Stenhams wouldn't get it.

"They're real estate developers," Kate explained. "And they've already got clearance to level the house and subdivide the property for condos. That's how sure they were that they would inherit. They tried to get Inga committed to a nursing home. And because they shot themselves in the foot with that charge of incompetence a couple of years ago, there was nothing they could do to claim incompetence now. I could totally see one of them breaking into your aunt's house to do some damage." She looked at Wayne, challenge clear in her hazel eyes. He sighed.

"I'll have a chat with them tomorrow. After I hear the results of the search. OK?"

Kate smiled approvingly.

Wayne added, "If they were involved, maybe a visit from the chief of police will be enough to keep them from trying again."

I nodded. "I appreciate it, Chief Rasmussen." I handed him the letter. "It arrived two days ago."

I watched as the chief of police opened the envelope and pulled out the single sheet of copy paper inside. His lips pursed as he read the message again. Kate, reading over his shoulder, looked from him to me and got to her feet.

"Come on, Avery. Let's get you settled in Shannon's room. You must be tired from the trip and everything that's happened. A good night's sleep will make you feel better. Everything will seem less difficult in the morning."

She put her hand on my back and guided me out of the kitchen. I went along with her, but I was thinking to myself that it was going to take more than a good night's sleep for me to feel OK about the fact that someone seemed to be threatening not only my property but my life.

Kate's Mr. Ellis showed up the next morning, and scared the bejeezus out of me while he was at it.

I had slept like the dead—Kate had some seriously comfortable beds in her establishment—and after breakfast, which she insisted on feeding me although I wasn't actually a paying guest, I walked up the hill to Aunt Inga's house and let myself in. Kate was right: everything did seem less scary in the bright light of day, and I wasn't too worried about being back there.

The cop Chief Rasmussen had sent over, a sweet young thing of barely twenty, with soft peach fuzz on his chin and a bright-eyed, eager look, had finished going over the kitchen for fingerprints. There was gray powder everywhere that I would have to wipe away once I had finished picking up the broken crockery. He hadn't found any evidence of forced entry; not surprisingly, as the key had been under the mat for anyone to find and use.

After young Officer Thomas had taken his leave, I dressed in old clothes and got busy picking up debris. Many of the broken dishes were in the Blue Willow pattern—creamy porcelain with hand-painted trees, birds, and bridges in gleaming cobalt blue—and while I threw everything else straight into the trash can, I kept those aside. I wasn't sure exactly what I planned to do with them, but the crisp pattern spoke to me. Maybe, when I found another design job, I could copy it for something. It would look lovely on a bed-spread, or pillows, or a dress. Or maybe I could even use the pieces themselves for something. Mosaic a picture frame or tabletop or something like that.

Aunt Inga owned an old-fashioned kitchen radio, dating from circa 1975, which I had managed to tune to a local sta-tion, and I was singing along with Bruce Springsteen, wig-gling my hips to the beat as I worked. I was standing like an ostrich, my derriere in the air and my head buried under the kitchen table, sorting through the pottery pieces that were there, when I happened to glance back and saw another pair of legs, encased in faded jeans and ending in a pair of scuffed work boots, standing behind me.

For a second I couldn't believe my eyes: someone else was in the house? Why hadn't I heard him come in? And then fear struck. Was this the same person who had broken in yesterday? Had he been looking for me then, and now he'd come back to finish the job?

My breath hitched in my throat as my fingers tightened around the dustpan, the most lethal weapon at hand. I con-sidered turning and slashing at him with it, before making a break for the front door, but I wasn't sure I could get up without braining myself on the underside of the table; plus his legs looked a lot longer than mine, and he'd probably catch me. Instead, I dropped to my knees and scurried under the table on all fours, popping up on the other side to face my intruder across the not-quite-large-enough expanse of enamel.

At first glance, he didn't look that scary. (Not unless one happened to be an unattached female with a soft spot for good-looking guys with melting blue eyes. In that case, all bets were off. Good thing I was fed up with men.)

"Miss Baker?" he said, apparently taken aback at my re-action.

I nodded, eyes wide.

"My name's Derek Ellis."

I blinked. From what Kate had said, I had pictured the handyman in his late middle years, between fifty and sixty perhaps, with a balding pate and a paunch. Someone who wore plaid shirts and chewed tobacco.

Derek did have the plaid shirt, open, over a well-washed T-shirt, and a pair of faded jeans that fit just right. But after that, my picture and reality parted ways. He was no more than three or four years older than me, and three-quarters of a foot taller. There was no paunch in sight, and he had all his hair, which was just a touch closer to blond than brown. It was thick and healthy and in need of a cut, and it curled around his ears and flopped over his forehead. I could imagine that many a woman's fingers might have itched to brush it aside. Mine twitched, too, around the handle of the dust-pan. "Wow," I said eloquently.

Derek Ellis's lips twitched. "I thought you knew I was coming."

I lowered the dustpan. I didn't seem to be in any imminent danger. "I did know you were coming. Although I thought you'd knock before you walked in."

"I rang the bell."

"Did you really?" I shrugged. "Like most everything else in this house, it probably doesn't work." The radio, blaring away on the counter, probably hadn't helped, either. I glanced at it but was unwilling—so far—to leave the safety of the far side of the table to turn it off.

Ellis didn't notice. He looked around at the cracked vinyl, rusty sink, and leaning cabinets. I did the same. And I know for a fact that the expression on my face was one of resigned horror. Ellis's was—there's no other word for it—inspired. His eyes, the clear blue of cornflowers, turned soft and dreamy.

"Kate says you helped her renovate her house," I said, laying the dustpan on the table.

He tore his eyes away from the siren song of broken floors and peeling paint long enough to pull a business card out of his pocket and hand it to me. I looked at it. "Waterfield R and R?"

"Not that kind of R and R." Either he was reading my mind or he had heard it before. "Remodeling and restoration."

"Kate says you're good."

"When she's right, she's right."

No false modesty there. "I suppose she told you that I have to get my aunt's house in shape before I can sell it?"

He nodded. "Not worth as much as you'd like, I understand."

"No," I answered, "I don't think you do. The Realtor I spoke to offered me a hundred thousand dollars. Kate told me that if I fixed the house up, it might be worth three hundred thousand. I'm out of work. I need to make some money to tide me over until I can find another job. I figure if I spend a couple of weeks and a few thousand dollars ..."

I stopped when Derek Ellis started chuckling. It was an

appealing chuckle, spontaneous and genuine. He had even, white teeth and a dimple, and under other circumstances, I might have found him attractive. At the moment, I was too busy processing the fact that he seemed to be laughing at me. "I don't understand what's so funny," I said stiffly.

"I can see you don't." He wiped away tears of amusement before he continued, his voice uneven. "If you're gonna renovate an old house, Tinkerbell, first thing you gotta learn is, it always takes longer and costs more than you think. Your couple of weeks will turn into a couple of months, and your few thousand dollars will turn into fifteen or twenty."

"I have twenty thousand," I said, "although I was planning to use some of that to live on…"

"Of course you were."

"And I planned to do as much of the work as I could myself, to save money. I may not be able to haul lumber or sand floors…"

"The sander would run away with you," Derek Ellis nodded, leaning against the counter with his arms folded across his chest, blue eyes assessing me. "You don't look like you weigh more than one hundred ten pounds soaking wet. And you'd probably cut the electricity to all of Waterfield if you tried to rewire the doorbell."

I bit my tongue—hard—before answering. "I'm sure the local library has one of those books, *Renovating for Dummies*."

He grinned.

"I'll need some help, though. If you don't think you're up for it, I'll find someone else."

I waited, but Derek was silent, allowing me to go on. "I don't have expensive tastes. I can live on canned tuna and tap water if I have to. I'll be staying here at the house, so I won't have to pay rent. And I don't have a car, so I won't have expenses for gas…"

"No car?" Derek interrupted. "How do you plan to get around?"

"Walk," I said succinctly. "This is a small town. Since I won't have much of a life outside this house…" The projects would be all-consuming, both the renovating and trying to discover what deep, dark secret Aunt Inga had died before she'd had the chance to impart. "I figure I can get around just fine on foot."

Derek quirked a brow. "And when you need two-by-fours from the lumber depot? How are you gonna get those home?"

I wasn't entirely sure what two-by-fours were, but presumably they were too big to carry. "Ask them to deliver?"

Derek rolled his eyes.

"Fine," I said. "So maybe I didn't think this through all the way. Give me a break, OK? It's the first time I've tried to renovate a house. I don't know all the details." I waited a beat before I added, "Bet *you* have a car, though."

"A Ford F-150," Derek corrected. When I looked blank, he clarified, "It's a pickup truck."

"Even better. So you could carry the…what did you call them?…two-by-fours back from the lumber depot no problem."

I smiled optimistically. The corners of Derek's mouth curled. "I suppose I could, if I were inclined to."

I batted my eyes, looking hopeful and girlishly coy. "What would it take to make you inclined to?"

He leaned a little closer, lowering his voice seductively. I admit it, I held my breath while I waited for him to speak. "Six hundred a week plus a twenty percent bonus when the house sells," he said.

So much for looking girly and cute. I squinted suspiciously. "Twenty percent of what?"

"The selling price, of course."

"That seems rather steep," I said. "A real estate agent only gets six percent." At least that's what Melissa James had wanted.

"A real estate agent won't have spent three months working his tail off. But if you prefer, you can pay me by the job. I charge fifty dollars to rewire the doorbell and three thousand to redo the kitchen. Plus materials." He looked around at the scattered porcelain shards, and added, "If you want help with the cleanup, that's thirty dollars an hour."

"Six hundred a week is fine," I said. He smiled, or maybe smirked is more accurate. Until I added, "And I'll give you a ten percent bonus, but only on the net." He shrugged.

"It was worth a try. I can start Monday. How is six A.M.?"

"Much too early. I never get up before eight."

"You'd better set your alarm, then. Unless you want me catching you in bed."

I shook my head quickly. That was a complication I could do without.

He grinned. "I'll see you Monday, Tinkerbell." He wandered toward the hall door, then turned when he heard me come trotting down the hallway after him.

"You don't have to see me out. I can find my own way."

"I want to make sure the front door is bolted behind you," I explained. "I'd hate for anyone else to walk in. The next person may not be as harmless as you."

His eyebrows rose, but he didn't comment. I stood in the doorway and watched him walk through the weedy yard before locking the door and fastening the security chain. Just as I was about to turn around and go back to the task of sort-

ing pottery pieces, I heard the growl of a large engine outside and paused for a moment to peek through the window
to watch Derek's vehicle pull away from the curb and into
the street. And when I headed back to the kitchen, I was
gnawing my lip thoughtfully. Turns out that a Ford F-150 is
a big truck, one with plenty of room in the back for two-by-
fours, whatever they may be. This particular Ford F-150
was black with tinted windows, and it looked very much
like the truck I had seen the first time I'd been here. The
truck that had taken off from the curb with that same impatient growl and that had nearly clipped the front of my rental
car in its hurry to get away from Aunt Inga's house.

. . .

Around dinnertime, I had another visitor. There was a knock
on the door, and when I looked out, I saw a cream-colored
Mercedes parked at the curb.

I managed to bite back a groan, but just barely. For a second I thought about staying inside and pretending I wasn't
home. I didn't want to talk to Melissa James. I had been
dreading this moment, when I'd have to face her and explain that I had decided not to sell Aunt Inga's house after
all. And I especially didn't want to see her when she was,
once again, dressed to kill in a Roberto Cavalli raw silk suit
and eight-hundred-dollar Manolo Blahnik pumps, while I
was wearing my oldest jeans, a dirty T-shirt, and no lipstick,
with my hair tucked under a scarf.

Too late. She had seen me peer out, and hiding would
have been childish. Instead, I opened the door and gave her
my best smile. I was a New York designer (out of work, ad-
mittedly, but still), and she was a provincial real estate
agent; I had no reason to feel inadequate. "Why, hello, Melissa. Won't you come in?"

"I'd love to," Melissa said. She stepped delicately over the threshold and into the house, giving the impression that dirt and dust was simply attaching itself to her leg as she did it.

"Have a seat." I indicated the worn love seat in the parlor. It must be where the cats hung out when they were home, because the gray velvet was covered with cat hair. I crossed my fingers surreptitiously, hoping that some of it might adhere to Melissa's elegant posterior. "What can I do for you?"

She sat down, crossed her legs—I had a momentary vision of Tara on Philippe's sofa—leaned back, and smiled. "You can accept my client's offer of one hundred ten thousand dollars."

I lifted an eyebrow. "The offer went up?"

Melissa shrugged elegantly. "When you didn't call me, I assumed it was because you weren't interested. So I spoke to my client and asked him if he wanted to sweeten the deal. He said he could go to one hundred ten thousand dollars and still come out OK."

Something in her voice sounded off, like she was having a private laugh. It seemed to me that maybe her client thought that one hundred ten thousand dollars would be a steal, and he'd come out OK at a much higher price. For a second I thought about calling her on it, but then I decided that it didn't matter. The house wasn't for sale. Not yet.

"I'm sorry," I said, not too sincerely, "but I've decided to hang on to the house for now. Make some repairs and do some updating. I don't want to off-load it to the first person who asks. Especially for so little money. This was my aunt's home, and I feel I owe it to her to treat it with respect."

Plus, I still had to discover Aunt Inga's secret and right whatever wrong she had mentioned in her letter.

Melissa didn't answer for a moment, just looked at me. "It's a big job," she said eventually, looking around. "Are you sure you want to take it on?"

I shrugged. "I want to try. If it doesn't work out, I can always sell it later."

"That's true," Melissa said with another bright smile. "I'll let Ra...my client know that the house isn't for sale at the moment, but that he's first in line when you change your mind."

That wasn't exactly what I'd said, but I let it go. Melissa stood up and extended her hand. "Stay in touch, Avery. Let me know how it goes."

"Sure," I said, gesturing her to precede me out into the hallway. When her back was turned, I stared intently at her perfect rear end, but to my disappointment, the silk was slick enough that the cat hairs just slid right off and landed on the floor. Something else I'd have to clean up. That figured.

• • •

"Of course," Mother said when I called her that evening, "of course I remember my cousin Mary Elizabeth. We didn't grow up together, but I'd see her at family gatherings and such. Why do you ask?"

"Her name came up," I said vaguely. My mother was on the other side of the continent, thousands of miles and several time zones away; there was no reason to worry her with the news that someone had broken into Aunt Inga's house and vandalized it. Or that I was getting what amounted to death threats. "I didn't realize I had family up here. Other than Aunt Inga, I mean."

"Your grandfather was born in Waterfield, dear. He moved to Portland when he was a young man. His sister

Catherine was already married then. For as long as my father was alive, we'd go back to visit occasionally. Once Daddy passed on, the visits became fewer, and then, when Aunt Catherine died, I had even less reason to visit. Mary Elizabeth and I were never close, and I was living in New York by then; the trip was longer and more difficult. I'm sure you don't remember, but the reason we went to Waterfield when you were five was to pay our respects to Aunt Catherine."

"That's when Aunt Catherine died? Did I go to the funeral?"

"Oh, no," Mother said. "You stayed at the house with Aunt Inga and the cats while I went to the funeral."

"Why didn't Aunt Inga go to the funeral?" Waterfield wasn't a big town now and must have been smaller then; Inga and Catherine had to have known each other.

"Oh, dear." I could practically hear Mother biting her lip. When she answered, her voice was lowered, as if she were afraid that someone would overhear. "Catherine and Inga didn't get along. They'd had some sort of falling-out years ago, and never mended the relationship. Something about a young man, I believe. I think Catherine may have stolen Inga's beau or something."

"Gosh," I said, thinking of the leggy Tara, "that would certainly be enough to make me want to avoid her for the rest of my life." I think I'd probably go to her funeral, though. To make sure she was really dead, and to dance on her grave. OK, maybe that was a little harsh. "Why didn't you and your cousin Mary Elizabeth get along?" Had Mary Elizabeth tried to steal Mother's boyfriend at some point, too?

"I didn't say we didn't get along, just that we were never close. She's five or six years older than me, and we only saw each other occasionally. I left Portland at eighteen to go to college. By then, Mary Elizabeth was already married and settled in Waterfield with her husband. A couple of years later they had twins."

"That's what I hear," I said. "The police chief…" I bit my tongue, but it was too late.

"Police chief?" Mother repeated. "You've been talking to the police? Why? Nothing's wrong, is it?"

"Nothing I can't handle. Chief Rasmussen is dating the woman who runs the B and B where I stayed last…" I hesitated for a tenth of a second. "…week. They were telling me about the Stenham brothers. Mary Elizabeth's children. Apparently they tried to have Aunt Inga declared incompetent a few years ago, so they could get their hands on her property."

Mother snorted. "I can imagine how well that must have gone over. Aunt Inga was sharp as a tack. Physically, she may have been wearing down, but there was nothing wrong with her mental capabilities."

I nodded. "The doctor must have agreed with you, because the Stenhams didn't get her power of attorney. From what I understand, they assumed they would inherit when she died. They were all set to tear down the house and build condos when they discovered that she had left it all to me." The Stenhams were probably the relatives Mr. Rodgers had mentioned, who had threatened to sue. "I can't really blame Aunt Inga, though," I added. "If someone tried to have me declared incompetent, I wouldn't have left them my house, either."

"Not only that," Mother said, "but they tried to shave poor Prissy once."

"Prissy?"

"One of the cats. It's more than twenty years ago now;

I'm sure Prissy is no more. The twins would have been twelve or thirteen, I think."

"Gosh," I said, fascinated in spite of myself, "what happened?"

"Oh, not much. When poor Prissy came home, practically bald, Aunt Inga paid a visit to Mary Elizabeth and saw that Ray and Randy had scratches all up and down their arms. She threatened to report them to the police and the ASPCA if it happened again. Mary Elizabeth was quite upset."

"I can imagine." If they had been my children, I would have been upset, too. Not to mention embarrassed to claim them as my own.

"Oh, not because they were nasty little beasts who had hacked most of the fur off that poor animal, dear. Because she thought Aunt Inga was making a mountain out of a molehill." Mother paused. "I guess you don't remember Ray and Randy, do you? You met them that summer we were up there."

"I did? No, I don't remember that at all."

"You've probably blocked it. They were thoroughly awful little boys. Three or four years older than you, and big for their age, while you were on the small side even then..."

I nodded. I was always the shortest kid in my class, and things haven't changed much since I was little. No pun intended.

"They came over to play while Mary Elizabeth and I went to Catherine's funeral, and of course they ran roughshod over you. You had bruises all over your little legs when I came back, so they must have been throwing rocks..."

"Not rocks." I shook my head, remembering now. "Those hard, green apples. There's a tree in the backyard, remember? They tricked me into playing cowboys and Indians and left me tied to the tree for hours while they pelted me with apples..."

Mother sat in sympathetic silence while my voice shook. Oh yes, I remembered the Stenham twins now. Two nine-year-old bullies with black curly hair, red cheeks, oversized teeth, and braying laughs.

"So how are things going?" Mother asked divertingly. "Are you getting settled in all right?"

I wriggled my aching body a little farther into the soft pillows on the bed. "I suppose. The place is a horrible mess. I've spent all day scrubbing, and all I've managed to do is clean the downstairs and arrange a bedroom for myself. I found an upstairs room with a view of the garden, where I think we stayed when we were here before. There's something familiar about it. It has an old-fashioned twin bed and a matching toilet table with a mirror, and a whole lot of vintage clothes in the closet, mostly from the 1940s and '50s. Aunt Inga's, I guess. Great old fabric in good condition. I'll keep them, if you don't mind."

"That sounds fine, dear," Mother said. "Offhand, I can't think of anything of Aunt Inga's that I'd like to have, but if you find family photographs or letters or anything like that, you'll keep those aside for me, won't you, Avery?"

"Of course," I said, slightly indignant. "I wasn't planning to sell Aunt Inga's personal correspondence on eBay. I'm not totally lacking in common courtesy or family feeling or whatever."

"Of course you're not, dear," Mother said soothingly. "I didn't mean to imply that you lack either sense or sensitivity. Just keep anything related to the family aside for me, if you don't mind."

I promised I would, and we said our good-byes and hung

up. And then I flopped back on the bed with a dispirited groan. Mother and Noel were on their way out to a romantic dinner, with wine and candlelight and the sound of waves crashing against the shore, and in New York, Philippe and Tara were probably hand-feeding each other pieces of *Cuisses de Grenouille à la Provençale* at Le Coq au Vin. Or, knowing Tara and her juvenile tastes, and Philippe and his, *Pissaladière* (pizza with tomatoes, onions, and anchovies) in bed. While all I had to do tonight was crack open a micro-waveable box of frozen macaroni and cheese. Alone. Sometimes, life just isn't fair.

—6—

Derek Ellis showed up as advertised, before dawn on Monday, with a truckful of tools and an attitude that came close to being the death of me. I'm not a morning person, and I was worn out from working hard all weekend. On Saturday, after cleaning all the pottery shards off the kitchen floor, I'd emptied the ancient, harvest gold refrigerator humming loudly in the corner. This had been a supremely unpleasant task, due to the fact that some of Aunt Inga's food had been sitting there for long enough to congeal and grow entire forests of green mold.

In addition to tackling the downstairs, I had also walked to the grocery store and returned dragging a couple of bags of food and more cleaning supplies. After that, I spent the rest of the day making sure I had somewhere to sleep and clean sheets to sleep on, which was a production number in itself, given Aunt Inga's circa 1960 washing machine. It must have taken ten minutes just to figure out where to pour the detergent. And then I pretty much collapsed into bed to make my phone call to California. I hadn't even had the energy to get back up to microwave the contemplated mac and cheese. On Sunday morning, I had scrubbed the ancient, footed bathtub before soaking my aching body in rusty, sulphur-smelling water. Thus restored, I had gone on to clean the rest of the bathroom. I had also cleaned the rest of the upstairs and tried to restore it to some semblance of order.

By the time I had done all this it was past dinnertime, and I didn't feel like I could move another muscle. So I gnawed on a dry bagel and fell into bed again, exhausted. When Derek showed up the next morning, I was blinking sleep out of my eyes as I stumbled down the stairs to let him in, wearing yesterday's dirty jeans and T-shirt and with my hair straggling over my face.

Unlike me, Mr. Ellis must have gotten his full eight hours of beauty sleep. His eyes were clear and bright, his hair was freshly washed and flopped distractingly over his forehead, and he filled out the plain, white T-shirt quite nicely, thank you. A tool belt was slung low around his hips, and he was obviously looking forward to getting to work.

"Morning, Tinkerbell." He grinned at me in passing. "I'll start tearing out the kitchen floor, if that's all right."

"Sure," I said, turning to look after him. "What do you want me to do?"

"Whatever you want. Go shopping or something." *Something female,* his tone seemed to say.

"I was thinking I could help…" I began. He stopped at the end of the hall, framed in the doorway.

"No offense, but unless you know what you're doing, I'd just as soon you'd stay out of the way. Wouldn't want you to get hurt." He ducked inside the kitchen. Irritated, I headed up the stairs to the second floor. Chivalry is well and good, but not when it interferes with my newfound resolutions.

By the time I got back downstairs, after washing and brushing and putting on clean clothes, I could hear prying and banging noises from the kitchen. When I stopped in the doorway, I saw that Derek had already ripped up several square feet of ancient vinyl. As I watched, he inserted his forked metal bar under another section of flooring and heaved. The muscles in his upper arms strained against the sleeves of the T-shirt, and the vinyl groaned. I smiled appreciatively. His personality might benefit from a few weeks at charm school, but there was nothing wrong with his looks.

The floor uncovered by the removal of at least three layers of ugly, outdated vinyl was another story: dried-out hardwood, almost black with age and old, hardened glue. I eyed it with disappointment. It bore no resemblance to the gleaming hardwoods in Kate's house, or even to the dusty and scuffed wood floors in the rest of Aunt Inga's house. No wonder it had been covered. Derek might as well just put another layer of vinyl over it. Or maybe some tile. Or even industrial tile, the kind in video stores and health centers. The whole industrial look was popular in New York at the moment: lofts and warehouses being turned into living space, with exposed ductwork crisscrossing the ceiling and stainless steel everywhere. Aunt Inga's house, with its tall windows and taller ceilings, would be a great candidate for the loft look.

"What are you doing?" Derek asked curiously. He had stopped working and was looking at me.

I flushed; apparently I had been standing like a statue, staring into space, muttering to myself. Bad habit. "Sorry. I was just redesigning the kitchen in my mind. You know, picturing a new floor and new cabinets..."

"What do you want new cabinets for?" Derek wanted to know. "Nothing wrong with these. Solid wood, custom built sometime in the 1930s, by the look of 'em." To prove his point, he thumped the nearest cabinet door with his fist. The resulting thud was certainly solid.

"They look like something the cats dragged in," I objected and went on to elaborate, colorfully, "off the beach, somewhere. From a hundred-year-old shipwreck."

"Nonsense," Derek said dismissively. "They don't make cabinets like these anymore. Not unless you're willing to pay a craftsman a lot of money. You clean 'em, you sand 'em, you stain 'em or paint 'em...they're good as new." His hand slid caressingly along one cabinet front, the way another man might touch some shapely part of his girlfriend.

"I was thinking maybe something more modern...?" I said. "The industrial look is very popular right now. My... um...someone I know in New York just redid his kitchen with a concrete counter and industrial tile on the floor. Very current. Very hip. Very urban."

Derek's face congealed. "Industrial look?" he repeated.

I nodded brightly.

"Did you say a *concrete* counter?"

"And stainless steel appliances. Exposed brick walls, air ducts running underneath the ceiling; very utilitarian. The industrial look is the hottest thing in interior design in New York this year."

"Right," Derek said. "You may not have noticed, Miss Baker..."

"Call me Avery." Or Tinkerbell. Anything was better than the formal Miss Baker.

"...but you're not in New York anymore."

"Still," I said, "Miss James told me that stainless steel and granite is popular here in Waterfield as well..."

Derek's eyes narrowed. "Who?"

"Melissa James. You know, the real estate agent?" From the way she'd talked, I had assumed that everyone in Waterfield knew Melissa James.

"I know Melissa," Derek said. It could have been my imagination, but it looked like his hand tightened on the crowbar. I took a prudent step backward. "Melissa told you to tear out the old kitchen cabinets and put in stainless steel and granite?"

"Well...she didn't exactly tell me to do it. Not in so many words. It was more of a suggestion, I guess. She said that's what buyers are looking for."

Derek muttered something. From the look on his face I assumed it would be unprintable, so I didn't ask him to repeat it. "Listen, Miss Baker," he said. I opened my mouth, and he added, quickly, "Avery, I mean. Avery, there's nothing wrong with these kitchen cabinets. They're solid wood, well made, much better quality than anything you'll find these days, and there are plenty of 'em..."

"But they're a little old-fashioned, don't you think?"

"Nothing wrong with being old-fashioned," Derek said stubbornly.

"Of course not," I agreed, although I tend to think there are all sorts of things wrong with it. "But if we're going to try to sell this house for top dollar, to get us both as much money as possible—and you're getting ten percent, remember?— don't you think it would be better to give the people what they want? It's not like either you or I will be living here a few months from now. *We* don't have to look at it."

"I'm not putting in a concrete counter," Derek said. "I

don't care how urban and hip you say it is. This is a Victorian house; a concrete counter wouldn't look right."

"But it's *my* Victorian house. And *my* money you're using to renovate it. Don't you think that gives me the right to have whatever kitchen counter I choose?"

"Not if I'm doing the renovations," Derek said.

"Then maybe I should find someone else to do the renovations."

He grinned. "Maybe you should. Good luck finding someone else who'll do it for six hundred dollars a week."

I scowled. "Fine. Have it your way. I'm going to tackle Aunt Inga's desk. I'll be in the front parlor if you need me."

I didn't wait for an answer, just turned on my heel and marched down the hallway, ignoring his chuckle. Had there been a door to slam, I would have slammed it. The parlor had doors, but they were the sliding kind—solid wood pocket doors—and they didn't make anything like a satisfying bang when they met in the middle. Still, they served to keep me in and Derek out, and muffled considerably the sounds of his labor as I sat down at Aunt Inga's ugly 1970s desk and began tossing things around.

. . .

My aging aunt may have had a method to her madness, but if so, it wasn't discernible to me. The desk was just as disorganized as the rest of the house. The top surface was a jumble of receipts, opened and unopened mail—the unopened presumably brought in by Mr. Rodgers in the days since Aunt Inga's death—grocery coupons from Sunday's newspaper supplement, and little pieces of paper with scribbles on them, where Aunt Inga had added or subtracted numbers from her checkbook or written little reminders to herself to buy cat food or lightbulbs.

The top drawer was in a similar state, with the addition of about a half dozen pens and blunt pencils, some rubber bands, assorted paper clips and other fasteners, a bottle of Elmer's school glue, a wooden ruler that looked like it dated back to Aunt Inga's own school days, two rolls of Scotch tape, and a slew of other small items of the sort that most people accumulate over time and keep around to make their lives easier.

The bottom drawer held hanging file folders for Aunt Inga's bank account statements, income taxes, paid bills, and the like. I gave them a cursory glance, but as Mother had said, Aunt Inga hadn't owned much. I didn't find anything to contradict that impression.

Derek had gone to lunch sometime between eleven and noon, and I had taken advantage of his absence to sneak into the kitchen to see what he'd accomplished. So far, so good: the vinyl floor was gone, and so was the ugly half-circular sink that had hung on one wall. Or not gone, exactly; there was a big pile of debris on the lawn outside, but at least it was out of the house. I'd made myself a sandwich while I was out there, and had eaten it standing on the blackened floor, leaning against one of the (well-made, perfectly good) kitchen cabinets that Derek had insisted on saving. Now I was back at Aunt Inga's desk, turning over papers, digging for anything that might give me some idea why Aunt Inga had summoned me to Waterfield and what the big secret might be.

I was just lifting out a thick manila folder labeled with the word *Cats* when there was a knock on the front door. Startled, I jumped, and the file slipped from my hand and hit the edge of the desk, where it exploded all over the parlor floor.

"Damn!" I muttered, as papers flew everywhere. Then I raised my voice, "Yeah, yeah. Hold on, I'm coming."

I assumed it was Derek, back from lunch, and I was rather looking forward to taking some of my bad mood out on him. But instead, I saw the bright curls and brighter eyes of Kate McGillicutty through the window in the front door.

"Hi!" she said brightly when I opened the door. "I brought you your critters." She'd offered to keep them for the weekend, until I was settled in.

I looked around. There was nothing in her hands, not that I expected the regal Jemmy to have allowed himself to be carried. Or that Kate would have wanted to haul his bulk around. "Where?"

Kate waved a hand toward the street. "They took off as soon as I opened the car door." I looked past her to the tan station wagon parked at the curb. "They'll be back when they get hungry. Don't worry about them; they know how to get around." She peered curiously over my shoulder into the semidarkness of the house.

"In that case," I said and took a step aside, "would you care to come in?"

Kate grinned. "I thought you'd never ask."

"You've been here before, right?"

Kate nodded. "I came with Wayne to pick up the cats after your aunt . . . you know."

"Well, I've cleaned, and Derek Ellis has torn up the floor in the kitchen and removed the sink, but that's pretty much it so far." I wandered along the hallway toward the kitchen as I talked, with Kate trailing behind. "He refuses to take down the old cabinets; says they're constructed better than anything I'll be able to find these days. Never mind the fact that they're ugly as sin and not at all what I want. I was tempted to borrow that crowbar thing he's been using, and try to take them down myself, but he took it with him when he went to lunch." He'd been grinning when he walked out with it over his shoulder, too, as if he'd known what I was planning.

Kate giggled. "He isn't the easiest person in the world to get along with."

"No kidding."

"Although if you let him have his way, he might surprise you."

"It's *my* kitchen!" I said.

"But he's been doing this a lot longer than you. He knows his business. Just don't let him talk you into using real milk paint when it comes time to paint the walls. It stinks to high heaven and is really hard to apply. Unless you buy the powdered kind; that's not so bad. But he talked me into painting my kitchen with the real thing, put together from old, curdled milk and lime and powdered brick. It's beautiful, and it'll last forever, but what a horrible experience!"

"Surely it can't be any worse than the air in New York," I said bravely but nonetheless slightly nauseous at the thought of applying curdled milk to my walls.

"I wouldn't count on that," Kate answered. "You know, there are things you can do to the existing cabinets to jazz them up. You're a designer, right? I'm sure you can think of something fun. They're your basic picture-frame construction, see?" She pointed to a cabinet door, which did indeed look something like a framed picture, with a thicker border around a flat middle panel. "You could pop out the panel and put in something else, like glass or beadboard paneling. Paint the whole thing a funky color or two, and voilà, new cabinets!"

"That's true," I said, my eyes going glassy as I pictured the possibilities. Glass, beadboard paneling...fabric? Meanwhile, Kate wandered back down the hallway to the door to the parlor, and peered in. "What happened here?"

"Oh, right." I hurried after her. "Derek won't let me help him in the kitchen, so I decided to go through Aunt Inga's desk instead. You startled me when you knocked on the door, and I dropped one of the files." I sank to my knees on the floor next to the desk and began piling the contents of the cat file into an untidy stack.

"What sort of file?" Kate plopped down next to me to help.

"Medical histories and CFA registrations and stuff like that for the cats. Looks like they go to the veterinarian on Broad Street for checkups." I held up a bill for feline distemper vaccinations administered sometime in the past year.

"It's the best vet in Waterfield." Kate nodded, grabbing a few stray pieces of paper and adding them to the stack.

Halfway under the desk, I saw a small, white rectangle and reached for it. I assumed it would be the veterinarian's business card, filed away with the other cat-related paperwork, but I was mistaken. Oh, it was a business card, all right; it just didn't belong to Dr. Piedmont, the vet on Broad Street.

"Huh," I said.

"What's the matter?" Kate peered over at me, her hands full of paper.

"Found this under the desk." I handed it to her. "Martin Wentworth. That's the missing professor, right?"

Kate added her papers to the stack and took it. "Sure is. What's Martin Wentworth's card doing in your aunt's cat file?"

"I was hoping you'd be able to tell me that."

Kate shrugged. "Your guess is as good as mine. Maybe he liked Maine coon cats. Maybe he was writing an article about them and interviewed your aunt. Or maybe Jemmy and Inky got lost one day, and he found them and brought them home."

"How did your boyfriend's trip to Boston go last week? Anything new on the professor's disappearance?"

Kate grimaced. "Unfortunately not. Wayne went to talk to some of the staff at Boston University. That's where Professor Wentworth did his graduate work. But they haven't seen him. And neither has anyone else. He's still missing. Wayne's upset. Once they've been gone over seventy-two hours, the chances of finding them alive decrease every hour."

"Huh," I said.

Kate watched me for a moment. "What's the matter, Avery?"

I shrugged. "Probably nothing. It just seems a little strange that my aunt should write to me and ask me to come visit her, because she had some important family secret to share with me. But by the time I get here, she's dead, and Professor Wentworth is missing."

"That doesn't mean there's a connection."

"His card was in her desk," I said, holding it up. If that wasn't a connection, I didn't know what it was.

"Professor Wentworth probably just stopped by to talk to her about the history of Waterfield. She was very old. She probably knew a lot."

"Maybe. So you don't think we ought to call Chief Rasmussen to tell him that we found the card here?"

Kate shrugged. "I'll mention it to Wayne when I see him tonight. I don't suppose there's a date on the card, or anything like that? It might help if we had some idea when they met."

"I'm afraid not," I said, turning the card over. "Aunt Inga doesn't seem to have kept an appointment calendar, either. Didn't have many appointments to keep track of, I guess."

"I guess not," Kate agreed. "I'm not sure whether the professor kept a calendar, but if your aunt's name had been in it, I'm sure I would have heard."

I nodded. Most likely.

Kate opened her mouth to say something else but closed it again when the front door opened. I'd been so engrossed in our conversation that I hadn't heard Derek's truck drive up or the truck door slam outside. I watched as he sauntered into the hallway and spared a glance in our direction. When he saw that I wasn't alone, he did a comical double take that made me smother a laugh.

"Kate." Damned if he didn't blush, too.

"Hi, Derek," Kate said sweetly. "Long time no see."

Derek shrugged, scuffing the floor with the toe of one well-worn boot. "Been busy."

"Good for you. I'm glad you could find the time to help Avery." She smiled.

"My pleasure." He shot me a look.

"I'll bet," I said.

Kate looked at me with amusement lighting her hazel eyes.

"I'd better get to work," Derek added. "See you around, Kate. Don't let the door hit you on the way out."

He disappeared from the doorway, and we could hear his steps recede down the hall toward the kitchen. I waited for the sound of tools starting up back there before I broke the silence.

"Is he always this charming?"

Kate giggled. "Pretty much, yes. You can't say I didn't warn you."

I shook my head. No, I couldn't.

7

The days settled into a groove. Derek showed up bright and early every morning with a disgustingly cheerful greeting and went to work in the kitchen or basement while I continued to sort through Aunt Inga's accumulated stuff, of which there was a lot. The Dumpster that Derek had ordered was filling up rapidly with discarded galvanized pipes, ratty vinyl, old newspapers, and ugly, broken furniture and knickknacks. Kate got into the habit of stopping by for a few hours in the afternoons to help me get the house habitable and—I think—to tease Derek. On Wednesday morning Wayne Rasmussen dropped in, too, to tell me what Officer Thomas had determined regarding my break-in, and also what he had found out from examining the envelope and threatening letter I had received.

"First off, Brandon found no evidence of forced entry when he was here on Saturday morning. Not that anyone would have needed to break in with the key under the mat."

I shook my head. And here I'd thought small towns were supposed to be safe.

"There were no fingerprints that didn't belong here. Yours, your aunt's, Mr. Rodgers's, a few of ours from when we found her. And, interestingly, Martin Wentworth's."

"Really?" I said.

Wayne nodded. "We snagged them from his condo when we first realized he was missing. Just in case of . . . well, you know."

I nodded. I did know, or if I didn't, I could make a good guess. Just in case they had to identify him by his fingerprints whenever they found him.

"Of course," Wayne added, "his prints here don't mean anything. We already suspected that they'd been in touch from the business card you found. Good job on that, by the way. But the card, along with those prints, could have been left anytime between September and now."

"That's true," I admitted. Assuming my aunt hadn't cleaned house in the eight or nine months before she died, anyway.

"As for your letter, we had no more luck there, I'm afraid. Lots of fingerprints, but none we could identify. The envelope and paper are basic, available in any office supply store, grocery store, or drugstore. The CVS and the Walgreens carry them, and so does Shaw's Supermarket. The letter could have been written on pretty much any computer in town, including those down at the police station, and printed on pretty much any printer, with standard black ink. The staff at the Waterfield Post Office couldn't identify who sent it. They don't remember seeing it before. And seeing as there are mailboxes all over Waterfield where it could have been deposited, there's no reason why they would."

"So there's no way to know who sent it to me?"

He shook his head. "You gave Mr. Rodgers your contact information before you left, and you signed the guest register at Kate's B and B with your New York address. And anyone who knew your name could have looked you up through the White Pages. I did, and you're listed."

"What did the Stenhams say when you spoke to them?"

Wayne made a face. "That they had nothing to do with the break-in and that I couldn't prove that they did. And I can't."

"So that's it?"

He nodded. "Afraid so. I'll keep an eye out, but for now, that's all I can do. You'll have Derek here during the day," he glanced toward the kitchen, where my handyman was once again hard at work, "and I'll have the patrol cars drive by a few times each night. If anything happens, don't hesitate to call 911."

I promised I wouldn't, and he took his leave. I went back to sorting through junk.

The coon cats had settled into the utility room, with their bowls and their kitty chow. To my amazement, there was no litter box to empty every few days. Jemmy and Inky weren't effete house cats, and they did their business out-of-doors. In fact, I saw them very rarely. As long as I kept their food and water dishes filled and didn't try to pick them up and cuddle them, they stayed out of my way. There was no snuggling up in bed at night; if they came home at all, through the cat flap in the back door, they preferred to sleep downstairs on the sofa in the parlor. Occasionally, I'd see one of them— the striped Jemmy or the coal black Inky—stalk away from the house, plumed tail waving, but mostly I forgot that they were there. Unless I forgot to feed them, and then they hunted me down, complaining loudly, and proceeded to twine themselves around my legs to trip me until I caught on to what they wanted and provided it.

Whenever I got bored with Aunt Inga's things or I wanted an excuse to move around and work out the kinks, I went to wherever Derek was and offered to help him. He invariably turned me down, with anything from a distracted frown to an amused grin depending on how his work was progressing that day. Occasionally, he'd allow Kate to make a suggestion, but for all intents and purposes, I was invisible. It irritated me. So much so that by Thursday afternoon, I was ready to scream.

"You know," I said when he was coming down the hallway toward the front door, ready to leave for the day, "this isn't how I planned it."

He stopped in front of me. There wasn't a whole lot else he could do, unless he wanted to move me bodily out of his way, which, obviously, he didn't. "No?"

I shook my head. "I'm happy that you're here, because I wouldn't know what to do without you. I mean, I wouldn't know how to do what you're doing if you weren't here to do it. But I thought I'd get to do some of the renovating myself, too." The fun parts. The parts that didn't involve replacing corroded pipes or scabbing rotted wood.

He grinned. "You just said you wouldn't know how to do what I'm doing if I wasn't here to do it."

"I'm not talking about redoing plumbing or shoring up walls," I said, rolling my eyes. *Jeez!* "I just want to do something simple. Something creative. Something that doesn't require specialized knowledge or really big muscles. I'm not a moron, you know. I can manage to swing a hammer without hitting my thumb. I can even use a brush for something other than painting my nails."

"Fine by me," Derek said. "Tomorrow, you can start taking down the wallpaper in the hall. It doesn't take strength or any special knowledge. It's just a boring, time-consuming, messy job that has to be done before the walls can be painted."

"Couldn't I just paint over it?" I suggested. "I know some great texturing techniques. You wouldn't be able to tell there was anything but plaster underneath." A couple of layers of thick oil paint ought to do the trick, with some appliquéd flowers or stars on top, maybe. My creative juices percolated.

From the expression on Derek's face—a kind of incredulous, half-pitying horror—you might have thought I'd suggested a spot of bank robbery.

"Guess not," I said.

Derek shook his head firmly. "No, Tinkerbell. You don't paint wallpaper. Ever. It makes it twice as hard to get off later. Plus, it just isn't *right*."

"It's not like anyone would know," I said.

"*I'd* know," Derek answered.

I rolled my eyes. "Other than you. You know, I know what your problem is."

He cocked his head. That irritating lock of hair fell into his eyes. "You do, huh?"

"I do, yes. You're a perfectionist. And a control freak. And set in your ways. And you have a problem with women. I don't know who turned you this way, and I don't care, but it wasn't me, so I'd appreciate it if you'd cut me some slack. I *am* paying your salary."

His lips twitched, but he managed to control himself. "That's true."

"So you'll let me do something?"

"I told you. You can strip the wallpaper in the hallway. When I get here in the morning, I'll give you what you need and help you get started."

"OK," I said happily. If I were a puppy, I'd probably wag my tail. As it was, I gave him a bright smile. "Have a good evening."

"Yeah."

I stepped away from the door, and he grabbed for the handle. His "You, too," was an afterthought, thrown over his shoulder as he walked briskly down the steps away from me.

• • •

No sooner had the Ford F-150 disappeared down the street than a late-model Mercedes, cream-colored and sleek, rolled up to the spot it had vacated and stopped. I bit back a groan. Why was it that whenever Melissa James dropped in, I always looked my worst?

However, this time she didn't seem interested in me. When she came up the walk, her attention was still focused on the street. "Was that Derek's car I saw?" were the first words out of her immaculately painted lips.

"I beg your pardon?" I said.

"Derek Ellis. I thought I saw his car."

"That's a truck," I said. "An F-150. And I hired him to do some work for me. That's not a problem, is it? He came highly recommended."

"Oh no," Melissa said, and I swear she was grinding her perfect teeth, "there's nothing wrong with his work." I don't think I imagined the slight emphasis on the last word.

I hid a smile. "Yes, Kate told me he's good with his hands."

When Kate had used that same expression a week or two ago, she hadn't seemed to recognize the double entendre. Melissa had no such problem. Her eyes narrowed for a second, although she didn't comment. "How is it working out?" she asked instead.

I shrugged. "As far as I can tell, just fine. He does his work; I stay out of his way. He tells me when he comes and goes, and that's pretty much it."

"Same old Derek," Melissa said indulgently. "Won't notice you unless you're outfitted with a plug and an on switch." She sent me a sympathetic look.

"Oh, I don't mind *that*," I answered cheerfully. "If he likes his tools better than me, that's fine. It's what I'm paying him for, isn't it?" I smiled brightly. "So what can I do for you, Melissa? Are you coming by to check progress?"

Melissa smiled depreciatingly, her glossy bob swinging. "Sorry, Avery. I have investors who are interested in the house, so any time you feel that you've gotten in over your head, just say the word, and I'll bring you an offer."

"Thanks," I said, "but Derek seems to know what he's doing."

"That's good to hear," Melissa answered, but she didn't sound like she meant it. "Well, I saw you out here and just wanted to say hello." She turned on her heel, preparatory to going back to the Mercedes.

"Would you like me to give Derek a message?" I asked her elegant back. "Tell him you stopped by?"

She turned again at the bottom of the steps. "It's much better for everyone if you just don't mention me to Derek, I think."

"I see," I said.

"I'll see you around, Avery. Take care of yourself."

"Right," I said, watching her sashay away, the long grass brushing her slender calves, "you, too." And I wished, I admit it, that she'd stumble over something under the overgrown weeds and, if not actually break her ankle, at least break the heel on one of her obscenely priced Manolos.

Once she was gone, I braved the grass myself, shuffling around the corner of the house to the backyard. There was a little shed at the end of the property, and I thought there was just a chance that there might be an old push mower or something back there. Hard to imagine Aunt Inga, at almost ninety-nine, pushing a manual mower around her own yard, but it was worth a look.

I wasn't entirely sure what I planned to do if I did find a push mower, or for that matter any other kind of mower, because it wasn't like I'd ever used one before. I wouldn't know how to turn it on, and I certainly couldn't imagine myself walking around the half-acre yard with it. Still, I thought I'd better look. So I waded through the grass down to the shed, removed the open padlock that held the door latch closed, and peered into the dark interior.

I needn't have worried. There was no lawn mower in the shed. Mostly, it was full of gardening tools: spades, hoes, pitchforks, and shears, plus about a thousand terra-cotta pots of various sizes. Aunt Inga must have enjoyed gardening before she got too old and infirm to keep up with the weeds and grass.

The only other thing of note was a bicycle. It was parked right in the middle of the small shed and looked incongruous sitting there, rubbing elbows with the well-used, rusty tools. It looked fairly new, a mountain bike with nubby wheels and some sort of lightweight frame. Maybe Aunt

Inga had bought it as a surprise for me, for when she expected me to visit. It looked more like a man's bike than a woman's, but maybe Aunt Inga didn't know the difference.

I contemplated taking it for a spin but decided against it. I really had to do something about the grass. Instead, I went inside the house and called Kate, whose grass was just as manicured and lovely as the rest of her B and B. Maybe she'd be able to tell me the name of the person she used to cut her lawn. However, I caught her on her way out the door, late for a date with Police Chief Rasmussen. "Ask Mr. Rodgers," she said quickly. "I do my own yard, but he has a huge house with at least two acres of grass around it, and I doubt he cuts it himself. Sorry, Avery, but I've got to run. Wayne's waiting in the car." She hung up before I could tell her about the bike I'd found.

So I dug out Mr. Rodgers's number and dialed the attorney. After I had explained my predicament, he offered to call a lawncare person for me.

"Oh, you don't have to do that," I protested.

"It is my pleasure, Miss Baker. I will arrange to have someone come out tomorrow to give you a quote."

"Thank you very much," I said.

"Is there anything else I can do for you, Miss Baker?"

"I don't think so," I answered. "Unless..."

"Yes?"

"I was just wondering...Did you ever have any contact with Professor Wentworth from Barnham College? Or know what he might have been doing in Aunt Inga's house?"

Mr. Rodgers was silent for a moment. "I don't believe so," he said eventually. His voice was somehow cautious, as if maybe he shouldn't be discussing Aunt Inga's business with anyone.

I tried to explain.

"See, I came across his business card the other day, when I went through Aunt Inga's desk."

"Oh?" Mr. Rodgers said.

"It had fallen into Aunt Inga's cat file. Where she kept her cats' vaccination records and kennel club registrations."

"I see," Mr. Rodgers said.

"And then Wayne—the chief of police—told me that they'd found Professor Wentworth's fingerprints in Aunt Inga's kitchen."

"Dear me," Mr. Rodgers said.

"And I was wondering if maybe the reason Aunt Inga wrote to ask me to visit had something to do with Professor Wentworth and with the history of Waterfield."

Mr. Rodgers didn't answer.

"But if you never met him, and Aunt Inga never talked about what they were doing, then I guess you can't help me."

"I'm afraid not, Miss Baker," Mr. Rodgers said.

"Thanks anyway."

"My pleasure, Miss Baker. Is there anything else I can do for you?"

"No," I said, "I don't think so. Unless... you didn't happen to give out my address to anyone during the time I was in New York, did you?"

Mr. Rodgers's tone became even stiffer. "Certainly not, Miss Baker."

"I didn't think so," I said apologetically, "but I thought I'd better ask. Someone sent me a threatening letter, and I thought perhaps one of my cousins..."

"Indeed not, Miss Baker. No one asked me for your contact information. I did, however, have a consultation with the Misters Stenham last week, when they came to discuss their desire to contest Miss Morton's will. I happened to step outside my office for a moment to use the copy machine, but of course it is not my intention to accuse anyone of anything."

"Of course not," I agreed, thinking that for someone whose intention it hadn't been to accuse one or both of the Stenhams of snooping through his desk for my contact information, he'd certainly managed to leave the impression that that's what they'd done.

Mr. Rodgers asked again, with commendable patience, whether there was anything else he could do for me. When I told him there wasn't, he said, "In that case, I will arrange to have someone come to your aunt's house tomorrow to give you a quote on the yard. And please don't hesitate to contact me if you need anything else."

I promised I wouldn't—hesitate, that is—and hung up before I could think of anything else I wanted to ask, so as not to keep the old gent from his dinner any longer.

My own stomach had started making plaintive noises, so I decided to take a walk into downtown to get some dinner. The weather was lovely, clear and cool. I'd been good all week, preparing and eating meals at the house, and I felt virtuous. Plus the fridge was almost bare, and I wanted something other than a tuna sandwich or macaroni and cheese for a change.

Aunt Inga's house was located three or four blocks from the center of Waterfield. As I walked down the steep street toward downtown, between rows of Victorian cottages spilling flowers out over and through picket fences, with a fresh sea breeze teasing my hair into snarls, I wondered if I would ever start thinking of it as *my* house and not Aunt Inga's. Or if maybe it would be better if I didn't. It wouldn't stay my house for long, and the less attached to it I was, the easier it would be to leave it at the end of the summer. When I returned to my shower, my working kitchen, and the hot and aromatic canyons of New York City.

Breathing deeply of the fresh air, nice while it lasted, I turned my attention to other things. As Mother had told me, Waterfield is the third-oldest town in Maine. The two older ones are Kittery and York, just FYI. Waterfield is smaller than either of them, with well under ten thousand inhabitants, although there was a lot of new construction going on, and the population of Waterfield was growing daily. Add to that the summer people, the ones with vacation cottages in the area, and there was plenty of activity around, with people wandering along the streets, in and out of the storefronts, as I threaded my way down Main Street. I could hear soft Southern accents and Texas drawls and even a few foreign tongues, along with plenty of the clipped downeastern dialect.

Waterfield's main drag is a whopping two blocks long, built at the turn of the century. Last century. Late-Victorian commercial buildings lined the street, two and three stories tall with storefronts and offices on the main level and storage, apartments, or offices above. Everything was beyond quaint, so cute and clean and pretty that it looked like a movie set. I detected Melissa James's guiding hand in some of the more outrageous loveliness, like the baskets of velvety petunias hanging from all the lampposts, as well as the boxes of free real estate magazines on every corner.

I had passed the offices of Waterfield Realty and was on my way past the Grantham Gallery when someone bumped into me and knocked me rudely backward a step or two. I didn't exactly fall, although I stumbled, and it took me a moment to regain my balance. Once I had, I spun around, ready to do battle.

The man was tall and broad, and like me, he had curly hair. Unlike mine, his was short and dark, expensively cut and gelled, and he was wearing designer khakis and a short-sleeved, black polo shirt. Stenham Construction was embroidered across one pectoral in loopy script.

"Randy, I presume? Or is it Ray?"

Ray—or Randy; I never could tell them apart, even as a child—showed me all his teeth. They were less oversized than they used to be, but there were still a lot of them. If it was intended as a family-friendly, reassuring grin, it failed miserably. And of course he refrained from making my life any easier by telling me whether he was in fact Randy or Ray. "Evening, Cousin Avery," he said instead. "I'd have known you anywhere. You haven't changed much in thirty years." The implication was that I was still short, skinny, and easy to push around.

"Twenty-six years," I corrected, not bothering to sound friendly. If he wasn't going to be nice, why should I? I may be short and skinny, but I'm not as easy to push around as I used to be, especially by someone who implies that I look older than I am.

He folded muscular arms across his chest. "I hear you're renovating Aunt Inga's house."

I looked up at him. Way up. He was almost a full head taller than me and correspondingly broad. "She left it to me, so I figure I can do what I want with it."

Ray—Randy?—grinned nastily. "How's it going?" he asked.

"Slowly. With all the things Aunt Inga never got around to fixing, and the furniture and boxes everywhere, not to mention the mess that someone left in the kitchen..."

I watched him, hoping he'd give himself away, but I was disappointed. He nodded. "I heard about that. Wayne Rasmussen stopped by. He seemed to think that my brother and I might have had something to do with it."

"And did you?"

"Would we do something like that?"

"I don't know," I said. "Would you?"

His eyes turned a flat, muddy brown, like pebbles, and he lowered his voice as he leaned closer to me. "A word of advice, Cousin."

"Sure," I said, trying not to show that the way he towered over me made me feel uneasy. He must have guessed anyway, because his lips curved unpleasantly.

"We've been working construction for eighteen years now. There isn't much we don't know about houses, including everything that can go wrong with them. Electrical shorts, plumbing leaks, falling bricks hitting people on the head…" He paused to let those visuals sink in, before he continued. "A single woman living alone can't be too careful. You should consider leaving…while you can." He smiled, but it didn't reach his eyes.

I would have stepped back if I could, but I was already pressed up against the brick wall of the gallery, with nowhere to go. "Are you threatening me?" I asked, and I'm afraid my voice sounded just as shaky as I felt.

My cousin straightened up, feigning shock.

"Of course not, Cousin Avery. It's just a friendly bit of advice. Between family, yeah?"

"Right," I said. He opened his mouth, but before he could say anything, someone else spoke. "Everything OK, Avery?"

8

I recognized the voice, and so, obviously, did my cousin. He was smiling unpleasantly when he turned around. "Evening, Ellis."

"Stenham." Derek nodded curtly, but his eyes were examining me. I forced a smile.

"Hi, Derek. Sure. Everything's fine."

"We're just having a friendly conversation," Ray/Randy explained, inching a little closer to me, putting him and me on one side, Derek on the other. "About a family matter." He put emphasis on the word *family*.

Derek didn't seem at all intimidated by the larger man, and his smile was every bit as unpleasant as Ray's had been. "I think under the circumstances we're almost family, don't you?" He waited for a moment to hear Ray's reply, but when Ray didn't make one—in fact, it looked like he flushed angrily—Derek continued, his voice gentle. "I know just as much about old houses as you and your brother. More, since those replicas you're putting up these days are held together with spit and plumber's putty. And if anything happens to Avery's house while I'm working on it, and I think you had something to do with it, there isn't a hole deep enough for you to hide in, Stenham."

"Ooooh!" Ray grinned, squaring his shoulders. "I'm quaking, Ellis."

It was Derek's turn to flush angrily, but without sounding like he was twelve years old and about to get involved in a schoolyard squabble, there wasn't much he could say. His fists clenched, but he didn't move, and Ray smirked as if he had won some kind of victory. He swaggered off, bumping Derek with his shoulder in passing. We stood and watched him make his way down the sidewalk, edging people aside as he went. He got into a black truck similar to Derek's and pulled away. I got a glimpse of a white sticker on the door and recognized the Stenham logo from Ray's—Randy's—shirt. Derek turned to me. "You OK?"

I nodded. "Thanks for rescuing me."

He shrugged. "You didn't look like you were doing too badly on your own."

"How much of the conversation did you hear?" My hands were a little unsteady, and I shoved them in my pockets.

"Enough. I used to get into fights with Ray and Randy when I was a kid. They're not concerned about fair play, and they've never heard that it's wrong to pick on someone smaller."

"I've had run-ins with them before, too." I nodded. Granted, there is a bit of difference between the tricks they played on me when we were small and what Ray (or Randy) had seemed to threaten tonight, but I didn't want Derek to think I was one of those damsels in distress, incapable of taking care of myself.

"Then you know what you're dealing with. Keep your eyes open on the way home."

I promised I would and watched him walk away across the street before I turned and hurried up the hill toward Aunt Inga's house again. The whole incident had made me re-evaluate the comfort of a bowl of macaroni and cheese be-hind my own closed door.

· · ·

"You wanna do *what*?!" Derek said.

It was the next morning, and we were standing in the kitchen. I had spent at least half the night tossing and turn-ing, my mind abuzz with the unsettling encounter with my cousin. It had been worth it, though. Those hours lying awake trying to think of other things had given me an idea for what I wanted to do with Aunt Inga's broken pieces of Blue Willow pottery. And Aunt Inga's kitchen counter. That idea was what had gotten this response from Derek.

"I thought you'd be happy," I said. "It's better than a con-crete counter, isn't it?"

Derek muttered something. I waited. "I suppose," he said eventually.

"It's not like I'm asking *you* to do it," I pointed out. "I'll handle it myself. I've done mosaic before. On smaller sur-faces, and with little pieces of glass, but I'm sure it's a simi-lar process. All I need is for you to tell me what materials and tools I need. And maybe just stand by when I'm starting out, to make sure I'm doing it right."

"That's all, huh? You sure there isn't anything else?"

I shook my head. "I think that ought to do it. Ex-cept...you could be a little more encouraging. I'm not stupid, you know. When it comes to interior design, I probably know more than you do. No offense, but it's my field. I majored in textile design, but one doesn't graduate from Parsons summa cum laude without picking up a few interior design credits along the way."

"I'm sure," Derek said. "Here." He handed me a funny-looking plastic and metal tool, round with a small serrated wheel underneath. When I stared at it blankly, he added, "It's a scoring tool. When you run it over the wallpaper in the hallway, it makes little holes. Then, when you spray the walls with adhesive remover, it'll seep into the holes and make it easier to take the wallpaper down."

"My kitchen counter . . ." I began, with a sideways glance toward it. Now that I'd had the idea of turning Aunt Inga's broken dishes into a countertop, I was eager to get started.

"Can wait till next week." And with any luck, his tone said, by then I would have forgotten all about it and gone on to some other fleeting fancy.

"Fine," I said. "Be that way." I did a precise about-turn on my heel and stalked out into the hallway where I took out my frustrations by running the scoring tool violently up and down and all around the walls. Derek laughed and got busy.

The rest of the day progressed in the same manner. Silently. Apart from spending a few minutes talking to Mr. Todd, who came to give a quote on cutting the grass, I didn't speak a word. Derek clanged and banged down in the basement, redoing the kitchen plumbing, and I seethed. He went to lunch at his usual time, and I had my usual tuna on whole wheat at the now-controversial kitchen counter. At four forty-five, he cleaned up his tools and asked me to pay him for his first week's work. I was still laboring over the walls, tediously peeling off slivers of paper that had been there for one hundred years and were loath to relinquish their hold on life. I was coming to see the truth of what Derek had told me: renovating a house always takes longer and costs more than you think. Writing the check was painful; not because he didn't deserve the money but because I knew it was only the first of many such checks I'd have to write.

Derek left to get to the bank before it closed, and I went back to stripping wallpaper. It was tedious and annoying work, although strangely satisfying.

Between yanks I kicked myself. Dammit, what was it with me and men? Why did I always end up working with these egotistical jerks who made a career of preventing me from doing what I wanted? I was paying Derek's salary, dammit; didn't that entitle me to some say? If I wanted new kitchen cabinets, and I was willing to pay for them, shouldn't I be able to have them? And I'd bowed to his wishes and found a compromise for the concrete counter, but now he'd ix-nayed that, too. He was just like Philippe: nothing was ever good enough unless it was his idea. For fifty cents I'd fire him, except I needed him. He worked damned hard for his $600 a week, and if he could make Aunt Inga's house look like Kate's B and B when it was finished, that was worth quite a bit of aggravation. Still, I wished he could be a little easier to get along with. And not quite so good-looking. Because, let's face it, the fact that I found him attractive only served to make his attitude toward me more irritating.

By seven o'clock, I'd had enough. I'd missed enjoying dinner out yesterday, so I figured I'd treat myself tonight instead. And instead of heading into downtown, in case I ran into Ray or Randy again, I pulled the bike I'd found out of the shed and pedaled in the other direction instead. I ended up at a cinder-block place called Mario's, out beyond the edge of town, where I indulged in several slices of shellfish pizza, telling myself I'd work them off on the ride home.

By the time I was coming back to town, it was going on ten o'clock, and things in Waterfield were dark and quiet. As I pedaled along the ocean road, all I could hear was the crashing of the waves below the cliffs, the rhythmic sound almost drowning out the soft whirring of my textured bicycle wheels. There was no moon in the sky, but the stars were brilliant, and the black sea rippled with foamy crests. The cool breeze puckered the skin on my arms and whipped my hair across my face, and I breathed deeply, enjoying the change from the stuffy streets of New York. Other than a few guests whiling the time away on Kate's front porch, I didn't see a soul.

Leaving the bike propped up against the corner of Aunt Inga's house, I made my way up onto the front porch. I hadn't turned on any lights before going out, and by now, everything was dark. It took a minute to fumble the key into the lock and open the door. I snaked my hand around the jamb, searching for the light switch, and found it eventually, but although it switched over with an audible click, the light didn't come on. The bulb must have burned out, or maybe the electricity was off. Maybe Derek had shut it down at some point during the day and had forgotten to turn it on again before he left. Just to make sure, I tried the switch again, several times, with no luck.

As I was standing there, I heard a sound from down the hallway. It sounded like a footfall, and then a shadow moved in the darkness. I froze, and a voice broke the silence.

"Mmrrrow?"

All the air left my body on a whoosh, and I sagged. Behind me, the front door swung shut as I bumped it with my elbow. The lock latching with a snick made me jump again.

"Dammit, cat," I said weakly, leaning against the closed door, "you scared me half to death."

The cat sneezed. As it came closer, soft feet padding on the hardwood floors, I realized it was Jemmy, coming to wrap himself around my ankles, the tip of his striped tail tickling the back of my knees. I had forgotten to fill his bowl before I left, and now he was making nice to get me to feed him. I choked back a slightly hysterical laugh and bent to run my hand across his head and ears. "OK, Jemmy. I'll get you your food. Just head for the kitchen. I'll be right behind you."

My eyes had gotten a little more used to the darkness, and I could make out shapes of furniture and boxes as I shuffled along behind Jemmy, working hard not to step on him or kick him inadvertently. When I saw a movement out of the corner of my eye, I jumped another foot or so, and then started breathing again when I recognized myself in the gilt-framed mirror Aunt Inga had hanging in the hallway. Another cat-shaped shadow met us just inside the kitchen door. Inky must have been waiting there, daintily allowing Jemmy to take care of things, as a proper lady should. As soon as I stopped, they both began twining themselves around my legs, loudly demanding sustenance.

The kitchen light didn't work, either, so I decided that the problem was with the electrical system itself, and wasn't just an issue of burned-out bulbs. I'd have to go down to the basement and have a look-see. Derek had shown me the breaker box earlier in the week, just in case something like this happened, and I was pretty sure I'd be able to figure out which breaker to flip.

Both felines were vocalizing impatiently, wondering why I didn't just get them something to eat. The dark was no problem for them, of course. The idea of handling a

manual can opener in the dark, and slopping wet and smelly
cat food into two bowls without being able to see what I was
doing, was a daunting task, however. I decided that they
certainly wouldn't starve if I made them wait five minutes
while I lit a candle and went down to the basement to see if I
could get the lights turned back on. If Derek showed up tomorrow and discovered that the cause of the blackout was a
tripped breaker that I'd been too chicken to reset, I'd never
live it down.

Two minutes later, I was standing at the top of the basement stairs peering into the black void below. The flicker-
ing flame of the fat, scented candle I had taken out of the
bathroom gave a faint glow to the top two rickety steps, but
beyond that, all was darkness. And whereas I wouldn't say
I'm afraid of the dark, I'm at least respectful of things like
mice and spiders. The dirt basement gave off a musty, earthy
smell, and it took real effort to convince myself to take the
first step onto the stairs. So far, so good. I took another,
and—when the wood under my feet wobbled—shot out my
free hand to grab the makeshift railing. When it gave, sepa-
rating from the stairs and swinging out into the dark, I hung
on for dear life, until the piece I was holding broke off in my
hands, and I plummeted with it, the candle falling in an arc
from my hand and my voice shrieking uselessly.

Things went black after that, although it wasn't because
I lost consciousness, just because the candle went out. I hit
the floor like a sack of cement, with a groan and a grunt, and
lay there, catching my breath and marveling at the fact that I
was alive. When I thought I could move again without doing myself further injury, I rolled over and began taking
stock. My hands smarted, but I couldn't feel anything worse
than some abrasions with gravelly dirt from the basement
floor embedded in them. My face hurt as well, but it seemed

to be due to yet more scratches and not anything serious, like a broken nose. One of my legs twinged—probably because I had landed on it—and upon investigation, I discovered that I had ripped my favorite jeans and skinned my knee. It protested loudly when I tried to get up, so I stayed where I was a little longer, and contemplated my situation.

Things could have been worse. I was still very much alive, if not entirely whole. But my injuries were minor compared to what could have happened. I hadn't broken anything. The stubby candle had been snuffed out on its way down, so the house wasn't on fire. And the dirt floor had probably been more forgiving than a concrete floor would have been.

Still, I didn't want to spend the rest of the night on it. Groaning, I pulled myself up and half crawled, half walked over to the steps, pushing aside broken pieces of railing as I went. Damn Derek, anyway; he'd been up and down these stairs every day for a week: if the railing was loose, shouldn't he have reattached it? I knew he'd been busy with other things, and repairing a broken basement railing isn't glamorous or fun, not like redesigning a kitchen or restoring a stained glass window, but shouldn't it have occurred to him that the loose railing was a safety hazard and that I could fall down the stairs one day and break my neck? It had happened to Aunt Inga. All right, so maybe my aged aunt hadn't been as steady on her feet as me, not to mention that her bones had probably been a lot more brittle, but still, oughtn't Derek to have taken care of it? It was what I paid him for, wasn't it?

Grumbling and complaining under my breath to take my mind off the pain in my knee and my smarting palms and face, I managed to make it over to the steps and to feel my way up. Because the railing had fallen, I kept to the inside of the staircase, trying not to wince as my arm brushed against the cold, dank brick of the foundation.

The steps themselves were primitive, just thick planks of rough wood nailed to risers. They scratched my already abraded hands, and I had to be careful not to pick up any splinters. Just as the hallway was in sight—so to speak; the darkness was a little less solid up there because of the windows—the step I was creeping over wobbled under my knees, and for a moment, I thought I'd go rattling back down to the bottom. Only my death grip on the threshold kept me steady, and I was able to crawl on, up into the hallway, where I lay on my stomach, panting, for longer than I care to admit.

Eventually, I gathered myself together to feed the cats, before pulling off my jeans and washing my various injuries in the pitch dark. That done, I crawled onto Aunt Inga's bed, still sitting in the middle of the dining room, and dropped off to sleep.

The nightmares began toward the wee hours of the morning. I was falling, tumbling over and over like a rag doll, from step to step, before landing on the hard floor of the hallway with an impact that jolted my teeth together. Lying there, dazed and blinking, I heard the slam of a door, and then footsteps, coming closer. My mind screamed for action—*Someone's coming! Get up and run away!*—but I couldn't move or do anything but lie there, paralyzed.

The steps halted, and a dark shadow loomed over me. With a strangled cry, I wrenched my eyes open and forced my aching body to obey the panicked dictates of my mind. Flailing my arms wildly, I felt my fists connect with something soft and heard a voice. "Whoa! Easy!"

My arms were grabbed and held, and I blinked owlishly in the weak morning sunlight slanting through the sheer curtains. The shadow wasn't dark after all; it resolved itself into a blue T-shirt and a forelock of sun-streaked hair, under which a pair of blue eyes peered at me.

"Oh," I said, slumping, "it's you."

Derek released me, and I flopped back on the bed. He stuffed his hands in his pockets. "What the hell happened to you?"

"Fell down the stairs," I said. He arched his brows. I added, "The railing broke."

"What railing?"

"The railing on the basement stairs. You know, as much as you've been up and down those stairs this past week, I would have thought you could have spent thirty minutes making sure..."

He was already on his way out the door to the hallway. "While you're down there anyway," I called after him, as I heard the basement door creak open, "have a look at the breaker box. The lights were off last night as well."

He didn't answer, just started down. I could hear a soft curse when the second to the top step wobbled, but then he continued past it. A minute later all the lights on the first floor blazed on.

I grabbed the excuse to swing my legs over the side of the bed and limp toward my torn and muddy jeans, crumpled on the floor. I had flopped down on Aunt Inga's bed in just a T-shirt and panties last night, and before Derek came back upstairs and could notice my state of undress, I wanted to cover up.

"What are you doing?" he asked from behind me as I stood there, balancing on one foot while trying to bend the other knee far enough to fit the hurt leg into the pants. Surprised, I lost my balance, and would have fallen flat on my face had he not grabbed me. "Careful."

"I'm just trying to get dressed," I said, my cheeks hot.

"Not on my account, I hope?" He grinned.

"Well…"

"Let me have a look at your knee first, OK?" He pulled me gently over to the edge of the bed and knelt on the floor in front of me. "That's a nasty bruise. Does this hurt?" He twisted my knee, and I squealed. He let go again and sat back on his heels, looking up at me. "Probably need to see the doctor."

"The emergency room?" This early on a Saturday, it would have to be. "I'm not sure I can afford that."

"We'll figure something out," Derek said, standing. "Upsy-daisy." He scooped me up, and I found myself floating across the room, like a bride across the threshold.

"My pants!" I yelped, squirming.

"Oops." He put me back down and turned his back, gentleman-like, while I sat on the edge of the bed to finish putting on my torn jeans.

When I announced I was decent, he swung back toward me, and I added, quickly, "I'm sure I can make it to the truck on my own. You don't have to carry me."

His face was solemn. "That's OK. You don't weigh much."

"One hundred and ten pounds soaking wet," I said. He grinned.

"I'm sure I can manage to stagger out with you."

"If you insist."

"I really think I must, yeah? You should stay off that leg as much as possible."

He lifted me again and headed toward the door. This was as close as I'd ever been to him, and I noticed that he smelled of shampoo and Ivory soap, overlaid with a hint of something astringent, like paint or mineral spirits. Simple and uncomplicated. Nice.

"I thought you'd have plans today," I said when he had loaded me into the truck and had climbed into the driver's seat himself.

He sent me a look. "Like what?"

"Well, it's the weekend. I was thinking maybe a romantic outing with your wife, if you have one. Or girlfriend. In some out-of-the-way place that only the locals know about."

"Nope." He turned the key in the ignition, and the truck roared to life.

"You don't have a wife? Or you don't have plans with her today?"

He shot me another flash of blue eyes. "Why all the questions about my personal life?"

"No reason." Kate hadn't mentioned a Mrs. Ellis, and he wasn't wearing a ring, but in his line of work, with his hands constantly dealing with sticky and corrosive substances, maybe he preferred not to. "Just making conversation."

"And here I thought you were checking to see if I'm available," Derek said with a grin.

I flushed.

He drove and I pouted until we pulled to the curb outside another immaculately restored Victorian, pale green in color and surrounded by masses and masses of blooming flowers. I looked around for a sign telling me this was a doctor's office or medical clinic but didn't see one.

"Where are we?" I asked when Derek came around the truck to open the door for me.

"Birch Street. This is where the doctor is, when he's not up at the medical center."

"His house? Won't he mind us dropping in like this?" Maybe it would be better just to go to the emergency room after all.

Derek smiled. "He won't mind at all. Loves me like a son. C'mon."

He scooped me out of the car and closed the door with his hip before heading up the immaculate walkway to the front door, holding me to his chest. I looped my arms around his neck and enjoyed the ride.

9

Waterfield's doctor was a good-looking older man with graying hair cut short and a friendly, open face with round glasses. He was casually dressed in wrinkled khakis and a faded blue golf shirt with a crocodile on the pocket. A napkin tucked under his collar was stained with yellow, and he had a fork in one hand. When he saw us, he took a step back, eyes wide behind the lenses. "Derek. Good morning, son. What's going on?"

"Morning, sir," Derek said, walking right in. "This is Avery Baker. I'm helping her renovate her aunt Inga's house over on Bayberry. I found her looking like this when I came to work this morning."

"Mercy." The doctor looked around for somewhere to deposit his fork and ended up putting it and the soiled napkin on what was either an outstanding reproduction or a

genuine mahogany-veneered Hepplewhite sideboard standing in the hallway. Philippe would have been green with
envy. "You'd better put her in the parlor."

He stepped out of the way. Derek headed into a room on
the right with the doctor following. "On the couch, please."

The couch was a pristine example of a 1770s Federal-
style straight-back sofa upholstered in yellow damask. It
might even have been a Sheraton. Again, Philippe's mouth
would have watered, and he would surely not have approved
of the way Derek unceremoniously dropped me onto the old
seat. The doctor, whose sofa it was, didn't turn a hair. "What
seems to be the problem, young lady?"

"I fell down the stairs," I explained. "Last night. The
lights were out, and when I went down to the basement to
flip the breaker, I fell and banged myself up a little."

"More than a little," Derek muttered.

"I scraped my hands and my face, and my knee hurts," I
added.

"Would you mind?" The doctor gestured to my leg with
a pair of scissors that he had pulled out of a knitting or embroidery basket next to the sofa.

"What? Oh...Sure, if you have to." I watched as he
sliced into my favorite jeans, forever ruining them. A hole
at the knee is one thing; a slit from the bottom all the way up
to thigh level is something else. The doctor crouched in
front of me and began poking and prodding. Derek folded
his arms across his chest, his eyes narrowed as he watched.

"Why don't you go on into the kitchen, Derek?" the doctor suggested over his shoulder. "Say hello to Cora and give
me a chance to talk to your friend here. If I know you, all
you had this morning was a pot of coffee."

Derek hesitated for a moment, but then he gave a short
nod and wandered off.

"Gotta remind the boy to eat," the doctor said with a friendly wink, "just like when he was little. He'd get so caught up in things, he'd forget." He smiled, probably to distract me while he twisted my knee. "So you're Inga Morton's niece?"

I nodded. "Great-niece. Yes. My great-grandfather and her father were brothers. Ow."

"Sorry." He sat back on his heels, peering up at me over the glasses. His eyes were the same shade of blue as Derek's, but with a darker ring around the iris. "The good news is, your knee is going to be fine. You bruised it when you fell. It'll be discolored and swollen for a few days, but there's no significant damage done. I can put a couple of Band-Aids on the scratch, if you want."

"That's not necessary." I touched it gingerly. "It's already starting to scab over. What's the bad news?"

"The bad news is it'll take a few days to get well. You should go to the drugstore and buy yourself a knee brace. Stay off it as much as possible, and when you do have to move around, try not to put any undue pressure on it."

I nodded. "Thank you, Doctor."

The doctor grinned. "Call me Ben. Any friend of Derek's is a friend of mine. Plus, I treated your aunt, you know."

"No," I said, "I didn't. Did you know Aunt Inga well?"

"Fairly well. I was her physician, just like my father before me. We've been doctors for generations."

Derek, sauntering in just in time to hear this, pressed his lips together as he put a hand under the older man's arm and helped him to his feet.

Dr. Ben continued, with a nod and smile at him, "Your aunt was the oldest resident of Waterfield; she went through several generations of doctors and lawyers in her lifetime. You've met Mr. Rodgers, I'm sure?"

I nodded.

"Before him, old Horace Cooper was her attorney. Graham Rodgers was his protégé, a fatherless boy from Thomaston whom Horace took under his wing because he didn't have any children of his own. He put Graham through law school and then took him on as a junior partner, and when Horace died, Graham inherited the Cooper family home along with the law practice."

"Nice work if you can get it," Derek remarked.

Dr. Ben smiled. "Have you seen Cliff House yet, Avery? As someone who likes to renovate, you'll appreciate it."

I shook my head, reserving judgment on whether I actually *liked* to renovate. "Kate McGillicutty told me he has a big spread outside town."

Dr. Ben nodded. "It's another of our historic homes, like the B and B. The Cliff House was built in the early 1800s. Beautiful place. You worked there recently, didn't you, Derek?"

"Painted the damn thing last fall," Derek said. "From top to bottom. All sixteen rooms."

"Wow," I said. "That sounds like quite a job."

Derek shrugged.

"He painted this house, too," Dr. Ben said, with a proud look around that encompassed Derek himself. "Every wall, every baseboard, every inch of trim."

I looked at the ten-foot ceilings, the carved molding, the plaster walls. It was all pristine and beautiful. "Good job."

Derek didn't answer. A grouping of small oil paintings on the far wall caught my attention, and I peered at them for a second. There was Dr. Ben's house, Kate's B and B, and a big, white house with a red door, which looked Federal or Georgian in style. Someone in the Ellis family liked to paint pictures as well as walls, it seemed. I wondered if this was

Derek's work, as well, but before I could ask, a cluster of redbrick buildings in another canvas resolved themselves into a faithful reproduction of Barnham College, complete with minuscule gargoyles, and took my thoughts in a different direction. I turned my attention back to Dr. Ben. "This may be an odd question, but would you happen to know what was going on between my Aunt Inga and Martin Wentworth?"

"The young professor who disappeared a couple of weeks ago? I'm sorry, I have no idea."

"What makes you think something was going on?" Derek asked.

I glanced at him. "I found Professor Wentworth's card in the desk in the parlor, and Wayne found his fingerprints in the kitchen. I was wondering what they were discussing."

"Your aunt was the oldest resident of Waterfield," Dr. Ben reminded me. "She could remember things that everyone else had forgotten. The smuggling during Prohibition, the Roaring Twenties, even World War I, when she was just a girl. Stories and local scandals that nobody else remembered anymore. And although her body was becoming feebler, her mind was still sharp. And I must admit I was quite shocked when Wayne Rasmussen called and told me she had passed on. I know she was almost one hundred, but I thought she'd be around for a while yet."

"There wasn't anything suspicious about her death, was there?"

The doctor's voice was cautious when he answered. "Nothing I saw was inconsistent with an accident, and the M.E. in Portland confirmed it. Do you have reason to suspect otherwise?"

"Not really. It's just that some weird things have been happening." Like Aunt Inga's cryptic letter to me, and her death so quickly afterward, not to mention the threatening note I'd received and the broken china...

The doctor nodded. "The only thing that struck me is to wonder what she was doing upstairs in the first place. The stairs were almost impossible for her to manage anymore. Occasionally, she'd ask me to bring something down for her, but to my knowledge, she hadn't ventured upstairs herself for several years."

I nodded. "Wayne Rasmussen told me that my cousins tried to have her declared incompetent a couple of years ago. Kate said it was so they could get their hands on her property."

"They didn't succeed, though. I testified before the judge in the case, and the Stenhams didn't stand a chance. They've never been remarkable for their wits, have they, Derek?"

Derek shook his head with a quickly suppressed grimace.

Dr. Ben added, "All they succeeded in doing was ensuring that they didn't get the house after she died, either. She left it to you instead." He smiled, seemingly pleased that the Stenhams had thus shot themselves in the foot.

"Ray Stenham accosted me the other day," I said. Derek muttered something, and I turned to him. "Excuse me?"

"I said, that was Randy. Not Ray."

I squinted. "Are you sure?"

Dr. Ben shot him a glance. His expression was partly laced with wry amusement and partly something else that I couldn't quite pinpoint. Derek remained impassive. "Positive. I grew up with 'em both; I can tell 'em apart."

"Oh." I bit my lip. "I thought it was Ray." Good thing I hadn't actually called him by name.

"What did he want?" Dr. Ben asked.

I turned my attention back to him. "He *said* he wanted to

warn me about all the things that could go wrong when renovating a house. What he actually wanted, I think, was to scare me into leaving town, and giving or selling Aunt Inga's house to him and his brother."

"Interesting." Dr. Ben turned to Derek, and they exchanged a look.

"What?" I said, glancing from one to the other of them.

Derek looked away. "Nothing. You ready to go?"

"I guess." I looked at Dr. Ben, who nodded.

"Just take it easy for a few days. Try not to use that knee any more than you have to. Sit and watch while Derek does the work."

Derek rolled his eyes.

I grinned. "Don't mind if I do. Thanks, Doctor. How much do I owe you?"

"I don't charge for doing a favor for a friend," Dr. Ben said with another smile. He clasped my hand for a moment when he said good-bye, before Derek hoisted me again, and headed back out to the truck.

"Nice man," I said when we were rolling down the street in the direction of Aunt Inga's house again. "He called you son. He's your dad, right?"

"He's my dad." Derek glanced left and turned right at the corner.

"Your dad's a doctor, and you're a handyman?" As soon as the words were out of my mouth, I wished I could take them back.

He shot me a look. "You have a problem with that?"

"Of course not. I guess I'm just surprised that you didn't follow in his footsteps." Especially since Dr. Ben had said that the family had been physicians for generations.

"You're not one of those girls who won't get involved with anyone but a doctor or a lawyer, are you, Tinkerbell?"

"That's a fine thing to ask," I answered. "My former boy-friend was a furniture maker, for your information."

"No kidding," Derek said. "What happened?" He twisted the wheel to make another turn.

"What do you mean, what happened? We broke up. Just before I moved here."

"Mutual?"

I hesitated. "In the end, I guess it was." Philippe had cheated, and I'd chosen not to forgive and forget.

"Do you still have feelings for this guy?"

"You know," I said, "I could turn all snarky and say that's none of your business."

"But?" He smiled.

"But I'm a nice person, so I won't. Sure, I have feelings for him." Feelings of wanting to kill him, mostly. "He's six hours away, with someone else, so I also have some perspective."

"Makes sense," Derek admitted.

A few minutes later we pulled up outside Aunt Inga's house. He opened his door. I did the same, scooting out before he could pick me up and carry me again. Frankly, I was enjoying the experience a little too much, and I thought it better to nip that in the bud. But the moment I put any weight on my bum knee, it buckled, and Derek had to move quickly.

"Of all the stupid, pigheaded, stubborn..." he muttered. The rest of the litany of my failings was drowned out by my outraged squeal as he tossed me over his shoulder like a sack of grain and strode up the walk, kicking open the gate on the way.

After dropping me back onto Aunt Inga's bed, he sat down next to me. "Tell me again what happened last night. In detail."

I sighed. "I already did. There's nothing more to tell."

"Humor me," Derek said in a voice that left no room for argument. I rolled my eyes but did as he said.

"After you left, I stripped the rest of the wallpaper from the hall. Then I took the bike from the shed and rode out to this place called Mario's for dinner."

"I know it. Down the ocean road apiece."

I nodded. "When I came home, I discovered that all the lights were out. I thought maybe you'd turned them off and forgot to turn them back on before you left." In his eagerness to cash his check or something.

He shook his head. "I didn't turn them off yesterday. And I wouldn't have forgotten to turn them back on if I had."

"You flipped the breaker this morning, though, and the lights came back on. Right?" He nodded. "So they really were off last night. If you didn't turn them off, who did?"

I intended it as a rhetorical question, but Derek chose to answer it. "That's what I'd like to know, too."

A beat passed—was he serious?—and then I said, "Couldn't it have been an accident? A power surge, something like that?"

"Anything's possible." But it didn't sound like he meant it. "So you came home, and the lights were out. Then what happened?"

"Then I thought about going to bed and calling you to come and deal with it this morning, but I was afraid of what you'd think of me if you found out that I'd been too chicken to go down to the basement by myself. So I lit a candle and headed down, and when I leaned on the railing, it broke."

Derek nodded. "I saw the pieces."

"I'm sure you did. And I think you ought to have taken care of it before now. I'm paying you to take care of things like that. If you knew it was unsafe, you should have fixed it."

"If it had been unsafe, I would have fixed it," Derek said. "There was nothing wrong with those stairs yesterday."

He looked at me. His eyes were clear and guileless, and I decided that he was either honest or a much better liar than I gave him credit for. "A power outage couldn't have done that," I said.

Derek shook his head. It sounded like he was implying that someone had been in my house last night and had turned off my lights and tampered with my stairs. But who could have done such a thing? And why?

A name came immediately to mind. Or rather, two. If what happened was anything but an accident, it was probably caused by one or both of the Stenham brothers, trying to scare me out of town. Randy had brought up the possibility of accidents. He hadn't specifically mentioned the danger of my falling down the stairs and breaking my neck, but he had warned me about all the things that could go wrong in an old house and said I should get out of Waterfield while I could. And since the Stenhams were family, it wasn't impossible that they had a key to Aunt Inga's house and could come and go at will.

If it wasn't the Stenhams, maybe it was Melissa James; not that I could picture the elegant realtor crawling around my basement in her designer suit and Manolo Blahniks. But Kate had mentioned Melissa's temper and said that she wasn't above a bit of vandalism when in a mood, and she certainly did seem set on selling my house. Her last words to me on Thursday had been to take care of myself. I probably shouldn't discount her entirely, although I had no idea how she might have gotten in.

Much as I disliked the idea, I couldn't totally discount

Derek as a suspect, either. Of everyone, he'd had the best opportunity to rig the stairs. Everyone else would have had to break in, but he'd been here all day yesterday already. Working in the basement, no less. I'd heard him banging and cursing down there, but I certainly hadn't checked up on him, and I had no idea what he'd been doing. For all I knew, he could have been sabotaging my stairs while I was scraping wallpaper in the hallway above his head. But there was nothing in it for him, was there?

I shook my head. "Surely not even the Stenhams are stupid enough to try to hurt me just so they can get their hands on Aunt Inga's house. And when it comes to Melissa James..."

Derek's eyes narrowed. "What about Melissa James?"

I tilted my chin up. "She was here the other day. Asking for you. Ogling the house."

"Huh," Derek said. His face had darkened, and he seemed to be in the throes of an internal struggle.

"What?" I inquired. He scowled at me for a second, then his face cleared and his voice turned dismissive.

"Melissa may be the center of her universe, but she's not stupid. She wouldn't try to hurt you."

"Dear me," I answered, annoyed, "I didn't realize you two were so close. Is she an old flame, or something?"

"Something." He seemed to chew on his tongue for a moment, and then he added, a little less curtly, "When was she here?"

"She stopped by on Thursday evening, just after you left. Said she had seen your truck outside, and wanted to know what you were doing here."

Derek's mouth curved in a faint smile. "What did you tell her? That I was working on your plumbing?"

Something about the way he said it made a blush

creep up into my cheeks. "As a matter of fact, I guess I did. Sort of."

Derek chuckled, and I added, not knowing when to quit, "Let me guess. Did you used to work on her plumbing, too?"

"Happens I did, yeah." His glance at me was challenging.

"Well," I said, aware of a feeling of disappointment, "it sounded like she'd be interested in picking up where you left off. Funny, I wouldn't have thought you two were one another's type. Not that it's any of my business."

"Let's keep it that way," Derek said. "If you're all set, I think I'll head out. I have a couple of errands to run. Anything I can do for you before I go?"

I shook my head.

"In that case, I'll see you later." He left. Less than a minute later, he was back. "Is that your bike outside?"

"The one leaning up against the porch? I found it in the shed yesterday. I guess it must have been Aunt Inga's." Although what my ninety-eight-year-old aunt had been doing with a twenty-six-inch, carbon-frame mountain bike, I had no idea.

"The shed out back?"

I nodded.

"Huh," Derek said and disappeared again.

I waited until I had heard the impatient roar of his engine before I limped down the hallway to lock the front door.

10

When there was a knock on the door thirty minutes later, I assumed it was Derek coming back. Grumbling and complaining, I levered myself off the bed and inched my way toward the front door. My progress was slow, and the person outside must have been impatient, because by the time I got to the door, it opened. I came face-to-face with Graham Rodgers, who looked just as surprised to see me as I was to see him. "Miss Baker!" he exclaimed. Then his cool, gray eyes widened as he took in my bedraggled appearance, and he stepped back. "Dear me, what happened?"

"I fell," I explained. "Stumbled on the stairs last night, in the dark."

"Oh, dear." He winced, looking so perturbed that I hastened to assure him.

"It's not as bad as it looks. No broken bones, no major

injuries. Derek took me to see his dad, and Dr. Ben said I'll be sore for a week, but otherwise I'm fine."

"That's wonderful," Mr. Rodgers said. "My apologies, Miss Baker, for barging in like this. I came to ask if Mr. Todd stopped by yesterday, and when no one answered the door, I became concerned."

"No problem. If Derek hadn't happened to come to work this morning and found me, you might have had the pleasure of taking me to the doctor yourself." I smiled.

After a moment, Mr. Rodgers smiled back a little stiffly, as if the sensation wasn't familiar to him.

I continued, "But yes, Mr. Todd came by yesterday. He gave me a quote on the grass and said he'd be back Monday or Tuesday to mow."

"Excellent," Mr. Rodgers said, taking another step back. "In that case, I shall go and leave you alone. You should rest, Miss Baker."

"I intend to," I said. "Before you go, though..."

"Yes?"

"I was wondering if you might be willing to answer a question for me."

Mr. Rodgers indicated, in his lawyerly way, that it would depend on the question, but that he'd be pleased to listen and then determine whether he could, in fact, tell me what I wanted to know. I hesitated, trying to form the question in a way that wouldn't give offense.

"The first time we met, you said that you had already drawn up a will for my aunt Inga many years ago." Mr. Rodgers nodded, his thin face wary. "I was wondering if you'd be able to tell me anything about it."

"I'm afraid not, Miss Baker," Mr. Rodgers said. "That information is protected under the attorney-client privilege."

"Even if Aunt Inga is dead?"

Mr. Rodgers inclined his head. "May I ask why you desire to know?"

"Oh," I said, "I was just thinking. If the beneficiary of that will was resentful of Aunt Inga's new will, and of me inheriting everything, I thought maybe that person could be behind all the things that have happened to me. The threatening letter, the broken dishes, the stairs..."

I glanced up at him to gauge his reaction. Mr. Rodgers's gray eyes were opaque behind the lenses of his glasses, and his face was impassive, giving nothing away.

"I guess I could just suggest it to Wayne Rasmussen," I added, when he displayed no reaction at all. "See if he can figure it out."

"That won't be necessary, Miss Baker." Mr. Rodgers's voice was cool. I guess he didn't appreciate my gentle blackmail. "The beneficiary under Miss Morton's first will was her cousin, Catherine Kendall. When Mrs. Kendall passed away, a new will was drafted, with an old friend as the beneficiary. This person is also now deceased. I assure you, he has not come back from the grave to cause harm."

"Oh." I blushed, feeling ashamed of myself. "I'm sorry."

"Indeed. And now, Miss Baker, if you will excuse me." He stepped back out onto the porch.

"Sure," I said. "Sorry, Mr. Rodgers. I didn't mean to upset you. Have a nice weekend."

"And you, also, Miss Baker," Mr. Rodgers said, but he didn't sound like he meant it. He turned and walked down the buried walkway to his Cadillac, back straight. I closed the door, feeling like a heel.

. . .

I had barely made it into Aunt Inga's room and onto the bed when there was another knock on the door. This time I was

sure it was Derek returning, and as I shuffled along the hallway, I was already planning what I was going to say to him
in return for making me come open the door yet again. But I
was thwarted once more: this time I found Kate McGillicutty and Wayne Rasmussen on the welcome mat. Both of
them looked concerned, and both of them looked at me like
they thought they had reason to be.

"You look like hell," Kate said bluntly.

Wayne glanced at her, amusement lighting his dark
eyes.

They were both casually dressed in jeans and sneakers,
she with a green blouse that made the most of her vivid coloring, and he in a short-sleeved, gray T-shirt that brought
out the platinum streaks in his dark hair. It was the first time
I'd seen the chief of police in anything but a uniform, and it
took some getting used to.

Kate added, a little more kindly, "How are you feeling?"

"The way I look," I answered, rubbing my scabby nose
irritably. "Like I got dragged backward through a hedge."
Or fell down a staircase onto a dirt floor in the dark.

"Have you seen a doctor?" This was Wayne's con-
tribution.

I nodded. "Derek took me to see his dad. Dr. Ben said to
take it easy and stay off my knee. I was supposed to buy a
knee brace, but I haven't gotten around to it yet. Come on
in, and let's sit down." I moved aside.

"There's a key in the door," Wayne pointed out as he
stepped over the threshold. He pulled it out and handed it
to me.

"It must be Mr. Rodgers's key. He was just here." I
dropped it in the desk drawer.

Wayne picked up the conversation when we were all

seated on Aunt Inga's uncomfortable parlor furniture, me on the straight-backed desk chair upholstered in nubby tweed, and the two of them side by side on the worn, gray love seat. I hoped most of the cat hair would stay where it was and not stick to the chief's posterior when he left.

"Where's Derek now?"

"Running errands. He didn't say what or where, and I didn't ask. Did he call you?" Someone had to have called the police, and it hadn't been me.

Wayne nodded. "Tell me what happened." He might be wearing civilian clothes, on his way home from a little league game or headed out to lunch with his lady friend, but he had pulled the policeman's notebook and pencil from his jeans pocket and was ready to take notes. "From the beginning."

Presumably Derek had given him the basics over the phone, but I repeated the story, with all the details I could remember.

"Derek seemed to think that someone had done it on purpose," the chief remarked when I was done.

I nodded. "So he said. Although that doesn't make any sense. I don't have any enemies, and though there are a lot of people who seem to want my house, it's not like I'd give it to them if I got hurt and had to leave town. I'd give it to Mr. Rodgers to manage before I'd hand it over to the Stenhams or Melissa."

"Sounds like you're pretty sure the Stenham brothers are behind it," Wayne said.

I shrugged, not too apologetically. After the other night, I didn't feel too bad about shopping the Stenhams to the police. Randy had done his best to intimidate me, and as far as I was concerned, he deserved what he got, whether he was behind my accident or not. "I ran into Randy the other day, and he threatened me. Said I should get out of town while I still could."

Kate glanced at her boyfriend. "Sounds like you might want to have another talk with Ray and Randy, love."

Wayne nodded. "What were you saying about Melissa James, Avery?"

I shrugged. "She was here the other day. Asking questions. Wondering if I'd gotten in over my head yet. Telling me that whenever I want to sell the house, she's got someone lined up to buy it. Oh yes, and making snide comments about Derek. If I didn't know better, I'd say she was jealous."

Wayne's lips quirked, and Kate snorted. They exchanged a look. Kate opened her mouth, but before she could say anything, Wayne got to his feet. "If you girls are gonna gossip, I'm leaving. To the basement to take a look at your stairs, specifically." He nodded to me.

"Be my guest," I answered, watching him walk out of the room on long legs. "Watch your step on the second riser, it's loose."

I turned back to Kate, who was watching me with a grin on her face.

"So," she said, "what's going on with you and Derek?"

"What do you mean?" I answered promptly. "Nothing. Absolutely nothing. He's a nice guy, I'm sure, but not my type." And not actually that nice, either. He'd been helpful enough about getting me to the doctor and back home again this morning, although I could have done without being carried over his shoulder like a sack of feed.

"So why are you interested in him and Melissa?"

"I'm not," I said. "I'm just surprised that she'd be interested in him. Or vice versa. I wouldn't have thought they'd have a lot in common."

"You'd be surprised," Kate informed me. "That's how Melissa ended up here, being a guiding light to all of Waterfield."

"I beg your pardon?"

"They used to be married, didn't you know? Met in college, had a whirlwind romance—I can quite see how Melissa could sweep a man off his feet if she tried, can't you?—and then they got married, and when Derek finished his residency, they came back here."

"Married?" I repeated stupidly. "Residency?"

"He studied medicine. Planned to take over his dad's practice. Went through medical school, did his residency and everything, and then decided he was happier being a handyman."

"I'm not surprised, since his bedside manner is a little lacking." I smiled, doing my best to keep my cool in spite of the fact that I was so surprised I could hardly speak. So much for the small-town carpenter I thought I'd met.

Kate grinned. "From what I've heard, his bedside manner isn't lacking at all."

I forced back a blush. "You know what I mean. So what happened? They're not married anymore, are they?"

"Oh, no." She shook her head. "The marriage lasted a total of four or five years, I think. Most of it while he was a resident. With the crazy schedule he kept, I guess they never spent enough time together to get sick of each other. But then they got back here and settled into a normal life, and they decided they didn't have much in common after all. It wasn't much later that Melissa started dating Ray Stenham."

"Melissa's dating Ray Stenham?"

Kate nodded.

"Gosh," I said and fell silent. This explained Derek's cryptic statement to Randy the other day that under the circumstances, they were almost family. Melissa was Derek's ex-wife, and now she was dating my cousin Ray. No wonder Derek hated the Stenhams. And no wonder he acted so weird whenever I mentioned Melissa's name. I guessed maybe Melissa still felt a proprietary interest in him, and that was why she'd been checking up on him.

It would be only too easy to start feeling bad for him, being jilted like that, and I reminded myself to stay vigilant against any undue sympathy. Whatever had happened in his personal life, he was still on my suspect list. "You don't suppose *he* could have . . . ?"

"Could have what?"

"The stairs, the basement . . . ?"

Kate opened her hazel eyes wide. "Derek? I wouldn't think so. Why would he want to hurt you?"

I shrugged. "No idea. He's here, that's all. Whoever did it had to have gotten in somehow. I've lived in New York my whole life; I don't leave my doors unlocked. What about Melissa? Could you see her breaking into my house and sabotaging my basement stairs?"

"Sooner than I could see Derek doing it," Kate said loyally.

"Is she still interested in him, do you think?" If so, she might have misunderstood our relationship and thought she needed to get rid of me.

"As far as I know," Kate said, "she's content with Ray for now. That's not to say that it wouldn't gratify her to no end to think that Derek was still carrying a torch for her."

I nodded. I could certainly understand that. It would be gratifying to me to have Philippe come crawling back begging for forgiveness, too. Not that I'd grant it. At least I didn't think so.

"But he's not, right?"

Kate shrugged. "Who knows? If he is, he hasn't said any-thing about it. He's had a few dates since the divorce, but nothing serious. I never thought it might be because he's still in love with Melissa, but I suppose anything's possible."

"Great," I said with a grimace, then turned as Wayne came back down the hall toward us. He stopped in the doorway.

"This bicycle Derek mentioned, is it in the dooryard?"

"Bicycle?" Kate repeated.

"I found it in the shed in the backyard yesterday," I said. "It's in the front yard now, leaning up against the side of the porch. I rode it last night."

Wayne headed for the door, and I added, to Kate, "It's a little big for me. If Aunt Inga rode it, she must have been considerably taller than I am."

"She was taller than you," Kate said, measuring me with her eyes, "but not by that much. A couple of inches, maybe. You're on the short side, and she was tall for a woman born almost a hundred years ago. About average height these days, I'd say. But it can't be her bike. She could barely keep her balance walking; there's no way she'd be able to ride anything. Unless . . . it isn't a three-wheeler, is it?"

"Of course not," I said, giggling. "It's an all-terrain bike. Looks new."

"Interesting," Kate said.

"Why? Has somebody reported a missing mountain bike?"

"Not exactly, but a man riding a mountain bike went missing a couple of weeks ago. Professor Wentworth, re-member?"

"A bike-riding professor? How quaint." A picture formed in my head of Sean Connery as Indiana Jones's dad, riding an oversized three-wheeler.

"I think you may have gotten the wrong idea," Kate said. "Professor Wentworth was young. Not much older than you. Fresh out of school, healthy, in good shape. He kept a car for the winter months, but when the weather was good, he liked to ride his bike. He rode it the morning he disappeared."

"Why would Professor Wentworth leave his bike in my aunt's shed?" I asked.

Kate shrugged lightly.

"I don't suppose there's any news?"

"None I've heard," Kate said. "Although if that's his bike outside, that might be a break in the case."

"How is your daughter holding up? You know, I wouldn't mind meeting her sometime. If she knew Professor Wentworth, maybe she'd be able to tell me what he and my aunt had in common."

Kate sighed and shook her head. "She's spending more and more time down at the college. I hardly saw her at all last week. If Barnham wasn't such an upstanding place, and her friends such nice kids, I'd worry. Thankfully, she's too smart to get in the sort of trouble I was in at her age."

I arched my brows inquiringly—she had brought it up, after all, so it wasn't like I was prying—and she added, "I got pregnant at eighteen. By the time I was Shannon's age, I was juggling classes and diapers and a part-time job I needed to make ends meet. I dropped out of college after a year, although I did go back and finish up later. With a different major, of course."

"Why 'of course'?"

Kate grinned. "Shannon's father was French. I was going to study business, but then I met him and decided to study French instead. All it took was being called *mon petit chou* once." Her pronunciation was totally different from what I was used to hearing.

"His name wouldn't happen to be Philippe, would it?" Philippe had called me his little cabbage (*chou*), his little flea (*puce*), and his little rabbit (*lapin*), as well as just plain his little one (*ma petite*). You'll notice the common denominator. Amazingly, the condescension had never occurred to me before. Guess I never made it past the sexy accent.

Kate shook her head. "Gerard Labadie. Why do you ask? Who's Philippe?"

"Ex-boyfriend. Recent breakup. What happened to Gerard?"

She waved a vague hand. "Oh, he's around. Somewhere. Last time I saw him was when Shannon was three, and I came home and found him in bed with my roommate." She said it like it didn't matter, although at the time, I imagined it must have mattered quite a bit. Which just goes to show that in sixteen years, I will probably be able to hear Philippe's name without wanting to strangle him, too.

"Men," I said.

"Can't live with them," Kate agreed, without finishing the classic saying. I smiled.

Although I have to admit that some men aren't so bad. When Wayne came back inside, he had Derek with him. Derek had a couple of long pieces of wood over his shoulder—two-by-fours, I hazarded a guess—and Wayne was carrying several smaller pieces of wood under one arm, and a plastic bag from the local hardware store in his other hand. They dumped it all on the floor in the hallway and came into the parlor. Wayne sat down next to Kate again, and Derek leaned a shoulder against the doorjamb and looked at me.

"How are you feeling?"

I told him I was feeling OK, and he added, "I brought you a present."

"From the hardware store? How sweet of you!" I wondered what it might be. A pound of nails? A hammer? Some new PVC pipe for the bathroom?

Kate and Wayne exchanged a glance, and Derek sent me a jaundiced look. "Don't overdo it, Tinkerbell," he warned.

"I was trying to be sarcastic," I explained.

"I should have guessed. Here." He tossed me a plastic-wrapped package, and I managed to get my hands up in time to catch it.

"A knee brace? Wow, that's . . . That really *is* sweet!"

He shrugged. "Dad said you should have one, and I figured you didn't feel like going out and buying one yourself."

"You're right about that. I appreciate it."

I had changed into a pair of shorts, so ripping open the package and sliding the brace up over my calf and knee was a simple matter. It had a hole in the front to circle the knee-cap, so it didn't even bother my scratches. I glanced up. The dark blue T-shirt made Derek's eyes appear even more vivid than usual, and that damn lock of hair was hanging over his forehead. "Thank you," I said demurely.

"My pleasure." He had a hint of color in his cheeks, and the suggestion of a grin in the curve of his mouth. It occurred to me to wonder if he'd been looking at, maybe even admiring, my legs.

Derek turned to Wayne. "Can I start working on the stairs now?"

Wayne nodded. "The wood is too rough to take fingerprints, so there's no sense in even testing it. Stay away from the breaker panel, though. I'll send Brandon out to dust it on Monday. Just in case we get lucky."

Derek grimaced. "I probably ruined any luck you were likely to have when I reset the breakers this morning."

"It's worth a try," Wayne said. "And it keeps him busy. I'm always worried that he'll leave us and sign on with the Boston PD if I don't give him enough to do." He smiled.

"I'll get to work, then." Derek swung on his heel. We heard him walk down the hall and open the basement door. After a minute, hammering and sawing started down there.

"What about the bike?" Kate wanted to know.

Wayne turned his attention to her. "Bikes aren't like cars, Kate. They don't have to be registered, and they don't have VIN numbers we can run. I'll have to talk to witnesses who saw Wentworth on his bike frequently and see if they can identify it. I'll have Brandon dust it for fingerprints, too. Avery," he turned to me, "tell me about it."

"The bike? There's nothing more to tell. I found it in the shed the other night. I was looking for a lawn mower, and there it was. I hadn't been in the shed before, so I don't know how long it's been there. Didn't you look for it when Professor Wentworth went missing?"

"In your aunt's shed?" Wayne said. "Of course not. Why would we?"

No reason, I guessed.

He added, "We looked for the professor, as well as the bike, in all the logical places: parking lots, all around campus, along the road, in the woods, at the bus and train stations. But we didn't go door to door or check private property. We can't do that, not without some kind of solid connection between the missing person and a particular place. It would take too long, for one thing, and we have to respect people's privacy, for another."

I nodded. "So is this a solid connection? Do you want to search the house now?"

"I've already been over the house," Wayne reminded me. "When your aunt died, remember? We didn't go over it with a fine-tooth comb, but we looked well enough to make sure no one else was here. Professor Wentworth was already missing then, although I don't think we'd started searching for him; it all happened at much the same time. The last time anyone saw him was the day before Mr. Rodgers found your aunt dead." He paused, looking pensive.

I felt a frisson down my back. "Let me see if I understand this. Professor Wentworth left home on his bike one morning, and no one's seen him since. The next day, Mr. Rodgers found my aunt dead. My aunt had Professor Wentworth's business card in her desk, and now I've found his bike in her shed? Have you ever thought that maybe he had something to do with her death—and now he's on the run?"

Wayne said, "I know what you're thinking, Avery. And it's suggestive, I'll admit, but we can't assume that Professor Wentworth pushed your aunt down the stairs and then ran."

"It makes sense to me," I said.

Kate hid a smile.

"Of course it does," Wayne answered. "But that's because we don't have enough information yet. We're not going to rule it out, OK? But we're not going to ride off in all directions with the assumption that that's what happened, either. First I'm going to take the bike with me downtown and try to confirm that it is, indeed, Martin Wentworth's bike. After that, we'll know a little more. And if it is his bike, then we can start looking for a connection between your aunt and the professor. You can help with that."

"I'll keep an eye out for anything around here that might

connect to the professor," I promised. "You'll let me know what you find out about the bicycle, right?"

Wayne told me he would, and then he and Kate left, taking the mountain bike with them. I shuffled along the hall to the cellar door and peered down into the basement. Derek looked up at me. "Go lie down," he ordered. "There are a couple of DIY magazines in one of those bags on the floor. They'll keep you busy. I don't want to hear your feet touch the floor again until I'm finished down here." His voice was stern. I resisted the urge to ask, smartly, if these were doctor's orders, but only because the thought of lying down sounded really, really good.

11

After rebuilding the cellar stairs, Derek spent the rest of the afternoon replacing the locks on the back and front doors, while I lay on Aunt Inga's bed flipping through the magazines he had brought me. One of them had detailed step-by-step directions for how to mosaic a tabletop, and I couldn't help but wonder if Derek had picked it up on purpose to give me a crash course in the technique of decorative tiling.

The more I looked at the photo spread, the more I liked the idea I'd come up with, of using the broken pieces of Aunt Inga's Blue Willow china to create a one-of-a-kind kitchen counter. It seemed fitting somehow, and it would probably look pretty good, too, especially if I did something funky, like coloring the grout cobalt blue to match the pattern on the china. If that was even possible. Any grout I'd ever seen came in boring colors, like white and sand and gray, but surely there was a way to make it a little more exciting? Derek would know. I decided to ask him when I was feeling better. Until then, there wasn't much I could do about the counter, anyway.

He finished what he was doing in the midafternoon and stopped at the foot of Aunt Inga's bed to ask if there was anything I needed before he left. When I said no, he said good-bye and sauntered out. "I'll lock up," he tossed over his shoulder. "The new keys are on the desk in the parlor. Minus the one in my pocket."

I stuck my tongue out at his back, but I didn't complain. If he was willing to lock the door so I wouldn't have to get up, more power to him. It wasn't like I was concerned that he was planning to abuse the privilege of having a key. He wouldn't be walking in on me in the bathtub anytime soon, more's the pity.

After I'd read the DIY magazines cover to cover, I cracked open Aunt Inga's book about Marie Antoinette. I'd finished the novels I'd brought along, and it was the only other book in the house, or at least the only one I'd found, and although it isn't the sort of thing I usually enjoy, it kept my attention. By bedtime, I knew more about the doomed queen of France than I had ever wanted to.

Some of it was information I'd actually heard before. Philippe had been enamored with the dead queen and had made me sit through many of the movies made about Marie Antoinette. He'd argued vehemently against Hollywood's accusations of selfishness and greed. Until Philippe set me straight, so to speak, I'd always been under the impression that Marie Antoinette exclaimed gaily, "Let them eat cake!" when the citizens of Paris were starving. Not so. According to Philippe, that was Maria Theresa of Spain, and brioche— the French word she used—isn't properly cake, it's a sweet roll that is sometimes used as a basis for desserts and meat dishes.

As I read, the evening ebbed away, and before I knew it, I was three-quarters done with the book. Chapter ten described the French Revolution's 1789 beginning. First, the royal family was moved from the fabulous palace of Versailles to the old, dilapidated Palace de Tuileries in Paris. By 1791, Marie Antoinette and King Louis-Auguste had seen the writing on the wall and decided to take their children and their valuables and flee abroad. With the dauphin's governess taking on the role of a Russian baroness, the queen playing her maid, the king her butler, and the royal children her offspring, the family made their escape. But when they stopped for a change of horses in Varennes, someone recognized the king's profile from a coin, and they were sent back to Paris under guard and reinterred in the Tuileries.

I sipped a cup of hot chocolate as I read about how Louis was beheaded in January 1793, and in August, Marie Antoinette was placed in the Conciergerie prison to await trial. There was a failed rescue attempt later in August, called the Affair of the Carnation because the plan for the rescue was hidden among the petals of a flower smuggled into the prison for the queen, and in October, Marie Antoinette was tried for treason against the new Republic. The trial was a mockery and the verdict a foregone conclusion; the queen was executed on October 16, two days after the trial started.

Not too long after that—just about the time it would take a fast ship to make it across the Atlantic—a schooner by the name of *Sally*, captained by one Samuel Clough, arrived in Wiscasset, Maine, just a few miles up the road from Waterfield. Ostensibly, *Sally* was engaged in the lumber trade, but instead of lumber, below her decks were fabulous clothes, French furniture, and other expensive treasures, and—as Kate had mentioned—six long-haired cats, the French queen's pride and joy. Well, what do you know, I mused to myself as I closed the book, said good night to Jemmy, who was making an unusual appearance in the doorway, and drifted off to sleep.

· · ·

"I owe you an apology," I told Kate the next afternoon.

"You do? Why?" She glanced over at me. We were in her car, headed toward Barnham College, where at my request I was going to talk to Kate's daughter, Shannon, about Professor Wentworth. I wasn't quite sure what I was hoping to learn, but I thought it worth a try. If Shannon had known the professor well enough to work with him on "special projects," maybe she'd know what the connection was between him and my aunt.

"Remember when you told me that Jemmy and Inky could be descended from Marie Antoinette's cats?" I said. "I thought you were pulling my leg." I repeated what I'd read in Aunt Inga's book the night before.

Kate giggled. "If I'm going to try to be funny, I'll try a little harder than that. Some people really do believe it. I'm not so sure. It seems to me that when Marie Antoinette's things were being loaded on board the *Sally*, her cats would have been history."

"So maybe the whole thing is a fairy tale," I said.

Kate shook her head. "I don't think so. Or if it is, at least it has some basis in fact. Captain Clough did work for Colonel Swan, ferrying lumber to Paris, and the *Sally* did come back to Maine in 1794 full of French furniture and other expensive things. The Swan family still has some items. There's even a chair down at the historical society. You should go take a look at it."

"Where is the historical society? Are they open today?"

"I doubt that very much," Kate said. "Old Miss Barnes is quite active in her church. She wouldn't open the museum on a Sunday."

"Seems to me Sunday would be an excellent day to open the museum. It's when most people are off from work and have the time to do things like visit museums and galleries."

"Tell that to Miss Barnes," Kate said and turned the car through the open wrought-iron gates of Barnham College.

I had passed Barnham on my way into town the first time I was here, but I'd been too preoccupied with finding my way to take a good look at the college as I flew past. Now I did, and I found it to be almost too picture-perfect, the kind of small private school you see in the movies. A half dozen redbrick buildings with tall, gothic windows, clay-tiled roofs, and gargoyles hunched on the corners were ranged around a central quad, where small groups of students were hanging out on this warm Sunday afternoon. They were the one incongruous note, dressed in faded, ripped jeans or frayed shorts, with their ratty T-shirts advertising anything from beer to the virtues of education.

Kate zeroed in on a young couple standing toe to toe on the far end of the quad, their noses a scant few inches apart. A few feet away, another girl—petite and blonde—was looking from one to the other of them. She had her back to me, so I couldn't see her face, but her posture expressed concern.

"There they are," Kate said.

"The couple?"

She nodded. "They're not really a couple, though. That's Josh, Wayne's son. Between you and me, I think he'd like for them to be, but she's not biting." Kate shrugged.

The closer we got to Josh and Shannon, the more heated their argument seemed. Josh had his dad's lanky height and dark, curly hair, and he was scowling down at Shannon through wire-rimmed glasses, his lean cheeks flushed. She, meanwhile, was glaring up at him, her gestures emphatic. She had inherited her mother's red hair and centerfold figure but had yet to develop the heaviness of hip and thigh that twenty years and childbirth had given Kate. Shannon's hair was a deep mahogany, vivid against her milky white skin, and her eyes were blazing green fire at Josh.

"Who's the other girl?" I asked.

"The little blonde? That's Paige. She and Josh have always been close, and when Shannon came into the picture, the two of them pretty much adopted her."

I wasn't entirely sure whether she meant that Josh and Paige had adopted Shannon or that Shannon and Josh had adopted Paige. From the way it looked right now, the latter was true: Shannon and Josh looked like the parents, arguing, while tiny Paige stood in the background, all but wringing her hands.

We were still a few yards away, too far to hear what was being said, when Josh became aware of our approach. He said something to Shannon and straightened. She swung on her heel, her smile bright, but not sincere enough to reach her eyes. "Hi, Mom."

"Hi, baby," Kate said, her eyes on Josh. "Hi, Josh. Paige."

"Afternoon, Kate," Josh said politely.

Paige murmured something.

"We'd better get going. Have fun with your mom, Shannon. You ready, Paige?"

Paige nodded, and he flung a long arm around her shoulders to lead her away across the grass, his dark head bent to her fair one. Just before they turned the nearest corner, Paige looked back at us.

"What's going on?" Kate wanted to know, her attention on her daughter now. "What were you two arguing about?"

"Who says we were arguing?" Shannon said. "You know Josh. Always such a worrywart." She smiled at me. "You must be Avery. My mom's told me about you."

"Likewise," I said. "Nice to finally meet you."

"I hear you're renovating your aunt's house. With Derek." Her eyes were dancing.

"Shannon likes Derek," Kate explained. "If he were ten years younger, I'd worry."

"If he were ten years younger, there'd be no reason to worry," Shannon pointed out cheekily. "So, Avery, what can I do for you? My mom said you wanted to ask me some questions about Professor Wentworth."

"If you don't mind." I explained about finding the professor's business card in my aunt's desk last week, and his bicycle—or at least what I suspected was his bicycle—in her garden shed a few days ago. "I'm trying to figure out what the connection is," I said. "Especially since she died and he disappeared at the same time."

"Really?" Shannon glanced over her shoulder in the direction where Josh and Paige had vanished.

I nodded. "I don't suppose you know whether Professor Wentworth was doing anything that might involve my aunt? Researching something, perhaps?"

Shannon shook her head, throwing another glance after

Josh and Paige. I got the impression that she really, really wished she was with them instead of here with us. "I didn't really know him very well," she offered.

"I see. I thought maybe, since your mom told me you'd been working on a special project with him over the winter…"

For a second, Shannon looked like she had no idea what I was talking about. Then she flushed. "Oh, right. No, that had nothing to do with your aunt."

"I know it's a lot to ask," I said, "but I don't suppose you'd show me his office? Just in case there's something there that ties in to my aunt's death?"

Shannon hesitated.

"Wayne and his crew have already been over the professor's office," Kate reminded her, "so I don't think it would do any harm to let Avery have a look."

"I'm not sure Wayne would agree with you," Shannon muttered, but she started moving. "It's in this building over here. And he's not dead—not that we know of—so the dean's kept it the same, just in case he comes back. If he doesn't, the college will have to give the office to the history professor they're bringing in after the summer, but for now, everything's still there." She drew her dark brows together. "Wayne wouldn't even tell Josh whether they were treating the disappearance as suspicious. Although if they've found his bicycle, then I'd think that'd be suspicious, don't you, Mom? It's not like he'd be able to get anywhere without it, and his car's still parked at the condo."

While she talked, she walked us across the quad and into the building she had indicated. Like all school buildings everywhere, it was high-ceilinged and dark, permeated by an odor of glue, paper, and dust from old books. A central hall ran down the middle of it, with doors coming off it on either side. They were made of heavy, dark wood and had textured glass panels in the upper half.

"This is it." She stopped outside a door on the right. Kate and I bunched up behind her.

"Aren't you going to open it?" Kate said after a moment.

"Nuh-uh." Shannon shook her head. "You open it. I'm in enough trouble already."

"What kind of trouble?" Kate asked.

Shannon shrugged. "I'm gonna go find Josh and Paige. Bye, Avery. It was nice to meet you." She turned on her heel and walked off.

"Huh," Kate said. She turned a questioning glance on me.

I nodded. "Go ahead. I'll meet you at the car."

Kate took off down the hall after her daughter. "Shannon, wait!"

Shannon peered back over her shoulder and increased her pace. Kate did the same. In a matter of seconds, mother and daughter were both gone, down the stairs and out of the building. I heard the heavy front door slam shut behind them.

So there I was, by myself, outside Professor Wentworth's office, in the middle of a lazy Sunday afternoon with no one else in sight. With nothing to stop me from opening the door and having a look around. Nothing but my own sense of right and wrong, that is.

Naturally, I opened the door and stuck my head in. And recoiled. "Whoa!"

The word came out sounding a lot louder than I had expected, and I clapped a hand over my mouth and looked around guiltily, just in case someone had heard me. Nothing happened. No one stirred or came to ask what I thought I was doing there. After a moment, I pushed the door open enough to slide into the room beyond. The door closed behind me with a soft *snick*.

I stopped just inside and looked around again, totally overwhelmed. My friend Reba in New York, the pack rat, had nothing on Professor Wentworth. His desk was overflowing with untidy piles of papers, and shelves of books, shoved together helter-skelter, took up one entire wall behind the desk, with more books sitting in stacks along the walls. A coat tree in the corner was buried under clothes, the outermost layer holding the mandatory professorial corduroy blazer with leather patches on the elbows, along with a couple of winter hats, a few scarves, and a wool overcoat. A corkboard on the wall bristled with so many pieces of scrap paper and thumbtacks it resembled a pin cushion. There were lists of names and telephone numbers, probably those of his students. Shannon was listed, and so was Paige, with a last name of Thompson. Josh wasn't. There were college memos, cutouts from the local newspaper, and receipts for things like copy paper and toner cartridges.

Among the items was a replica of a painting of a woman with a powdered wig, dressed in a burgundy velvet gown with a gold brocade undergown and a lacy fichu. I'm no expert, but I was pretty sure I recognized Marie Antoinette. Granted, any portrait of an elegant eighteenth-century lady with powdered hair and nice clothes looks very much like another, but I'd spent a large part of yesterday reading a book with a painting of Marie Antoinette on the cover, and I was fairly certain that's who I was looking at.

That was another connection with my aunt, then. They had both been interested in the late queen of prerevolutionary France.

I spent another few minutes looking around, but without

knowing what I was looking for, it was a futile endeavor. A person could spend days in here, going through paperwork, and still have nothing to show for it. It made me wonder just how thoroughly Wayne and company had searched the office after Martin Wentworth disappeared. What I was looking for could be right under my nose, and I'd never know it. So I contented myself with shuffling through the top layer of papers on the desk, to see if anything jumped out at me, and when nothing did, I started pulling out the drawers. They were better organized than the top of the desk, but not by much, and if Professor Wentworth had been doing research on either Marie Antoinette or my aunt, there was no evidence of it.

I was just about to leave when I came across an envelope in the top drawer, half buried under pencils, erasers, and rubber bands, and practically covered with cryptic notes saying things like "Utensils—RB?" or "Bergère—Fraser House." When I opened the envelope, it turned out to be full of photographs. Snapshots, blurry and out of focus. For a moment I was afraid I'd come across the professor's private stash of dirty pictures, but a quick look dispelled that idea. The photos were of things, not people. A small footstool standing on a wood floor. A chaise longue in some dark corner somewhere, embroidered with ribbons and swags of flowers. A hairbrush and mirror set on what looked like a blue blanket. A set of hair combs on a tabletop. An exquisite tapestry hanging on a background of tartan plaid in shades of green, orange, and royal blue.

I brought the tapestry photo closer, eyes narrowed and nostrils quivering. It was quite possibly the ugliest wallpaper pattern I'd ever seen, and I'd had plenty of opportunity to judge. I'd spent most of Friday stripping Aunt Inga's hallway of it. But there had been no antique tapestry hanging in the hallway then.

• • •

Kate wasn't at the car when I got back to the parking lot, so I settled in to wait. It didn't take long; only a few minutes had passed when she came striding across the grass at a good clip. I stuck the stack of photographs back in my handbag. Kate might be OK with me going into Wentworth's office, but I wasn't sure she'd feel the same way about my absconding with possible evidence, so I thought it better to keep that part of it to myself. Still, I wanted to be sure I would recognize these things if I ever came across them.

"Everything all right?" I asked when she was within hailing distance.

"Fine."

"Is your daughter OK?"

"Fine." She wrenched open the driver's side door and slid behind the wheel. I hurriedly got into the car on the other side as she cranked the engine over and zoomed backward.

"Are you OK?"

She opened her mouth, probably to say "Fine" again, and then thought better of it. Instead she sent me a sidelong look under her lashes. "Sorry. She just makes me angry, you know."

"Wouldn't talk to you?" I asked sympathetically.

Kate grimaced. "Swore up and down that nothing was wrong. She and Josh had a fight, about nothing important, and she won't tell me anything else."

"I remember being nineteen," I said. "There was a ton of stuff I thought I couldn't tell my mother."

Kate nodded. "I thought that if I didn't say anything about

the parties and the alcohol and the sex, my folks wouldn't know what was going on. Of course, all that changed when I got pregnant." She pulled the car out of the college grounds and onto the main road again. After a moment she added brightly, in an obvious effort to change the subject, "So, did you find anything exciting in Professor Wentworth's office?"

The photographs were burning a hole in my purse, but I shook my head. "I'm afraid not. There was enough stuff there to occupy several people for several weeks. There was no way I could go through it all in just a couple of minutes. He had no file on my aunt; I did look for that. Although, like my aunt, he had several books about Marie Antoinette and about Maine history."

"Sounds like maybe the professor was looking into the legend," Kate said. I nodded. It sounded exactly like that.

.   .   .

After Kate dropped me at Aunt Inga's house and had helped me carry in the couple of bags of groceries I had asked her to stop for, she went back to the B and B, and I made myself an early dinner. When my empty plastic bowl and plastic fork were safely deposited in the trash can, I made double sure the back and front doors were locked before I made my way up the stairs to the second floor. My knee still hurt a little, but the brace was doing a bang-up job in keeping it supported, so I already felt a lot better. Still, the rickety, steep steps up to the attic were more of a challenge than I wanted. I made it, though, and pushed open the plain plank door after unlatching the hook and eye that kept it closed. It screeched like a soul in agony, and I jumped and then sneezed as a cloud of dust wafted up from the floor when the bottom of the door skimmed over it.

There was nothing as helpful as a light switch inside the door here; I had to shuffle into the middle of the attic and pull on the chain that hung there. The glare from the naked hundred-watt bulb cut across my retinas, and I squeezed my eyes shut until I could see again without hurting myself. Then I opened my eyes and looked around.

Aunt Inga's attic was the equivalent of Professor Wentworth's office: bigger and dustier, but just as full of junk. Boxes and barrels, furniture and clothes. A rather nice old walnut rolltop desk—far superior to the more modern monstrosity downstairs—was sitting just inside the door, and I gave it a pat on my way past. I should look through it sometime to make sure my aunt hadn't left any paperwork or anything else important in it.

That wasn't what I was looking for now, however. I had brought the snapshots from Professor Wentworth's office for reference—not that I could mistake the tapestry if I found it—and I was on a mission. The tapestry wasn't anywhere in the downstairs part of the house, or I would have found it by now. It wasn't in the basement, it wasn't in the garden shed, and the attic was the only other possible place it could be, provided it was still on the premises. Hence my trip up here to look around.

It took a while, and I found lots of other interesting things, including what I thought was a wedding veil tucked away at the bottom of a box, but no tapestry. I did find the chaise longue, though. Eventually I realized that the closet built along one wall of the attic didn't extend all the way back to the roof. It had a back wall, which left a roughly triangular space in the very back of the attic, comprised of floor, closet wall, and sloping ceiling. And that's where the chaise longue was, tucked behind the built-in closet, on the other side of the chimney, and buried under two different furniture covers and a pile of assorted Christmas junk. I had to climb over boxes and under racks of clothes to get to it. When I got there, I discovered that the innermost cover was made from a special nonacidic material, the kind museums and collections use to protect especially old and fragile fabrics. At first glance, the chaise longue wasn't prepossessing; it was reupholstered, badly, in the most god-awful example of 1970s orange and brown tweed I had ever seen, which clashed horribly with the curvy, elegant lines of the carved legs and headrest.

I picked at the edge of the seat and undid a few uneven stitches, peeling the tweed aside to expose a corner of the original fabric. And then I sat back on my heels and stared, my eyes wide.

I'll be the first to admit that antique furniture isn't my forte. Working with Philippe had taught me the basics, though. Plus, there was fabric involved here, and I do know fabric.

This fabric, with its needlepoint embroidery of stylized flower arrangements, swags, and ribbons, dated from the second half of the eighteenth century, as did the burlaplike underside: 1750–1800, in other words. Right around the time Samuel Clough and *Sally* were ferrying their load of Marie Antoinette's favorite things across the Atlantic.

12

"*Ma petite chou!*" Philippe exclaimed five minutes later, when I had made it downstairs to the main floor and had dialed his number. "How are you, *ma chérie?*"

"I'm fine," I said shortly, wrinkling my brows. He sounded much too happy to hear from me, although that wasn't what had given me pause. Something he had said sounded wrong, but I couldn't put my finger on it. "Do you call Tara your little cabbage, too?"

He must have thought I was jealous, because Philippe chuckled warmly. It trickled over my skin like a gentle mist, but it didn't go any further. No telltale tightening in my chest or my stomach this time around.

"*Mais non, chérie. Naturellement!*" He sounded shocked, although I wasn't entirely sure whether it was the idea that he'd call her by *my* pet name, or the idea that he'd call the coltish Tara a cabbage in the first place, that was surprising to him. He lowered his voice to an even more throbbing register. "I miss you, *ma petite.*"

"I miss you, too," I answered automatically. In truth, what I missed wasn't Philippe himself, it was just someone I could talk to, and laugh with, and turn to when I was happy or sad or scared or worried.

"When are you coming back, *chérie?*"

"I'm not sure," I said. The way things stood, the likelihood of my going back to Philippe was slim to none, unless he fired Tara and came groveling on his hands and knees, and even then I didn't think I wanted him back. Still, I didn't feel up for an argument, especially when I had a favor to ask. "There's a lot to do up here. And I may go out to California to visit Mom and Noel before I come back to New York. It's been a while since I've been there."

"But *chérie*—" Philippe said, and I knew that he was pouting like a disappointed five-year-old. Things must not be working out with Tara.

I interrupted. "I was actually calling to ask your help. Since you're such an expert on both antique furniture and French history."

"*Oui?*" It's always possible to shake Philippe out of a case of the sulks by appealing to his ego.

"Remember when you said that maybe I'd find a valuable treasure in my aunt's house?"

"*Oui?*" He was beginning to sound decidedly cheerful.

"Well, I don't know how valuable it is, but I came across this old fainting couch up in the attic. You know, a chaise longue." I gave it the French pronunciation. "It's made in France, I can tell that much, and in the late eighteenth century..."

"Tell me about it," Philippe commanded, his accent almost missing in his excitement. I did my best to describe the piece of furniture I had found, and when I wasn't doing it to Philippe's satisfaction, he asked me increasingly detailed questions, including one about what I thought might be a maker's mark burned into the underside of the couch. After several minutes of interrogation, he seemed satisfied.

"So?" I demanded when he fell silent. "What do you think?"

"Where would your aunt get such a thing?" Philippe asked.

"I guess I forgot to mention that part." I told him—briefly—about Samuel Clough and *Sally* and the French cargo. "Local legend has it that it was Marie Antoinette's stuff, things she was going to use to start over in the New World."

"*Trés interessant*," Philippe said.

"I don't know what the connection is between Captain Clough and my aunt, but maybe the families were related a hundred years ago, or something."

"With a provenance," Philippe said, pronouncing it in the French manner, "the chaise longue would be more valuable, *naturellement*."

"Naturally," I agreed, grimacing at my own face in the mirror. Before—by which I mean while we were dating—I had always found his sprinkling of Gallicisms quaint and sexy, but tonight I must admit they struck me as calculated and irritating. After living in New York for ten years, he should be able to speak proper English.

"Without, it might still be worth many thousand dollars. But if the provenance could be proven, and especially if it could be traced back to Antoinette..."

"Right," I said briskly. "I should see if I can find a provenance. Maybe I can find out how the couch came to be in my aunt's possession. Thanks for your help, Philippe."

"But *chérie*—" Philippe said. And that was the last thing I heard, because I hung up the phone. And just so I wouldn't be tempted to answer when he called back—which I was pretty sure he would, persistence being one of Philippe's more prominent traits—I immediately dialed California.

"Hello, dear," Mother said. "How are you?"

I thought it safer not to mention my accident and told her I was fine. "I wanted to ask you a question."

"Of course. Do you have another call?"

"I don't think so," I said.

"Are you sure? I could have sworn I heard something...?"

"I'll call them back. Listen, Mom, I wanted to ask you something. When you were growing up, did you ever hear the story about Captain Clough and *Sally* and a whole bunch of furniture and other things that came over to Maine from Paris during the French Revolution?"

"Of course," Mother said. "It's a Maine legend. Are you sure you don't want to get that? They sound persistent."

"I know who it is, and no, I don't want to get it. It's no one important." Hearing me say that Philippe was unimportant would probably make Mother happy, since she'd never liked him, but I didn't want to derail the conversation.

"If you're sure." She didn't sound entirely sure herself, but she stopped asking, and eventually, the insistent beeping on the line stopped, too. "Where were we? Oh, yes. There are items all over coastal Maine that the owners claim came over from France on the *Sally*. Captain Clough had a house on Edgecomb Island, so a lot of things ended up there, but I know that Colonel Swan and his wife owned something they called the Marie Antoinette bed. And one of their children married a Knox, so there's a sideboard or buffet at Montpelier in Thomaston, as well. There's even a chair or something at the Fraser House in Waterfield, I think."

"How about the Mortons?" I inquired. "Any connection there?"

"To the Cloughs or the Swans? None I've ever heard of. Why do you ask?"

"I found this fainting couch," I said, and I went on to explain what it looked like and what Philippe had said about it. Mother sniffed eloquently when she heard his name, but she refrained from comment.

"If we're related to the Cloughs or the Swans," she said when I'd finished, "I've surely never heard about it. Of course, that doesn't mean it's impossible. I don't know as much as I'd like about the Mortons, and if it was a distant connection two hundred years ago, there's no reason why I would have known. One would have thought the possession of a piece of Marie Antoinette's furniture would be a topic of conversation in the family, though."

One would think. "So maybe it isn't Marie Antoinette's couch at all. Maybe it's just a generic French fainting couch that never belonged to anyone important. Maybe it's a reproduction. It looked eighteenth century to me, but I'm not an expert on furniture, and although Philippe confirmed that it sounded eighteenth century, he hasn't seen it." And wouldn't, because I didn't want to see him.

"A pity you can't ask Aunt Inga," Mother remarked. "She knew everything that ever happened in Waterfield."

I nodded. "I know, the doctor told me." And then I bit my tongue, but it was too late.

"Doctor?" Mother repeated. "What's wrong? You aren't ill, are you, Avery?"

"Not at all," I said. "I fell down the stairs on Friday. It was no big deal. I hurt my knee, but I've had it taken care of. Dr. Ellis looked at it and told me to take it easy for a week, and that I should be completely fine by then."

"I remember Dr. Ellis," Mother said. "I saw him once or twice when I was a girl. He's still practicing?"

"This is his son, I think. His name is Ben, and he's around sixty. He told me his family has been doctors for generations."

"Of course," Mother said. "I remember Ben Ellis. He's a few years older than me, so I didn't know him well, but I remember him. Didn't he have a son, as well?"

"Derek," I answered. "He's been helping me with Aunt Inga's house."

"That's nice of him," Mother opined.

"I hired him. It's what he does for a living."

Mother dismissed Derek as soon as she found out that he wasn't a doctor like his father, and that he wasn't helping me out of the goodness of his heart.

"What a shame," she said, sounding just a little disappointed.

"I doubt he'd agree," I answered. "He studied medicine but decided not to go into practice. And just in case you're getting ideas, I'm not looking for a new boyfriend quite yet. Especially not in Waterfield. I'll only be here until the end of the summer, so it doesn't make sense to get involved with anyone."

"Of course not," Mother agreed. "Although love doesn't always make sense, does it, Avery?" I knew she was thinking of her own late-in-life love affair with Noel and following him across the country to California. "You wait, when you least expect it, the right man will come along."

"I'm sure he will," I answered. "And in the meantime,

I'm staying busy with Aunt Inga's house. I'll stop by the historical society tomorrow to have a look at the chair, and if I discover anything interesting about the Mortons, I'll let you know."

"You do that, dear," Mother said. She wished me good luck and hung up. I went to bed.

• • •

"Sure," Derek said the next morning, after I had asked him if he knew where the local historical society was located.

I waited, but when he didn't continue, I added, "Would you tell me where it is?"

"You going there?"

"That's the plan."

"Now?"

I rolled my eyes. "Of course not now. It's barely seven o'clock in the morning. Officer Thomas is supposed to come by to fingerprint the electrical panel downstairs, so I have to be here to let him in. And I'm not exactly dressed to go out, in case you hadn't noticed."

He contemplated me. I'd still been in bed when he let himself in, and I had come down to greet him in what passes for my "pajamas," a pair of shorts and a rumpled T-shirt. My hair was once again arranged à la crow's nest, and I wasn't wearing makeup or even a bra underneath the shirt.

The corners of his mouth tilted up. "I'd noticed."

I flushed and folded my arms across my chest. "There's no need to be rude."

The grin widened. "I wasn't being rude."

"For your information," I said, "when I had to go to work every day, I always managed to look appealing." Of course, back then I had been dressing to impress Philippe, but that was none of Derek's business.

"Oh, I'm not saying you don't look appealing, Tinker-bell." I felt slightly mollified by that until he added, "You look like you just rolled out of bed. What could be unappealing about that?"

He winked and brushed past me, and I turned to look after him as he sauntered—there's no other word for it—down the hallway. He was wearing a royal blue T-shirt today, and his usual faded jeans, and of course that heavy tool belt that rode low on his hips. I considered following him into the kitchen but changed my mind when he turned and threw me a knowing grin over his shoulder. Instead, I closed my mouth with a snap and scurried up the stairs as fast as I could.

It was tempting to pull out all the stops, to really show him what I could do when I tried, but I managed to resist the temptation. Instead, I pulled on a clean pair of jeans (which just happened to fit perfectly), and a baby-doll top in turquoise silk, hand-dyed by *moi*, which made the most of what little figure I have. I turned my head upside down and brushed my hair until it crackled, and then I spent several minutes in front of the bathroom mirror painting my face, covering the sprinkling of freckles across my nose and giving myself that natural glow that made me look like I was radiant all on my own, without the benefit of makeup at all.

When I came downstairs again, Derek had hoisted a bag of grout and a plastic bag from the local hardware store up on the kitchen table and was busy sorting through several small plastic-wrapped packages of something.

"What's in the bags?" I asked.

"A couple of extra dead bolts and security chains for the doors, and new locks for all the windows. If someone's out to get you, I don't aim to make it easy for them. I also picked up a tube of tile adhesive and a ten-pound bag of grout. I figured you could get started on your kitchen counter." He glanced over at me. "It's something you can do without moving around too much, and it'll keep you from going crazy with boredom."

"I thought you didn't want me to mosaic the kitchen counter," I said. Although I had suspected a softening in his attitude on Saturday, when he'd given me the magazine with the instructions.

He shrugged. "It's your counter. You can do what you want with it. Maybe it won't look so bad."

"What a ringing endorsement," I said.

He smiled. "I'll get you set up, and then I'll go to work on the doors." He turned toward the counter and began showing me the proper way to arrange the pottery shards. I only half listened, preoccupied with the movements of his hands. They were slender, with long fingers and blunt nails, one of which was jagged, and another which was blue, from where he had hit it with a hammer the other day. I'd heard the curse and gone to the cellar door to ask if he was all right, but his answer had been curt enough that I hadn't asked for details.

"OK?" he said now, turning to look at me. I nodded, although I hadn't the faintest idea what he'd said. "I'll leave you to it, then." He straightened up.

"Um..." I said.

"Yeah?"

"Could you maybe go over it one more time? Just in case I didn't catch it all?" As I'd told him once, I had in fact done mosaic before, but I enjoyed watching him demonstrate.

"You gonna listen this time?" He didn't wait for me to answer, just launched into his spiel again. I didn't think I could get away with asking a third time, so when he turned to me to make sure I understood what I was to do, I nodded and looked capable.

"Let me know if you run into any problems."

I promised I would.

"When you're ready for the grout, let me know, and I'll mix it for you."

"Thank you," I said.

"No problem. I'll be around if you need anything."

I watched him grab a set of burglar-proof dead bolts and chains and saunter out the door. Shortly afterward, I began hearing sounds of drilling in the hall. I turned back to the counter to manipulate china shards, wondering whether Derek wasn't being just a little *too* friendly and helpful (and flirtatious) all of a sudden.

OK, so on TV, the heroine's near demise at the hands of the villain might make the hero realize how he's felt about her all along. But this was real life, and although I was most likely the heroine, at least in my own life, Derek was just as likely to be the villain as the hero, even if I couldn't think what he might have to gain by causing me to fall to my death.

Could he be trying to impress Melissa? I wondered, as I arranged the porcelain shards in various combinations to create a pleasingly random pattern across the countertop. She had left him. If he wanted her back, and he knew she wanted Aunt Inga's house, maybe he thought getting rid of me would make her happy. Hard to believe he'd attempt murder for the woman who'd jilted him for his schoolyard nemesis, but as Mother said, love doesn't always make sense. Maybe he was still pining. He had tried to divert suspicion from her, telling me she couldn't possibly be behind my accident, not that I was about to take his word for it.

It seemed more likely that Melissa was working with the Stenhams, though, since she was dating Ray. Or maybe that relationship was going south? If she was happy with Ray, why would she care that Derek was working for me? But if she wasn't happy, and she wanted Derek back, and perceived me as a threat, then maybe...

"Looks good," Derek's voice said near my ear.

I jumped. "Thank...thank you."

My voice got caught in my throat. I'd like to claim it was because he startled me, but I'm afraid it was really because he was standing too close, leaning over my shoulder. If I tilted my head back, I could almost kiss him. If he met me halfway, at least.

He didn't. But he did stay where he was a second longer, looking down at me. Long enough for my eyes to flick down to his lips and back up to his eyes. He grinned and straightened. I turned back to the counter, my cheeks hot.

"I just wanted to tell you that Officer Thomas has arrived," Derek said. "I took him downstairs." He sounded blessedly normal, although, of course, that fact irritated me, too. Breathless and stammering might be too much to expect, but it would have been nice if he'd been not entirely unaffected.

"Thank you," I said.

"Your front door's secured. I'll start putting locks on the windows now."

He turned to the table, where the paraphernalia he'd brought earlier still lay, scattered across the enamel surface. I watched as he gathered up a half dozen small packets of window hardware and stuffed them in his pocket. "See ya." He wandered out.

"Later," I said to his back, rolling my eyes in exasperation as he disappeared into the dining room. A few seconds later the power drill kicked on again. I went back to my broken shards and my dark thoughts.

. . .

Officer Thomas finished his work just before lunch and headed out with his fingerprinting kit and a plastic container full of bits and pieces of broken railing that Derek helped him carry to his cruiser. Of course he wasn't able to tell me whether he'd found any interesting prints downstairs, not until he could process them—and Derek's, for comparison; he already had mine, from the last time someone had broken in—but I did get him to confirm that the bike I'd found in Aunt Inga's shed had belonged to Martin Wentworth. The police had pulled the professor's fingerprints from his condo after the disappearance, in high enough numbers to ensure that they were actually his, and there were matching prints on the bicycle. I had obliterated any prints on the handlebar and brakes when I rode the bike the other night, but the professor's prints remained on the tires and frame. "It was a lucky break for us that it's been inside the shed this whole time," Brandon Thomas said, "or the rain would have washed away anything useful long ago."

"What are you planning to do now?" I wanted to know. Brandon said they'd go over Professor Wentworth's condo and office again, looking for anything that might tie my aunt to the professor. I tried not to feel guilty about walking off with the photographs from the desk as I asked him to please keep me updated on what he found.

"Ready to go?" Derek asked when Officer Thomas had driven away. I turned to him.

"Go where?"

"I thought you wanted to stop by the historical society today."

"Oh," I said. "Right."

"I'll buy you lunch."

"You don't have to do that," I protested, although I allowed myself to be led out of the kitchen and down the hall toward the front door by his hand at the small of my back.

Derek drove the three blocks into downtown, parked the truck on a side street, and walked me to a small, utilitarian deli just off Main Street. It must have been a place where the locals hung out, because the proprietor greeted him by name. Derek ordered a lobster roll, while I tried unsuccessfully to negotiate for turkey on whole wheat as a change from the tuna. Apparently downeasterners, as the local Mainers are known, weren't into turkey, and I had to settle (hah!) for another lobster roll, along with chips and a Diet Coke. We ate sitting across from each other on hard plastic orange chairs, and although the ambiance may have been lacking, the quality of the food wasn't. The lobster was some of the best I'd ever had: fresh, succulent, and flavorful, with a side of melted butter. Le Coq au Vin couldn't have done better.

"How's the counter coming?" Derek asked when he'd eaten a few bites and had to take a break for a sip of Moxie soda.

I swallowed before I answered. "You looked at it before we left. Didn't it look OK?"

"It looked fine. I wondered how you felt about it."

"Oh," I said. "I feel good. I still think it's going to look nice. Although it's going to be hard to get an even surface. You know, for cutting and things like that."

He took another bite of the sandwich before he answered. "Would you consider using your scridgens for a backsplash instead?"

"My what?"

"Pieces."

"For a backsplash?" I thought about it. With a solid countertop—maybe a bright blue Corian or eco-friendly resin—doing the backsplash in a pattern of broken Blue Willow might look quite good. "That might work."

"Something to think about." He crunched a chip.

"How long have you been doing renovation work?" I asked, partly to keep the conversation going but mostly because I was interested.

"Full time for about five years now. I started doing it in high school, to make some money over the summer, and then I got good at it. It seemed a shame to stop." He grinned.

"Especially when all you had to look forward to was taking over your dad's medical practice," I nodded. "Just out of curiosity, why didn't you ever tell me you went to medical school?"

"Not because it's a secret. I figured you already knew. Everyone else does. And you talk to Kate, and Kate knows everything. She's not shy about telling people, either."

I hid a smile. "She's not, is she?"

He shook his head, and that wayward lock of hair fell into his eyes again. I busied myself by picking up my sandwich and taking another bite. "You two seem friendly," I remarked when I had swallowed. Kate had been in and out of the house almost every day for the past week, and their relationship had seemed casually affectionate: half sisterly indulgence on Kate's part, half brotherly exasperation on Derek's, with some easy flirtatiousness thrown in for good measure.

He grinned. "Is that a roundabout way of asking if we've been involved? Just because I told you how long I've been working on houses doesn't mean you can ask for all my secrets, Tinkerbell."

"I wouldn't dream of it," I said. "Besides, I know enough about your love life already."

"You do, do you? Like what?"

The grin was challenging, and like a fool, I took the bait. "Like the fact that you and Melissa James used to be married." That efficiently wiped the smile off his face, and I added, wishing I'd kept my mouth shut, "I'm sorry."

"So am I," Derek said. And added, "It was a long time ago."

"Four or five years, Kate said."

"Kate says entirely too much." His voice was free of rancor, however. "I'll tell you about it sometime."

"Why not now?"

He pushed his chair back. "Right now we've got other things to do. You ready?"

"I guess I can be." I'm a small person; I don't need much fuel to make it through the day.

"I'll walk you over to the Fraser House. It's just a few blocks away. Think your knee can handle it? And then I'll head down to the hardware store for some supplies."

"Sure." I followed him out the door. The middle-aged woman behind the counter, the same one who had made our sandwiches, called out a "See ya," as we left.

13

The Waterfield Historical Society was located in the Fraser House, a lovely old building just off Main Street, and the desk in the lobby was manned by a dragon. A dragon in a beige twinset and pearls, but a dragon nonetheless. Seventy if she was a day, but still as straight-backed as if she had swallowed a broomstick, and with thick, iron gray hair piled on top of her head. When I walked through the door, she looked me over a few times, from top to bottom and back—taking note of my tight jeans, painted toenails, and bare shoulders—before she inquired what my business was.

"My name is Avery Baker," I explained. "I'm Inga Morton's niece."

"Ay-yup?"

"I'm renovating her house over on Bayberry."

"Ay-yup?" The local colloquialism sounded funny coming from such a dignified lady.

"I was wondering if you had any information about the family." May as well ask.

"I'm afraid the Mortons haven't done much to distinguish themselves," the docent said dismissively.

"I'm sure that's true." I smiled. I wasn't a kid anymore, and this throwback to my middle school days didn't frighten me. Much. "Still, I'd like to see anything you have."

She sniffed. "I'll have to check the files."

"Take your time," I said and watched as she turned away to a utilitarian metal filing cabinet that looked out of place in the high-ceilinged, Greek Revival foyer. "I'll just have a look around while I wait. Someone told me you have a chair, supposedly from France, from back when Captain Clough brought Marie Antoinette's furniture and things over."

"In the parlor."

"Through there?" I indicated the room beyond two lovely Grecian columns.

The docent inclined her head regally.

"Thank you." I wandered in that direction while she went back to her files.

The chair I was looking for was situated between two tall windows in the parlor, out of the damaging rays of the sun and behind a rope. Do Not Touch!!! said a little sign that hung from the rope, with no less than three exclamation points following the command. I bent as close to the chair as I could without touching it, my nose twitching.

Philippe had created something similar to this last year. It wasn't rococo, exactly; it was the style that had grown out of the rococo period, after Louis XVI—Marie Antoinette's husband—had succeeded his grandfather, Louis XV, to the French throne. XV was the great-grandson of the famous

Sun King, Louis XIV, and he shared his ancestor's taste for luxury and extravagance. However, when shy, dull Louis-Auguste came to power in 1774, furniture gradually changed from playful and sinuous to staid and straight. Influenced by neoclassicism, cabinetmakers produced angular versions of the forms popular in the earlier part of the century. What I was looking at was one of those. A symmetrical armchair, scaled down to fit in the intimate salons so popular under Marie Antoinette, with straight legs and arms in carved gilt wood, upholstered in peach damask. A bergère, just like in the notation on the envelope in Professor Wentworth's office. I recognized it from one of the snapshots I'd liberated, too. And although I'm no expert, the tiny maker's mark, burned into the frame underneath the seat, where it wouldn't be noticed, looked exactly like the maker's mark on the chaise longue in Aunt Inga's attic.

When I came back out to the reception area, the elderly docent had finished her search through the files and was flirting—yes, flirting!—with Derek. Or maybe it would be more accurate to say that Derek was flirting with her, and she was responding in kind. He did everything except kiss her hand, and she was visibly eating out of his.

"There you are," he said with a dazzling grin when he saw me.

"Yep. Here I am." I smiled back. It was impossible not to. "I didn't think I'd see you so soon."

"It doesn't take long to buy some sealer and a package of paint mix."

"Paint mix?" I felt my smile slip. "Oh, no! You're not going to make me smear curdled milk on my walls, are you? Kate told me about this. She says it looks gorgeous and lasts forever, but it stinks to high heaven."

"Your ancestors used milk paint," the museum docent

pointed out. "If it was good enough for them, surely it's good enough for you."

"They didn't have anything else!" I turned to Derek. "Can't I just have normal paint instead? The kind that comes in a can?"

"I can put it in a can," Derek said.

"That's not the same thing!"

"We'll talk about it," Derek promised. I rolled my eyes. I knew what that meant. He continued, "You ready to go home? Lots to do this afternoon."

"Almost." I turned back to the docent, who informed me that the historical society had precisely one slim file of information about the Mortons. When I did a preliminary flip through it, I saw that it contained not much more than a family tree, which ended with Aunt Inga, as the last living Morton. There was her obituary, which someone must have cut out of the local paper after her death; a few other, older obituaries; and some old photographs and copies of marriage licenses and death certificates, that sort of thing. No diary, no bundles of letters, nothing exciting.

"You may take it home," the docent said graciously, "by signing here." She flipped open a huge ledger and pointed to the last line on a page. I didn't really want to take the file home—it didn't seem to contain anything interesting, and I had enough old junk in the house as it was—but I didn't want to say no, either, when she'd gone to the trouble of finding it for me. So I put my John Hancock on the line, and skimmed my eyes up the page to see who else had been interested in my family. Not surprisingly, the last entry before mine bore Mr. Rodgers's name. I don't know what he thought he might find among the Morton family papers, but he was Aunt Inga's executor, so it wasn't unreasonable that he should want to go through the historical society's things as pertained to her. He'd been here the day after my aunt died, the day before I first came to Waterfield.

More interestingly, the signature before Mr. Rodgers's, dated some months previously, said M. Wentworth.

"Was Professor Wentworth interested in the Mortons?" I asked casually as I pushed the book and pen back across the counter. Derek leaned an elbow on the desk and took a look at the entry for himself. The docent's face clouded.

"The professor was interested in the history of Waterfield, of which your aunt knew a great deal."

"Do you know if he met Aunt Inga?"

"I believe he had," she said. "In fact, I suggested it to him, back when he first came to town. Inga Morton knew more about the town and its inhabitants than anyone, and although I held out no great hope that she would agree to talk with the professor, being so reclusive and—pardon me—old, I thought it worthwhile to ask."

"Do you have any idea what happened to him?"

She shook her head. "I'm afraid I don't. The last time I saw the professor was when he was here last, in February. Such a lovely man." She shook her head sadly.

"I'm sure he was," I said. "You know, he disappeared at the same time as my aunt died. The same day, practically. You don't suppose . . . ?"

She sent me a look that could have peeled the milk paint right off the wall. "Please be sure to bring the file back intact. There is an inventory written on the inside of the flap, with a list of everything that belongs in the file. Please do not lose any of the papers. They're irreplaceable."

"Of course," I said, tucking the folder under my arm. "That chair in the other room, the French one? What's its provenance?"

The dragon lady looked slightly more affable now.

Maybe she was pleased to be able to lecture. "Jeremiah Fraser built the Fraser House between 1839 and 1842. He was a sea captain engaged in the China trade. The captain's wife, Patience, was related to the Cloughs, and the chair was part of her dowry. Among several other things, of course. Smaller things. Some jewelry, a hairbrush, hair combs, a fan encrusted with diamonds. All of which we have lost, unfortunately." Another cloud passed over her wrinkled countenance.

"Lost?" I repeated, aghast. How could a museum lose important artifacts like those? It's not like a diamond-encrusted fan is something you just happen to throw away in a moment of distraction.

"The museum suffered a robbery back in 1934. All the smaller valuables were stolen at that time."

"Gosh," I said, "I'm sorry."

She nodded stiffly.

"Well...thanks very much for your help."

"My pleasure." She simpered, although it was directed more at Derek than at me. "Take care of the file. And you, young man..." She turned to Derek, "You take care of yourself."

"Yes, ma'am." He gave her another blinding smile before ushering me out the door with a hand at my back.

．　．　．

"Who's she?" I asked as we headed back to work. Bless him, he had gone back and picked up the truck before coming to get me. It was waiting at the curb when we came out of the Fraser House.

"Miss Barnes? She used to teach at the high school." He looked right and left and right again before easing the truck across the intersection of Main Street and Oak.

Point for me, I thought, making a check mark on the air with my finger. I'd had her pegged as either a retired school-teacher or an old librarian. "You must have been a good student, if she still remembers you."

"I was OK, I guess. I liked history."

"And Miss Barnes obviously liked you. It's a good thing she's almost old enough to be your grandmother. If you flirted like that with someone your own age, they might get the wrong idea."

Derek grinned. "Why do you think I don't?"

I rolled my eyes.

When we got to the house, I headed for the kitchen.

Derek was right on my heels. "About the milk paint," he said.

I shook my head. "I don't want it. There's no reason why you can't use oil or latex instead. Something normal."

"Milk paint *is* normal. People used it for centuries. It goes on beautifully and lasts forever. And the coverage and clarity of color is wonderful."

"I don't want curdled milk on my walls!"

"But as you've often pointed out, they won't be your walls. We're only renovating the house to sell it again, remember?"

I grumbled, but he was right; I had said that. Much to my chagrin, I was starting to feel possessive of Aunt Inga's house. Derek added, "Authenticity is important. Any Realtor will be overjoyed to be able to tell her clients that the house is painted with time-authentic milk paint."

I narrowed my eyes. *Her* clients? "If you think I'm going to give the house to your ex-wife to sell when it's ready, you can forget it. I'll slap a For Sale by Owner sign in the yard and try to sell it myself first. And if that doesn't work, I'll find someone else. She can't be the only Realtor in Water-field."

He shrugged. "Fine by me. I don't owe her any favors." He turned to the kitchen counter, where all my china shards were laid out in the prettiest pattern I could manage. "The counter is about the same width as the backsplash is tall. You can transfer your pieces directly from the horizontal to the vertical. Are you ready to start grouting?"

"I guess," I said. And added, wistfully, "I don't suppose you can give me blue grout, can you?"

He grinned. "I thought you might ask, so I picked up some colorant, just in case. I'll mix it together."

He did, while I watched, just a little amazed that he knew enough about me to guess that I'd want blue grout. And not only to guess but to be so sure of himself that he actually went out and bought what he'd need to give me what I wanted.

He handed me a pair of thin rubber gloves and a spatula. "Here's what you want to do . . ." He waited until I had pulled the gloves on, and then he showed me how to squeeze a bit of tile adhesive on a piece of china, tack it to the wall, and then apply the grout, pushing the thick mixture between the pieces of porcelain and wiping the excess off with a damp cloth before it set. Gingerly, I got to work. I'd done something similar before, so it shouldn't have been a big deal, but Derek stood there, watching me, and it unnerved me.

After a few minutes he decreed that I seemed to be doing an OK job.

"How very condescending of you," I said.

His lips twitched. "I do my best."

"I bet. So what are *you* planning to do this afternoon?"

Hopefully something more useful than looking over my shoulder, making me nervous.

"I thought I'd start priming the hall. Get a clean base coat that'll take the colored paint well. I bought a can of Kilz, too, while I was at the store. But first..."

"First what?" I asked, glancing over my shoulder when I heard the rustle of cloth. And then I dropped my spatula, loaded with grout, onto the countertop with a clatter. "What are you...yowser!"

"I often get undressed when I'm getting ready to paint," Derek explained blandly, yanking the T-shirt he'd just taken off over my head, blocking out the brief glimpse I'd gotten of a flat stomach and taut muscles. "And you need something to cover up with. That top's too nice to get gunked up with adhesive and grout."

I couldn't help noticing that the shirt smelled like him and was still warm from his body. It settled on my much smaller frame like a soft sack, covering everything from shoulders to midthigh, and my arms all the way past my elbows.

"I don't care if you're used to painting in the altogether," I managed when my head popped out on the other side, "don't you dare take off anything else!"

"Wouldn't dream of it," Derek said solemnly. And then he grinned. "I'll be in the hallway if you want me." He walked off, jeans riding low on his hips and every muscle in his upper body moving in perfect harmony. I stayed where I was, trying to get my breathing under control as I watched, running his words over in my head. He'd be in the hallway if I wanted him. Right...

• • •

By late afternoon I had pretty much managed to recover. To enough of a degree that when the doorbell rang, I made an instinctive move to answer it, and then stopped when I caught a glimpse of Derek's half-naked form through the open door.

"I'll get it," he said.

"Thank you," I answered. I heard his steps go down the hall, then the various locks and bolts clicking open. A moment of silence followed as Derek opened the door, then, "Good afternoon, Mr. Ellis," came Mr. Rodgers's soft, educated voice.

"Hi, Mr. Rodgers," Derek responded affably.

"May we come in?"

"Sure." Derek stepped aside, and I heard two sets of footsteps file into the hallway. I put down my spatula and was just about to head out to see who had come to visit when Mr. Rodgers spoke again. "May I introduce Philippe Aubert? Monsieur Aubert, this is Derek Ellis, our local handyman."

Oh, Lord. I stopped abruptly.

I could just imagine the tableau. Mr. Rodgers, dapperly conservative in a dark business suit, wing-tip shoes, white shirt, and tasteful tie, with his thin, gray hair meticulously combed across his balding head, and Philippe, flamboyant as an actor playing a Frenchman, in hand-tooled boots, black beret sitting jauntily on top of his shoulder-length hair, snug pants sculpting his muscular legs, and some shimmery satin shirt open at least two buttons farther south than was strictly decent...

As I rounded the corner, I saw that his square jaw sported yesterday's sexy five-o'clock shadow. His voice, with its pronounced French accent, was the throaty, raspy purr of a caged lion. "Avery! *Ma petite puce!*"

Derek made a sound like a quickly smothered snort and then cleared his throat innocently. The third figure in this weird tableau, he looked relaxed and at ease. There was primer on his hands and a smear of white across his taut stomach. His hair was dusty and stood up in choppy spikes where he had run his fingers through it. His jeans were so worn and faded as to be practically threadbare, and although they fit him like a glove, they were hardly the height of fashion. Still, he looked content and comfortable. And real, unlike Philippe, who came across more like an actor who had inadvertently walked onto the wrong television set, dressed to play the hot, new love interest on *Sex and the City,* and instead finding himself taking over for Carter Oosterhouse on HGTV.

"What are you doing here?" I asked, torn between amused anger and irritation.

"You called me, *chérie.*" He looked reproachful.

Derek arched his brows.

"I called to talk to you," I corrected. "About the fainting couch, remember? I didn't ask you to come here."

"I heard your loneliness, *ma petite.* I knew you missed me as much as I missed you." He looked soulful.

"Right," I said, suppressing the urge to roll my eyes.

Derek turned away, and I could see his shoulders shaking.

"Just out of curiosity, where's Tara?"

"Who's Tara?" Derek asked, his back still turned. His voice was uneven.

"The new girlfriend. She's twenty-two."

"Ah." Derek didn't say anything else, and I shifted my attention back to Philippe.

"How did you know where to find me? I didn't give you my address."

"Monsieur Aubert contacted me through his attorney,"

Mr. Rodgers interjected. "Miss Lee phoned this morning to say he was on his way to Waterfield."

"I see." It had never occurred to me that Philippe could get my address by asking Laura Lee. I should have told her not to give it to him, but frankly, it hadn't occurred to me that he'd want it.

"*Chérie*," Philippe said, "what's this you are wearing?" He took a slip of Derek's shirt between two fingers and wrinkled his nose.

"Oh," I said, flushing, "it's Derek's." I pulled the T-shirt over my head and gave it back to its owner, who put it on with a wink.

Philippe lowered his voice as he bent closer to kiss me on the cheek, "And who is this Derek?"

I allowed the kiss—barely—but sidestepped the arm that reached for my waist. "He's helping me renovate Aunt Inga's house." For money, but I wasn't about to tell Philippe that. If he thought Derek was here because of my own sweet self, then that was no more than he deserved. Philippe, I mean.

Derek smiled. A dazzling grin, bringing out dimples and crinkly eyes and everything nice. He stuck out his hand. "Derek Ellis. Nice to meet you, Phil."

It was my turn to snort and cover it with a hand and a ladylike cough.

"My name is Philippe," the latter said stiffly. "Philippe Aubert."

"Of course it is." Derek continued to pump Philippe's hand enthusiastically, no doubt transferring all the paint he possibly could. "Avery has told me all about you."

"*C'est ça?*" Philippe sent me a narrow look, while at the

same time continuing to give as good as he got with the handshaking.

"Ay-yup." If Philippe's grip bothered him at all, Derek didn't let on. I wondered if Philippe was suffering. "So what are you doing here, Phil?"

"Avery called me," Philippe said.

"About the chaise longue," I added.

"Right." Derek glanced at me. I hadn't told him about finding the couch, so he had no idea what I was talking about.

"The couch is in the attic," I said. "In fact, since you're both here," two young, strong, able-bodied men, obviously set on proving their individual strength and superiority, "maybe you'd be so kind as to help me carry it downstairs?" It didn't look heavy, but it was unwieldy, and it was the least Philippe could do, after dropping in on me like this, without warning. With any luck, maybe he'd throw his back out coming down the stairs. Or, on second thought, I'd rather he didn't. If he couldn't drive back to the city, he'd have to stay here, and I didn't want him under my roof—Aunt Inga's roof—any longer than I had to.

"Sure," Derek said readily.

"*Mais naturellement*," Philippe added.

They broke the death grip each had kept on the other's hand and stepped away from each other, exchanging wary glances.

"Great. This way." I headed up the stairs. Philippe followed, after Derek stepped aside with an ironic bow. Mr. Rodgers straggled behind.

"My pardon, Miss Baker," he said while we were standing side by side watching Philippe and Derek gently wrestle the fainting couch from the depths of the attic. Philippe's cheeks were flushed. I could tell by his behavior that I was likely to be right in my theory that the couch was eighteenth-century French, and valuable. He hadn't even blinked when his shiny eggplant-colored satin shirt got caught on a nail and tore.

"Yes, Mr. Rodgers?" I moved my eyes away from the boys to the dignified lawyer.

"This fainting couch...is it valuable?"

"That depends," I said. "As an example of eighteenth-century French furniture, it's probably worth a few thousand dollars. But if it can be proven that it was part of the cargo that came over from France in 1794, and that it might even have belonged to Marie Antoinette, then it could be worth a lot more."

"So that's what you're on about," Derek remarked, as he and Philippe came within hearing distance, each carrying an end of the chaise longue. I shrugged unapologetically.

"Kate told me about the legend. I know that the Knox family has a sideboard at Montpelier, and the Swans have, or had, something they called the Marie Antoinette bed at their house in Dorchester. And of course I saw the chair at the Fraser House this afternoon. There are pieces that supposedly belonged to Marie Antoinette all over coastal Maine. Why not here?"

"More pieces than would have fit on ten *Sally*s," Derek agreed. "Forget 'why not here.' Do you have any reason to believe your family knew either the Swans or the Cloughs well enough to be given any of Marie Antoinette's things?"

"That's what I was doing at the historical society this afternoon," I explained. "Trying to make a connection between the Mortons and either the Cloughs or the Swans."

Mr. Rodgers looked politely intrigued, maybe even slightly alarmed. "Dear me, Miss Baker. Were you able to make such a connection?"

I shook my head. "Not so far. Miss Barnes gave me the Morton file to take home, but there doesn't seem to be anything of interest in it. Not that I've had a chance to look very closely. I noticed you looked at it a couple of weeks ago, just after Aunt Inga died."

Mr. Rodgers nodded. "To my knowledge, no Morton ever married a Clough or a Swan, and neither a Clough nor a Swan ever married a Morton."

"Of course not," I said with a wry look, "that would have been too easy." I glanced at the couch, making its slow way down the steps in front of us, and added pensively, "I wonder if the tapestry that used to hang in the hallway was of this vintage, too...?"

Mr. Rodgers shot me a startled glance. He missed a step and knocked into me. I stumbled, and for a second I was afraid I wouldn't regain my balance. One end of the fainting couch thumped on the stairs as a strong arm caught my waist and kept me from falling. "Easy," Derek said into my hair.

"Thanks," I answered shakily. Philippe, far from expressing any concern that I might have fallen and broken my neck, directed a glare at Derek.

"Careful! This chaise longue is potentially invaluable."

"But maybe not quite as valuable as Avery?" Derek suggested.

Philippe muttered something but didn't argue, although I was quite sure he didn't agree.

They picked up their respective ends of the couch and continued their cautious way down.

"Tapestry, Miss Baker?" Mr. Rodgers prompted.

"Oh, yes." I thought fast. I couldn't tell him I'd looted Professor Wentworth's office and found the professor's stash of photographs, so I lied instead. "My mother told me

Aunt Inga used to have an old tapestry hanging in the hall-way. I don't suppose you know anything about it?"

"I'm afraid not, Miss Baker," Mr. Rodgers said. "Miss Morton did have something like a tapestry hanging in the hallway for a while, but I think it was modern. She took it down some months ago, I believe."

"I see," I said. The tapestry in the photograph had pictured knights on horseback hunting unicorns, as far as I had been able to make out, so this didn't make any sense. But maybe someone else in town had the same ugly tartan wallpaper in their house, and the tapestry in the picture hadn't been Aunt Inga's at all. I turned my attention to more immediate things. We had reached the bottom of the stairs, and I had to decide where to direct the chaise longue.

"You can put it in the parlor, please," I said. "Through the double doors on the right."

The men headed for the front room with their burden and placed it lovingly—more so on Philippe's part than on Derek's—in front of the window. We all took a step back and cocked our heads.

"It's wicked ugly," Derek said after a moment.

"That's just because of the tweed," I answered. "What's underneath is much nicer."

"I'll take your word for it." He turned to Philippe. "What do you think, Phil?"

Philippe didn't have to answer; his feelings were plainly written across his face. It was the same expression Derek had had the day he first beheld my aunt's kitchen. Rapt. Worshipful. Avaricious. "It appears genuine," he said reluctantly. "Of course, the only way to be sure is to take it to New York and have someone authenticate it. Someone at Christie's or Sotheby's, maybe. One of the big auction houses. I know a girl at Christie's . . ."

He probably knew girls in a lot of different places, girls he'd never taken the time to tell me about. "Not on your life," I said. "This is *my* couch; it stays here."

"But, *chérie*..."

"I'm sure there's someone in Waterfield who can authenticate it. There are antique shops all up and down Main Street, and Derek's dad has a lot of antiques in his house. And if not, I'm willing to trust my own instincts. The fabric is eighteenth-century French. The needlework pattern is classical. Even the burlap on the underside dates from that period. It's a pity it's torn, but after two hundred years, I guess that was inevitable."

Mr. Rodgers shook his head, clucking. "Dear me, I cannot believe I overlooked this. It was the fact that it was hidden in the far corner of the attic, I suppose, under so many other things..." He sounded genuinely distressed at the oversight.

"Don't worry about it," I said, patting his arm. "We've found it now, and that's all that matters."

"Indeed." But he still looked glum.

I opened my mouth to say something comforting, but before I could get the words out, there was a knock on the door.

"Expecting someone else?" Derek asked.

I shook my head.

"I'll get it."

"Thank you." I watched him walk out of the parlor, and then turned my attention back to the couch and Philippe. He looked up and met my eyes, and I could tell from the slight accusatory look he gave me that he'd noticed me watching Derek. I looked accusatory right back. What did he expect, after all? That I'd sit up here in Waterfield licking my wounds and lamenting the fact that I'd lost him?

Out in the hallway, high heels clicked on the wood floor, and for a moment I was afraid that thinking about her had brought Tara to my doorstep, along with Philippe. A second later a vision in creamy white appeared in the doorway, followed by a stone-faced Derek.

Melissa stood for a second looking around, bathing Mr. Rodgers and me in the radiance of her teeth, before her gaze fell on Philippe. I could see her visibly doing a double take, her lovely deep blue eyes widening, before she hastily focused her attention on me. "Avery! How are you, dear? Wayne came and told us about the accident. How horrible for you!"

"Hi, Melissa," I said politely.

"A little behind the times, aren't you?" Derek inquired softly. Melissa pretended she couldn't hear him.

"I brought you some flowers. Would you mind, baby?" This last was directed at Derek, along with the bouquet of daisies. He didn't have any choice but to accept them, as well as the casual—and condescending—endearment, but it was obvious from his expression that he could have done without both. Philippe, meanwhile, distracted from his contemplation of the fainting couch, looked up and saw Melissa.

She smiled. "Hi, I'm Melissa James." She held out her hand.

"Philippe Aubert. *A votre enchanté.*" Philippe clicked his heels together—Derek rolled his eyes—and bowed over Melissa's hand. "A pleasure, madame."

Melissa tinkled gaily. "Oh, mademoiselle. Please."

It was my turn to roll my eyes.

Derek glanced over at me and arched his brows.

I shrugged.

Philippe was explaining that he had just arrived from

New York, and Melissa was exclaiming over the long drive and how tired he must be. "I know!" she said, as if this was a brilliant idea that wouldn't have occurred to the rest of us. "Why don't we go and get some dinner? Unless you and Avery want to be alone, of course?"

She tittered coyly. I hastened to say that no, we didn't. Philippe sent me another reproachful look, hardly effective, since he was busy basking in Melissa's admiration.

"Avery and I have plans," Derek said.

I turned to him in surprise. "We do?"

"Sure. Don't you remember? You asked me about that romantic, out-of-the-way place that only the locals know about?"

Of course I remembered. I hadn't expected him to use it as an excuse to get out of having dinner with Melissa, though. Not that I begrudged him any excuse he could come up with. In fact, I was grateful that he had invented one that covered both of us. "Oh. Yes, of course."

"Oh, are you taking Avery to your place?" Melissa cooed. Derek's cheeks darkened, and so did Philippe's. I sent Melissa a dirty look and turned to Mr. Rodgers, standing mostly forgotten beside me, still looking at the fainting couch.

"What about you, Mr. Rodgers? Do you want to come to dinner with us?"

Melissa had the good grace to look ashamed of her behavior and of the fact that she'd totally ignored Mr. Rodgers.

"Dear me, no," the lawyer shook his head. "I have plans for tonight, I'm afraid." He glanced down at the couch, probably marshalling his excuses, then added, "In fact, I think it is time for me to leave. Miss Baker, Miss James, always a pleasure. Mr. Ellis, nice to have seen you. Monsieur

Aubert, welcome to Waterfield. I feel certain that between Miss Baker and Miss James, you will be well taken care of, but if there is anything I can do, please do not hesitate to contact me."

We watched him chatter his way to the front door and bow himself out.

"Have you had a chance to see any of Waterfield yet, Philippe?" The way Melissa pronounced his name was positively caressing. "Would you like me to show you around while Avery and Derek do their thing?"

"Why not?" Philippe said, looking darkly from Derek to me before turning a blinding smile on Melissa. "I would love it if you would show me around, *ma belle*. Avery..." He smirked, "I will see you later, *oui*?"

"I'll be here," I said. Melissa hooked her hand through Philippe's arm and guided him out, albeit not without a triumphant look back over her shoulder. To be honest, I wasn't sure whether it was directed at Derek or at me, and what's more, I didn't care.

$$-14-$$

"So that's the boyfriend," Derek remarked when the door had closed behind the two of them. I nodded.

"Ex-boyfriend. Yes."

"Phil."

"Philippe. Yes."

"Bah," Derek said.

I laughed, surprised. "What do you mean, bah?" No one had ever actually said bah to me before.

"If he's French, I'm Coco Chanel."

"Of course he's French," I said.

Derek arched a brow.

I added, "I mean, just listen to him talk!"

"So he has a French accent. One he forgets when he gets angry. And he's picked up a few French words that he sticks into the conversation when he thinks they sound good. That doesn't make him French."

"Of course he's French! He told me he grew up in Paris. He translates the menu at Le Coq au Vin. He spent two weeks in France just a few months ago."

"I spent a year in France once, too," Derek said. "Didn't make me French."

"Well, of course not, but... What were you doing in France?"

"Exchange program. Last year of high school. Don't change the subject."

"I wasn't changing the subject. Just trying to determine what makes you qualified to decide. What makes you think Philippe isn't French?"

Derek shrugged. "Nobody who's really French is that French."

"You've got to be joking."

He shook his head. "Nope. He doesn't talk right. But you don't have to take my word for it. Kate's daughter speaks wonderful French, and Kate's is good, too. They'll tell you."

"You want me to ask Kate and Shannon to determine if my old boyfriend is really French."

"That's right," Derek said. "Kate's good. She'll be able to tell. Back when Kate and I were dating..." He stopped, flushing.

"Oh, ho!" I said. "How long were you together?"

He squirmed. "Not long. And we weren't together. We just went on a few dates. When she moved to town five years ago. Just after Melissa left. It's not important. Where were we?"

"We were talking about Kate," I said. "And you. Dating."

"Let's just move past that, OK? Kate speaks French. Shannon speaks it almost natively. Her father was French."

"I know; Kate told me. So what you're saying is that my boyfriend, the one I've worked with and dated for four months, is a fraud?"

"Afraid so."

"I don't believe you," I said flatly. "You're just..." I hesitated. I wanted to say *jealous*, but I didn't dare.

Derek declined the bait. "Bet you I could prove it. Shannon owes me a favor."

"Did you date her, too?" I probably sounded snide, but I was beyond caring. Derek looked shocked.

"Of course not. She's nineteen. I'm thirty-four. And besides, Kate would kill me."

"That didn't bother Philippe," I said. "He's thirty-eight, and Tara is twenty-two."

"I'm not Phil. And besides, we've already decided that he's a fraud. Why are you surprised that he'd sleep with a girl young enough to be his daughter?"

"*Almost* young enough to be his daughter."

"Bah," Derek said.

I smiled.

He added, "What do you say we finish up for the day and go grab dinner?"

I widened my eyes. "Are you asking me out?"

"I told Melissa we had plans to go to the Waymouth Tavern. If we don't go, she'll find out. You don't want Melissa on your case, do you?"

"Decidedly not. I'll get busy with my backsplash."

"You do that," Derek said.

• • •

The Waymouth Tavern turned out to be situated outside town, on top of the cliffs Mother had warned me about when I was little. If I had felt especially energetic the other night when I pedaled out to Mario's for pizza, and if I had continued down the ocean road another three miles or so, I would have come to it. It looked like a log cabin with lots of windows, and the inside was dark and cozy, with imitation Tiffany lamps and seating in individual booths along the walls. The view over the Atlantic was breathtaking. Tiny lights bobbed on the water where fishing boats were headed out for a night's work, and a thin sliver of moon hung high in the sky. Thanks to Derek's boy scout trick of keeping a clean shirt in the truck, after a washup and a finger comb, he looked a lot less scruffy, and the food wasn't bad, either. I had a crab cake sandwich and clam chowder, and Derek had a workingman's hamburger and fries. I like to talk, so I kept the pauses from getting too long and uncomfortable by making observations about the food, the restaurant, the view, and the weather, along with the house, the renovations, the fainting couch, and my surprise that Philippe had driven all the way up from New York to see it. If Derek didn't answer, I tried not to take it personally. Melissa and Philippe were nowhere to be seen, though, and I couldn't help but wonder if maybe Derek regretted having gone to dinner with me when there was nobody around to notice.

No sooner had the thought entered my head than I heard a voice: "Well, well! Look who's here."

Oops! I glanced over at Derek, who was scowling. "Don't get all excited, Kate. We're just having dinner."

"Of course you are," Kate said and winked at me.

I made a face. "Hi, Kate. Chief Rasmussen. Would you care to join us?"

"Oh, we wouldn't want to intrude," Kate said coyly.

Derek muttered something.

I raised my voice. "Don't worry."

"Well, if you don't mind." Kate didn't need any more urging; she scooted into the booth next to Derek, bumping him companionably closer to the window with her hip. "How are you?"

"Fine."

"How are the renovations coming? Business is picking up at the B and B now that school's out, or I'd be over there helping you."

Derek shrugged.

I turned to Wayne Rasmussen, who had moved onto the bench next to me. "Evening, Chief."

"How are you, Avery?" If Kate's mixture of sisterly in-dulgence and friendly flirtation toward Derek bothered him, the chief of police didn't show it. "Everything OK? Nothing else has happened at the house, I hope?"

I shook my head. "Nothing at all."

"Except her boyfriend's arrived," Derek said.

Kate looked over at me, eyebrows disappearing under her copper curls.

"Boyfriend?"

"Phil," Derek said.

"Philippe Aubert," I corrected.

"I remember you mentioning him. So where is he?" She looked around, as if expecting Philippe to materialize in midair.

"Melissa took him on a tour of Waterfield," Derek said. "She just happened to drop in; I guess she smelled money. Either that or his cologne. She's probably hoping to get him to buy one of her obscene condos."

Wayne looked from him to me and back. "Why does he need a condo if Avery already has a house?"

"Derek isn't explaining it right," I said. "First, he's my ex-boyfriend. I dated him for four months, and then he cheated on me. We broke up just before I came up here. Secondly, the only reason he's here is because I called him last night to get his opinion on a piece of furniture I found in Aunt Inga's attic. It's a French fainting couch, eighteenth century, and Philippe is French as well as a furniture maker, so I figured he could give me some information over the phone. I didn't ask him to come here; he just decided to drive up on his own. And it's not because of me, it's because of the couch. If he was still interested in me, he wouldn't be spending the evening with Melissa."

"And you wouldn't be spending it with me," Derek said.

I ignored him, addressing Kate and Wayne. "Derek thinks Philippe is a fraud. He says Philippe acts too French to actually be French. It's ridiculous."

Kate smiled indulgently, and Derek flushed. She turned to me. "Don't worry, Avery. Wayne can look into him. Right, Wayne?"

"Sure," Wayne said. "Can't have people going around pretending to be Frenchmen. Not in my town." He grinned at me.

"Fine," I said. I wasn't ready to believe that Philippe had fooled me for months, but if Wayne could prove that he was exactly who and what he said he was, at least I could prove to Derek that I wasn't such an idiot as he thought.

"I'll check him out tomorrow morning. Tell me what you know about him." Wayne pulled a pencil and his tiny notebook from his pocket, and I told him everything I knew about Philippe. As I went over it, I was amazed at how little it was. I knew that he liked French food and red wine and foreign movies, but I'd never seen his driver's license or his passport, so I had no actual proof that the name he'd given me was his real name. He'd said he grew up in Paris and studied at the Sorbonne, but I had no idea whether it was true or not. I had never spoken to his mother and I didn't know her name or where in Paris she lived. Now that Derek had sown the seed of doubt in my mind, I was questioning everything Philippe had ever said, and I wondered, with a sinking feeling, whether Derek could be right, and I was wrong.

"I feel like a fool," I said.

Kate sent me a sympathetic look, and Derek a scowl, but Wayne shook his head.

"Don't. We don't know anything yet, and even if he turns out to be a fraud, you're not the first or last person to be taken in by one. At least he didn't take you for anything valuable."

"Just my confidence," I said, but not loudly.

Derek glanced at me across the table but didn't speak.

I forced a smile and turned back to Wayne. "Any news on the missing professor?"

Wayne shook his head. "Nothing new, I'm afraid."

"Have you thought any more about the possibility that he might have pushed my aunt down the stairs and then disappeared to avoid being arrested?"

"If we had some proof that your aunt was pushed down the stairs," Wayne said, "I'd be more inclined to think about it. Do you have any reason to believe she was?"

"Not really," I admitted. "Except for the scary letter I got. And the fact that Dr. Ellis told me he was surprised when he learned that Aunt Inga had fallen down the stairs. He said that when she needed something from upstairs, she'd usually ask him or someone else to bring it down."

"Anything else?" Wayne said.

"Martin Wentworth was looking into the history of the Morton family. When I visited the historical society today, I saw that he had taken the Morton file home earlier this year. The docent said she had suggested that the professor talk to Aunt Inga."

"So?"

"What if they had an appointment that morning, and she said something he didn't like, and he pushed her? Or maybe she just fell, but he was afraid that he'd be accused of pushing her, and so he thought he'd better disappear? Maybe there was something in his past that would make it more likely that he'd be convicted, and he didn't want to take the chance."

"That's not a bad theory," Wayne admitted. "There isn't anything like that in his background, though. Everyone I've spoken to agrees that he's a nice young man from a decent family trying to get on in life. He's never even had a parking ticket."

"You've gone through his things, right?"

Wayne nodded. "Both the office at the college and his small condo on the other side of town. Nothing in either place that shouldn't be there, and no clues where he went. Lots of research materials, though. We made an inventory, so I'll check and see if we have anything about your family."

"I'd appreciate that. I'll go through the folder from the historical society tonight when I get home and see if I can figure out what he was interested in." I nibbled on a crust of bread before I added, "Did he keep a date book? With records of his appointments and things like that?"

"I'm told he did," Wayne said, "although we haven't

found it. We found last year's book, ending in December, but Miss Morton wasn't in it. We're assuming he had this year's book with him when he left."

"That makes sense," I admitted.

Wayne nodded.

"What do you think happened to him? Off the record. Did he just leave? Or did someone do something to him?"

"I'm hoping he just left," Wayne said. "If he killed your aunt, accidentally or on purpose, that's likely what happened. If so, he'll resurface sooner or later when he gets tired of hiding or when someone recognizes him."

"But?"

"But it's almost impossible to disappear without a trace. Most people who vanish eventually turn up dead. They had an accident, out of the way somewhere, and no one's stumbled on them yet, or someone killed them and hid the body. There are secret rooms and tunnels all over Waterfield, where someone could hide or be hidden."

"Secret rooms and tunnels?" I repeated, my eyes big.

Derek groaned and put his head in his hands.

"A few of the older houses around here have tunnels going down to the sea," Kate explained. "There was a lot of smuggling going on in the old days. And as recently as Prohibition, for that matter. Cliff House, the Willard place, Morganmeade..." She sighed enviously. "Wish I had a secret passage in *my* house!"

"Wouldn't you be worried that someone could get into your house that way?"

Kate shook her head, but it was Wayne who answered. "All the public access points are padlocked. The coast guard checks them regularly. Once in a while we get some idiot trying to do a bit of smuggling on the side, so we have to keep up."

"I guess there's no way Professor Wentworth could have accidentally wandered into one of them and gotten locked in, then. And here I thought I had solved the case for you."

Wayne smiled. "It's not a bad idea, actually. It sounds like something he might have been interested in. I'll check with the coast guard to make sure everything's been locked up tight for the past couple of months. If one of the entrances was ever open, maybe we should check it out."

"Glad I could help," I said and glanced over at Derek.

He took the hint. "I guess we should go."

Wayne stood up to let me slide out of the booth, and I said, as he sat down, "I'll give you a call in the morning."

He nodded. "If you make it late morning, maybe I'll have some information on your boyfriend, too."

"Ex-boyfriend," Kate and I said in unison. I looked at her, and she grinned and winked and slid her eyes to the inscrutable Derek. I blushed.

"That's Mr. Rodgers's house right there," Derek said on the way home, pointing to a Federal-style home about halfway between the restaurant and Waterfield proper. It was situated at the end of a long drive overlooking the ocean. The house was big and white and perfectly symmetrical, with eight tall windows on either side of the green front door and with two matching chimneys, one in each half of the house.

"Wow," I said, "you painted all that?!"

"Just the inside. By the time I was done, it was too late in the year to start on the exterior." He shrugged.

I felt a pang of guilt. "I'm not keeping you from taking on other work, am I? If you need to work for other people, too, I don't mind."

Actually, I did mind. I had come to think of Derek as my own personal handyman, but of course I didn't say so.

He glanced at me. "You're paying me, aren't you? No, I don't need to work for anyone else. I suggested painting the outside to Mr. Rodgers a few weeks ago, as a matter of fact, and he put me off. Unless there's an emergency of some kind, I just tell everyone that I have to finish Miss Morton's house first, before I can get to theirs. They don't mind waiting."

"Must be nice to be so popular," I remarked.

He grinned. "You have no idea. Most of what I do is one-offs—clean this stained glass window; refinish this floor; paint this room—and getting to redo a whole house is a treat. The little stuff pays the bills, but seeing a house turn from abused and neglected and run-down to beautiful is priceless. Sorry if I sound like a commercial."

"No," I said, "that's nice, actually. So how come you're not renovating full time?"

"On my own dime, you mean? Can't afford it. Being a full-time renovator takes money, and I'm not getting rich laying tile and hanging drywall. That's why . . ." He stopped abruptly, and flushed. I looked confused for a moment before I realized what he'd been about to say.

"That's why Melissa divorced you and took up with Ray instead. Because of the money."

Derek hesitated, but I guess he didn't see the sense in denying it. "He's raking it in with his construction company and their shoddy condos. She wanted to be married to a rich doctor, but once I wasn't gonna be a doctor anymore, let alone rich, it was all over."

"Sorry," I said. And in an effort to change the subject, I added, "So there are tunnels under Mr. Rodgers's house?" I gave it one last glance over my shoulder before it disappeared behind the pine trees. All the lights were off, save for the one in the entry, its yellow glow stream-

ing out through the arched fanlight above the green
door.

Derek nodded. "Alexander Cooper, the man who built
the house two hundred years ago or so, was a smuggler.
He'd tie up below the cliffs at night and take his contraband
into the house through the tunnels, and then he'd take the
legitimate cargo to the harbor in the morning. Smuggling
was a way of life along the coast back then, and nobody but
the officials thought there was anything wrong with it. Have
you ever heard of William King?"

I shook my head.

"He was Maine's first governor, elected in 1820. In 1824,
when he was up for reelection, his opponent decided to try
to discredit him by publishing a pamphlet about how King
had traded with both the British and the Americans during
the War of 1812."

"That's treason, isn't it?"

"Of course it is. There's a fine line between free enterprise
and selling goods to the enemy, though, and people sometimes step across it. Especially in a place like this, where half
the population had relatives across the border. Anyway, the
plan backfired, because nobody cared. Everyone was involved in smuggling back then, and the people who weren't
wished they were. So King got reelected anyway."

"Interesting," I said. "You weren't joking when you said
you liked history, were you?"

"Guess not. I'm not much for sitting around reading,
though. I'd rather be doing something useful. Restoration
scratches both itches for me."

"I'd rather be doing something useful, too," I said.

He glanced at me. "Your backsplash is looking good. Tomorrow we'll seal it and make sure it's nice and smooth.
Then we'll get on with the cabinets."

"Right. About the cabinets. I had this idea..."

"Here we go again," Derek said, rolling his eyes.

I grinned.

• • •

"I'll check the house," he said when I opened the front door of Aunt Inga's house. "You get busy looking through the file."

"You don't want me to walk through the house with you?"

He grinned. "Are you offering to hold my hand in case I get scared, Tinkerbell? Or are you afraid of being alone, and you want to hold mine?"

"Neither. Knock yourself out."

"Suit yourself." He sauntered down the hallway. I turned into the parlor. And stopped with an outraged shriek just inside the pocket doors.

"What?" Derek appeared in the doorway behind me, looking around wildly. "What?!"

"Look!" I pointed.

"Where? There's nothing there."

"Exactly! The fainting couch was there when we left!"

"Damn," Derek breathed. "What the hell...?" He examined the room, as if maybe the couch had decided to move over to stand in front of another wall instead.

"Someone took it!" I said.

"How can someone have taken it? The door was locked."

"I don't know. But it didn't walk out on its own."

He didn't answer.

"Maybe someone swiped one of the new keys. They're over there, on the desk."

"Bet you it was Phil," Derek said.

"My money's on Melissa. What was she even doing

here? Like you said, it was a little late to bring flowers; it's been three days since I fell."

"Yeah, but why would Melissa want an ugly chaise longue? It's not her style, believe me."

"I don't know, and I don't care. She was here, so she had opportunity. Who else could have done it?"

"I'll say it again," Derek said. "Phil. You know he wanted it. He was practically wiping drool off his chin. He probably stuffed it in the back of that fancy car he drove up in, and he's halfway to New York by now."

I shrugged. Maybe, maybe not.

"Call Wayne," Derek added. "I'm going to have a look around."

"I'll come with you. What if whoever is still here?"

"You planning to take a bullet for me?" But he didn't stop me from following him out the door and down the hall-way. And when I fumbled for his hand, it was right there. Maybe he wasn't as unaffected as he seemed. We walked through the house holding hands, looking into every room and behind every door. Nothing was out of place, and with the notable exception of the fainting couch, nothing was missing.

"Call Wayne," Derek repeated when we were once again standing in the front parlor, looking at the empty space where the couch had stood. "Or better yet, I'll do it."

He pulled his cell phone off his belt and punched in the number. I could tell by the way he jabbed the buttons that he was angrier than he looked.

"He's on his way," he announced when the terse conver-sation was over. "Along with Dudley Do-Right and—unless I miss my guess—Kate."

"Dudley Do-Right?"

"The kid who does the fingerprinting and collects the cigarette butts."

"Officer Thomas," I said. The young forensics cop who had dusted my kitchen for fingerprints after the first break-in, and the breaker box after the second. "Right."

"Excuse me a minute, won't you? I need to hit something, and I don't want it to be you." Derek strode out the front door. A few moments later I heard a muffled curse. I deduced that one of Aunt Inga's trees had taken a fist, but Derek had gotten the worst of it.

· · ·

Wayne and company made excellent time; it was no more than ten minutes later when they pulled up outside, blue lights flashing. Derek met them at the gate and walked them in, hands in his pockets. Kate immediately started fussing, first over me, then—when she got a good look at Derek's hand—over him. She led him into the bathroom, and I watched from the doorway as she cleaned and bandaged his knuckles. Meanwhile, Wayne and Officer Thomas busied themselves in the front parlor, with their fingerprint powder and forensic equipment. I didn't expect their efforts to yield any results. The only people who could have taken one of the spare keys were Derek or Melissa, Philippe or Mr. Rodgers. All had been here earlier, so any forensic evidence would be useless. But at least Derek and I had been together all evening, so he couldn't possibly have stolen my couch. And if the same person had stolen the couch as had sabotaged my stairs, then he was off the hook for that, too. Not that I'd ever seriously suspected him.

"Melissa James," I said firmly when Wayne asked me if I suspected anyone in particular.

Kate hid a smile.

Derek shook his head. "No way."

"He wasn't asking you," I said.

"Melissa isn't interested in antique furniture."

"She's interested in money, though. You said so your-self. The couch is potentially valuable. And I'm sure the Stenhams would be happy to have it, as well."

"Who do you suspect, then?" Wayne addressed Derek.

I snorted. "Who do you think he suspects? Who else was here?"

Derek nodded. "That's right. The boyfriend."

"Phil," Wayne said. "Or Philippe."

Derek started ticking off damning coincidences on the fingers of his injured hand. "He drove all the way from New York, just to see the couch. And the way he acted when we were carrying it, I thought he was going to punch me when I let it fall. Avery refused to let him take it back to New York so someone he knows at Christie's could authenticate it. And we already know he's a lying, cheating bastard, so what's a little theft between friends? Yeah, I think he grabbed one of the keys from the desk when we weren't looking and decided to come back for it later. We told them we had plans for dinner, so he knew nobody would be here."

I whipped out my cell phone and dialed Philippe's num-ber, hoping he would pick up and then show up to exonerate himself. But there was no answer. I left a message demand-ing that he call me.

"What kind of car does he drive?" Wayne asked, tiny notebook and pencil at the ready.

"He owns a black Porsche. I assume he's driving that." I glanced at Derek, who shook his head.

"I saw him in a Range Rover. Red."

"Probably a rental," I muttered. "So he'd have something to put the fainting couch in."

"Not a lot of red Range Rovers in Waterfield," Wayne said. "Should be fairly easy to find. And while I'm at it, I'll tell everyone to keep an eye out for Melissa James's Mercedes, as well. Excuse me." He nodded politely before he turned away, fumbling for his phone.

"What are you planning to do tonight, Avery?" Kate wanted to know.

I had been watching Wayne, and now I turned back to her.

She added, "You're not going to stay here alone, are you?"

"Of course she's not," Derek said.

"I'm not?"

He shook his head. "In case it's escaped your notice, someone has a key to the house. So you're not spending the night alone."

"I suppose you're planning to spend it with her?" Kate inquired, arms folded across her chest. She was watching our exchange with indulgent amusement.

I blushed.

"If I have to," Derek answered without enthusiasm. "Though I was hoping she could go home with you. You've got room, right?"

"I guess," Kate said. I opened my mouth to say that under no circumstances should she feel obligated to put me up, that I was an adult and could take care of myself, but before I had a chance to, she had continued. "Shannon is home tonight, but Derek's right. It's the middle of the week, and I've got rooms available. You're always welcome, Avery."

"I don't want to intrude on your time with your daughter..." I began.

Kate smiled. "She goes to school less than ten miles away. I see her plenty. I'd rather have you come home with me than worry about you being here by yourself. Of course, if Derek was to volunteer to stay..." She arched a brow at him.

"I'd rather go home with you," I said.

"I'd rather you went home with Kate, too," Derek added. "That way I can get a good night's sleep and be ready to re-key all the locks tomorrow. Damn, but this is getting monotonous!" He turned on his heel and stalked out.

Kate and I looked at each other and giggled weakly.

.   .   .

"So what's going on with you and Derek?" she asked an hour later, as we were sitting across the table from each other in her streamlined, modern kitchen, sharing a pint of ice cream. I had rescued a robe from Aunt Inga's house, along with my toiletries, and was comfortably attired in terrycloth and with my hair straggling down my back.

"Didn't you ask me that question just a couple of days ago?" I retorted.

"I did. But it seems there's been progress since then."

I shrugged. "He's growing on me. He talks to me now. He's even told me a few personal things about himself."

"Really?"

"Really. Like the fact that you two used to date."

"Oh, God." She started laughing. "We went out a couple of times when he was working on the house, that's all. No chemistry. He's a sweet guy but not my type."

"Not mine either, really." Or at least not the type I'd always thought was my type. Then again, look where getting mixed up with Philippe had gotten me.

"Could have fooled me," Kate muttered. "Listen, Avery. No offense. I don't know you very well, but unless you're planning to stick around for a while—say, a year or three— do everyone a favor and don't get involved."

"I beg your pardon?"

"If you're just planning to have some fun for the sum- mer, find someone else to play with. Someone who won't mind when you leave."

"Oh," I said, silenced. I hadn't thought of it that way. Up until now, I'd been thinking I didn't want to get too close to anyone in Waterfield because of how difficult it would be for *me* when I left. I hadn't considered how the other person might feel. And especially if it was Derek, who'd already been left once before.

In the silence, the swinging butler door from the dining room opened, and a dark head popped in. "Hey, Mom... oh, I'm sorry, Avery. I didn't realize we had company." Shan- non and I exchanged smiles.

"I'm not exactly company," I clarified. "Your mother's putting me up for the night because the police are crawling all over my house."

"Gosh," Shannon said, coming all the way into the kitchen, "what happened?"

While Kate filled her in on the furniture heist, I contem- plated the girl. She seemed intrigued by the whole thing, making suggestions for what might have happened and aligning herself with Derek in thinking that Philippe must have been behind it. She wanted to meet him, she said, to check him out for herself. There was nothing cagey or eva- sive about her tonight; she entered into the game with gusto.

"By the way," I said in a lull in the conversation, "remember that bike I told you about last week? It was Professor Wentworth's after all."

Shannon nodded. "Josh told me. Brandon Thomas told him."

"I don't suppose you've heard any news, have you?"

She shook her head. "Just that the bike was Martin's and was found in your aunt's shed. So I guess they did know each other. But beyond that, I have no idea what was going on."

"Wayne said he used an appointment book to keep track of his classes and appointments. The police found the one for last year, but not the one he was using now. I guess maybe he had it with him when he left."

"Probably," Shannon agreed. She got up from the table without meeting my eyes. I noticed that she was blushing bright red. "Hey, Mom, is it OK if I take the car out? I won't be gone long."

"Sure," Kate said. "The keys are on the hook by the door. Drive carefully."

"Nice to see you again, Avery." Shannon disappeared without waiting for my answer.

Kate smiled apologetically. "Sorry, Avery. Ever since she started going to Barnham this fall, she's been more reluctant to talk about what's going on in her life. One of those coming-of-age things, I guess."

"I guess."

"She's a good student," Kate continued. "She's not pregnant, and she's not using drugs. I know the signs, and believe me, I look for them. And her friends are nice kids. Paige is so quiet you hardly notice her being there, and Josh is a sweetheart. No trouble with any of them."

"I'm sure," I said, and forced a smile. "Let's talk about

something else, OK? If you're finished grilling me about Derek, why don't I return the favor? Tell me about how you and Police Chief Rasmussen met."

Kate grinned. "It was a dark and stormy night..." she began. I popped a spoonful of mint chocolate chip in my mouth and settled in for the long haul.

—16—

I was sitting at Kate's dining room table the next morning, indulging in pecan pancakes and coffee, when Derek wandered in.

"Morning." He inspected the dining room thoroughly, leaving me not entirely sure if he was looking for someone or just reassuring himself that he'd done a good job on the renovations.

"Morning," I answered, around a mouthful of pancake. "Have a seat." I waved my fork at the chair opposite.

"Don't mind if I do." He turned the chair around and straddled it, eyeing my breakfast. "You know, I'd have married Kate for her cooking alone."

"Why didn't you?"

He grinned. "She wouldn't have me."

"I don't blame her. Nobody wants to be wanted just for their cooking."

"Oh, Kate has other assets, as well." He laughed when he saw my expression, but he didn't push the issue. "Sleep well?"

"Fine, thanks. You?"

"Not bad. Ready to go re-key all those new locks?"

I grimaced. "I guess."

"Finish your breakfast first. Maybe I can get Kate to feed me, too." He looked around.

"She's in the kitchen. Why don't you let her know you're here?" I speared another piece of pancake. "I'll be done in a few minutes, and then we can leave. We may have to make a stop on the way."

He stopped halfway to the door. "Yeah? Where?"

"I'll tell you later." I turned my attention back to breakfast. Derek shrugged and pushed open the door to the kitchen.

•   •   •

It was thirty minutes later when we finally got out of the B and B. As soon as Kate saw Derek, she insisted on making him his very own batch of pecan pancakes and a fresh pot of coffee, and she stood over him to make sure he ate every crumb. I wouldn't have been surprised to hear her mutter darkly about how thin he was.

"I thought Shannon would be here," he said between bites.

Kate shook her head. "She left early this morning. Before Avery got up. It's just as well; if you keep flirting with her, she'll never give up on the idea that she wants to marry you when she grows up."

"If she can cook like you, I just might do that. Of course, it's not right to marry someone just because of their cooking." He grinned at me.

"Damn right," I said.

"I think she might have a boyfriend, anyway," Kate added. "I caught her whispering with Paige on the phone a few times over the winter. Whenever she saw me coming, they stopped talking. Hopefully he's not some long-haired, tattooed musician."

"Hopefully," I said lightly.

Derek gave me a sharp glance.

"We should go. Thanks for breakfast, Kate." He stood, giving her a peck on the cheek, and she smiled up at him.

"Look out for Avery. Make sure nothing happens to her."

"I'll do my best. You ready?" He glanced at me.

I nodded.

"Let's go, then. See you later, Kate."

"Thanks for letting me stay here," I added. "When I sell Aunt Inga's house, I'll pay you back for all these nights of free lodging."

Kate smiled. "Don't worry about it. When the room isn't reserved, it's just sitting there, so you may as well use it. And I enjoy talking to you. Let me know how things go today."

• • •

"So," Derek said as soon as we were in the truck with the engine started. "You said we have to make a stop. Where are we going?"

"To talk to Shannon McGillicutty."

"Why?"

"I have a theory." He nodded for me to continue, so I did.

"Kate thinks Shannon had a boyfriend over the winter. She used to whisper with her friend Paige on the phone. Kate said she's been secretive and closemouthed ever since she started at Barnham last fall. She never mentioned her boyfriend's name or brought him home to see her mother. The only person she ever brought home was Professor Wentworth, because he drove her home after they 'worked on a special project together.'" I made quotation marks in the air with my fingers.

Derek looked over at me, but didn't say anything.

I continued. "She's been upset since Professor Wentworth disappeared, and she's also not whispering on the phone anymore. She has, or used to have, a crush on you, so she obviously likes older men. And when I asked her about him last night, she called him by his first name."

"Nice theory," Derek said. "But you're wrong."

I was? "How do you know?"

"Because he was seeing someone else."

I blinked, disconcerted. "Surely not my aunt Inga?"

Derek smothered a laugh. "Your aunt was ninety-eight, Avery. Professor Wentworth is younger than me. No, he wasn't seeing your aunt. Not that way, at least."

"So who was he seeing? And how do you know?"

"Saw him with someone. She looked young, but it wasn't Shannon." I looked at him, and after a moment he went on. "I was renovating someone's bathroom over in the condo complex where Martin Wentworth's apartment is, and I was working late, because I was hoping to finish the job that night. It was around eight o'clock when I heard a car door slam outside. I looked out, because I thought it might be my client coming home."

"But it wasn't?"

He shook his head. "It was a girl with blonde hair. Running across the courtyard while a car peeled away from the curb. I watched her knock on Professor Wentworth's door, and from the way she greeted him, if she was a student, she wasn't there for private tutoring." He hesitated for a second before he added, fairly, "Unless it was a different kind of tutoring."

"What did you do?" I asked.

"What do you think I did? I finished the job I was hired to do. None of my business what the professor was doing on his free time, was it?"

"I guess not," I admitted. If it had been Shannon, presumably Derek would have made it his business, but under the circumstances, I guess there wasn't a whole lot he could have done, really. "Was she someone you know?"

He hesitated. "I've seen her before, yeah. With Shannon and Josh Rasmussen."

"Must be Paige," I said. "She has blonde hair, and that would explain why she seemed so worried on Sunday, when I came to ask Shannon about Professor Wentworth. Josh took her away before I could talk to her."

Derek nodded. "You still want to go to Barnham?"

"Of course I still want to go to Barnham. The only difference is that now I want to talk to Paige instead of Shannon. Thank you very much for keeping me from sounding like an idiot when I accused Shannon of having an affair with her teacher."

"My pleasure." Derek grinned. "Hang on." He turned the wheel and made an illegal U-turn on Main Street. I was thrown against him and breathed in the scent of soap and shampoo for a second before I straightened up.

"Sorry."

Derek gave me a sidelong look, as if he knew that I wasn't really sorry at all. "This is gonna take time away

from renovating, you know. It'll be longer before you can
get back to New York and that new job and new boyfriend
you have to find."

"If Professor Wentworth pushed my aunt down the stairs
and killed her, I'd like to know," I retorted. "I think that's
worth a delay, don't you?"

"You're the boss." He glanced in the rearview mirror.
"Oh, damn."

"What?" I twisted around.

"Blue lights."

"Maybe they're after someone else. The siren isn't
on…"

No sooner were the words out of my mouth, than the
shrill sound cut through the crisp morning air. Derek made a
face. "Must have been that U-turn I made back there."

"Sorry."

He smiled. "Not your fault. With any luck, it'll be Officer Estrada—Ramona Estrada—and I can talk my way out
of the ticket."

"Do what you need to do," I said, leaning back on the
seat with my arms folded.

Derek chuckled.

However, the lanky form that extricated itself from the
black-and-white car belonged to the chief of police himself,
in full uniform. He adjusted his belt importantly, put his
mirrored sunglasses on, and swaggered over to Derek's
window. "Morning, folks."

I smiled at the display. "Morning, Wayne," Derek said.

"You're aware you made an illegal U-turn back there,
right?"

"Sorry. Avery remembered something."

"Uh-huh." Wayne didn't sound impressed with the
excuse.

"We were just on our way back to the house from Kate's," I said brightly, "when we remembered something we'd forgotten."

"Funny coincidence. I was just on my way to Kate's to talk to you."

Uh-oh. "What about?"

"Couple of things. First, Brandon Thomas worked on fingerprints all night, and the only ones he found in your house were the two of yours, Kate's, Graham Rodgers's, Melissa James's, and your boyfriend's. And a few of Miss Morton's, from before. Oh, and mine. And of course his own."

Of course. "But none of the Stenhams?"

Wayne shook his head. "Pretty much everyone had prints on or near the desk where the keys were, so we can't rule anyone out."

That figured.

"Add to that the fact that every Tom, Dick, and Harry knows to wear gloves these days, and you can't rule out anyone in all of Waterfield. Hell, all of Maine. Still, one good thing came of this."

"What's that?" I asked.

He smiled. "Since we had to identify and eliminate fingerprints, I put your boyfriend's prints through the database along with everyone else's, and I got a hit."

"You're kidding!" I exclaimed, at the same time as Derek said, "Let me guess. He's wanted in six states for fraud and impersonation."

Wayne chuckled. "Sorry to disappoint you. He has no criminal record at all. The only reason he's in the system is because he used to consult for the state of Tennessee, and the government fingerprints everyone."

"Tennessee?" I repeated blankly. Philippe had never mentioned living anywhere but New York and Paris.

Wayne nodded. "I found a copy of his identification card. Have a look. This is him, isn't it?" He handed me a sheet of paper. Derek and I both hunched over it. After a second, Derek began to laugh.

"Phil Albertson," he crowed.

"God!" I moaned, hiding my face in my hands. The paper fluttered down to the floor of the truck, and Philippe's face—Phil Albertson's face, I guess I should say—looked up at me, ten years younger and forty pounds heavier, sporting a full beard. Derek's pat on my back missed being comforting by a mile, as he was shaking with laughter.

"Once I knew who he was," Wayne added blithely, "it was easy tracking him. I have his birth certificate, his social security number, his work history, his education . . . He grew up in a small town in Tennessee and started working with his father, a local carpenter, right out of high school."

"Lord!"

"The consulting he did was on some sort of forestry project, ten or twelve years ago. Best I can figure, he left Tennessee after his father passed on. That's the last record I can find of him down there. Of Phil Albertson, I mean. Aubert Designs was incorporated in New York two years later. By the time you started working for him, he'd already been in business for a while and had started to build a following."

"I had no idea," I said, talking through my fingers. "I never suspected. I feel like an idiot!"

"Don't. By all accounts, he's very good at his act. He has to be, to fool so many people into thinking he's a French expatriate, when in fact he's never even visited France."

Derek could barely suppress his mirth.

"He went out of town for two weeks earlier this year," I said. "Where did he go, if not France?"

Wayne consulted his paperwork. "From what I can tell, he went to LaGuardia Airport and took a plane to Nashville and a rental car from there to Paris."

"Paris?"

"Paris, Tennessee. Population just over thirty thousand. Exporter of tobacco, soybeans, wheat, and corn. Located one hundred miles from Nashville in Henry County."

At this, Derek laughed so hard I was afraid he was going to choke. Personally, I was torn between crying and swearing. "Damn you," I said weakly, punching him in the arm, "this isn't funny."

"Sure it is."

"You wouldn't think it was funny if it happened to you."

"Maybe not, but…" He made an effort to pull himself together. "…just think of—what's her name?—Tara. And Melissa. Falling flat for that continental charm, and then it turns out he's a Tennessee hick who's never even been outside the country. He was born in Paris, all right: Paris, Tennessee! Oh God, Wayne; can I be there when you tell her? Please?"

In spite of my wounded pride, I found myself giggling, too. Thinking of stupid, young Tara and her adoration of Philippe—Phil—did make me feel better, and I could certainly sympathize with Derek's desire to rub Melissa's elegant nose in her faux pas. I wouldn't mind being there to see that myself.

"If I could find her, I might let you do that," Wayne said, "but we haven't been able to locate either of them yet. There's an unofficial APB out on both the Range Rover and the Mercedes, but so far, no sightings."

"Huh." Derek stopped laughing. "Wonder where they could be?"

"Holed up in a cheap motel room somewhere," I said sourly.

Wayne glanced at me and changed the subject.

"Where are you two going in such a hurry? You remembered something, you said?"

Derek and I made a point of not looking at one another. "We're heading down to Barnham College," Derek said.

"To see a man about a dog," I added. "It's not important. Do you need anything else?"

I could tell that Wayne was curious, but he shook his head. "I'll keep looking for the Range Rover and the chaise longue. After I write you," he turned to Derek, with a grin, "a ticket for a traffic infraction. Making a U-turn on Main Street is illegal, as you very well know."

Derek rolled his eyes.

．　．　．

Thirty minutes later we were sitting across from Paige Thompson in the cafeteria at Barnham College, nursing cups of bad coffee. She was a slight, pale girl with mousy blonde hair, dressed in an oversized denim shirt. Her eyes were red-rimmed, as if she'd been crying, and her hands were convulsively tight around the white cup. Shannon sat on one side of her, bristling like a mother hedgehog, and on the other sat Josh, tall and lanky in a Barnham College sweatshirt and round glasses. I recognized Wayne's steady brown eyes behind the lenses.

"You know, Shannon," I said with a smile, in an effort to lighten the mood and put the three of them at ease, "when I spoke to you last night, I suspected you'd been seeing Professor Wentworth on the sly."

For a second or two, Shannon looked totally shocked, while Josh hid a grin. Then her eyes started sparkling, and she grinned, too. "Me? You thought *I'd* been seeing Martin Wentworth? I can't imagine where you'd get that idea."

"Well," I said, "you called him by his first name, and your mother thought you had a boyfriend this winter, because you were whispering on the phone all the time. And then there was that 'special project' that you worked on together..."

"Right," Shannon said, her grin fading. "The special project." She and Josh were both careful not to look at Paige.

"Of course," I continued, smiling sweetly, "that was before I talked to Derek and realized that you weren't the one having the affair."

I moved my attention to Paige, who managed to look miserable and defiant all at the same time.

Shannon rolled her eyes. "That just figures, doesn't it? After all the trouble we went to, to make sure that no one guessed, it turns out that Derek's known all along."

"What can I say?" Derek said with a shrug and absolutely no attempt at modesty. "I'm brilliant."

"Or just lucky," Josh suggested. "You probably happened to see them together sometime, right?"

Derek grinned. "You got it."

Shannon turned to me. "She has enough trouble as it is, don't you think, Avery? Without you giving her any flak. I mean, her boyfriend's missing!"

"Please," I said, lifting both hands in the universal gesture of surrender, "I have no plans of giving anyone a hard time. As far as I'm concerned, she can date anyone she wants. That's her business. All I care about is finding out what happened to my aunt."

"Your aunt was Inga Morton, right?" Paige asked. Other than the initial, whispered greeting, this was the first time

I'd heard her voice. It was soft and wispy, the voice of a little girl. "Martin visited her several times. He was researching the Marie Antoinette legend—how Marie Antoinette's things came over from France after the revolution, but she didn't—and there was some kind of connection."

"Between my aunt and Marie Antoinette? Or the Marie Antoinette items?"

Paige shrugged, her pale hair falling forward. "Either. Both. I don't exactly know what it was, because he wouldn't tell me. Said it was confidential. But I know that he was working with your aunt on something. It had to do with some things she owned. Or maybe didn't own." She looked confused.

"I'm trying to determine when they met," I explained, "and if possible, what they discussed."

Paige didn't answer. I turned to Shannon, who said, "Josh and I don't actually know much about what Martin was working on outside class. He told us to call him that, by the way. Josh isn't even a history major, and that special project I told my mom about was just an excuse. The real reason he drove me home that night was because I'd just found out about him and Paige, and I'd been chewing him out. But of course I couldn't tell my mom that."

I nodded.

She continued, "He wrote down everything he did in that day planner you asked me about last night."

"The one that went missing when he did?"

The three of them exchanged a look.

"Oh, don't tell me," I said, "it's not really missing after all, is it?"

They looked guilty.

"The three of you stole Professor Wentworth's day planner?" Derek said.

Shannon grimaced. "Yeah."

"And you the son of the chief of police," Derek said to Josh. Josh shrugged, sipping his own coffee.

"I know that Brandon Thomas is the only forensic crime tech in the Waterfield Police, and as soon as I heard that he was on his way to the professor's condo, we went to the office and took the day planner. The door wasn't locked—it never is—and the girls made sure I wasn't caught."

"But didn't you realize that it might help the police find him?" I asked, at the same time as Derek demanded to know, "Why, for God's sake?"

Shannon chose to answer him instead of me. "We figured that Paige's name would be all over it. If Josh's dad got hold of it, everyone would know that she'd been seeing Martin."

"Do you still have it?"

I held my breath, hoping that these juvenile criminals hadn't thought to get rid of the planner to hide the evidence. It's what I would have done; at least I hoped it was. Anything else would have been stupid. I hoped very much that they were too young and inexperienced to realize that.

Josh and Shannon both turned to look at Paige.

She nodded.

Josh rolled his eyes behind the glasses.

"Probably couldn't bear to burn it," Shannon muttered.

I nodded. By now, the appointment book was all Paige had left of her boyfriend, and she must have been clinging to it. "Do you have it with you?" I asked.

She shook her head. "It's in my room."

"Can you go get it?"

"Why do you want it?"

"Because it will help me figure out what happened to my

aunt. And because we can give it to Wayne without getting you—any of you—in trouble."

"I'll talk to Wayne and get him to agree not to tell her parents," Derek added. "But the police need to see it. If he really wrote everything down, the planner might help them figure out where he went. Or what happened to him. Or what he did."

"What do you mean, what he did?" Paige's guileless blue eyes narrowed to thin slits.

Shannon looked apprehensively at her.

Derek glanced at me. He chose his words carefully, for all the good that it did. There's really no way to gently break the fact that you're suspecting someone's lover of being a cold-blooded killer and a coward to boot. "There's a theory that he killed Avery's aunt and then ran away to avoid the consequences."

"He'd never do that!" Paige said, spots of high color in her cheeks.

Shannon patted her on the back, reassuringly.

Derek raised both hands, palms out. "Hey, relax. I'm not saying he did it on purpose. Maybe it was an accident. Maybe he got scared. It could happen to anyone."

"He wouldn't!" Paige had closed her small hands into fists, and her soft voice was shaking. "He wasn't a coward. He cared about Miss Morton. He'd never hurt her. And if he did it accidentally, he'd call the police. He'd never run away and leave her there!"

"Then the police need to know that," I said, trying to inject some calm into the situation. "All I want to know is what happened to my aunt. If her death was an accident, that's fine. If it wasn't, I want to know who's responsible. If it wasn't Professor Wentworth, I have no desire to crucify him. Why don't you let me read the planner, and then I can decide whether there's anything in it that might help?"

"You won't give it to them without telling me?" Paige's eyes were beseeching. All three of them were staring at me, unblinkingly.

"I promise," I said.

Paige agreed to go to her dorm room to get the planner, and although she was reluctant to hand it over to us, she did it eventually. I thanked her profusely and promised I'd take good care of it, and only give it to Wayne if I thought it would help him find the professor or find out what happened to my aunt. Thirty minutes later, Derek and I were back in Waterfield, inside Aunt Inga's house. Everything looked the same as it had when I left the day before, except for Brandon Thomas's fingerprint powder all over the front parlor. It didn't look like anyone had been in the house since last night. Even so, Derek insisted on doing a walk-through before rejoining me in the kitchen. The unfinished mosaic backsplash looked reproachful, and I turned my back on it.

"I'll seal the backsplash," Derek offered, "if you want to work on the planner."

I squinted at him. "Are you sure?"

"I wouldn't offer if I wasn't."

"But don't you want to see what's in here?"

He grinned. "Oh, I'm sure you'll let me know when you find something. You're not exactly reticent, you know."

"Unlike you. Well, if you're sure you don't mind."

"Go ahead. I'll just get busy, and you sit right there and start reading. That way I'll be nearby if you find something you want to discuss."

"Deal." I settled onto one of the kitchen chairs and opened Professor Wentworth's day planner, while behind me, Derek got to work with sealer and brush.

What Paige had handed over was actually something more like a three-ring binder with a calendar, and what looked like most of a ream of blank pages in the back for jotting down notes. The calendar had two parts, one monthly, with all the days laid out in a grid, and the other daily, with a page per day, for hourly appointments and things like that. Almost every page was scribbled over with tiny, cramped handwriting. The only thing I can say for Martin Wentworth is that he was a tidy writer—especially compared to how messy he kept his office. His letters were small but extremely neat, arranged in ruler-straight lines, as precise as computer fonts. I had no problem reading what he had written.

Understanding what he had meant was, unfortunately, a different matter. He used abbreviations a lot, probably to save space, and most of them were unfamiliar to me. Some I could guess at from the context, but once in a while I'd come across something that made no sense. "What does VD mean?" I asked Derek. He left the counter to lean over me, one hand on my shoulder. I was wearing a skimpy tank top again, with my shoulders mostly bare, and his hand was warm and rough against my skin.

"Venereal disease?" he suggested. "I hope Paige knows about that. 'Checked into H for VD.' He checked into the hospital because he had venereal disease?"

"Or he checked into booking a hotel for Valentine's Day?"

"Or he might have looked into the vapor density of hydrogen."

"Is that something a history professor would have to do?"

"I wouldn't think so," Derek said, "although he might have been doing all sorts of things in his spare time."

"True." And had been, it seemed. "What about this one?" I pointed. "WC?"

"God." He rolled his eyes and blew out an exasperated sigh. "WC could mean any number of things. Water closet, an old word for a bathroom. White Castle, the hamburger chain. There aren't any around here, but there are some in Portland. Someone with the initials WC, maybe another of his students, or a teacher down at the college? World Cup. Water cooler. Wing commander. Workers' comp. Any and all of them. I'm sure there are more, too."

"It probably doesn't matter. I'm only at the end of January. If he disappeared in May, I'm not sure it matters what he did four months earlier."

"Maybe you should start with the last entry and work your way back," Derek suggested. I blinked. For some reason, this very logical approach hadn't occurred to me.

"You're not as dumb as you look, are you?"

He removed his hand from my shoulder. "I didn't drop out of medicine because I was too stupid to hack it, if that's what you thought. And you don't exactly look like a nuclear scientist yourself."

"I'm a girl," I said complacently. "I don't have to look smart. I just have to look pretty."

"I'd prefer a smart girl to a pretty one. Of course, if your next boyfriend's gonna be another Phil, you've got nothing to worry about."

He stalked to the counter and got back to work, his movements crisp. I looked at him over my shoulder for a moment, on the brink of a rejoinder, before I thought better of it and turned my attention back to the planner.

"Here it is," I said after a moment of turning over pages, going backward through time. "It says here that my aunt and the professor met several times during the spring, including the day before she died."

Derek wandered over. "What did they talk about?"

"No idea. He doesn't go into detail. There are just notations of 9:00 IM@h. Inga Morton at home, I guess. Every Wednesday for a while."

"He went missing on a Wednesday," Derek said.

"Did he really? There are cross-references to some of the note pages in the back of the book." I flipped there and found page upon page of minuscule writing. Abbreviations and symbols proliferated there, too. I wondered, if we had a question about anything, whether Paige would be able to answer it. Perhaps she'd had practice deciphering the professor's impromptu shorthand. Or perhaps he'd told her what was what during their periods of pillow talk.

"I'll leave you to it," Derek said, with a glance at the overfilled pages. "Let me know if you come across anything interesting."

I promised I would, and then he went back to the backsplash while I devoted myself to figuring out what Professor Wentworth had been researching in the months before his disappearance, and what connection there might be between that and my late great-aunt.

It became obvious rather quickly that Professor Wentworth had indeed been looking into the legend of Marie Antoinette. He had visited Montpelier and Dorchester and of course the Fraser House. He had also, it seemed, finagled invitations to a couple of the privately owned historic houses in the area, which had items that supposedly were brought over on the *Sally*. It looked like he was trying to compile a list of the various items that had arrived on that fateful voyage.

"Huh," I muttered.

Immediately, Derek was next to me. "What?"

"Look at this. It looks like he made a list of the cargo from the *Sally*. He probably looked up the ship's manifest, or something."

"Or it could be a list of the contents of someone's house. Or shop." He saw my expression and added, "OK. Yeah, it does."

"I wonder why. I mean, look here." I pointed. "Fraser House. Where the historical society is, right? Fan, mirror and brush set, utensils..." My voice ran down.

"What?" Derek said. I shook my head.

"Nothing. Just a stray thought. My point is, the historical society and the Fraser House don't have these things anymore. They still have the chair, but all the smaller things were lost in that robbery Miss Barnes told us about, remember?"

Derek nodded. "So maybe he was trying to come up with a list of what Marie Antoinette actually thought she'd need to start over."

"What good would that do? If those things went into limbo in 1934, who cares where they were before that?"

"Obviously he did," Derek said. "He was a history professor. Those things were probably interesting to him." He went back to the backsplash. I shrugged—maybe so—and went back to the appointment book.

All right, so I'd try a different angle. On the list of items from the Fraser House, the small bergère was missing. But the chair was actually still there, in the house. The fan, mirror and brush set, and utensils were listed, but were not in the house any longer. So maybe Professor Wentworth was interested in the missing items more than the ones that were still there.

That same stray thought tugged on my memory again. Something about that list from the Fraser House. I turned back a page and read it over.

"My mother told me that Aunt Inga sent her a set of antique lobster utensils for her wedding last year," I said, just as much to myself as to Derek. He glanced over.

"Your mom got remarried?"

I nodded. "My dad died when I was thirteen."

"My mom died when I was twenty-seven. My dad married Cora two years later."

"Must be difficult to be alone again after you've been with someone that long. I know it threw my mother for a loop, and she was still fairly young. Suddenly all the responsibility was on her shoulders. She had to do everything herself. Make all the money, pay all the bills, and still be there for me. And if you think a thirteen-year-old girl is easy for a single parent to handle, think again."

"That's how old Shannon was when she and Kate moved here," Derek said. "Believe me, I know."

"So how do you and Cora get along? Do you like her?"

Derek nodded. "She's great. But more importantly, my dad likes her, so even if I didn't, I'd find a way to make it work. How about you and...what's your stepfather's name?"

"Noel. And I never thought about him as my stepfather, although I guess he is, technically. They live in California, so I don't get to see them very often. I've only met him a few times. He seems very nice, though, and he worships the ground she walks on. Mom's very happy."

"That's good. So she invited your aunt to the wedding?"

"The Wedding. Yes. Aunt Inga couldn't make it—too old and infirm, or maybe just too afraid to leave home—but she sent a set of antique lobster utensils that my mom said were fit for a queen."

"Huh," Derek said. His eyes flicked up and met mine.

I didn't know how to answer the question he wasn't asking, but I was thinking the same thing, so I nodded. "How could we find out?"

"The *Chronicle*'s been around for a while."

"Is that the local newspaper?"

"One of them. The other one's the *Waterfield Weekly*. That's been around a while, too. I think they both date back to the teens. There's probably something in the archives about the Fraser House robbery."

"We could go see," I suggested.

"We could." He meticulously finished sealing another pottery piece before he replaced the lid on the sealer and wrapped the brush in plastic. "Let's do it now. If it takes a long time, I'll buy you lunch."

"Thanks," I said, getting up, "but if it's all the same to you, I'd rather come back here. There's a lot more research I need to do." I'd only just started looking at Professor Wentworth's notes; who knew what else I might find in his day planner?

Derek shrugged. "Suit yourself. We can pick something up and bring it back here if you prefer."

"Either. I guess it doesn't matter." I walked in front of him out of the house and stopped on the porch to lock the door behind us before shuffling down the walk in Derek's wake. The grass was still knee-high, and I really, really hoped Mr. Todd would be able to come soon to mow it.

The *Chronicle* newspaper offices were located on Main Street, just across from the *Weekly* newspaper offices. It was like they were squaring off, ready to do battle, although I guessed there was probably room enough for both of them in a town this size. They'd certainly both managed to survive for long enough. The plaque outside the *Chronicle* main entrance said, Since 1915, and when I wandered over to check the matching plate outside the *Weekly*'s entrance, it said, Since 1912.

"That's a long time," I remarked to Derek as we pushed through the doors to the *Chronicle* offices. He nodded.

The *Chronicle* archivist was another fan of Derek's, a round-faced woman in her fifties, with a thick gold band prominently displayed on her left hand. She looked delighted to see him, and when Derek turned on the charm, she couldn't move fast enough to do his bidding. In short order we were both sitting in front of a microfiche machine in a utilitarian back room.

This was my first experience with microfiche—textile design isn't a field where microfiche comes into play a whole lot—but Derek seemed to know his way around the machine. "I have to do some research once in a while," he explained when I asked. "Sometimes I have to pull permits to do certain types of renovations. Waterfield Village has a protective zoning overlay, and there are certain things I'm not allowed to do to the facade of the houses in the historic district. But if I can prove that there was something similar there at one time, or that the house was originally painted in what's considered a nonhistoric color, I'll get special dispensation to do it anyway."

"And there's microfiche involved in that?"

"Sometimes, yeah." He operated the machine, rolling smoothly through the pages of the *Chronicle*. I yawned.

I won't bore you with a blow-by-blow of the progression of events. Research is boring at the best of times, especially secondhand, like this. We hit pay dirt about an hour in, when we came across a small notice about a robbery in a neighboring town. Someone had broken into a private home while the owners were out of town for the weekend and absconded with several valuable items, among them a jewelry box full of gold and diamonds, as well as an Aubusson tapestry rumored to have come over from France on the *Sally*.

"Oh, my God!" I said, wide-eyed. "An Aubusson!"

Derek looked at me like he couldn't quite see why I had turned pale and my hands were shaking. "What's an Aubusson?"

"Aubusson is the name of a weaving and textile commune in France. Started in 1580 by weavers from Flanders who took refuge there. In the seventeenth century, the Aubusson workshop was given royal appointment status. They made tapestries for the kings and queens of France."

"Know a lot about it, don't you?"

I shrugged. "Maybe I'm not quite as stupid as I look, either. Textiles—fabrics—are my specialty. An antique Aubusson tapestry from the eighteenth century might be worth as much as two hundred thousand dollars these days. A royal commission Aubusson from the same time might be worth a whole lot more. If my aunt had one of those..."

"What makes you think your aunt had one of those?"

I hesitated, then came clean. "I looked through Professor Wentworth's office the other day." He arched his brows, and I added defensively, "The door was open. And I didn't take anything. Nothing important. Just a stack of photographs from the desk drawer."

"Photographs of what?" Derek asked, moving the microfiche along again, after printing out the article we'd found. Behind me, I could hear the printer on the other side of the room kicking into life.

"Antiques. A hairbrush and mirror set. Two hair combs. A *guéridon*—that's a small, three-legged table. A beaded footstool. The chaise longue we lost yesterday. And a tapestry hanging in Aunt Inga's hall. At least I think it was Aunt Inga's hall. The wallpaper was the same."

"The wallpaper you took down?" Derek said.

I nodded.

"The wall I painted yesterday? There was no tapestry there then."

"Believe me," I said, "there's been no tapestry there at any time in the past couple of weeks. Not for as long as I've been around. An Aubusson tapestry isn't something I'd overlook."

"But there was an Aubusson tapestry in Aunt Inga's house at some point. At least that's what it sounds like you're saying?"

I nodded.

"Someone must have removed it, then. Maybe she sold it."

"I told you how much they go for," I said. "If she sold it, where's the money?"

He shrugged. "No idea. I'm more interested in where she got it, anyway."

"Isn't that rather obvious? If it's the same tapestry that was lost in the robbery, anyway?"

"I guess." Derek stopped the microfiche again. "Here's another."

I leaned closer to the screen. "Thieves Strike Again" was the headline. This time the daring robbers had snuck into a home in the middle of the night, while the elderly inhabitants were upstairs, asleep. They hadn't heard anything and hadn't realized that anything was wrong until the next morning when they came downstairs and saw that several valuable antiques were missing. Among the stolen items were a small, three-legged table, a beaded footstool, and all of their silverware, including a set of utensils rumored to have belonged to Marie Antoinette.

Derek didn't say anything, just hit Print and kept going.

The next robbery we came across was the one from the Fraser House, in the fall of 1934. As Miss Barnes had told us, a hairbrush and mirror had been stolen, along with a diamond-encrusted fan and a few other small things. The thieves had left the chair, either because it was too big and unwieldy to remove, or because they were interrupted. Derek printed the article and moved on.

A month later there was another robbery, in neighboring Thomaston, and this time, the robbers got more than they bargained for. The homeowners, probably alerted by the previous robberies, had hired a security guard while they were out of town for Thanksgiving. The guard wasn't anyone official, just a local man out of work at the beginning of the Great Depression, whose wife was expecting and who had said himself was willing to make some extra money. He wasn't armed, and when he came across the robbers in the middle of the night, one of them hit him over the head with a piece of statuary. Then they proceeded to take what they wanted, including an embroidered chaise longue rumored to have come to Maine from France in 1794. When the owners came home the next day, the security guard was dead on the floor, and all their valuables were gone.

"Oh, my God!" I said, paling. "How horrible!" Not only had he failed to stop the robbery, but the thieves had killed him and left his wife a widow and his unborn child fatherless.

Derek nodded. "They were probably just trying to knock him out so they could finish the job they came to do, but they panicked and hit him too hard, and then they left him there. It's easy to do in the heat of the moment. If they'd gotten him to a hospital, he might have lived."

"It sounds like you know a lot about it," I said.

"Not because I go around hitting people over the head. I did an emergency medicine rotation during my residency, and I saw all sorts of things." He started the microfiche machine moving again.

"I doubt we'll find any robberies after this," I said, focusing on the screen. "They probably weren't professionals, and when the guy died, I bet they stopped."

Derek nodded. "We've pretty much found what we came for anyway, haven't we?"

"I guess we have," I admitted.

"You want to go across the street to the *Weekly* and see if they've got anything different?"

"I don't think that's necessary. I've got enough on my mind without adding to it."

"I don't blame you," Derek said, removing the microfiche from the machine. "Let's go home."

"Let's." I walked out of the room with my head held high, stopping only long enough to hand the microfiche back to the lady at the desk and confirm that Professor Martin Wentworth had indeed been there, sometime in October or November, and had, among other things, wanted to see the 1933 to 1934 issues of the *Chronicle*.

—18—

"I'll finish sealing the backsplash," I said when we walked into Aunt Inga's house again. "I'm sick and tired of looking into the past. You always find out things you wish you didn't know." Like the fact that your aunt's big secret was that she was sitting—literally, in the case of the chaise longue—on a pile of loot.

"I'll go pick up some lunch," Derek said. He hesitated for a second before he reached out and chucked me gently under the chin.

I smiled. Nice of him to try to cheer me up, even if it didn't work.

He was gone for at least an hour, but I didn't notice the passage of time. Too many things on my mind, too many unanswered questions. The stolen chaise longue and missing tapestry, the dead security guard, the missing professor, my dead aunt...and her criminal past.

To avoid thinking too deeply about any of it, I threw myself into a frenzy of physical activity. When I had finished sealing the backsplash, I pulled out the sewing machine and started constructing lace panels for the kitchen cabinet doors. The large piece of lace I'd found upstairs—Aunt Inga's never-used wedding veil?—was discolored and moth-eaten in patches, and I was grateful, because its condition allowed me to cut it up with a clear conscience. After lunch, I'd ask Derek to start taking the doors off the cabinets and popping the middle panels out.

Mother had told me that Aunt Inga never married. But if she'd had a wedding veil stashed in the attic, surely she must have thought about it at some point. Mother had mentioned a boyfriend, hadn't she? As I cut the old lace into squares and basted and then hemmed the edges, it occurred to me to wonder who Aunt Inga had been planning to marry. If she had ended up with some of the loot from the robberies, which it seemed she had, unless there were two eighteenth-century French fainting couches sitting around Waterfield, then maybe her boyfriend had been one of the robbers.

This led me to drop the lace and open the file I'd gotten at the historical society, containing information about the Morton family.

When Derek eventually knocked on the door again, I hurried out to open it for him and dragged him inside the house by his arm, almost causing him to drop the packages of food and drinks. "Look at this!" I bounced on the balls of my feet, waving what I had found in the file in front of him. Derek squinted as it zoomed past his nose. "It's a picture of

Aunt Inga when she was young. She's with a guy, and I'm thinking it might be her boyfriend."

"Makes sense," Derek said, grabbing my wrist and holding it steady, the better to see the picture. "She's got a very proprietary grasp on his arm, at any rate."

I wondered whether his grasp of my arm might be considered proprietary, too. He had his hand wrapped around my wrist, with his thumb against the soft skin on the inside of my arm, where my pulse was beating overtime. I decided not to worry about it.

"Of course," Derek added pensively, "so does this young lady." He indicated the third person in the picture.

The old black-and-white photograph showed three people: two young women, one young man. The two girls were dressed in the height of 1930s fashion: calf-length, narrow skirts; wide-shouldered, belted jackets; small hats. One was a tall blonde, the other a short brunette, and both had the same possessive grasp of the young man's arms. He was tall and broad-shouldered, his dark hair slicked back, his smile dimpled and devastating.

"That's Aunt Inga," I said, pointing to the tall blonde. "I'm not sure who the other two are."

"The guy looks familiar—so does the girl, now that I look more closely at her—but I can't place either of them." He dropped my arm and walked around me and down the hall toward the kitchen. When I got to the table, he was digging sandwiches, drinks, and desserts out of his bags. "Italians, Moxie, whoopie pies," he said.

"Excuse me?"

"Italian sandwiches. Cans of Moxie soda. And whoopie pies for dessert."

"Oh. Great." I suppressed a face. Italian hoagies are OK, even though in Maine the rolls are split open on top instead of along the middle, like in any civilized part of the world. And whoopie pies are delicious. Moxie soda, however, is an acquired taste, one I haven't seen the sense in acquiring, since Moxie isn't readily available outside New England.

Still, I sipped bravely, not wanting Derek to see that I considered his choice of beverage just slightly superior to battery acid and about on par with soapy water. Seemingly lost in his own thoughts, I doubt he noticed, and as usual, we ate without speaking much.

"What's the matter?" I asked eventually, when I'd had enough of staring at the way his eyelashes made shadows across his cheekbones.

He glanced up, a quick flash of blue. "What?...Oh. Nothing."

"You sure?"

"Sure I'm sure." He looked back down to his paper plate.

"Because you seem kind of...I don't know...pre-occupied."

He shrugged. "Got a lot on my mind."

I nodded. I could understand that. There was a lot on my mind, too. But I preferred to talk about it. Hash it out. Speculate. Try to figure out what it all meant.

By the time he had gotten to the whoopie pie, the food seemed to have mellowed him out a little, and he spoke around a bite of chocolate cake and vanilla cream. "Wayne called my cell while I was out."

Uh-oh, I thought. "Now what?"

"Melissa. He talked to her."

"She's back?"

"She was never gone. She dropped her car off at the dealership for some repairs yesterday, and they gave her a loaner. That's why Wayne's APB didn't turn it up."

"So where's Philippe? Phil, I mean?"

"Melissa doesn't know. They parted ways in the early evening. She assumed he went back here to wait for you, but if he did, he was gone by the time we got here at eight."

"And so was the fainting couch," I said.

Derek nodded. "Wayne said Melissa swore she doesn't have it. And I don't think she does. No appreciation for anything older than herself."

"I still can't imagine how the two of you got together." The words fell out of my mouth without conscious thought, and as soon as they were uttered, I wished I could take them back. However, not only did Derek answer, he answered civilly, without biting my head off.

"I was in med school, and she wanted to marry a doctor. She was pretty, and I was young and not too smart."

I smiled. "Kate said she swept you off your feet."

"I thought she was the prettiest girl I'd ever seen. I couldn't get over the fact that she liked me, when she could have had any man she wanted. Before I knew what happened, we were husband and wife. Kate probably told you it didn't last long?"

"Four or five years, I think she said. Long enough, she said."

"Long enough," Derek echoed. "It was pretty bad toward the end. After I quit medicine to do this." He glanced around, taking in my kitchen and beyond, his work.

"Next time, maybe you should marry someone who likes the things you do, now that you know what they are."

"I'll keep that in mind," Derek said with a grin, his eyes crinkling at the corners. "So tell me more about this photograph and why you think it's important." He pulled it toward him for another look.

I leaned back on my uncomfortable kitchen chair. "I

don't know how important it is, but it seems worth looking into. My mother told me Aunt Inga had a boyfriend when she was young. If she had a wedding veil stashed in the attic, maybe he was more than just a boyfriend. But apparently it didn't work out. Something to do with my aunt Catherine. After that, Aunt Inga pretty much became a hermit. Didn't go out much, didn't allow anyone into her house."

"Makes sense, if she didn't want anyone to know she had the fainting couch and the tapestry," Derek said.

I nodded. "I wonder what happened to the tapestry. Lately, I mean. The professor had a photograph of it, so it must have been here until recently. He was only in Waterfield since September. Unless the wall in the background was someone else's wall, but how many people would buy orange, green, and blue tartan wallpaper, do you suppose?"

Derek shrugged.

I added hesitantly, "You don't think he took it, do you? Professor Wentworth? Pushed Aunt Inga down the stairs and then grabbed it and ran?"

"How much did you say it would be worth? Two hundred grand? Doesn't seem worth committing murder for."

"Tell that to that poor guard in Thomaston back in 1934," I said. "Whoever the robbers were, they didn't make a dime, since they couldn't very well sell any of the stuff they stole. Someone would have recognized the items, with all the press they got. Except for the jewelry, maybe. They could have taken all the stones out of the rings and necklaces, like the Comte de Lamotte did with Marie Antoinette's necklace, and sold just the gems."

"The Comte de who?" Derek said. I told him the story of Marie Antoinette and the infamous Affair of the Diamond

Necklace. "That makes sense, I guess," he said when I was finished. "Take the jewels out of the jewelry and sell them separately, but keep the antiques hidden where no one can see them."

"Until Professor Wentworth came along, wanting to talk to Aunt Inga about the history of Waterfield, and recognized the tapestry, because he'd studied the legend."

Derek nodded. Apparently this progression of events made sense to him, too. "I still say he wasn't the type to push your aunt down the stairs and make off with it, though. He had a good job and a nice little girlfriend, and he was a historian. He wouldn't steal an artifact."

"Unless he justified it by telling himself that they stole it first."

Derek shrugged. "Why didn't he make off with the chaise longue, too, then? He disappeared on Wednesday, and she wasn't found dead until Thursday. That would have given him plenty of time to drag it down from the attic."

"And do what with it?" I asked. "The bike was in the shed, and his car is still at the condo. You've carried the chaise longue; could he have put it on his back and staggered down the street with it?"

"Not without someone noticing," Derek said.

"But he could have kept an eye on the place, and when he saw that we found it and brought it downstairs, he showed up with a rental car and made off with it then."

"I suppose he could have," Derek admitted reluctantly, "but I still think that was Phil."

"Or Melissa." Derek opened his mouth to argue, and I continued, "She may not be interested in it herself, but maybe the Stenhams are. They're part of the family, too, and they've lived here their whole lives. Maybe they knew

Aunt Inga had these things. Maybe the Stenhams have been trying to get rid of me so they could get their hands on the antiques. They've certainly tried hard enough to get the house. Razing it and developing the land for condos may be just an excuse. Or an added bonus."

"There isn't much I would put past Ray and Randy Stenham," Derek agreed. He dug a flat carpenter's pencil stub out of a compartment in his tool belt and turned Aunt Inga's picture over, preparatory to writing something on the back of it. Then he stopped, squinting. "Is there something written on the back of this?"

"Is there?" I grabbed for it.

Derek held on. "Come over here if you want to look."

"Fine." I got up, hurried around the table, and leaned over his shoulder, trying not to be affected by the heat from his body and the smell of soap and shampoo. "What does it say?"

"It says, 'Independence Day 1934,' " Derek said, looking up at me. "And then it says 'Bath, ME. Inky, Jemmy, Cat.' "

I blinked. "Inky and Jemmy? Those are the names of the cats."

"Obviously more than the names of the cats," Derek said.

"Aunt Inga named the cats after herself and her boyfriend?"

"If he was her boyfriend."

"Why would she do that? No, never mind. She did it so that when she died, she could write in her will to her heir—me—that she had every confidence I would know the right thing to do about Inky and Jemmy."

"That's a clue if I ever heard one," Derek said.

"Maybe so. But what is it she wants me to do?"

He shrugged. "Beats me. Maybe we should try to figure out who Jemmy was, and see what he has to say."

"He has to be dead, don't you think? If Aunt Inga was almost ninety-nine, he couldn't be much younger. Not if he was breaking and entering in 1934."

"Would your mother know?" Derek asked.

I shook my head. "I doubt it. My aunt Mary Elizabeth might know, although I don't relish the idea of asking her."

"Mary Elizabeth Stenham? No, you don't want to do that. I'm sure we can figure it out some other way."

I started gathering the remains of the lunch. I was standing anyway, so I figured I may as well. "Your dad wouldn't know, would he? He said he spent time with Aunt Inga once in a while."

"She would have had to have told him," Derek said. "He's only fifty-nine, so it all happened long before his time."

"Would he be able to tell us, if she did? What about patient-doctor confidentiality?"

"That only applies to medical information," Derek said. "Unless you're a priest, then everything told under the confessional is privileged...wait a minute."

"For what?" I pitched the crumpled papers and empty Moxie cans in the trash.

"I'm thinking. If your aunt Inga and her boyfriend were getting married, there'd be records of that, right?"

"I think so," I said.

"In the old days, the church would announce the banns for three weeks prior to the wedding. Not like these days, when you can get a marriage license, wait three days, and then get married."

"Or go to Las Vegas and get married the same day."

"So if the banns were read, the church might have a rec-ord of it. You up for another break?"

I glanced out the kitchen window. "It looks like a nice day."

"A perfect day for a stroll through the churchyard, I'd say. And a chance to work off that whoopie pie, too." He stretched, both arms over his head.

"I don't see that being a problem for you," I said, watch-ing, "but I'm game."

"Glad to hear it. Let's go, Tink." He held out a hand.

"Just out of curiosity," I said, taking it, "why do you call me that?"

"Tinkerbell?" He looked down at me as we walked toward the front door. "It seems to fit, don't you think?"

"I don't know. Does it?"

"She's little and cunning and pouts a lot, with a whole lot of yellow hair piled on top of her head." He tweaked the messy pile on top of mine. I had scooped my hair into a sort of bun earlier, because it was getting in my face while I was sewing, and I had forgotten about it.

"Cunning?" I repeated, letting my hair down and leaving the scrunchy around my wrist for later. I'll admit to being small, and I had probably pouted more than usual lately, but it was the first time anyone had called me cunning.

He grinned. "Cute."

"Cunning means cute?"

"Sure. Colloquialism."

"In that case," I said, "thanks."

"My pleasure." He opened the garden gate and bowed me through. I passed him, glowing a little more brightly than usual, just like Tinkerbell whenever Peter Pan was around. He thought I was cute...

. . .

The church, one of those tall-steepled, white New England churches I'd seen in so many photographs, was a few blocks away, and we took the truck. Derek parked outside the white picket fence that circled the graveyard and came around to open the door for me. "Been here before?"

I shook my head, embarrassed. "I should have been, I guess. Mr. Rodgers told me that Aunt Inga didn't want a fuss, so there was no funeral and no graveside ceremony. But she gave me her house, so I ought to have found the time to put some flowers on her grave."

"Now you know where it is, you can come back." He opened the little white gate and ushered me through. "The older graves are down here, near the street, while the newer ones are up there on the hill. I'm not sure where your aunt would be."

"I'm not sure, either," I admitted. "Maybe, if we go inside, someone can tell us."

"Worth a try," Derek opined. "We'll have to go in anyway, to find out about the parish book."

The interior of the little white church was whitewashed like the outside, hushed and cool, with dark wooden pews and tall stained glass windows, shining like gems where the sunlight slanted through them. "I worked on those," Derek said. "Cleaned off more than a hundred years of grime. Took me some time, but I got them looking pretty good, I think."

"I'd say. They're lovely." I looked around. "This is a pretty church. Restful."

"That's what a church is supposed to be, yeah? The offices are in the back. C'mon." He headed down the aisle with me right behind. A small door half hidden behind the wall-mounted pulpit took us into the utilitarian, unadorned part of the church, down a short set of shallow stone steps and along a murky corridor. Derek raised his voice. "Anybody home?"

"Someone is always home in the Lord's house," answered a resonant baritone from behind one of the open doors.

Derek grinned. "Afternoon, Barry." He stuck his head into an office on the right.

I followed, a little diffidently, to peer past his shoulder.

"Nice to see you, Derek." The speaker was a man of Derek's age, a little beefier in the shoulders and with a little less hair, seated behind a steel-and-fake-wood desk piled high with papers. He saw me, and continued, "And who's this?"

"Avery Baker," I said politely.

Derek added, "Inga Morton's heir. I'm helping her fix her aunt's house over on Bayberry. Tink, this is the Reverend Bartholomew Norton, better known as my buddy Barry from high school."

"Nice to meet you, Reverend Norton," I said.

Barry Norton inclined his head. "And you, Miss Baker. I'm sorry for your loss."

"Thank you. I didn't know her well, but I wish I had."

"We're looking for her final resting place," Derek said. "Avery doesn't know whether there's a family plot somewhere or if her aunt's buried on the hill."

"Inga Morton was buried in the family plot near the southwest corner." Reverend Barry gestured through the thick stone wall of the church. "The burial took place almost two weeks ago, with no fanfare. The last of the Mortons." He shook his head sadly. Derek glanced at me. I recognize a smooth segue when I hear one, and this one was as smooth as could be.

"My mom told me that Aunt Inga had a beau when she was younger. I even found her wedding veil packed away in the attic."

The Reverend Barry nodded.

"I have no idea what happened, or even who he was, but I was wondering if there is any way to find out. If banns were read, maybe. Just on the off chance that he's still alive."

"Back in those days," the Reverend Barry said, "banns would have been read. Unless your aunt and her beau planned to elope, of course." When he got up from the desk, he turned out to be just a few inches taller than me. From the powerful voice and the broad shoulders, I had expected someone much more imposing, but the Reverend Barry was at least half a head shorter than Derek.

"The marriage, birth, and death book is in the entry," he continued over his shoulder, as he passed through the door into the dusky hallway on short but powerful legs. "You passed it on your way in."

Derek stepped aside and bowed me through the door ahead of him. We trooped back out the way we'd come in, up the stairs and into the church itself, back up the aisle between the glowing stained glass windows, and into the entry. Reverend Barry stopped by a huge book—two feet by one and a half by four inches thick—sitting on a small table off to one side of the heavy front door. "It goes back to the beginning," he explained, and added, before I could ask, "the beginning of this church, I mean. Not the beginning of time, nor even the parish. Just back to 1887, when the church was finished."

"That's long enough," I answered. Aunt Inga hadn't been born until 1910; any banns read for her would have taken place well after that.

"Help yourself." He stepped aside and gestured me up to

the table. I started turning pages while the Reverend Barry and Derek caught up on what had been happening in their respective lives lately. I wasn't listening with more than half an ear, and as a result, I didn't catch more than half of what was said. Melissa's name came up once—maybe Barry was asking how she was doing—and although I didn't hear Derek's answer, his tone of voice seemed to shut the subject down flat.

"Find anything?" he asked shortly thereafter. I shook my head.

"I started in 1934, since...well, you know. I'm down to 1933 now, and there's still nothing...wait a second."

He was next to me in a heartbeat. The Reverend Barry, with his shorter legs, took a little longer, but I had barely had time to point to the handwritten names before he was hanging over my other shoulder. "Where? Oh, yes. Well, what do you know?"

"Huh," Derek said.

I nodded. A part of me had suspected it, but it was still a shock to see the names there, next to each other. Banns for the marriage of Inga Marie Morton to Hamish Kendall, to take place on New Years Eve, 1934.

19

"So," Derek said when we were outside, wandering along one of the gravel paths underneath towering oaks and maples and the bowl of a clear, blue sky, "Aunt Inga was engaged to Hamish Kendall."

I nodded, looking right and left as we walked, reading the names on the gravestones along the walkway.

"The same Hamish Kendall who married your aunt Catherine. Mary Elizabeth Kendall's father. Ray and Randy Stenham's grandfather."

"If you say so."

"But old Hamish died years ago," Derek continued, "so he's definitely not out to get you. He couldn't have killed your aunt, unless he did it from beyond the grave. And neither could his wife. She's been dead even longer."

"I'm not sure anyone killed my aunt," I admitted. "Maybe

my imagination is running away with me. She was very old, and they're very steep stairs. If she fell, it's not unlikely that she'd die."

"That's true."

"I mean, why would someone want to kill someone who's almost ninety-nine and could go at any moment? It doesn't make sense."

"Not unless someone was afraid of what she'd tell you when you came to visit," Derek said.

"But if so, they'd have to have known she was writing to me, and why."

"She might have asked whoever it was to mail the letter for her," Derek suggested. "She couldn't get around very easily anymore, so maybe she gave it to someone else to put in the mailbox."

"But then that someone could have just kept it instead of mailing it. And she didn't die for another two weeks, anyway. If she had put the right amount of postage on the letter, it would have reached me in a couple of days, and I might have been in Waterfield a week before I actually came. While Aunt Inga was still alive."

A stab of guilt and grief hit me in the gut. I knew it wasn't my fault, that I'd come as soon as I could, but I felt like I had failed my aunt. She had reached out to me for help, for absolution, for *something*, and I hadn't responded quickly enough. If only the letter had gotten to me sooner, if only I had dropped everything and run right then . . . if . . . if . . . if.

"Tell me again everything that's happened," Derek said. "From the beginning. I have a feeling I'm missing something."

I took a breath, then laid everything—the whole case— out for him as we wandered between the old gravestones with their angels and crosses. The letter from Aunt Inga, the phone call to my mother, the trip to Waterfield, only to discover that Aunt Inga was dead. Mr. Rodgers crawling on the floor, looking for her will...

"On the floor?" Derek interjected. "Why would he think it would be there? The logical place to look for a will would be the desk, wouldn't it?"

I nodded. "That's what I thought, too. In fact, that's what I told him. And that's where it was."

"Huh," Derek said. "Seems strange."

"It does, doesn't it? You know, I could make a doozy of a case against Graham Rodgers if I wanted to. He was at the house when we brought the fainting couch down from the attic. He said he didn't know how he could have missed it, remember?"

Derek nodded. "If the keys were on the desk, he could have taken one while Melissa was performing her big scene. We were all too busy looking at her to notice what anyone else was doing."

Humph, I thought, although I didn't say it. "He also had a key to the house while I was in New York, when someone came in and broke all Aunt Inga's china."

"What?" Derek said.

"Don't you remember? You walked in on me sweeping up, the first day you came to the house."

"I remember you sweeping, but I didn't realize someone had broken in. Too busy admiring the scenery, I guess." He grinned.

I remembered that when he came in that morning, I'd been standing bent over, my butt in the air, wiggling to Bruce Springsteen. Hopefully that was the scenery he was referring to, and not Aunt Inga's kitchen. "What did you think? That I'd had a hissy fit and smashed everything myself?"

Derek didn't answer, but he blushed, and my jaw dropped. "Oh, you...you...that's just insulting! I'd never do that! Who do you think I am, your ex-wife?!"

"You do have a bit of a temper," Derek said. "You yelled at me, yeah?"

"You scared me! And then you talked down to me. You laughed at me, too."

"That was before I knew you," Derek said.

"Well, Graham Rodgers was the one who put the key under the mat for me. He tried to get rid of me before that, too. He offered to have the house cleaned out and put on the market for me, so I wouldn't have to be bothered. I thought it was nice of him, but it could certainly look like he was trying to keep me away. And that night someone rigged the stairs. He showed up the next morning, remember?"

"To make sure Mr. Todd had come by to talk to you about the grass, wasn't it? Why do you think that's sinister?"

"Well, he had his own key. When I didn't answer the door quickly enough, he began to let himself in. If this was a TV show, he'd be the murderer returning to the scene of the crime to make sure I was dead. Or to discover my body, like he...Uh-oh!"

"What?"

I grinned. "I was going to say, like he discovered Aunt Inga's. But they had a standing lunch date every Friday, right?"

"Did they? I thought it was Thursday."

I wrinkled my brows. "Why would you think that?"

His voice was patient. "Because Martin Wentworth went missing on a Wednesday, and Mr. Rodgers found your aunt the next day."

"On Thursday? Are you sure?"

"Positive. It's just a couple of weeks ago. But I'll call and check with Wayne if you want." He put his hand on his phone.

I shook my head. "That's not necessary. I probably just made a mistake." It's difficult, not to say impossible, to remember every word someone has said, especially when it doesn't seem significant at the time. After all, who could seriously suspect dapper, gentlemanly Mr. Rodgers of anything?

"Shouldn't be too hard to figure out," Derek opined. "Either they went somewhere together, or he picked up food somewhere and brought it to her. If it happened on the same day every week, all we have to do is ask around. In a town this small, someone will know their routine."

He tilted his head. That sun-streaked lock of hair fell into his eyes, and this time—dammit—I lifted my hand to brush it aside. I caught myself, but not fast enough. He chuckled.

"Sounds like a lot of work," I said, putting both hands behind my back and pretending, without much success, that nothing had happened. "Wouldn't it be easier just to call and ask him?"

"No, because then he'll know we're on to him."

"On to what? You don't really think he's done anything, do you?"

"I don't know," Derek said. "With this much evidence, I think it's worth including him as a suspect for real."

I giggled. "Don't be silly. He was Aunt Inga's friend. And he's always been helpful to me."

"That's exactly what he would do," Derek answered, "if he was trying to lull you into a false sense of security."

I shook my head, amused and exasperated. "You know, if carpentry doesn't work out and you don't want to go back to medicine, you should try writing thrillers."

"I'm just trying to make sure you don't do anything stupid," Derek said, turning toward the small family plot surrounded by a knee-high wrought-iron fence. I glanced up at him, smiling.

"You know, if I didn't know better, I'd think you cared."

"If you weren't leaving once we sell your aunt's house, I might."

I blinked. After a short, piercing glance, he wasn't looking at me, just staring straight ahead at the tall stone marking the final resting place of the Mortons, and his expression was approximately as stony as the old granite. I opened my mouth and closed it again.

For something to do, I turned my own attention away from Derek and to the monument. It was a big slab of granite, and at its head was the name Frederick William Morton, with dates of birth and death in 1855 and 1919, respectively. His wife, Rose, was born a few years after him and died a few years before.

Below Frederick, the inscriptions divided. On one side lay Edward and his progeny, among them my grandfather John and his sister Catherine; the latter with a death date the year I turned five. On the other lay William, born 1886, dead 1967, along with his wife, Constance, 1889–1964, and his daughter Inga Marie, 1910–2008. The fresh carving of Aunt Inga's death date was like an unhealed wound, dark and sharp in contrast to the weathered and softened edges of the older inscriptions.

There were some flowers, mostly wilted, on Edward's side of the stone—maybe my aunt Mary Elizabeth had put them there, for her mother—but there was nothing on Aunt Inga's side. I looked around, disconcerted.

"Here."

Derek walked over to the picket fence surrounding the

churchyard and bent. When he straightened back up, he was holding a motley bouquet of weeds, wildflowers, and a few irises he must have yanked out of a bed on the other side. The mixture was lovely, especially considering its impromptu arrangement. "This should do for now, yeah?"

I nodded. "Yes." My voice was froggy, and to my horror, my eyes were turning misty, too. "Thank you."

"My pleasure." He looked down at me, and then smiled. "C'mere." Shifting the flowers to the other hand, he put his free arm around my shoulders. "We'll come back some other time with a proper bouquet, OK?"

"OK," I sniffed. He was just the right height for the back of my head to fit perfectly into the crook of his shoulder. "Sorry for being so wet."

"You've had a lot going on in the past few days. You're due." His voice was easy, and when he didn't say anything else, I snuggled into his side and had a good if subdued cry.

If this had been a sappy romance novel, one thing would have led to another, and when I raised my lovely, dewy-eyed face to his, he would have kissed me and everything would have dissolved into pink mist. The reality wasn't quite so glamorous. I'm not lovely in the best of circumstances—cute sometimes, but never lovely—and by the time my self-indulgent moments of grief, guilt, and overwroughtness were over, my eyes were red and puffy, and I looked not so much dewy as drowned. He kissed me anyway. On the forehead. "Feel better?"

"I guess." I took a step back and swiped my eyes with the backs of my hands. "Sorry."

"We'll try it again sometime. Where do you want these flowers?"

"Oh. Um..." I looked around. "I guess just under Aunt Inga's name. John was my grandfather, so whenever I come back, I'll bring something for him, too, but for now, let's just give them to Aunt Inga."

"Done." He straightened up. "You ready to go back to work? We should try to get a little more done on the house today, yeah? The sooner we get finished, the sooner you can go back to New York."

"Right," I said. He looked at me, a smile tugging at one corner of his mouth, but he didn't say anything else. I squared my shoulders. "Let's go."

We spent the rest of the afternoon working on the kitchen. The backsplash was done, and the kitchen cabinets were next. While Derek popped the panels out of the upper cabinet doors—and "popping" makes the process sound a lot simpler than it was—I continued constructing lace panels, which Derek attached to the cabinets with a staple gun before reattaching the doors to the rest of the cabinets. We labored in companionable silence, only broken by the buzzing of the sewing machine and banging and prying sounds from Derek, interspersed with the occasional muffled swear word.

Five o'clock came and went without fanfare, but around six, Derek started making noises about quitting for the day. I nodded and smiled. I wanted to suggest having dinner together again, but I didn't dare.

"You OK?" he asked.

I nodded.

"Going to be all right alone tonight?"

"Are you offering to stay?" I wanted to know.

He looked at me for a moment in silence. "Do you want me to stay?"

I was tempted, I admit. "I wouldn't mind if you stayed," I said at last. "But I think maybe, under the circumstances, it would be better if you didn't."

He didn't pretend not understanding what I meant. "With you leaving soon, and all."

I nodded. "With me leaving soon, and all."

"I'll see you in the morning, then. You have my number if there's anything you need." He hesitated for a second before he reached out and brushed a wild strand of hair off my cheek. "Sleep well."

"You, too," I said and walked with him down the hallway to the door.

I watched him get in the truck and pull away from the curb. He waved as he drove off. And then I headed back into the house, pulling my cell phone out of my pocket and dialing as I went. Much as I didn't want to, I really had to pass Professor Wentworth's day planner off to the appropriate authorities. But now at least I didn't have to put Derek in the middle of it. He'd have to live with these people, probably for the rest of his life, while I only had to put up with them until the end of the summer. "Wayne? This is Avery Baker. Do you have a minute? I have something for you."

"And what might that be?" Wayne's deep voice responded.

"Professor Wentworth's day planner. With his schedule. The one you couldn't find."

Wayne was quiet. Ominously so. "Where did you get it?" he asked eventually. "Somewhere in your aunt's house?"

"Someone gave it to me. I'll tell you about it when you come to pick it up, OK?"

"This had better be good," Wayne said. "Don't move. I'm on my way." He hung up. I used the time while I waited to call Paige to let her know what I'd done.

"Any news about Philippe—I mean, Phil Albertson?" I asked ten minutes later, as I let Wayne into Aunt Inga's house. Philippe still hadn't returned my phone call. Wayne shook his head.

"I'm afraid not. I've had law enforcement in five states keeping an eye out for him all day, and so far, no one has reported a thing."

"Have you tried calling his office?"

Wayne said he had. "I spoke to the receptionist, Miss Hamilton, and to the attorney, Miss Lee. Neither of them has heard from him since yesterday."

"Tara must be upset," I said happily.

"That the new girlfriend?"

"That's her. She's twenty-two and looks like Melissa James. Or like Melissa must have looked back in college, when she swept Derek off his feet. And speaking of Melissa James..."

"She said they parted ways around six," Wayne said. "She went home to her condo, alone. She assumed Mr. Albertson went to look for you, since you were all he talked about. You and that couch, of course."

"Of course." The fainting couch was the only reason for his rekindled interest in me, and I was well aware of it. "So the last time anyone saw him was last night around six, when he left Melissa? Where did he spend the night? Did he have reservations anywhere?"

"None I've been able to find," Wayne said. "Miss Lee said he didn't ask her to make any. Miss Hamilton assumed he planned to spend the night with you."

"Hah!" I said. If Philippe thought I would welcome him back into my bed after he cheated on me with Tara, he was even more self-absorbed than I had suspected. Although I won't deny it cheered me to imagine Tara's chagrin at the thought. "Did you think to ask Mr. Rodgers? He showed

Philippe the way to my house—Aunt Inga's house—
yesterday."

"You told me," Wayne nodded. "And I tried to call, but
he didn't answer. Went out of town, most likely. He has relatives in Thomaston that he goes to visit occasionally."

"What about B and Bs? Hotels? Motels?"

"I've checked all the hotels, motels, and B and Bs as far
away as Portland. The police and the highway patrol in every state between us and New York have kept an eye out for
the Rover since last night. I had the NYPD knock on his
door this afternoon. I even called Christie's and tracked
down the girl he said he knew. Nobody's seen or heard from
him. At this point, there's nothing more I can do. Just wait."

"Just like Professor Wentworth," I muttered. "Into thin
air."

Wayne didn't answer. "So about this day planner..." he
said. I indicated the kitchen table, and he ambled over and
began turning pages. "I see he had plans to meet with your
aunt the day he disappeared," he remarked after a moment.

I nodded.

"Probably got here, too, if his bike in the shed is any in-
dication."

"Probably so," I agreed. "He left home on it that morning, didn't he?"

"So I've been told. Nice, sunny day, warm. An easy ride
from the condo, level terrain except for the last half mile or
so, up the hill from downtown. He left home just before
eighty thirty, probably got here right at nine o'clock. Put the
bicycle in the shed, so no one would see it. Could mean he
didn't want anyone to know he was here."

"Or just that he didn't want anyone to steal it while he
was busy doing whatever it was he had to do," I answered.
"If you look back through the pages, you'll see that he'd

been visiting my aunt every week for a while. His...
um...the person who gave me the day planner said they
were working on some sort of project together. Something
to do with Marie Antoinette and Samuel Clough and the
Sally."

Wayne's gaze sharpened when I mentioned the person
who had given me the planner, but he didn't push. Not yet.
"What do you think this means?" he asked instead, pointing
to the entry for the Wednesday one week before the day
Aunt Inga died. Next to 9:00 IM@h, it said SOL with three
question marks following it.

I hadn't noticed it earlier, and now I squinted at it for a
moment, running acronyms over in my head. "Standard of
living? Society for Organized Learning? Latin word for the
sun? He was big on abbreviations. The appointment book is
full of them. Derek and I had a lot of fun figuring out what
some of them meant, earlier."

"In my line of work," Wayne said, "SOL would be statute of limitations." I blinked, and he added, "This person
who gave you the planner...Who would that be?"

I hesitated. "Do I have to tell you?"

"Unless you want me to arrest you for obstruction of justice, yes."

"You wouldn't do that, would you?"

"Probably not," Wayne admitted. "Although I might.
Then again, spending the night in jail probably wouldn't be
enough to convince you to talk, seeing as you live with the
bare minimum as it is. Just let me ask you one thing. When I
saw you this morning, you and Derek were on your way to
Barnham College. That's what you said, wasn't it?"

I made a face. "Yes."

"So did you get this from someone at Barnham? A student? It wasn't Shannon, was it?" I shook my head, and he

looked relieved. "At least I don't have to worry about keeping secrets from Kate. Josh probably wouldn't have been
happy, either."

"He likes her, doesn't he?" It was a futile attempt to
change the subject.

"Josh? Likes Shannon? Worships the ground she walks
on. But if she'd gotten mixed up with her professor, I think
he would have told me." He looked at me in silence for a
second, and then he added, "They're all over eighteen, you
know. And although getting involved with a teacher may
not be smart, it isn't illegal. Whoever the girl is, I can't tell
her parents or arrest her."

"How about obstruction of justice?" I wanted to know.
"And removing evidence?" The things he had threatened
me with, in other words.

"Oh, well." He shrugged.

I did the same. "Her name is all over the planner, so I
guess it doesn't matter. Abbreviated, of course, like everything else, but it wouldn't take you long to figure it out. Her
name is Paige Thompson."

Wayne rolled his eyes. "That figures. She never did have
the sense God gave a flea. I'll talk to her."

"Be nice," I said, as I walked him down the hall toward
the front door again. "She seems pretty broken up."

"Always been delicate," the chief of police agreed. "Lost
her mom when she was a kid. Suicide. And her dad's not the
easiest person in the world to live with."

"I wondered why she had a dorm room at the college
when she's from Waterfield originally. I guess that's why." I
opened the door and let Wayne pass through. He kept a tight
grip on the day planner, as if he was afraid I would change
my mind at the last minute and snatch it back from him.

"Thanks for this." He lifted it. "I'll put young Brandon

on it, see what he can come up with. And I'll talk to Paige, in case she knows something she didn't tell you."

"Let me know how it goes," I said. Wayne promised he would and took his leave. I wandered slowly back inside, gnawing my lip.

The chief's suggestion for what SOL might mean made a lot of sense, unfortunately, especially with what I knew and he didn't. A statute of limitations is the legal precedent that decides for how long after the fact someone can be charged with a crime. In order to prosecute for theft, for instance, the theft has to have taken place within just a few years. On the other hand, if I remembered correctly from watching crime shows on TV, there is no statute of limitations at all on certain crimes. Like murder. What if Professor Wentworth had been researching the statute of limitations to see if he could have my aunt arrested and charged with killing that security guard in Thomaston in 1934?

But no. That would give my aunt a good reason for killing Professor Wentworth, but why would he kill her? Unless it really was an accident. If he told her what he planned to do, and she got upset, and they fought, and she fell down the stairs, and then he snatched the tapestry from the wall and ran. But wouldn't it have made more sense for him to leave it there, and then call Wayne? The tapestry—and the chaise longue in the attic—were proof that he was telling the truth, at least about the thefts and the dead watchman. If he had no prior history of violence, why run? Without the tapestry—and now, without the chaise longue—I wasn't sure how one could prove any of it.

Dammit, what had happened to the chaise longue? And where the hell was Philippe? If he had left Melissa at six P.M. last night, he'd had time to drive to New York and back twice by now. That Range Rover could probably burn up the road, and Philippe had a lead foot. He might have gone somewhere else—back to Tennessee, maybe, or across the border into Canada—but why? The fainting couch was valuable, but I doubted it was valuable enough to entice him to discard the business and identity he'd spent ten years building.

But if he wasn't in New York, and he hadn't gone any-where else, where was he? Not with Melissa, or so she said. Not with me. He had no acquaintances in town who might put him up for the night. He hadn't rented a room. Unless he had driven his car off the road into the ocean, where might he be?

Good Lord, I thought, stopping dead halfway down the long hall, what if he *had* driven off the road? My face paled as I imagined the sleek Rover zooming down the ocean road away from town, Philippe behind the wheel and my chaise longue lovingly tucked in behind him. I pictured him glanc-ing over his shoulder at it, gloatingly, just as the road turned, and the car not turning with it, but instead whizzing across the gravel and grass toward the guardrail, hitting it dead-on at ninety miles per hour. There's a lot of horsepower in a Range Rover; the guardrail would give, and both rail and car would go flying over the edge, hurtling down toward the cold water forty feet below. How deep was the sea just be-low the cliffs? If the smugglers had brought their boats in there in the old days, it would be more than deep enough to consume a Range Rover. Both Philippe and the fainting couch might be disintegrating in the frigid water of the At-lantic right now.

But surely someone would have noticed if the guardrail had been broken anywhere along the coast road. Wayne's squad had been up and down and all around all day, not just on the lookout for Philippe and the Rover, but also keeping an eye on anything else that might be going on in Water-field. They'd have noticed if someone had driven off the road into the ocean. Right? And even if they hadn't, with no car, and no bike, it wasn't like I could do any searching my-self. Derek might agree to drive me around, but it would be the utmost in insensitivity for me to ask him to help me search for my ex-boyfriend when he had just told me that he liked me himself. Or that he *would* like me, if I had any plans of sticking around. Which surely meant that he *did* like me, he just didn't want to.

So what was I going to do about Derek, I asked myself as I entered the kitchen to nuke another bowl of instant mac and cheese for dinner. I couldn't deny that I liked him back. We'd gotten along well the past few days. We worked well together, once he'd allowed that occasionally I might know what I was talking about. The joint productions of kitchen backsplash and kitchen cabinets were going to look great. He had bought me a knee brace, and picked flowers for Aunt Inga's grave, and held me while I cried. When I thought he was going to kiss me, my stomach had quivered, and my breath had stuttered in my chest. And—the dead giveaway—my hand twitched every time that damn hank of hair fell into his eyes.

So yes, the attraction was definitely there, and mutual. The problem was, of course, that he'd made it very clear that he didn't want to act on it unless I was planning to stay in Waterfield beyond the summer. And how could I do that? Selling Aunt Inga's house might net me a couple hundred grand, maybe, once Derek had gotten his share and once the Realtor had gotten his or her commission. But then I'd be homeless, and if Kate was right about Waterfield's real es-tate prices, I couldn't afford to buy another place to live.

And I had to have a job. Something fun and fulfilling. I hadn't gone to Parsons for all those years to ring up groceries at Shaw's Supermarket or wait tables at the Waymouth Tavern.

The microwave dinged, and I pulled my plastic bowl of gooey macaroni out and sat down at the kitchen table, digging in with a plastic fork. This probably wasn't the best time to think about it. I had more important—or at least more immediate—concerns. Like, where the hell were my erstwhile boss-slash-boyfriend and my antique chaise longue? Not to mention the missing professor who may or may not have killed my aunt?

Wait a second, though. I sat up straighter on the uncomfortable kitchen chair. What if I was looking at things the wrong way? What if Professor Wentworth had been researching the statute of limitations on the theft, but not on the murder? And not because he was trying to have my aunt arrested, but because—yes!—he was trying to help. My aunt was getting on in age, and knew she wasn't going to live forever. Maybe she wanted to come clean before she died, and she asked Professor Wentworth to help her get the antiquities back where they belonged. That would explain why he had a list of them, and photographs, as well. It would also explain the letter I'd gotten, and Aunt Inga's statement about wrongs needing to be set right. She was getting old—more than old; ancient—and wanted to take care of things before she died. Martin Wentworth had been trying to figure out where the various items belonged so he could return them there. Maybe Aunt Inga had already given him the tapestry to return to the robbery victims' descendants in Wiscasset, and that was why it was no longer on the wall in the hallway. Maybe he had left his bicycle in the shed and taken a bus or a train to Wiscasset, where something had happened to him. Or maybe he had hitched a ride with someone who realized the value of the tapestry and who had knocked him over the head and tossed him in the ocean, and in a week or so, he'd float into Boston Harbor. Maybe Aunt Inga had simply stumbled and fallen, and it was all just a tragic accident.

Who might Professor Wentworth have spoken to about the statute of limitations?

One name came immediately to mind: Graham Rodgers, Aunt Inga's old friend and faithful family attorney. After quoting chapter and verse to me when I asked him about holographic wills, it seemed Mr. Rodgers was well trained in the ins and outs of Maine law.

It was the work of a moment to call him; however, at this point my luck ran out. The attorney didn't have a cell phone. When he didn't answer his home phone, I left a brief message—"Hi, Mr. Rodgers. This is Avery Baker. I had a quick question about statute of limitations. Would you give me a call when you have a minute?"—followed by my number, and then I hung up.

No sooner had I closed the phone and put it on the table than it rang again. I picked it back up, sure it was Mr. Rodgers answering my call. It wasn't.

"Look outside," Derek commanded.

"I beg your pardon?"

"Look out the front door."

"Why?"

"You'll see." He didn't say anything else, and since it seemed like a fairly small thing to ask, I shrugged and got to my feet.

"Where are you?" I asked as I wandered along the hall toward the front of the house.

"None of your business. Are you there yet?"

"Almost." I undid the locks, opened the door, and peered out.

I had thought he'd be at the curb, holding flowers or a pizza or something—so sue me; I've watched too many sappy sitcoms—but he wasn't. He was nowhere in sight nor was his truck. "I don't see anything," I said.

"You're not looking in the right place. Look right. I mean, left."

I looked both ways, just to be safe, and still didn't see him. I did, however, see something else. "What...? Is that...? Oh, my gosh, is that for me?"

"It used to belong to one of Cora's daughters," Derek explained with a chuckle at my obvious surprise and pleasure. "She doesn't live in Waterfield anymore, so Cora thought you might like to have it, since you don't have a car. She came by a while ago, but Wayne was there and she didn't want to intrude. Is everything okay?"

"Everything is fine. I was handing over Professor Wentworth's appointment book. And of course I'd love to have it. Tell her thank you and give her a kiss from me."

Derek promised he would. "I'd offer to come back out there, so you could pass on the kiss in person, but I can tell that at the moment I'd be superfluous. Enjoy." He hung up. I stuffed the cell phone into my pocket and sank to the porch floor to commune with my new bicycle.

20

Ten minutes later, I was on my way out the ocean road at a good clip. The bike was a better fit for me than Professor Wentworth's had been, and although the injured knee grumbled a little at being bent and straightened repeatedly, it beat the heck out of walking. And doing something, even if it was riding around willy-nilly, hoping to sight the Range Rover or Philippe, was better than sitting at home doing nothing.

This day felt like it had gone on forever. It was amazing to think that just twenty-four hours ago I'd been having dinner with Derek at the Waymouth Tavern. We hadn't yet realized that the fainting couch was gone or that Philippe was missing. Or for that matter who Philippe really was. Or any of the other bombshells that had exploded in my life today. As I pedaled, I reflected on what a difference a day makes.

Of course I also kept an eye out to the left and right—
mostly the right—for signs of skid marks or breaks in the
vegetation or guardrail along the ocean road, as well as, of
course, for the Range Rover itself. By this time, it was dusk;
not dark yet, not so far north in the summer, but just starting
to turn from day to night. The stars were beginning to twin-
kle above, and lights began to come on in the houses I
passed.

After a couple of miles, I came upon Mr. Rodgers's
spread and slowed down. He still hadn't returned my phone
call from earlier, although there was a light on in a couple of
the downstairs rooms. As I rolled past the wrought-iron
gates, spelling out the name Cliff on one side, House on the
other, a shadow passed in front of the window. I slowed to a
stop.

There was no sign of Mr. Rodgers's Cadillac in the driveway, although I could see what must be a carriage house inside the fence, just to my left. These days, that was probably
in use as a garage. Maybe Mr. Rodgers had pulled the Caddy
inside. But if he was home, why hadn't he called me? And if
he wasn't home, but in Thomaston visiting family, as Wayne
had suggested, who was moving around in his house?

The gate was closed but unlocked I found when I tried to
open it. It moved smoothly without making a sound, and I
pushed it open just enough to wheel the bicycle through and
prop it against the fence post inside.

My first stop was the carriage house, a smallish structure
with three double doors and what looked like a dovecote in
the middle of the roof, topped by a weather vane. It was
painted white and green, like the main house, and the paint
was peeling in places. Mr. Rodgers really ought to have had
Derek paint it when he'd offered.

The three doors had six windows each, near the top. So

near the top, in fact, that I had to stretch as high as I could just to peer through. The interior was dark, but I was able to make out the outline of a car behind the first door. It was big, boxy, and light-colored, so was probably Mr. Rodgers's white Cadillac.

Behind the second door, there was nothing but garden tools: outlines of spades and hoes, garden hoses, and a wheelbarrow. I moved on to door number three.

There was another car behind door number three. Bigger than the Caddy, bulky and imposing. For a second, I couldn't believe my eyes. What was Mr. Rodgers doing with a brand-new Range Rover? Why drive the old Cadillac if he had this at home? And then my sluggish brain added two and two together. Not Mr. Rodgers's Range Rover, Philippe's.

Stunned, I went back down on my heels and just stood for a second, as my brain raced to keep up. OK, so the Rover was in the garage at Cliff House. That explained why Wayne's APB hadn't turned it up. Just like Melissa's Mercedes, it was off the road for the time being.

And if the Range Rover was here, then presumably so was Philippe. It made sense, really. Laura Lee had contacted Mr. Rodgers to tell him that Philippe was coming to Waterfield. Mr. Rodgers had shown Philippe the way to Aunt Inga's house. He might even have offered Philippe a place to stay in the event that Philippe wouldn't be staying with me. Philippe may not have realized that the writing was on the wall, and that I wouldn't welcome him back with open arms, but Mr. Rodgers, who had seen me with Derek for the past week, had most likely caught on to the fact that I was no longer interested in Philippe. His last statement to Philippe, back at the house the night before, had been for Philippe not to hesitate to call if there was anything Mr. Rodgers could do for him.

Or—I paled—what if the situation was less friendly? What if Mr. Rodgers had happened to drive by the house on his way home last night and had seen Philippe trying to make off with the fainting couch? What if Philippe had panicked and had hit Mr. Rodgers? He was half Mr. Rodgers's age, and thanks to his carpentry work, almost twice his size. Maybe he had taken him back here, to lie low until all the hoopla over the missing chaise longue died down—because he must have realized that he'd be the obvious suspect once we found it missing—and now he was holding Mr. Rodgers hostage in his own home. Maybe that's why Mr. Rodgers hadn't been answering his phone today. Maybe he hadn't gone to Thomaston to visit his family at all.

Something skittered quickly through my brain and out on the other side. I tried to grab it and hold on, but without success. And then I jumped as a voice behind me said, "Miss Baker?"

For a second, I felt dizzy. Then I swung on my heel, a big smile on my face. "Mr. Rodgers! You're all right!"

"Indeed, Miss Baker." Mr. Rodgers nodded cordially. "May I ask what you are doing in my yard?"

"Oh." I flushed and bit my lip. "I left you a message earlier, but I didn't hear back from you. And Wayne Rasmussen said he'd called you, too, but he hadn't been able to get hold of you, either. He said you'd probably gone to Thomaston. And when I saw that the light was on in the house, but that there was no car in the driveway, I got worried that someone had broken in. Between the break-ins at Aunt Inga's house, and…um…" I paused, not quite sure how to proceed. The other burglaries had taken place more than seventy years ago, perhaps before Mr. Rodgers was born; it was only in my mind that they were something recent.

"I see," Mr. Rodgers said. "Very considerate of you, Miss Baker."

"No problem. Um . . . is that Philippe's car in the garage?" I hooked a thumb at door number three.

"Indeed, yes. Monsieur Aubert has spent a very uncomfortable night and day." Mr. Rodgers lowered his voice delicately. "A reaction to the escargot at Pierre's, I believe."

"That figures," I muttered. Trust Phil Albertson to insist on eating snails, when every restaurant in town, including the college cafeteria, had Maine lobster on the menu.

"He is still in a bit of a tight spot, I'm afraid, but if you would care to come inside, I'll take you to him." Mr. Rodgers gestured toward the house.

"Sure," I said. I was there; I may as well see Philippe. If he looked pitiful enough, I might even reconsider my plan to slice him to ribbons with my pinking shears, although that was by no means a sure thing.

·   ·   ·

The first thing I saw when I walked into Cliff House was the fainting couch. It was sitting up against the wall in Mr. Rodgers's foyer, sans tweed upholstery. It was the first time I'd seen it entirely in its original form, and I stopped and stared. It was gorgeous, even though the once off-white fabric was yellowed with age and some of the embroidery had worn out. Frayed ends of golden yellow and pale green, rose, and blue thread were sticking out in places. Murmuring endearments, I squatted in front of it. "I thought I might never see it again," I told Mr. Rodgers over my shoulder, as I traced one of the embroidered flower swags with my finger.

"Monsieur Aubert was in possession of it when he arrived last night," Mr. Rodgers explained. "He indicated that you had relented and agreed to allow him to take it to New York after all, to be authenticated. We brought it in overnight, to keep it safe."

"Thank you," I said, getting to my feet again. "And don't worry, I don't blame you at all. It sounded reasonable; there was no way you could have known that he was lying through his teeth." The bastard. Just wait until I got my hands on him. I looked around the foyer, my hands fisted.

"He was lying?" Mr. Rodgers raised his eyebrows. "Then I'm glad you're here. This way, Miss Baker," Mr. Rodgers said, gesturing me down the hall. "Through here, please."

He opened a door and stood aside. I headed for it, not paying too much attention to where I was going, too busy looking around. The Cliff House was old, and built in a Federal style. The details were less frivolous than in Kate's house or Aunt Inga's. Kate's fireplace mantels were of dark wood, tall, with oval mirrors sunk into the top, and the fireplace surrounds and hearths had gorgeous glazed tile in shades of brown and green. Here, everything was less ornate: white-painted wood with slender columns on plinths supporting a broad, high mantel, around a fireplace surround of basic plaster. The hearth was simply red bricks laid in rows, uneven and unsealed. The floors were of broad wood planks and the windows a lot shorter than the tall, skinny Victorian arches. They were six over six, and sunk into the thick walls. Through a door on the right, I caught a tantalizing glimpse of an antique tapestry on one of the walls in the room beyond, and I almost stopped dead in my tracks, wanting nothing more than to go and examine it more closely. Even from a distance, I could tell that it was quite old and in remarkable condition. But Mr. Rodgers was waiting for me to catch up. "After you, Miss Baker."

He stood aside politely. I walked through the doorway,

only to find myself in another small hallway, less ornate than the one outside. Part of the old servants' quarters, maybe?

Mr. Rodgers followed, then moved past me with a murmured apology. The smaller hall ended in another door, which he also opened and, once again, bowed me through first. "The light switch is on the wall just to the right of the door, Miss Baker."

I stepped in, fumbling on the wall inside. No sooner had my heels cleared the threshold than the door slammed shut behind me. Outside, I could hear Mr. Rodgers throw the locks and bolts.

For a second I was too shocked and astonished to react, and then I threw myself at the door. "Shit!" It isn't a word I use often, but the circumstances seemed to demand it. I added a few more choice curses as I hammered my fists against the reinforced steel. Nothing happened; not that I had expected it to. Still, it was disconcerting. "Mr. Rodgers?" I tried. "What's going on?"

There was no answer. I had no idea whether he could hear me or whether he'd left after shutting me in. I certainly couldn't hear him. Was he standing just outside the door, listening to me freak out, or already calmly going about his business? "Shit!" I said again. It seemed to sum up the situation nicely, even if my voice was shaking.

"Avery?" a voice said from the darkness, followed by the sound of a door closing. I spun around, squinting, my nose wrinkling as a whiff of something sickly sweet wafted toward me.

"Philippe?" Old habits are hard to break.

"Ma petite chou!"

"Oh, come off it," I said rudely. "I have it on good authority that your name is really Phil Albertson and that you've never even been to France." He didn't answer, and I added, "What are you doing here?" Obviously he was not on his deathbed, suffering from poisoning by bad snails.

"That dirtbag Mr. Rodgers offered me a place to stay last night, and then he locked me in here," Philippe said with only a trace of his fake accent.

"Why?"

"How am I supposed to know? Why did he lock *you* in?"

I pulled a face. "I made a mistake."

"What mistake?"

"I thought you had stolen my chaise longue and that he caught you in the act, and now you were holding him hostage. Obviously I was wrong."

"Obviously," Philippe said. I could hear him come closer, but I couldn't see my hand in front of my face.

"Are you OK?" I asked belatedly. "He didn't hurt you, did he?"

"Something in my drink," Philippe said. He reached out a trembling hand and found my waist. "Do you still care, *chérie*?"

"Not so much that you'd notice," I answered, twisting away. I felt sorry for him, but there are limits. "You took care of that when you cheated on me with Tara. I'm glad you're not hurt, though. If we're to have any hope of getting out of here, we both have to be mobile. And speaking of mobile..." I fumbled for my cell phone. It showed me it was going on 9 P.M., but there was no signal.

Philippe sighed heavily. "I'm sorry to have to tell you, *chérie*, but there is no way out of here."

"There has to be!" I said and moderated my voice. "Have you looked around?"

"As well as I can in the dark. The room we're standing in is small, perhaps six by eight feet. Because the ground slopes up behind the house, we're underground, so there are no windows. There's a door on the other wall that leads into a tunnel. I followed it for a few yards, and then it, also, ended in a door. That's where I was when you arrived." No wonder he hadn't returned my phone call. His voice was strained. Maybe he had a touch of claustrophobia. After twenty-four hours down here, I might have a touch of claustrophobia, too. Hopefully it wouldn't come to that.

"Is it like this one?" I asked, thumping the door behind me. "Reinforced steel?"

"I'm afraid so, *ma petite*," Philippe said. I rolled my eyes but didn't comment.

"So there are two ways out. Through the door we came in, or through the door at the other end. Has Mr. Rodgers come back at all since he put you down here? With food or anything?" If so, maybe we could bash him over the head next time he showed up.

"Not until he brought you," Philippe said, accompanied by a complaint from his empty stomach.

"Well, he'll have to feed us eventually," I said.

"I'm afraid not, *chérie*. He didn't feed the other fellow."

"What other fellow?"

"There's a dead man at the end of the tunnel," Philippe said, all trace of French accent gone now. I gulped. Yep, that put things into perspective. Philippe wasn't claustrophobic. He just didn't like being locked in here with a corpse, coupled with the knowledge that that corpse might have been living and breathing when it arrived here, too.

Pushing nausea and fear aside ruthlessly, I tried to focus on what was important. "You tried the door, of course?"

Philippe assured me that he had. "*He* did, too. That seems to be what he was doing down there. Trying to claw his way out."

I swallowed. "Thanks. That picture will stay with me for a while." Philippe didn't answer. "Show me the way," I added.

Philippe gulped. "You want to go down there?"

"I don't *want* to. But I know there's no way out through *this* door. If there's a door down there, I want to check it out."

"There's no way through that door, either," Philippe said. "The guy is still here. And he hasn't been dead very long. There's still a lot left of him."

Another mental image I could have done without.

My voice trembled as I said, "I wonder if it's Martin Wentworth. He was a professor at Barnham College until he disappeared a couple of weeks ago."

"Unless someone else has disappeared in the last few weeks," Philippe said, "that's probably who it is. Or was."

"He must have been here this whole time. Poor guy." I shivered. Philippe must have felt the movement, because he reached out and put an arm around my shoulders. This time I didn't shake it off.

It turned out to be a long night. I fell asleep eventually, worn out by fretting. I was sitting on the cold floor, leaning on the cold wall, with Philippe's head in my lap. It didn't seem worth the trouble to tell him to move. I needed to conserve all my energy for getting us out of there in the morning, and I didn't need to waste any on Philippe.

As for how I was going to accomplish that feat, I had no idea, but I had to try, because Philippe sure as hell wasn't. He seemed resigned to just sit and starve. I wasn't. I was cold, tired, overwhelmed, and scared out of my mind, but there were too many things I still wanted to do to give up without a fight. I had a house to renovate, a new job to find, and a man to kiss. Because now that I was looking at the possibility of never getting the chance to do it, suddenly I wanted very much to kiss Derek. The idea that the rest of my (short) life would be a continuation of this moment, stuck in the dark with Phil Albertson, getting hungrier and colder and weaker as time wore on, was depressing. It was also an incentive to come up with a way to get out.

About halfway through the night the batteries on the cell phone gave out from being on continuously. There were no tools anywhere, and Mr. Rodgers had thoughtfully removed Philippe's Rolex for safekeeping, so we didn't even know what time it was after that. As the hours passed, I became increasingly disoriented. In the solid blackness under-ground, it could have been midnight, dawn, or high noon. Mr. Rodgers never did come back with food or anything else, and I never heard a single noise from the rest of the house. The room we were in must be soundproofed, proba-bly back in the days when Alexander Cooper had been smuggling gypsum, flour, blankets, and other necessities into Maine from Canada and ports beyond. Some of those blankets would have come in handy right now, but no such luck. The door Philippe had mentioned, in front of which lay the body of Professor Martin Wentworth, must lead far-ther into the tunnel and eventually down to the sea. That would be the best way out, it seemed. I had seen the door we'd have to go through in order to get back into the house, and it seemed impenetrable. Also, there was the small mat-ter of Graham Rodgers on the other side of it. I hadn't seen the door to the tunnel, although if Martin Wentworth hadn't been able to get through it, I didn't know how Philippe and I would manage. Still, it seemed we'd have to try. Otherwise, we were looking at being another kind of SOL, one I hadn't mentioned to Wayne earlier: shit outta luck.

I contained myself until Philippe woke up, and then I

told him the plan. He wasn't impressed. "The door is locked, Avery. Bolted. Chained. And there's a corpse lying in front of it. I'm not going back there."

"Fine," I said. "I'll go."

"You can't go down there by yourself!"

"It's either that or sitting here. You can do what you want, but I'm going to find a way out." I got to my feet, wincing, and shook out my stiffened arms and legs. "I don't suppose you have any idea what time it is?"

"Six o'clock?" Philippe suggested. "Seven? Eight?"

"Thanks." He obviously had no clue. I started feeling my way toward the other side of the room, trailing my fingers along the wall as I went. Eventually I smacked up against the opposite wall and found the door. My hand fumbled for the handle, and I pulled the door open, only to stop on the threshold, gagging, as the reek of death wafted up from beyond, sweet and strong. "Oh, Lord!"

"Told you," Philippe's voice said from several feet away.

"You did. Thanks." I shook my head from side to side in an effort to dispel the dizziness. There was nothing I could do about the stench, unfortunately. Pulling my shirt up over my nose helped a little, but not enough. "I'm still going down there. And if you had any backbone, you'd come along instead of letting me go alone."

"I've already been down there," Philippe said.

I sniffed and regretted it immediately. "Suit yourself. If I don't come back up, you'll know I found a way out. By then, maybe you'll have developed enough guts to follow. If you're not dead by then." I took a deep breath and plunged into the tunnel. Philippe stayed where he was, the bastard.

The passage I had entered was narrow and sloped down toward the ocean. I could keep one shoulder brushing the wall on one side, and the fingers on the other hand touching the opposite wall, with one hand stretched out in front of me to make sure I didn't walk into anything. Still, it was slow going. The smell of decomposing flesh became stronger as I walked on, but it also became more bearable, as my nostrils got used to it and my brain shut down to the fact that there was a rotting corpse up ahead.

To distract myself, I thought about Derek. If Philippe's internal clock was right, even marginally, Derek had either just come to work, or he'd be getting to Aunt Inga's house soon. What would he do when I didn't come down to open the door for him? Kick it in? Call Wayne? And when he realized I wasn't there, what would he think? That I'd packed my bags and hightailed it back to New York, petrified of commitment and the idea that he wanted me to stay in Waterfield? Or would he realize that I hadn't gone willingly? That I wouldn't leave without telling him? Would he try to find me or write me off without a second thought? Would I ever see him again, or would my last memory of him—and his of me—be my turning down his offer to spend the night?

Cheery stuff. I shuffled on, in stygian, smelly darkness, until my toes touched something squishy while simultaneously my hand met the cold metal of another reinforced steel door. I jumped back. That was too close.

The next few minutes were some of the most unpleasant I've ever lived through. Going through the pockets of a dead man isn't ever much fun, and this dead man wasn't even fresh.

It was worth it, though, because Martin Wentworth turned out to have all sorts of things about his person. Mostly useless, true, but not entirely. There was a cell phone with a battery as dead as mine. There was an assortment of pens and scraps of paper—notes, perhaps, but unreadable down here. There was a set of keys; I doubted they'd be of any help, but I pocketed them anyway. There was a wallet, and if we ever got out of there, that would help to identify him; it was either that or his teeth, most likely. As Philippe had said, there was quite a lot left, but what there was was probably past the point of being useful. There were coins, a half dozen little screws, a paper clip or two, a sealed square of what felt like a wet wipe; in short, the usual array of odds and ends that people keep in their purses (women) and pockets (men).

In one hand—and I use the word loosely—the corpse had something more useful. Very carefully I took it away from him, used the wet wipe to clean it off (thanks, Professor!), and examined it like a blind person reading Braille. Unless I missed my guess, Professor Wentworth had been locked up still in possession of equipment of some kind. It wasn't a Swiss Army knife, but it was similar. Something with a lot of attachments. Maybe a miniature bicycle tool kit...? Wrenches of various sizes, blades, even a bottle opener and a corkscrew. Most of the blades were broken off, unfortunately, and I surmised that he had been using the knife to try to chisel, pry, or gouge his way out through the door.

Something that wasn't a knife blade was broken, too, and it took me a moment to figure out what it was. This attachment was slim and round, not flat, like a blade. Similar to the corkscrew, but not twisted. Eventually it dawned on me: it had been a small screwdriver. And then I remembered the array of tiny screws in the dead man's pocket, and it all made sense. He hadn't been trying to chisel his way through the door; he'd been taking the door off its hinges.

Philippe had told me that he'd already checked the locks,

and it wasn't that I didn't trust him, exactly, but I checked again, just to be sure. He was right. The door was padlocked, several times, and every padlock was in place. But when I fumbled my way to the other side of the door, where the hinges would be, I had more luck. Almost all the screws were out of the top hinge, and several were missing from the bottom. Perhaps Professor Wentworth had started his work standing up, but as time wore on and he got weaker from hunger and thirst, he'd ended up sitting on the floor, still working to get out. It was horrible, and pathetic, and inspiring, all at the same time.

"How are you, *ma petite*?" Philippe's voice asked from the darkness. His curiosity must have gotten the better of him, to bring him down here after me. His voice was nasal, as if he were pinching his nose shut.

"How do you think I am?" I answered. "I just rifled the pockets of a dead man. How would you be?"

He wisely didn't answer. "Did you find anything?"

"Lots of stuff. No magic teleportation device, unfortunately. But I think he'd been working on taking the screws out of the door hinges. More than half of them are gone. If we can take out the rest, we may be able to pull the door far enough into the passage to squeeze through. Or push it out."

"I doubt that very much, *chérie*," Philippe said.

I rolled my eyes, not that he could see me in the dark. "Are you always this encouraging? No, never mind. Don't answer that." Thinking back on the time I'd known him, I realized that yes, he *was* always that encouraging. Or discouraging. Every time I'd come up with an idea for a new piece of furniture or a fun, new fabric pattern, or even a new restaurant for dinner, he'd told me why we should just do it his way instead.

Philippe huffed. I ignored him. "Help me move the body," I said instead. He took a step back. I could hear the heel of his hand-tooled boot scraping on the floor when he moved. His voice was stuck somewhere between rebellious and whiny.

"Why?"

I sighed. "Because he's lying in front of the door. I don't want to have to step around him while I'm trying to get the rest of the screws out." Or worse, on him.

"I'm not touching him!"

"I can't move him by myself. If I try to drag him, something might fall off."

"Gack!" Philippe said, and if the situation hadn't been so dismal, I might have enjoyed knowing that I wasn't alone on the verge of throwing up. However, the darkness and the smell were already bad enough without that.

"Sorry," I said. "Look, you don't have to touch the body, OK? Just grab his shoes or something. I'll take the shoulders."

I didn't wait for him to agree, just bent. After a few moments of mutinous silence, he did the same.

The process wasn't pleasant, but it got done. We managed to move the late professor ten feet farther up the passage without losing any bits and pieces, and then we returned to the door. I started picking at the screws, improvising with the few attachments left on the Swiss Army knife, while Philippe stood by and made useless comments. When my fingers were bleeding and I had broken half my nails as well as another knife blade, I ordered him to take over, and he did, albeit reluctantly. I sat down on the floor to rest, listening to the tiny sounds he was making, making sure he kept working.

"That guy you were with the other day," he said after a while.

"Derek Ellis." I leaned my head back against the cold stone and closed my eyes.

"Are you involved with him?"

It wasn't any of his business, but I answered anyway. "Not yet. If we get out of here alive, I'll give it serious consideration."

Philippe didn't answer. The tiny scratchy noises continued. "Will he realize that something's wrong and come looking for you?"

"I don't know," I answered truthfully. "I've only known him for a couple of weeks, so I can't be sure. I think so." But even if he did realize that something was wrong, would he think to look for me here? Martin Wentworth had been down here for two weeks, and no one had found him.

"Can I ask a question?" I asked a few minutes later, when my thoughts became too dismal to bear considering any longer. Philippe assented, although his voice was wary. "Why didn't you tell me that your name is not really Philippe Aubert and you're not actually French?"

"Oh. Um…" The sounds of progress halted for a few seconds, before he started working again.

"We dated for four months. I thought we were close. I told you private things about myself. Did you think I'd like you less if I knew you were just plain Phil Albertson from Tennessee?"

Well, duh! Of course he had. I actually felt kind of sorry for him. It had to be awful to feel so insignificant that becoming someone else seemed like a reasonable choice. Especially when, I had to grudgingly admit, he did have a real talent and expertise.

"That's the last screw," Philippe said eventually. "The top hinge is off the wall."

I jumped to my feet and grimaced when my knee protested. The cool dankness down here wasn't helping the stiffness at all. "Maybe we can push it a little bit. Get it to bend."

"I doubt it," Philippe said, still he did his best. "It has a little give, but not enough to open," he reported. I nodded. I could see a thin sliver of . . . not light, exactly, but a less dense darkness, up above.

"I'm ready to try again. I'll work on the bottom hinge, and you can rest. You did a good job." He moved, and I settled down on the floor in front of the door and went back to work. It was an almost impossible process in the dark: first I had to locate the head of the screw with my fingertip, then I had to guide a dime from Wentworth's pocket—what we were down to using at this point—to where the screw was, and then try to keep the dime in the tiny groove on the head of the screw while I twisted it. It slipped again and again, and my fingers were soon just as bad off as they had been. I managed to unscrew two more screws, though. It seemed to take forever, and I wondered how many hours had passed since Mr. Rodgers has shoved me in here. Twelve? Twenty-four? More?

"Ssssh!" Philippe said.

I froze.

"Listen."

He held his breath. I did the same, straining. At first I heard nothing, but then my ears detected noises. Or voices. They were faint and far away, and I glanced over my shoulder up the passage. Was it Mr. Rodgers, coming back to finish us off? Was he on his way down the passage toward us right now?

"I think it's out there," Philippe said.

"Out where? Outside the door?" I listened again. Maybe he was right. But how could anybody be outside the door? If Philippe hadn't been hearing it, too, I'd worry that I was hallucinating.

And then I remembered my conversation with Wayne Rasmussen at the Waymouth Tavern the other night. I had suggested that Professor Wentworth might have gotten stuck in one of the tunnels, and Wayne had said that he'd talk to the coast guard about having an extra look around next time they patrolled.

"Lift me up on your shoulders," I said frantically. "Quick."

"I don't think that's going to work," Philippe said, predictably, but he did as I asked. I braced myself with a hand against the wall and put my mouth right up to the tiny crack between wall and door, so close that I could feel cool metal against my lips. An almost imperceptible trickle of fresh air was coming through, and I filled my lungs with it, thankfully. The voices were a little more audible up here, too. I couldn't recognize words, or tell how many people were out there, but at least I could confirm that they were, indeed, voices.

"Helloooo!" I fluted through the crack. "Is anybody there?"

The voices outside ceased. My heart sank. Had they left without hearing me? "Hello?" I tried again, into the silence. "Anybody? Can you hear me?"

I heard noises from outside. Then a voice spoke, closer now. "I can hear you. I just don't know where you are."

I smiled. The cavalry had arrived.

21

"I found the stack of photographs on the kitchen table," Derek explained twenty minutes later. His face had been the first I'd seen when Wayne Rasmussen and his crew broke down the door into the tunnel, and for the first few seconds, his presence was the only one I registered. I walked straight into his arms. Only a rudimentary sense of decorum, plus the fact that we were surrounded by cops and members of the coast guard, stopped me from kissing him right then and there. Still, I clung to him like a limpet while Philippe staggered out of the tunnel behind me, shielding his eyes against the weak sunlight filtering in through an open metal gate a few yards closer to the sea. Beyond it, I could see the gray green waves of the ocean.

We were standing in a cave. For the uninitiated, it looked like the tunnel from the sea ended here. It had taken Wayne several minutes to figure out how to move the fake wall—painted to look like stone—to expose the continuation of the tunnel and the door we were stuck behind. After that, it had been a simple task to get us out. A blowtorch cut straight through the remaining hinge on the door, which fell with a crash. I tumbled out into Derek's arms. Philippe followed, while cops swarmed over the fallen door into the second half of the tunnel, their flashlight beams crossing on the walls, floor, and ceiling.

"Here's the corpse!" someone yelled, and Derek's arms tightened around me.

"I think it's Martin Wentworth," I mumbled against his shirt, shivering.

"Don't think about it." His voice was a low rumble against my ear. "Just be happy that you got out, yeah?"

"Sure." I sniffed. "The professor did most of the work, actually. He'd been taking the screws out of the hinges. If he hadn't done that, it would have taken us much longer. We probably wouldn't have heard you talk. You would have come and gone without ever realizing we were back there."

"We would have found you," Derek said. "Before you ended up like him."

I found the conviction in his voice comforting. "How did you get here, anyway?"

"I went to the house this morning," Derek said. "When you didn't open the door for me, I used the key I kept to let myself in. I saw that your bed hadn't been slept in, and I didn't see the clothes you wore yesterday. It didn't seem right that you would wear them again today."

"Gosh," I said, "I can't believe you remembered what I wore yesterday!"

"I spent all day looking at you. How could I not remember? Especially the way these jeans fit, yeah?" He grinned, a hand skimming across my posterior for a second. I grinned back.

"Thanks for looking out for me, Derek."

"My pleasure."

Beyond the metal door, someone had found the wallet I had left in the corpse's pocket and pronounced that it belonged to Martin Wentworth. No surprise there.

"You want to tell me what happened?" Derek added.

I shrugged. "I took the bike out for a spin. When I got here, I had a look around and saw Philippe's Range Rover in the garage. Mr. Rodgers told me Philippe was sick, with food poisoning, and had been in bed all day, and like a fool I believed him." I hesitated a moment, thinking back. "Actually, he only implied the part about the food poisoning; what he actually told me, was that Philippe had spent an uncomfortable day and night. Boy, was he right! And then he told me he'd take me to see Philippe, but instead he locked me in the storeroom. Philippe was already there. I'm not sure why Mr. Rodgers locked him up, though. He changed the subject when I asked, and since I was stuck with him, I decided not to push it."

"We could ask now," Derek suggested, with a look at Philippe, who was huddled under a blanket looking small and quite unlike himself.

"Wayne can do the asking," I answered. I didn't want anything more to do with Philippe. "Explain to me how you came to be here instead."

"Well, when I couldn't find you," Derek said, "I called Wayne and told him about that discussion we had yesterday, about how so many things that have gone wrong pointed to Mr. Rodgers. I know you didn't take it seriously, but when I told Wayne, he thought there might be something to it. Then we remembered the tunnel."

"And convinced the coast guard to let you in?"

He nodded. "We didn't want to tip Mr. Rodgers off by searching his house, so we had to wait for him to leave first. He drove off about an hour ago, and as soon as we got word, we pulled out on the water."

Wayne Rasmussen came out of the tunnel just as Derek put his arm around my shoulders again. He kept it there while I went over everything that had happened, in more detail, while Wayne wrote everything down. Next, Wayne walked over to Philippe, who explained that he had come upon Mr. Rodgers staggering out of my house with the fainting couch when he got back there after dropping Melissa off the other night. Mr. Rodgers had told Philippe I'd asked him to take charge of it, for safekeeping, and Philippe had believed him. When Mr. Rodgers invited Philippe to spend the night at Cliff House, Philippe had accepted with alacrity. He hadn't made reservations anywhere else—and although he didn't say so, it was obvious to all of us that he had expected a more welcoming reception from yours truly—and he didn't want to make the long drive back that night. So he followed Mr. Rodgers back to Cliff House, helped him unload the fainting couch and place it in the foyer, and then they both sat down in the parlor for a well-deserved drink. When Philippe started feeling groggy, Mr. Rodgers had led the way down the hall, making Philippe believe he was taking him to a bedroom. Instead, the same thing happened to Philippe as happened to me: he was locked in the dark storeroom, with no idea what was going on until I came along and explained it to him.

"We're gonna be busy here for a while," Wayne said, indicating the tunnel and the corpse, "but I guess you two would probably like to leave?" Philippe and I both nodded. "I'll have the coast guard take you back to town. We're not

quite ready to go up into the house yet. Mr. Albertson…"
Philippe winced but nodded, "I won't ask you to stick
around Waterfield. Your rental car has been driven to the
police station downtown. You may take it and go back to
New York. If I have any questions, I'll call you."

Philippe nodded. Wayne turned to me. "You'll be
around?"

Derek's arm tightened around my shoulders, but he
didn't speak. "For a while," I said.

We got a ride back to the harbor in the coast guard boat,
then we all piled into Derek's truck. I sat in the middle, with
my former boyfriend on one side and my maybe-hopefully-
future boyfriend on the other. Nobody said a word. When
we got to the police station, Philippe opened the door and
got out. For a moment I wondered if he was going to shut it
and walk away without saying anything, but then he turned
back. "May I have a word, Avery?"

"Sure," I said. "Excuse me a minute?"

Derek nodded, and I slithered out of the truck and faced
Philippe. In the bright noon sunlight he looked even worse
than I'd realized. Roughing it obviously didn't agree with
him. His wavy brown hair was tangled and dirty, his sexy
five o'clock shadow had turned into a scruffy beard with
touches of gray, and his fancy clothes were ripped and mud-
died. I was glad he'd come through the night relatively un-
scathed, though. I was no longer upset that he'd cheated on
me; in fact, Tara was welcome to him. For all his glitter,
there wasn't a whole lot of genuine gold there, and when
push had come to shove down in the tunnel, he'd been pretty
useless.

What he said was prosaic enough. "If you still want an
authentication on that fainting couch, I know someone who
can do it."

"That's all right," I answered. "Between then and now, I've found the provenance I need. Thanks."

He nodded. "Will you be staying here?" He looked around at the slow pace of Waterfield. Birds were singing, the air was clean, and a lady was pushing a baby carriage down the street past the police station. In the distance, the ocean blinked. Two little boys on bikes whizzed by, yelling to each other.

"For now," I said.

He nodded. "If you decide to come back to the city, you're welcome to come back to work for me. No strings attached."

"No offense," I answered, "but with Tara still there, I think I'd prefer not to."

He shrugged, but I could tell that he'd rather have me safely in-house at Aubert Designs than working for someone else who might worm his secret out of me. He needn't have worried. If word got out in certain circles that I'd been dating him for months, believing him to be a French designer when he was really from Tennessee, I'd never live it down.

"I'll let you know," I added.

He nodded. "I'd better get going. I don't suppose you'd be inclined to give me a good-bye kiss, for old times' sake?"

I smiled. "Better not. You take care, Philippe."

I gave him my hand. He kissed it, lingeringly, gazing soulfully at me. "You too, *ma petite*." And then he sauntered off to his car with a touch of his old insouciance in his step.

I stood and watched him get in the Range Rover and drive away, and then I crawled back into the truck. Derek grinned. "Good riddance, yeah?"

I shrugged. "I can't imagine what I saw in him."

"Same thing I saw in Melissa?" Derek suggested, cranking the car over and pulling out of the parking lot behind the Range Rover. "Something that wasn't there?"

"Like substance. You know, we really should tell her who he really is."

Derek smiled. "Sooner than later, yeah? So what do you want to do today? Work on the house? Get away for a while?"

"I'd rather just get back to work. Try to forget that I was ever locked in a basement with a con man and a dead body."

"Sounds good," Derek concurred.

"And I'd like a bath. And to brush my teeth. I feel grubby." I moved uneasily in yesterday's more-than-usually dirty clothes, aware that I looked awful and quite possibly smelled worse.

"I'll drop you off at the house," Derek offered, "and go pick up some lunch. That way you can get cleaned up, and when I get back, we can eat. Then we'll work on the kitchen cabinets."

"Sounds like a plan." I leaned back against the seat, content.

· · ·

Thirty minutes later, I was lounging in the bath, letting the hot water and soap clean away not only the dirt and dust but the fatigue and fear and the stench of dankness and death. When the water turned cold, I climbed out and dried myself, wrapping my terry robe warmly around myself before blow-drying my hair. Left on its own, it turns into something resembling a nest of angel-hair pasta. That done, I wandered out into the second-story hall with the intention of going into my room to get dressed.

I was just reaching for the doorknob when I heard footsteps downstairs. Derek must have come back with the food while I was using the hair dryer, and I hadn't heard him unlock the door and let himself in. I changed direction and went to the top of the stairs, a big grin on my face.

"Derek?"

The steps stopped and then came back. A shadow lengthened on the floor of the hall. A figure came into view, and the seductive smile dried on my lips. "You!" I snarled.

Graham Rodgers looked just as surprised to see me as I was to see him. He must have thought I was still tucked up nice and tight in his little chamber of horrors.

"Didn't think I could get out, did you?" I added belligerently, as he stopped at the foot of the stairs.

"Indeed, Miss Baker, I did not." He might have been a little paler than before but didn't look as rattled as I would have liked him to be. "Perhaps you would tell me how you managed, so I will know better for next time?"

"Oh, there won't be a next time. The police and coast guard are swarming all over your tunnel, processing the body of Martin Wentworth. Poor man."

"Bah," Graham Rodgers said. "Officious busybody."

"Yes, well, if it hadn't been for him, we wouldn't have made it out of the tunnel. You never went back to check on him, did you?"

"That would have defeated my purpose," Mr. Rodgers said coldly.

"Well, if you had, you would have seen that he had managed to take almost all the screws out of the hinges on the ocean-side door before he died. It took us just a few hours to deal with the rest. After we had dragged the body out of the way, of course."

Mr. Rodgers looked unrepentant. "What happened was his own fault," he said. "Meddling in things that weren't any of his business."

"How so?" I figured I might as well seize the opportunity to get some information out of him, while I waited for Derek to get back. Mr. Rodgers's voice turned colder than a downeast winter.

"He was trying to get your aunt to give back the items that were stolen in 1934."

"Well, why shouldn't she? They were hers." Sort of.

"They were mine!" Mr. Rodgers said, a pair of spots appearing high on his sunken cheeks. "I earned them!"

"What do you mean? You weren't even born in 1934."

"Actually, Miss Baker, I was born in December of that year."

"So . . . ?" I began, and then the brick dropped. "In Thomaston, right? Dr. Ben told me you're from Thomaston, and Wayne mentioned that you have family there. Your father was that security guard, wasn't he? The one who was killed during the robbery."

Mr. Rodgers nodded. "Indeed he was, Miss Baker. Times were lean during the Great Depression, and my father thought to pick up some extra money by guarding the mansion while the owners were away. When Mr. Kendall and Miss Morton arrived . . ."

"Miss Morton?" I repeated, my eyes big. "You mean, my aunt Inga took part in the robberies?"

"The idea for the robberies came from Mr. Kendall originally. Your aunt Inga went along with them because she was afraid that if she didn't, Mr. Kendall would break off the engagement and marry someone else."

"But he did anyway, didn't he? What happened?"

Mr. Rodgers's eyes turned even colder, the color and

consistency of steel. "My father happened, Miss Baker. When he caught Miss Morton and Mr. Kendall that night, he recognized them. They were the same age, and Thomaston isn't far from Waterfield. While Miss Morton tried to talk to my father, Mr. Kendall hit him with the statue."

"And killed him," I said, feeling sick to my stomach. Mr. Rodgers nodded. "And that's why Aunt Inga didn't marry him?"

Mr. Rodgers nodded. "She locked herself in her house, surrounded by her stolen antiques, and refused to have anything to do with anyone. She couldn't notify the police, because she would be arrested along with Mr. Kendall, but she also didn't feel she could marry him."

"And then Aunt Catherine married him instead. How do you know all this?"

Mr. Rodgers's face twisted. With rage, I thought. "From Horace Cooper, of course. When I graduated from high school, a poor, fatherless boy in Thomaston, Mr. Cooper offered me a job doing office work and running errands for him. Miss Morton put him up to it, I daresay. Guilty conscience. He taught me about the law and ensured that I passed the bar exam and could become his successor."

"And he knew about all of this?"

"He drew up Miss Morton's first will, leaving everything to her cousin, Catherine Kendall. It was Miss Morton's way of getting back at both Mr. and Mrs. Kendall. She planned for Catherine Kendall to inherit all the loot from the robberies, along with a letter explaining Mr. Kendall's role in the death of my father. But then Mrs. Kendall died, and a few years later, Mr. Kendall died, and Miss Morton had to make other plans. She wanted to give the antiques back to their rightful owners, but posthumously, of course. Mr. Cooper and Miss Morton decided that Miss Morton would leave her possessions to Mr. Cooper, and he would arrange the matter anonymously. Of course, he couldn't draft a document with himself as the beneficiary, so he asked me to do so."

"And then you killed him because you were his heir?" I ventured.

"Mr. Cooper died peacefully in his sleep." That didn't exactly answer my question, especially not considering the tone of voice Mr. Rodgers used when he said it, but I let it go.

"But you murdered my aunt, right? And Professor Wentworth?"

"In matter of fact, Miss Baker, I murdered neither. Professor Wentworth convinced your aunt to clear her conscience by returning the items immediately, rather than wait to do it posthumously. Of course I couldn't let her."

"Why not?"

Horace Cooper was beyond the long arm of the law, and Mr. Rodgers hadn't even been born when the robberies took place, so it wasn't like anything bad could happen to him.

"Because if Miss Morton returned the items before her death or changed her will so they didn't join the Cooper estate, I wouldn't inherit them. And they're mine. I've earned them." His voice was chillingly reasonable, as if this made perfect sense. In a twisted way, I guess maybe it did.

"But I guess you weren't planning to give them back to the rightful owners, were you?" I ventured.

Mr. Rodgers smiled tightly, a tacit admission.

"They're probably worth a mint. And they look so lovely in your inherited home. I guess you stripped them all after my aunt died, because as Mr. Cooper's heir, you thought they'd come to you anyway."

Mr. Rodgers inclined his head.

"But if Professor Wentworth convinced my aunt to return them right away, you'd miss out. So you killed them both."

"Indeed not, Miss Baker. Miss Morton's fall was an accident. Mostly. I hit Professor Wentworth with the fireplace poker and bundled him into the car; that much is true. With the assistance of Miss Morton's wheelchair, in case you were wondering how an elderly man like myself managed to move the body of a well-conditioned, much younger man."

"Actually," I said weakly, "I did wonder."

"The old smuggler storeroom seemed the best place for him. It is soundproof, you know, with no way in or out except through the house, now that the coast guard has locked the tunnel. And I did not imagine he would live long, with a head injury and no food or water."

I swallowed.

"But I did not, in fact, kill him. He was alive when I shut the door."

"Oh." It was all I could manage. Somehow, leaving the professor to die seemed even worse than killing him outright, but maybe that was just me.

A shadow of vexation crossed Mr. Rodgers's features. "While I took care of the professor, Miss Morton retreated to the upstairs. I felt certain she would go along with my suggestion that he just disappear—she had had no qualms about leaving my father to die, after all—but the years must have turned her squeamish, because she objected."

"So you pushed her down the stairs?"

"Dear me, no, Miss Baker. It was an accident, as I told you. We were standing at the top of the stairs, where you are now." He moved another couple of steps closer to me; I considered turning tail and locking myself in my bedroom but stood my ground, even as Mr. Rodgers's already cold eyes turned colder with remembered fury. "She refused to go along with my plan. When I couldn't convince her otherwise, it seemed better to let the matter die."

"You mean, let my aunt die."

Mr. Rodgers shrugged. "When I reached for her, she attempted to evade me. I left her on the floor in the hallway. It seemed fitting, considering that she did the same to my father. I made sure to tell her so. She was still breathing when I left, although I'm afraid her neck was broken. By the time I came back the next morning, she had expired." He said it with no more emotion than if he were talking about a fly.

"Just out of curiosity," I said, trying my best to match his dispassionate tone, without success, "I've been told that Martin Wentworth went missing on a Wednesday. I guess my aunt died on Wednesday, too?" Mr. Rodgers nodded. "You told me once that you had a standing lunch date with her every Friday. I guess you decided Friday would be too long to wait, so you came back on Thursday morning instead to make sure she was dead?"

Mr. Rodgers agreed politely. "Indeed I did, Miss Baker. Otherwise, someone else might accidentally stop in first, you see, and if she were still alive, that might be awkward."

"I can quite see that," I agreed.

Mr. Rodgers smiled tightly. "I am certain you also see why I now have to do something about you?"

"Actually," I answered, my heart starting to beat faster, "I'm afraid I don't. The police have found Professor Wentworth. They realize the only way he could have gotten into the tunnel was through your house. And I've already told them what happened yesterday. So has Philippe. Nobody's going to believe that I fell down the stairs and broke my neck. Plus, I'm not as easy to kill as my aunt. I'm almost seventy years younger, for one thing."

"Ah, but you fail to understand the satisfaction it would bring me." Mr. Rodgers's smile was like an ice cube down my back. "You ruined everything, you see. Until you showed up, I had everything under control. Miss Morton's death was considered an accident, and the police had no idea what had become of Martin Wentworth. He would have stayed down in the tunnel until there was nothing left but bones, and then I could have thrown those into the sea. But you arrived with the letter from your aunt, and saw me find the holographic will, which made it impossible for me to destroy it. Even then things might have worked out all right if you had agreed to sell the house to Miss James's boy-friend, or just allowed me the responsibility of packing everything up for you and moving it to a storage facility—of course removing anything valuable in the process—but you wouldn't even do that. Instead, you insisted on moving in and doing everything yourself, even after I tried to scare you away. And then you discovered Professor Wentworth's bicycle in the shed, and the chaise longue in the attic, and the whole story behind the robberies, and now everything is ruined."

He had slowly moved up the stairs as we spoke, almost—but not quite—without my noticing, and I hadn't been too worried. He was an old man, and I'm young and healthy, if on the small side. Still, when he put on a burst of speed over the last few steps, teeth bared, it took me by surprise. He had both clawed hands around my neck before I realized what he was planning to do, and then he squeezed. And he was stronger than I had expected. I couldn't catch my breath, and everything started to spin, while little specks of light, like colored confetti, danced in front of my eyes.

Somewhere in the back of my head, a roar built up. This man had done enough harm to enough people, and I was damned if I was going to let him do anything to me. I was not about to let myself be thrown down the stairs like a rag doll, the way he had thrown my aunt. I lashed out with my hands, kicked out with my feet, hit, clawed, and scratched like a wildcat, and drove Mr. Rodgers backward, to the edge of the stairs. Still, I'm not sure he wouldn't have taken me with him when he fell, but for one thing. As he lingered, unbalanced, a small, black form trotted up the stairs and between his legs. I twisted back, away from his grasp, and I could see his eyes widen as he realized what was happening. And then he tipped over backward and tumbled down, head over heels over head again, a thin scream issuing from his throat. Until he landed on his back and slid the rest of the way down the staircase, and out onto the hardwood floor. He ended up in a tangle of arms and legs and lay still. Inky, whose natural agility had allowed her to twist aside safely, sat down on the top step and tucked her tail around her neatly planted paws.

I waited for a minute, but Mr. Rodgers didn't stir, so I crept timidly down the stairs after him. Inky followed. After a detour into the kitchen to snatch up Derek's crowbar, I nervously crouched beside Mr. Rodgers. One of his legs was twisted, and he was out cold, but he was breathing, and I decided it was best to keep him that way. I wanted him to pay, and pay dearly, for what he had done to my aunt, to Martin Wentworth, and to Philippe and me, but I didn't want him to pay that way. I'd rather have him alive and regretting what he'd done, if only because he'd gotten caught. So I covered him with a blanket and called 911. Five minutes later, when Derek walked into the house carrying a pizza box and a liter bottle of Coke for me and Moxie for himself, he found me sitting on the bottom step of the staircase, my pale blue terrycloth robe snugged around me, a cat on each side, and the crowbar convulsively clutched in my hand, waiting for the ambulance to show up.

—Epilogue—

"So, Tinkerbell," Derek said, "what's it going to be?"

.   .   .

It had been nine weeks since Mr. Rodgers fell down my stairs, breaking his leg and his collarbone and giving himself a severe concussion. He was lucky; that same fall had killed Aunt Inga, so it could have gone a whole lot worse for him than it had. Or maybe not: he'd lived to see another day, but a day when he was tried for the murder of Martin Wentworth and the negligent homicide of my aunt Inga, not to mention the kidnapping of Philippe and me. He pleaded guilty—not only to those things, but to the trifling details of threatening me and sabotaging my stairs, as well as to breaking and entering and vandalizing Aunt Inga's house—and was sentenced to a large number of years behind bars. I don't expect to see him out and about any time soon. If he's an exemplary prisoner and lives to be as old as Aunt Inga, he might see sunlight again, but otherwise, no. And I don't feel too bad about that.

Wayne arranged for all the treasures we could find to be returned to the rightful owners. There was even a small finder's fee attached to a few of them. I didn't feel great about accepting money to right a wrong committed by my aunt in the first place, but I took the money anyway, with the caveat that it was going to go to a good cause.

Martin Wentworth's body—what was left of it—was processed and shipped back to his family in Rhode Island for burial. I never did have to look at it, a fact for which I will always be grateful. Poor Paige asked if she could, but was gently dissuaded by Wayne. He kept his promise not to tell her parents what had been going on; he even made sure she got Professor Wentworth's day planner back after the police were finished with it. It was all she had left of her boyfriend, and she clung to it and to her memories of their time together. When I saw her next, at the memorial service at Barnham College in July, she was dressed in unrelieved black from head to toe, looking like a bereaved widow.

After Mr. Rodgers's tumble, Derek and I went back to work on the house, of course also looking for any little trinkets we might have missed. But although we looked everywhere we could think of, and even checked the floors and walls for hidden rooms and cavities, we came up empty. If the jewel-encrusted fan was still around, we sure couldn't find it. We found lots of other great things, though. Beautiful oak floors throughout the first story of the house, equally beautiful but less formal heart of pine floors upstairs. Pristine plaster walls under the wallpaper. A wonderful—if horribly rusty and abused—fireplace screen in a corner of the basement, which Derek cleaned and affixed to the dining room fireplace. My special texturing techniques got shunted to the wayside—it just wasn't the right house for them—but we painted the kitchen floor in a diamond pattern of blue and white, to go with the Blue Willow backsplash and the gleaming cobalt counter, and even Derek admitted that it looked great. I got rid of Aunt Inga's 1970s furniture and replaced it with things from the attic, including the lovely rolltop desk and a pair of dark blue velvet curtains with tassels that I had to air out for several days before we could hang them. Once I had added a sprinkling of silver stars, they looked fabulous. I kept reminding myself that whatever I did had to appeal to potential buyers as well as to myself, but in truth, I ended up decorating and furnishing the house more to my own taste than anyone else's. Within reason, of course; Derek had managed to make me see that maybe the house wasn't the perfect blank canvas for *every* one of my whims.

He painted the outside a gorgeous robin's egg blue with cornflower and ochre trim, while I weeded the garden beds and planted flowers. And one crisp morning in mid-August, we were standing on the sidewalk in front of the house, looking at our handiwork.

"So, Tinkerbell," Derek said, "what's it going to be?"

I turned to look at him. He'd had a haircut since the events in Mr. Rodgers's basement, but his hair grew so fast that that irritating forelock still—or again—fell into his eyes. I'd gotten used to it by now. My hand hardly twitched at all anymore. "Your hair's doing it again," I said.

"Sorry." He grinned and tossed his head. "Don't try to change the subject. The house is finished. Or as finished as it'll ever be. There's always something more you can do.

But the summer's over. It'll start getting colder in a few weeks. You're going to have to decide, yeah?"

"About the house?"

"Of course about the house."

And about him. He didn't say it, but he didn't have to. We'd been skirting the issue for the past two months. I guess we'd been dating, sort of, but we'd avoided getting too close. We both knew that the end of the summer was coming, and neither of us wanted to start something we couldn't finish. Derek didn't want to get attached to me and then have me leave, and I didn't want to get attached to him and then either have to leave him or stay and maybe resent him because of what I'd given up. So we'd spent almost all our time together, but none of it horizontally (except for the time when we'd lain side by side on the dining room floor looking for Marie Antoinette's fan under a loose floorboard, but I don't count that). We shared the occasional kiss, and sometimes a quick snuggle, but so far we'd kept the relationship pretty casual.

"I've decided," I said. He turned to me.

"Yeah?"

"Yes." I took a deep breath. "I'm flying to New York tomorrow."

His face didn't change, but something moved in his eyes. Still, he kept looking at me, waiting for me to continue. "I had a call from my friend Laura Lee a few days ago," I continued. "A friend of hers sublet my apartment while I was here."

"And now she's leaving, so you can move back in?"

"Actually, she's found a job in New York and wants to stay. In my apartment. And make it her apartment."

"You're kidding," Derek said.

I shook my head. "I have to go pick up the rest of my stuff. Whatever she doesn't want to keep, which isn't much. And then start over somewhere."

"You can live here for free," Derek pointed out. "But I don't know that there's a lot of call for textile designers in these parts."

I shrugged. "That's OK. I thought maybe I'd try a career change. Be my own boss."

"Start your own design studio?"

"Maybe. Do some designing, teach a few courses on the side. I've already spoken to the people at Barnham and gotten the go-ahead to teach a class there next semester. It won't pay a whole lot, but it'll be enough to live on if I supplement with other things."

"And if I need a textile designer, or an interior designer, maybe you'd be available for consultation?" He was starting to grin.

"I think we might be able to arrange that," I agreed demurely. And then I grinned back. "Maybe we can even look for another property to renovate together, one we can actually sell and make a profit from. Between us, we'll probably have enough money to put a down payment on something, don't you think? If we put up Aunt Inga's house and your bachelor pad as collateral?"

"I wouldn't be surprised," Derek said. He put an arm around my shoulders. "You know, I could get into this idea."

"Glad to hear it," I answered, snuggling into his side.

"If we make it just one project to start with, and we discover that we can't work together, then we won't have lost anything."

"Exactly."

"But if we do work well together, we can keep doing it."

"That's right."

"I like this idea."

"Glad to hear it."

"How about we go somewhere to celebrate?" He glanced down at me, eyes very blue against his tanned face.

"What did you have in mind?" I asked.

His voice dropped. "I was thinking of someplace small and intimate, out of the way, that only the locals know about. Somewhere appropriate for celebrating our new... partnership."

I grinned. "Your place?" He lived in a converted loft above the hardware store in downtown. It had exposed brickwork, ducts running under the ceiling, even a concrete counter; all the things he hadn't allowed me to put into Aunt Inga's house for fear it would mess with the 1870s mojo. The first time I'd seen it, I had stared in openmouthed surprise for a few seconds, then burst out laughing.

"Yours is closer." He glanced at it.

"True. Sounds like you're in a hurry."

He shrugged unapologetically. "If you're leaving tomorrow, we don't have much time. Don't want to waste any of it."

"Of course not," I agreed. "Don't let me stand in your way."

"Never." He grinned. The next second I found myself hanging over his shoulder, giggling and squealing, as he kicked open the fence gate and strode up the walkway to Aunt Inga's—make that *my*—house.

—Home-Renovation—
and Design Tips

How to Mosaic a Tabletop, Counter, or Backsplash

1. Decide on your materials and a color scheme. Incorporating sea glass and shells or broken pottery may look fabulous, but if an uneven surface will drive you insane, stick with tiles that match.
2. Cover your surface with a single sheet of paper (any paper is fine, but something like plain newsprint will be less distracting). Cutting and taping is fine. Or use chalk to draw the pattern directly on the surface.
3. Arrange the pieces of tile on the paper-covered surface (no glue yet), working from the middle out to the edges and leaving $1/8$ to $1/2$ inch between the pieces. Think of it as a jigsaw puzzle and look for contrast and complement.

4. Leave it alone for a bit. Walk around it, see what it looks like from various angles, then rearrange the pieces if you change your mind.
5. Lift the paper (carefully!) with your entire mosaic on it off the tabletop/counter. Or, if you've not bothered with paper, move to the next step.
6. Transfer the pieces from the paper to the working surface one piece at a time, using tile adhesive to secure them and working from the middle out.
7. Allow to dry fully.
8. Mix your grout and apply it to the surface, forcing it in between mosaic pieces, molding it to irregular edges and smoothing it to the table's edge.
9. Wipe any remaining grout off the mosaic pieces with a damp cloth, turning it frequently.
10. Allow the grout to cure for at least a week before using the table or counter, misting frequently with clean water. Applying a layer of sealant is a good idea.

–Tips–

• Choose a sturdy surface (mosaic is heavy!).
• This technique can be used on just about any surface, but if you have a gorgeous marble tabletop, why would you want to change it? Your best bet is an unbreakable, porous one such as wood or particleboard. If the surface is very smooth (stone or glass), check the tile adhesive to make sure it will adhere to nonporous surfaces.
• Drawing a grid on your paper with a thick felt pen may help you lay out your design, particularly if you are

aiming for symmetry. (Or directly on the surface itself, with chalk or pencil.)

- If your mosaic incorporates odd-shaped pieces, you may want to apply the grout directly to the crevices bit by bit with your fingers. (Directions for grout always tell you to glop it on and then wipe it off; this works well for flat tile surfaces but not as well for irregular surfaces.)

Kitchen-Renovation Costs and Ideas

Renovating your kitchen is usually the most cost-effective upgrade you make to your home. Even in an old house, most people opt to renovate or replace rather than restore: *I like the look of an old coal-burning or wood-burning stove, but I want my dishwasher and garbage disposal, thank you very much.* But you can replace your kitchen in a way that is still sensitive to the age of your house.

–Cost Expectations–

If you are remodeling your kitchen as a face-lift prior to selling it, it is recommended that you spend no more than 10 to 15 percent of the cost of your house. If you are going to remain in your house for more than five years, spend 25 percent or more; in most cases you will recoup the entire cost of the renovation when you sell.

–It's Going to Cost *How* Much?–

Yep, kitchen renovation can be expensive. But there are ways to cut costs without sacrificing quality.

- Look for sales on everything!
- Use stock cabinets instead of custom cabinets or just reface the old cabinets. (Put on new doors, but keep the cabinets themselves.) Or give the existing cabinets a new look by painting or staining them.
- Simply putting in a new countertop can make a big difference.
- Keep the existing appliances if possible. If not, check out the scratch 'n' dent sales. Sometimes the dents aren't even visible, and you can save a bundle.
- Buy from the factory whenever you can, instead of going to a store. It's cheaper, and it takes less time to get your product.
- Try to keep existing plumbing and electrical, and don't make structural changes to the room; it's expensive.
- Make the most of small improvements like new paint, new wallpaper, new curtains, and decorations. Dollar for dollar, a new paint job gives you the biggest bang for your buck!

Use Lace to Create
Vintage Kitchen Cabinets

–Prepare Cabinet Doors–

THINGS YOU'LL NEED
- Screwdriver
- Jigsaw
- Safety goggles
- Medium-grit sandpaper
- Stain or paint

STEPS
1. Remove the cabinet doors from cabinets.
2. Take all hardware off the cabinet doors and store safely so you do not lose any fasteners or other small parts.
3. Wear safety goggles to cut out the center panel of each cabinet door with a jigsaw.
4. Sand down any rough edges using medium-grit sandpaper.
5. Apply a fresh coat of paint or stain to the cabinet doors now (if that is in your plans) before you add any lace insets.

> *Keep small children out of the area while working with the jigsaw.*

–Add the Vintage Lace Panels–

THINGS YOU'LL NEED
- Vintage lace panels
- Measuring tape
- Scissors
- Industrial stapler

STEPS
1. Measure the vintage lace and cut into panels approximately half an inch larger than the opening in the cabinet door.
2. Stretch the vintage lace over the panel opening on the back of the cabinet door.
3. Staple the lace to the back of the cabinet, using an industrial stapler.

> *If you don't have any vintage lace, you can make your own by soaking new lace in a solution of strong black tea. Soak the lace for at least an hour, and let dry flat.*

–Hang the Cabinet Doors–

STEPS
1. Reattach the hardware to each cabinet door.
2. Mount each door onto the cabinet frame.
3. Enjoy looking at your new kitchen cabinets every day!